DARK IN THE DAY

DARK IN THE DAY

Edited by Storm Constantine
and Paul Houghton

Stafford, England

Dark in the Day, edited by Storm Constantine and Paul Houghton, © 2016

Introduction – Storm Constantine © 2016
Wide Church of the Weird – Paul Houghton © 2016
Martina Bellovičová – Perhaps Their Parents Were at Fault © 2016
J. E. Bryant – The Vigil © 2016
Glynis Charlton – Brian © 2016
Matt Colborn – City in the Dusk © 2001
Danielle Collard – Wallace © 2016
Storm Constantine – The Secret Gallery © 2016
Louise Coquio – Listen © 2016
Elizabeth Counihan – Erlking and Crocodile © 2016
Krishan Coupland – The House of My Grandfather © 2014
Elizabeth Davidson – The Long Leather Boot © 2016
Siân Davies – Post Partum © 2016
Jack Fabian – A New Womann © 2016
Kerri Fender – Meta Wife © 2016
Paul Finch – Wicken Fen © 2012
Rosie Garland – An End to Empire © 2016
Jessica Gilling – Around the Apple Tree © 2016
Andrew Hook – A Life in Plastic © 2015
Paul Houghton – The Strange Case of Quentin Wilde © 2016
Rhys Hughes – Pyramid and Thisbe © 2016
Tanith Lee – The Beast and Beauty © 2016
Lisa Mansell – A Woman Talks to her Flesh as it Meets the Ground, For(uh)m, Carnivory, Angels of Anarchy, Catafalque © 2016
Kate Moore – Lift © 2016
Tim Pratt – Cup and Table © 2012
Nicholas Royle – The Dummy © 2008
Michael Marshall Smith – The Dark Land, © 1991
Paula Wakefield- In Touch © 2016
Ian Whates – The Piano Song © 2011
Liz Williams – The Hide © 2007

Cover Photograph: Michael Marshall Smith
Cover Design and Interior layout: Storm Constantine
Interior illustrations: Storm Constantine

Set in Garamond

IP0126
ISBN 978-1-907737-74-9

An Immanion Press Edition
http://www.immanion-press.com
info@immanion-press.com

CONTENTS

Acknowledgments

The editors would like to thank all the contributors for donating stories to this collection. Thanks also to Mike Ashley, Elizabeth Counihan and Ian Whates for putting us in touch with some 'weirdests', who subsequently became contributors. Thanks to Greg Shephard of Stark House for his advice and help – and for introductions to editors and writers. Thanks to Michael Marshall Smith for the cover photograph, and to Louise Coquio and Paula Wakefield for assisting with the editing and production.

Introduction

Storm Constantine

The idea for this anthology originated during one of my regular sessions as a guest lecturer in Creative Writing at Staffordshire University. I often speak about the day to day running of an independent press, explaining to students how books are created and all the work that goes into them once the actual writing is done. I thought it would be an interesting idea to involve the students in the creation of a book and what better way than to publish a short story collection that included some of their work? I decided that asking established writers to donate a story to the anthology would enable the up-and-coming contributors to reach a wider audience. I spoke with Paul Houghton, the Senior Lecturer in Creative Writing at Staffs Uni, and he liked the idea. I invited him to co-edit the book with me. As both Paul and I are keen fans of 'weird fiction', we thought it would be good to do our own anthology in this vein.

My first encounter with weird fiction was with Robert Aickman's *'The Swords'*, in my teens, when I collected all volumes of *The Pan Book of Horror Stories* and *The Fontana Book of Ghost Stories* – Aickman edited the first eight volumes of the latter. Each of the Fontana collections included a story by him. *'The Swords'* haunted me for a long time after I'd finished reading and led me to seek out more of Aickman's work.

Regarded as somewhat more respectable than simple horror, examples of weird fiction can be found in the work of Truman Capote (*Miriam*) and Flannery O'Connor (*Good Country People*), as well as many other ostensibly mainstream, literary writers. The genre has a distinguished lineage, including as it does the work of Algernon Blackwood, E. F. Benson, Shirley Jackson, Edith

Wharton and Oliver Onions, to name but a few. Collections dedicated solely to weird fiction are now regularly published – not just the odd (usually very odd) story cropping up in genre anthologies.

But it seems what constitutes 'weird' differs between writers, and many of the submissions we initially received for our book were – to us – ghost or horror stories rather than weird. Even those that didn't fit precisely either of those genre definitions, and were skilled stories, lacked the indefinable 'something' we were looking for. A weird piece by its very nature often evades labelling. I'm repelled by the majority of modern horror, which often relies too much on blood and guts, perhaps intending to invoke disgust in the reader. Weird fiction is quirky, thought-provoking, disorientating, but rarely visceral. Guts are too crude a prop for this genre.

A weird tale makes you think. It might require the reader to work a little for its meaning, or it might have multiple meanings, or even – in its most surreal examples – none at all. It *might* have aspects of the supernatural, horror, or science fiction. It might be a mystery, or a historical piece. Or it might even have a mainstream setting with no obvious otherworldly props. In some stories, the weirdness is experienced only by the reader rather than the characters, who themselves are strange. The weirdness doesn't come from a story's trappings but from within. What it *does* have is an almost indefinable atmosphere, a breath that brushes your skin, which lingers after you finish reading.

A writer of the weird looks for the unfamiliar in everyday situations and people. The protagonists are often hapless victims, who find themselves in a reality that's fallen out of balance. The world *looks* the same, but it's not. They are seeing beneath the skin of the world, or seeing *through* it. There might be hints that what they experience is entirely subjective, but is it? That's the magic of the weird.

The most intriguing weird stories reward you if you read them more than once. The first time through you might think 'what??', but the story has got under your skin. You *want* to understand it, so read it again, perhaps this time intuiting more of what might be going on. The author doesn't tell you. It's almost as if they flirt with you, beguiling your senses, laughing off-stage as you attempt to penetrate the mystery. You think about the story afterwards. You discuss it with friends. 'What do *you* think?' you might ask. I love that aspect of the weird. After reading Capote's '*Miriam*', I was desperate to talk about it with others who'd read it. The tale was almost maddening, yet utterly bewitching. I *had* to talk about it. Ultimately, with many stories of this genre, the reader must decide for themselves what the meaning is – and perhaps sometimes there are as many meanings as there are readers.

Some of the authors in this collection are new to writing – and this might be their first published work. Others are established writers who have generously donated a piece for us to reprint – or, as with Rosie Garland and Elizabeth Counihan, have offered us a previously unpublished work. We've also been able to print a story of Tanith Lee's that as far as we know has not been published elsewhere.

The book also includes a new story by me, which came unbidden, insisting it be told, even when I'd already selected a previously-published but little-known story of mine to include in this collection. Once it was done, off it went again, out into the evening of its world, its secrets only half explained.

I believe Weird should be regarded as a distinct genre – and not just among its fans and aficionados. To any readers of this book who haven't read much weird before (you'll have read at least *some*, if you read any genre anthologies at all), there is an enormous amount of writers and stories to discover out there. You can start by looking at the catalogues of publishers such as Stark House and Undertow Publications. I hope this collection gives you a tantalising taste and the urge to discover more.

Storm Constantine
June 2016

THE WIDE CHURCH OF THE WEIRD

Paul Houghton

The weird is, arguably, a wider church than some of the associated genres that weave in and out of it: the gothic, magical realism, horror and Sci-Fi. It doesn't have as many fixed tropes, and a low dosage of weird can work very well, just beneath the surface, or by being evident in one or more of the story elements: its main character, the setting, style, or an unexpected narrative incident. Sometimes you don't even know you're reading a weird story, until it takes that strange turn you always hope for but can't anticipate.

During its run between the mid-20s and 1950s it was the American pulp magazine *Weird Tales* that championed the weird story as its own distinct genre. Now it's being recognised again, and right here, too! Here are contemporary masters of the genre and craft, and writers entirely new to it. They sit well side by side, because they sit weirdly side by side. What do the stories have in common? Unusual people, strange, atmospheric places and odd events.

As well as weird fiction writers, there have always been established writers who occasionally write weird fiction. You would be forgiven for not knowing that an obscure weird story, 'Man Overboard,' was written by a certain Winston Churchill in his earlier years. It was originally published (and eerily illustrated) in *The Harmsworth Magazine*, volume 1, 1898-1899 (and the story is now readily available on the net). Equally, some of the late D.H. Lawrence's stories were distinctly weird. Published posthumously in 1946, 'The Lovely Lady' of the title story is anything but, in a tale that is charged with eerie atmosphere and warped psychology.

In one of my earliest tutorials with Angela Carter at UEA, she asked me, 'Have you read Celine?'

'No,' I said. I hadn't heard of him then, having mostly read British and American authors.

'He's a fascist bastard but I think you'd like him,' she said. 'Start with "Death on the Instalment Plan."'

She was right of course; it was wildly grotesque, and as funny as it was fierce – and definitely weird. To this day I remember his mother coming down the stairs with her cane: *Tip, Tap, Plonk!*' I had imbibed everything by Carter and McEwan and of course, Angela had written some of the weirdest stories you could hope to find. In 'Reflections' from *Fireworks*, her first story collection, a woman is not only knitting the woods but stitching time – before a giant phallus makes an appearance.

One day, in UEA's foyer I saw a blackboard announcing that Angela was reading at the Norwich Art School that very evening, when suddenly, *'BOO!'* she sprang from behind the blackboard. 'You're reading...' I stammered.

'Any requests?' she asked.

'Oh yes, the Lizzie Borden one.'

'The Fall River Axe Murders' is a weird, meticulously researched documentary story, so saturated in atmosphere, detail and tension, that it takes you right inside the house and head of Lizzie Borden, just before her famous *faux-pas* – enthralling to hear read live, in that piping voice, in a creaking art studio with a transfixed audience. Houses, and the atmosphere in them, loom large in this collection also.

As a reader who always wanted to be writing, I was either always discovering or rediscovering Bainbridge, Banks, Ballard, Ray Bradbury, Peter Carey, Marco Denevi, Hawthorne, Shirley Jackson, Flannery O'Connor, Bruno Schulz, Spark and Capote, Patrick McGrath, Nathanael West... the list is endless. But then I discovered Southern Gothic and knew it was the weird for me, because all the weirdness was located in the characters and the landscape they inhabited. Katherine Anne Porter, Flannery O'Connor, Eudora Welty, and the startlingly brilliant contemporary writer, Tim Gautreaux. 'Sorry Blood', the first story I read of his five years ago, was in the *Virginia Quarterly*, and I read it standing up, transfixed, in a library in Virginia. It may seem unlikely, but many of those stories and their characters from the American South reminded me of my rural upbringing in Worcestershire, England. There were plenty of strange folks around the wilder edges of that tourist town, Stratford-Upon-Avon! Door-to-door salesmen, God-botherers and just odd people, walking to the next village... My mum's friend found an escaped convict in her outdoor privy, and you can't get more Southern Gothic than that!

Weird writers come from all corners and the weird is wider than you ever imagined. But is the weird *respectable?* Is it getting respectable? Who cares? Chomp, chomp go the genres: they're mutating as we read. And who in their right mind would swap the strangely beautiful for the rational? When so often it seems the literary elite (of London, England!) is still entirely devoted to respectable middle class realism, perhaps a few chinks have at last opened up in that all too often spectacularly uninteresting facade.

My thanks go to everyone who has risen to the challenge here, and to Storm for both providing the platform, and working so hard at producing it at her mythical and magical publication house, Immanion Press. Thanks to Lou for editing.

Paul Houghton
Senior Lecturer in Creative Writing
Staffordshire University
June 2016

FOR(UH)M

Lisa Mansell

in the iamb of razors
he arias toward the basque-clad bosom of a black-flaxen crow
a harrow of vizier with sphinx-cloaked wing
that sea-shores the flex-tide and shale-scars
where the ships salt through the
rip

on the bardic lido of the tiled bastille
talmud-dumb butlers loiter
lucid in the barren rub of dulcimers
they rondeau yiddish and drone in the dante of tablas
they ague   and purge with gusto in the gutspit of their tug

the rhythm of nihil quells liquid-sip and lacquer
and livid   the butlers scribe with battled quills
a shard dance in the
sand
arabian   schism   in the musk-blossom of squill-flowers

The House of my Grandfather

Krishan Coupland

My grandfather built his house himself. Every brick, every
floorboard touched by his hands. His signature inside stud walls,
behind wallpaper, on the underside of the mantelpiece. Times
were different back then, I'm told. In those days everyone built
their house themselves.

We go to visit, my fiancée and I. Her name is Charlotte, and I
worry that Grandad will not approve. She puts on earrings, and
swaps her nose stud for a clear plastic spacer. Smiles. There's
nothing I can say to her about me and my grandfather that she
doesn't know already.

It's a long drive to his house, which stands out in the middle of
patchwork countryside, tall and gothic. The fields around are still
dusted with snow, the furrows white-capped. Few other cars to be
seen on the road.

"We should have brought something," says Charlotte as we
pull up on the gravel outside.

"He wouldn't have liked it," I say.

We ring the bell and wait, but it's cold outside and the door is,
as ever, unlocked. The entrance hall is dark, the bulb in the ceiling
blackened and dead. I walk along, opening the heavy velvet
curtains to let in white winter light. We hang our coats on the
rack, shuck our boots. A fire is burning in the front room grate. A
ledger sits open on the table beside a tray set with glasses and
wine.

"He'll be back soon," I say, but he's not. We go looking. Tiptoeing our way from room to room. All high-ceilinged, all dressed
in walnut and green felt. Tall bookcases stacked with folio
editions. My grandfather is a rich man with little to spend his

15

fortune on. Our feet, clad only in socks, slide on parquet flooring. The study is empty, and the dining room. The kitchen an echoing emptiness of terracotta tiles and shining pans. We wander through a library thick with the smell of leather, through storerooms stacked with dusty tins and jars. We crack doors cautiously, giggles brimming in our stomachs like trespassing children.

There are rooms here that I've never seen before. Quiet rooms, layered with dust. At the back of the house we find a second staircase that winds upwards in a tight spiral. We wander through bedrooms, endless bedrooms and bathrooms and offices. All are imperiously neat, echoingly empty. We think about calling his name, but then think again, not wanting to hear how little impact our voices might have on the tombstone silence of the house.

Another set of steps, another floor. And here we find the accumulated detritus of a life. Paintings and plaster statues and pieces of furniture. Rolled carpets stacked in piles. Panes of glass and dusty boxes containing ancient board games, tattered suitcases stuffed with clothes, boxes overflowing with tins and bottles and yellowed newspapers. Bedframes and mattresses and filing cabinets full of typewritten papers. My grandfather's memories stored up here in cardboard boxes, gnawed away at by rats.

At the far end of the attic a door opens into a narrow, bright room. Pigeons coo in hutches stacked along each wall, preening and brooding in their little piles of straw. They are beautiful, chests like oil spills, horny beaks and glass marble eyes. They smell of lime and musty straw. When he was my age my grandfather used to breed homing pigeons in the garden shed. Beautiful creatures, he told me. Beautiful. He won trophies for them. I open one of the hutches and a bird struts out, hard sharp claws grasping my thumb. It takes flight when I try to stroke it, disappearing through an open window and wheeling away over distant fields.

We climb again. The next floor is a schoolroom, the desks in immaculate array. The blackboard is clean and beyond the window the playground is busy with running boys in short trousers. We sit and wait a while here, but no teacher arrives. We ascend to a smoky post office that looks out at a village green. The ink that sits in pads by each station smells like old books do. A giant, red, iron set of scales stands by the doorway.

"He owned all this," I tell Charlotte, and her eyes are wide and she does not speak.

The next floor is dark and confusing. It smells of gunpowder here and we wander through many bare and stonewalled rooms. Rusted bedsteads and broken furniture. Rubble is heaped in the corners and in the final room we come across a rifle propped against the wall. I reach out for it but Charlotte grabs my hand.

"It's not ours," she says. And she's right. I leave it be. As we head for the stairs we hear the heavy drone of plane engines in the distance.

Another floor. There are no rooms here, just one giant hall, where a wedding is taking place. The couple have yet to arrive. Everyone sits hushed in the pews, dressed in fine clothes. Scents of musk and rich, flowery perfume. There are two empty seats in the front row, but we cannot linger. If we stop here I'm sure we'll end up staying forever.

We pass through a train station. Through a smoky office with a view of the city. My legs ache from the climbing and beside me Charlotte's face is drawn. She looks frightened. We do not let go of one another's hands. I recognise a room filled with beige leather armchairs from sometime in my childhood, but I don't remember when. There are no people. We climb up and up through darkness.

The next floor is dark as well, and big. In the distance I can see a yellow cone of light, hanging in space as though cast by a streetlamp. We walk towards it, but it hardly seems to get any closer. We rest, then walk, then rest, then walk. The cone of light grows slowly until I see that it's a lamp suspended over a desk. My grandfather sits at the desk, writing lines in a ledger. He looks older and frailer than I have ever seen him.

"Grandad," I say. "I'm sorry we're late. We got lost."

He finishes his sentence and looks up. There is a small tray balanced on the corner of the desk, on which sit three wine glasses and an unlabelled bottle. He gestures to the seats before the desk, and Charlotte and I sit.

"This is Charlotte," I say. My voice is so small here, and I'm tired from all the stairs. "She's my fiancée. I thought you'd like to meet her."

My grandfather looks at her with fading eyes and nods his approval. He pours us all a glass of wine, and there we sit and drink.

THE STRANGE CASE
OF QUENTIN WILDE

Paul Houghton

I found him face down in the muddy car park. I lifted him by the arms and turned him over. Beneath his tangled red hair, he was grinning widely.

"The shine on your shoe says a lot about you," he said, and laughed with a little hiss.

His pale orange complexion spoke of tanning sessions, before he'd hit the bottle. The jaded blue eyes had the out-of-season wintriness of a swimming pool, while his cleft chin suggested he'd been shoved away with a violent finger. But he had hands, not hooves, and was dressed in a black suit, with highly polished shoes. Perhaps his pratfall had occurred on the way from a funeral? Easy enough to get upset and drunk.

"Aye, he's been at the cheeky water," growled the ruddy-faced woman standing nearby. "Can't keep aff it, *harharhar*." Her laughter was as choppy as a starter motor.

"Penny for 'em, Gov'ner?" he muttered, his small hands pathetically cupped, like Oliver asking for more.

"Got all his workin' parts, *harharhar!* £10 to sober 'im up."

"Fine." I fished out a tenner and she smiled sweetly, as if I'd just given her son his first job.

"Be sorry to lose the wee fella but he needs to move on. We all are. They're closing us down. We've only been here 200 years!"

As I helped him across the car park, he whispered: "Take me away from that ol' *mincey heid*."

I was used to the market characters: its sellers and customers with gold teeth, headscarves and trilbys, blurred, historic tattoos, hands covered with chunky rings: glittering with diamonds and shining with sovereigns. As for merchandise, where else would you get a suit for £10, or a prow of a ship cocktail bar, a shoal of perfectly preserved piranha or a zebra-hoof lamp? It had to be Paddy's Market, where the wit flowed freely:

"Had anything to eat, son?"

"Aye, a Glasgi Salad" – also known as a bag of chips.

Begun by the Irish in the 1700s, the market was on its last legs now, squeezed by the council for being 'too illegal'. Gentrification, more like. The bootleg harsh vodka and American cigarettes sold from tea chests were only fringe elements in the car park. There, one week, a white van pulled up and a guy opened the back to shout at me, "Right mate, cost yer twenty to look at, a hundred to buy." Inside, all laid out, ready for a game, was a large, antique chess set. Each piece was a fornicating couple in a different position. Together with the ornate fireplace, it looked as if it had been stolen from a stately home. Lord Bath was likely missing both.

"You need a wash, a brush up, some new threads…" Before I could finish, he was muttering something.

"I said, are you one of those faggots or what?"

I examined his jacket. "You touched up the seams with ink then?"

"A well-worn tradition, *har-har*. Good enough for Poe, good enough for me, *heh-heh.*"

"You've got an act already?"

His only reply was a shrug, and since he'd no intention of telling me his name, I came up with Quentin.

"Based on who?" he wanted to know. "The stately homo or film director?"

"Take your pick." It was my turn to shrug, though the name was based on his red quiff, and all those red ideas under the crest of it. Meanwhile, he didn't seem the least bit grateful I'd pulled him from the murk of that car park, where folks could have trodden on him, or ran over him in a car.

I got him a maroon-velvet dinner jacket from Oxfam – perfect for the Bohemian I took him for. Having washed his face and hands as you might a five-year old's, the taming of his wild red hair into unerring neatness, was the transformation of a drunk into a Mormon. Refreshed, he blinked, and his eyelashes fluttered like the feelers of a beetle on its back. He rocked on his heels and did a little Irish jig as if he was ready for a night on the town and deserved one.

"Women and song," he sang, admiring his reflection and running his tiny hands through his groomed hair.

When I reckoned on his favourite tipples as Guinness and whisky, it turned out to be right. It was all there in those droll, chlorinated eyes.

He sat in the snug of the pub and swung his leprechaun legs, waiting impatiently for the evening to begin. It was growing dark outside and a thick fog had pressed itself against the windows like the fur of an enormous silver cat.

I wanted to talk career prospects, but he wasn't in the mood. "We'd clean up," I said.

In one smooth movement, he turned his head. "Have freak shows made a comeback?"

"Yup. TV is all one freak show."

"That explains why you're out on the streets, then?" He blinked, but wasn't waiting for an answer. "You're saying we're quids in?"

Closures and cutbacks meant I'd lost my job two months before. It had been tough but educational. At last I had time to think and dream by daylight. I could contribute to an uprising, or at least a creative quake. Me and my new ally might put a few creases in reality, or at least arrange something surreal enough to subvert the light of day. It was a project I was ripe for. Like a lot of people, I wanted something I didn't have, like laughter, first thing in the morning and last thing at night. To begin with though, this night would unfold with a good deal of hysterical drinking; everyone slinging it back to cancel out their cares in the world.

Sandra barged into the pub after quite a few at another, and like smoke from a burning building, the fog billowed in after her. "Who's this wee fella, then?"

"Less of the wee, Missy. I might be wee but I'm big where it counts, and I might be a Bogtrotter, but you'll pardon me for breathing!"

"Friggin 'ell! Is it pull-cord?"

Quentin bolted forwards. "No I am fucking not!"

"Oh, right. I s'pose you're one of those intellectuals, then. Well, drinks?" Sandra wavered, pointing at me and him.

"Double scotch," rasped my new acquaintance, in an Irish

brogue. "On the rocks and make it snappy – I've a thirst to quench!"

"Right y'are, little love." Lightly, Sandra koshed him round the head before heading for the bar, situated in the centre of the pub, like a ship coming into harbour. Its glittery prow was lined with enough silver and gold spirits for the journey of a lifetime.

"But is he old enough?" Sandra plonked the whisky in front of him.

"I'll say. About 30."

"Oh, same age as me..."

"Oh aye, right enough!"

"'E's a cheeky wee bugger, to be sure."

He lifted up his whisky and toasted us all. "Cheer up! You're all dying."

"Your friend has the strangest sense of humour."

"It's not that he's anti-social exactly. He's just never socialised before."

"I'm not surprised! Ah, but bless him, has he got a name?"

"Quentin."

"Oh, sharp as razor blades they are. Better watch your back."

Dougie came in, not so fresh after Saturday afternoon with the lads. He didn't notice Quentin at first. "Whoa! Who's the guy?"

"Quentin will do for now," said Quentin, "and since I won't be on top of any bonfires any time soon, get used to it."

"Pure creepy, man! Looks like..." he thought for a moment, "the 70-year-old reincarnation of a toddler."

"Kindly refrain from talkin' about me as if I'm not here – it's awfie fucking *rude.*"

"Like that, is it?"

"'Fraid so pal – 'sides," Quentin turned his head to the door and ran his hand over his quiff, "I don't talk to the dead unless they approach me first."

Over the pub's last hour many drinks were drunk and, spiralling in draughts, the spectral fog had come rolling in so thickly the pub interior looked like the set for a Hammer horror. The drink had quelled many inhibitions, and despite or because of his prickliness, Quentin was the life and soul of the party; people couldn't get enough.

"Look at his eyelashes," said San to Dougie, "those eyes were put in with a sooty finger. He's really sexy." To prove this, she proceeded to grab hold of Quentin and snogged his face off. Quentin ran his little hand through her hair and it wasn't clear who was moaning.

"Oi!" Dougie stabbed her with a finger. "He's no bigger than a five year old, you mad cow!"

A transference of crimson lipstick meant that Quentin emerged, with a smile more rakish than ever. Perhaps Dougie was more shocked than jealous.

"Oooh, what's down there, then?"

"Wouldn't you like to know…"

Cautiously, Dougie leaned towards me. "Seems he brings out the hidden parts in people. It's bloody weird. Give us a go!" He snatched Quentin off San.

"Heyyyy!" she said. "It's yous whose are abusing a small child."

"Yeah? And what were you doin'? Teaching 'im the facts of life, I s'pose?"

"We've all gotta learn some time!" said Quentin, but it sounded like San.

San and Dougie glared at each other in a silent declaration of war. They'd not been getting on for some weeks and were drinking a whole lot more, usually in separate pubs

"So," Quentin interrupted, more American than Irish now, "Can any of you dummies tell me, where's the capital of America?"

"I dunno. Where is the capital of America?"

"*All over Europe!* Tut, tut – you ignoramuses need educating. Okay then, what's little and pink and hangs out your pyjamas?"

San and I shrugged.

"Your **MOTHER,** *DUMMY!"*

The all-smiling barman came to ask what the little man was drinking but everyone agreed – he'd had quite enough.

* Bite the tip of your tongue eight times.
   * Try to swallow your tongue eight times.
   * Make a trough with your tongue and stick it out eight times.
My jaw ached, and while Quentin was becoming a local celebrity with little help from me, I was getting nowhere with the exercises. I tried some of the movements prescribed for him:

Surprise: *Mouth open, body moves back a bit.*
Laughing: *Move headstick back and forth in jerks.*

23

Ashamed: *Head lowered, looks out of corner of eyes.*

Soon it was more difficult to go out without Quentin than it was with him.

"Oh, you should've brought Quentin," friends complained. Obviously he was better company than I was. They'd become hooked on the little petrified man, who not only told them exactly what he thought but also supplied a rare opportunity for everyone to disagree with themselves. People wanted to borrow him, but I explained that being no bigger than a four-year-old, he couldn't go anywhere unaccompanied.

A fortnight after Quentin arrived, a friend, Crumb, phoned to say he was opening a second-hand bookshop and needed a gimmick for the launch: something eye-catching for the window. I suggested The Creature from the Black Lagoon reading *The War of the Worlds*, Dracula reading *Dracula*, Action Man reading *A Farewell To Arms*, Barbie reading *Pride and Prejudice* and, if Quentin wasn't in too much demand, he could be the centrepiece, reading Wittgenstein in one of those miniaturised armchairs furniture shops used in their displays. Set off by weird lighting effects and a wisp of dry ice, the other figures suspended around him would represent figments of his imagination.

"Sounds about right," said Crumb who was bound to; this was a man who'd recently attended his brother's wedding, dressed as a rakish undertaker in top hat, fingerless gloves, and Marilyn Manson eyeliner.

It took an afternoon to fix the window, and when all the figures were in place and the spots switched on, it all looked suitably curious, and more like a curiosity shop than a book shop. Sporting a purple silk bow tie with his velvet smock, Quentin looked like a taxidermied version of James Harries, the child prodigy who ran his own antiques business at the age of ten, and by fourteen had published his guide to profiteering from jumble sales. Since then, he'd had a sex change.

"Just the job," said Crumb and it was soon obvious that the curious window was a magnet for children. Unfortunately, even the adults were more interested in the figures than the books. They were particularly taken with Quentin who read *Moby Dick* on Monday, *The Lovely Bones* on Tuesday, *Lady Chatterley's Lover* on Wednesday, *Tractatus* on Thursday and *Lolita* on Friday. At this rate, he'd soon have the equivalent of a college education.

He'd been reading intently for a week when the offer came.

"That grand little chap reading *Lolita*. How much is he?" said The Prick from the BBC, reaching for his wallet.

"As far as I know, he's not for sale," said Crumb who was, as usual, chewing gum.

"Shall we say £80?" I imagined the pristine notes waved under Crumb's nose.

"I couldn't say. He isn't mine."

"Let's say a hundred and be done with it."

"This is a bookshop. We only sell books." Crumb chewed faster, and gestured at the tomes, wall-to-wall and floor-to-ceiling, where they were arranged in great twisted columns because they were holding up the roof.

The Prick started to count out notes. "Actually, I need him for a film. Pretty bloody urgently."

"He belongs to the guy who did the display..." I imagine Crumb faltering like a light bulb; like me he was always short of cash and everyone has their price.

"Well? I presume you have a telephone number?"

"Not on me, no."

"You must give him my card and get him to phone me immediately."

"I don't have to do anything," said Crumb, staring him down.

"Here's another twenty for your trouble."

"I thought he might even try and steal him," Crumb told me later and reminded me to get him insured.

So Quentin had hit the big time, gone for the week, playing a wee Scotsman in a parody of *Whisky Galore* for BBC Films. Before hitting the TV, the film would enjoy a limited theatrical release. When I'd insisted that the little man was not for sale, the Prick had agreed to pay £100 to rent him for the week. Quentin's role was pivotal to the story and so he was following in the great tradition of his forefathers, who featured in films such as *The Great Gabbo*, *Dead of Night* and *Magic*.

In the meantime, I'd read that actress Candice Bergen had been raised as her dummy-brother's kid sister. Her father was a famous vent, Ed Bergen, and in her autobiography *Knock Wood*, she remembers her brother's room in the family home – his neat little bed, his wardrobe of monogrammed clothes, his desk, and above it a pin-up of Dorothy Lamour. She was obliged to sit on her father's left knee, and spar with her brother, sitting on her father's right knee.

While Quentin was assured a certain degree of fame, I was sure I'd never see him again. Although I'd taken the precaution of insuring him for three thousand pounds, and that policy would provide money I could well use, I'd miss the little blighter if he didn't come home. No amount of money could replace his mercurial personality, or the mischief it caused. With his soulful soullessness, he was the epitome of the projected self, the id over the ego. If he was to become more than an actor and become an act, he might need a more arresting stage name. Oedipal Wreck was one that I had in mind.

Just as I feared, when the day came for his return, there was no sign of him, no phone call, nothing. I phoned the Prick from the BBC continually.

"Hallo. You're through to Oliver Masters. Leave your message and I'll get back to you," all in that pompous-twat accent. Of the five messages I left, each one more abusive than the one before it, the last two threatened him with the police. Of course, the Prick never replied.

I went to Crumb's book shop. As an extra lure, he'd installed a coffee bar from which he served the strongest coffee in the Western hemisphere. Maybe it would help me think what to do next. I was going to suggest taking down that window display, as during the week I'd noticed it looked rather pathetic without its centrepiece. As I approached the book shop though, it was a great surprise to see Quentin just sitting there, reading *Eats, Shoots and Leaves* as if nothing had happened, as if that burst of stardom hadn't meant a jot.

Unbeknown to me, the Prick's secretary had dropped Quentin off the day before

"Sorry," said Crumb. "I should've let you know. But I had to go to an auction and it slipped my mind."

"So. How was it?" I asked Quentin.

"Champagne and bitches." He leaned forward, gesturing to the knife in his back, invisible to all but himself. Otherwise, he was all in one piece, as well as full of new ideas.

"Listen, pal, mixing with those media whores I got a great idea." He winked like some Hollywood producer by way of George Burns. "Why not become my agent? Here's the deal: you set up the bookings – I'll bring home the bacon. All you need do is balance the books, help me rehearse and develop my wardrobe. All stars need a walk-in wardrobe, right?"

I laughed at his audacity before considering it more seriously. After all, if Emu and Orville could be hands-up celebrity birds for years on end, Quentin was home and dry. He'd give that sloshed aristocrat Lord Charles a run for his money too. In 1940s America, Buffalo Bob Smith's sidekick Howdy Doody's TV show had run for *ten* years. Even more strangely, in Britain, there'd been a ventriloquist's radio show, *Educating Archie,* with the legendary Archie Andrews.

"Think you can make it on your own?" I asked.

"Dud did without Pete, didn't he?"

"For a while. But then he made crap films and died of brain shrinkage. The deal is usually co-existence. I'm the albumen, you're the yolk."

"Ugh, how faggy! Really, puh-lease!"

"Suit yourself."

"But you know it makes sense. I mean to say, it's only dummies who go to work. I'm even prepared to be one of the millions of dummies who go to work and get paid for just being there."

"Since you put it like that..." I remembered my old t-shirt which proclaimed in green B-movie typography: THE JOB THAT ATE MY BRAIN.

While Quentin smirked his way up the career ladder, I could be out and about doing something far more interesting.

Quentin went into hyperdrive. He never seemed to sleep, and his eyes moved in the dark, as he made his plans by night. There would be footsteps in the hall, and a light on where there shouldn't be. He was studying something. How to be human? Books went missing from the house and Crumb's shop, although they were mysteriously returned later. I wondered if Quentin was planning his escape.

Quentin took a great photo: he takes a great photo – he's photogenic from every angle, and like Dorian Gray never ages. At first, offers via *The Stage, Variety* and *Screen* were sporadic and not always generous. Film students wanted him for their no-budget shorts and theatre groups wanted him to pep up their lacklustre productions with a comic turn. In the lean meantime, he suggested various scams. That we should buy a consignment of illegal cigarettes and sell them at 300% profit, that I should take out life insurance and promptly disappear so *he* could claim it. But then he got a regular job as a TV warm-up man: good steady wages, women all over the place. Suddenly, his permagrin seemed all the more permanent. His teeth were whitened accordingly.

"Perhaps you should write a book," I suggested. "Recording your experiences from the gutter to the stars."

"Nah, you're alright. That's your department – poncing around with words. I'd rather sing."

This surprised me since his voice had the quality of a startled crow: the rusty razor blades of Tom Waits crossed with the cracked-posh-charlady vocals of Marianne Faithfull. Even so, his version of *The Boulevard of Broken Dreams* was becoming almost as legendary as hers – locally at least.

We or rather *he* was becoming popular at all kinds of occasions. At Sandra and Dougie's joint 30th, (fancy dress essential), Quentin was the only guest who would have been welcome to "Come as you are." Cleopatra, Jason King and Shaft joined Captain Kirk and a girl in a fur bikini smoking in the corner. The Grim Reaper was ordering drinks at the bar for himself and a girl with wobbling green snakes in her hair. Since Dougie and San had hired a small club called *The Traffic Light,* I wondered whether they would be on green or amber tonight – the way things were going I was surprised they'd got past red. Dougie had hired professional deejaying equipment, but his mates had no idea how to operate it, so records were coming on in a slurry of mixed speeds, the 33s at 45 and vice versa. But if the whole affair was akin to a wedding reception from Hell, everyone looked in their element and, in this off-set setting, people not only took Quentin for granted, they took him for real, here, where he was no stranger or more disconcerting than anyone else.

Dougie, who faintly resembled James Dean, had come to his own party as Dean after the accident, wearing a safety belt like a sash, his denims splattered with generous helpings of gore. San, who looked nothing like Jayne Mansfield had come as Mansfield also after her accident – she was carrying a cast of her own head, so at least they had arranged their deaths together.

"Did you know I was a witch?" she said. "Heavily involved in the black arts – they reckon that's why I was murdered."

"Well, together you're as old as a coffin dodger," said Quentin. "Though I must say, you're both looking very lovely tonight."

"Thanks, but what are you?" San asked him.

"You decide! A dodgy geezer on the margins of polite society or living proof that everyone's schizophrenic?"

"Dodgy geezer, definitely. But your get-up?"

With his square head, green complexion, dusty suit and big boots this should have been obvious.

"He's my creation?" I hinted. *"It lives?"*

"Ah! And you must be the Baron."

I bowed.

"Have you come on your own?"

"You're never alone when you've created someone," I said by way of conversation.

San laughed wildly. "I'm not alone either. I have two heads!"

I had to agree. As usual, she and Dougie had been truffling but they never gave the stuff out. They needed all they could get because those snowy powders had been propping up their relationship for some time.

"I like your bolt," she said to my square-headed sidekick. "But what has Wanky Frankie done to your poor head?"

"Egg boxes," said Quentin, whose boots were five sizes too big.

My own Baron Frankenstein was by way of Peter Cushing so I sported wedge-shaped sideburns, thin black lips, shadowy sunken eyes and those death-like over-pronounced cheekbones.

Emma Peel arrived in her skin-tight leather accompanied by an authentic Oddbod from *Carry on Screaming* who was busily discomfiting those sober enough to be discomfited; a giant werewolf creature in a disturbing bright blue boiler suit, he was the only barefoot guest, his claws clattering on the dance floor.

"Have they sorted that fucking music out yet?" San snarled at Dougie.

"They've fixed it," he said, and I heard him say "bitch queen" under his breath.

"Can I hold him?" said San.

"Sure." I handed Quentin over and in exchange, San handed me her head.

"Jesus! Talk about broody." Dougie took a disgruntled finishing swig from his beer.

"I'm so happy with my little man," said San, cradling Quentin like a child.

Dougie's belch was a deliberate comment.

"D'you know, I feel that Quentin is one of us now? A new friend in our circle. We are a mother!"

"I'm getting another beer," said Dougie before whispering to me, "never thought I'd be sharing my birthday with Margaret Thatcher."

"Let's sit down for a while." San made her way to the tables and I followed. She made Quentin comfortable in a chair behind a half-drunk pint of lager and he fell back into the pose of his annihilation.

"To say that he grows on you would be an understatement," she said.

A dense fug of marijuana drifted in the air and the colourful blaze of costumes made me think I was in a tank for tropical fish. There was even a shimmery green mermaid whose red hair was almost as long as her tail.

Emma Peel came up to the table and, striking a pose, aimed an imaginary gun at Quentin.

"Trample me underfoot or I shall go mad!" yelled Quentin but she moved on, amused and slightly alarmed.

"Fancy bitch," said San. "Taking a pop at my little man." She patted Quentin on the head and straightened his dickie bow.

At last the deejay equipment was working and, with the room filling, the dancing had begun. Since San couldn't hear what Quentin was saying, he indicated how, if she were to cup her ear with a hand, she'd be able to direct her hearing.

"Wow, I thought that was just a cod gesture from films but it really works. So, I hear you've got a new job?"

"Yup. God's business," said Quentin. "Warming up the audience or rather – making the dead grateful they're alive."

"You must be so proud of him," she said to me and I shrugged. "I mean, he's done so well in such a short time. Come such a long way."

"Yes, and I never went to a single parents' evening."

San leaned towards Quentin and said confidentially, "You're really quite a surreal fellow, you know."

"Madam," he announced, "I exist solely to reduce the hour to the minimum of sense."

After two hours of drinking, dancing and *outre* fashion, the lights went down with the music and a spotlight came on at the far end of the hall. Everyone gathered there and those whose costumes allowed squatted on the floor. This was to be the high point of the evening: an alternative revue in which a few people would take turns to entertain: singing songs, telling tales and whatever else occurred to them. Only me and Quentin knew that he was to be the surprise end act. The first live performance was a Swedish folk dance by a tiny, fair-haired girl dressed in a traditional costume: a black dress sprouting colourful florets. This was followed by great waves of applause before two bald scientists in white lab coats and Mr Magoo specs entered with a flip chart on an easel.

"While barnacles plague boat owners, cut your skin like razors and taste *awful,* in the world of marine biology, they're not only famous for spending their entire lives standing on their heads," said the one, as the other illustrated what he was saying with a red marker pen. "Starting out as free-swimming larva, when mature, like everyone else, they choose a home with the same species to serve as potential mates. Once *in situ,* barnacle larvae use cement-secreting glands to attach themselves – headfirst – permanently to a surface. James Joyce's father quipped about his son's future wife, one Nora Barnacle – 'She'll never leave him.' This barnacle cement has been of great interest to dental researchers.

"Every barnacle has male and female organs, but they don't fertilise themselves, oh no. Instead, a mature barnacle uncoils its colossal, snakelike penis and probes around in a reach-out-and-touch-style of mating. Barnacles then, have the biggest penises in the world! Furthermore, in ancient Hawaii, people who were highly attractive to the opposite sex were said to be clung to by barnacles."

"Oh baby, you can be my barnacle," said San to Quentin before the applause roared like a wild fire. This was soon flattened by a dour singer-songwriter with an out-of-tune guitar. His first song was called *Sweet Mushroom Pie* and it was safe to assume the species of fungi he meant. When his set finished with a song called *Giro Papa,* about lying in wait for a fortnightly cheque, the applause hinted at relief as much as anything else. Afterwards, a man and two girls in black leather introduced themselves as *Menage Abattoir* and did a mincing little dance to the theme tune of *The Magic Roundabout* which, half way through, turned into a hip-grinding version of The Stripper. The girls stripped down to their leather harnesses and fluffy slippers while the man got as far as his leather thong.

"Well follow *that!*" I said to a dole-faced Quentin, during the rapturous applause.

"Oh, he will," said San who seemed to know more about it than I did, although I'd equipped Quentin with all the gear he needed: a raggedy nightgown, a wig and red contact lenses. Brought to his senses, Quentin jumped off his seat and scurried off towards the dressing room. Captain James T Kirk of the U.S.S. Enterprise held the audience in position with mildly obscene jokes about Royalty and Michael Jackson.

Quentin's changed appearance was met with absolute silence. Not only could you have heard a pin drop, I heard someone carefully peeling the cellophane off a fag packet. Quentin had become Linda Blair and his red pupils glowed like hot coals from his panda eyes. His face and hands were caked with chalky white foundation and his lips were dark purple. On the front of the night shirt he had daubed in red letters *Help Me.* He didn't bother introducing himself and immediately broke into song:

"I've written a letter to daddy.
His address is Heaven Above –" he sang almost sweetly before rasping:
"Your mother sucks cocks in Hell!

I've written dear daddy we miss you
And wish you were with us to love
You're all gonna die down there!"

In his left hand, he swung a glittering crucifix perilously close to the hem of his nightshirt. After three more verses he bowed and struck a crucifixion pose and I noticed the palms of his hands featured stigmata. Apart from San, everyone was too stoned or stunned to respond. She clapped furiously and laughed like a hyena, before a few others joined in, nervously. Quentin flung the crucifix in the air, broke into a little Irish jig and began his second song:

"Comes the bomb you'll all be
Well-done chicken fricassee
Every soul down the hole
But not me, not me, not me!

You'll have anaemia, touch o' leukaemia
It'll be *deplorable!*
You'll be mutants from pollutants
But I'll still be *a-d-o-r-a-b-l-e!*"

Quentin ran his fingers through his rat's tail hair, as a very stoned girl with matching dreadlocks sitting up front said loudly to her boyfriend: "Isn't it strange what people's imaginations do? Creepy!" She shook her dreadlocks as if she could shake the whole thing out of her head.

When Quentin had finished the song, everyone clapped and he stood absolutely still. I thought he was going to make an announcement or tell a joke.

Then he started to sing very softly:

"They put you in a wooden box
And cover you up with dirt and rocks
Woo hoo woo hoo woo hoo hoo
The worms go in, the worms go out
They go in thin and they come out stout
Woo hoo woo hoo woo hoo hoo"

"More! More!" yelled San. "Wasn't he *fantastic?* I could feel my pulse during that."

"Yeah," I said, "He's full of surprises."

"God, how could you live with a weirdo like that?" Dougie tapped me on the shoulder.

"He's pretty quiet most of the time. Sits there with a fag dangling from his mouth. Doesn't even bother lighting it."

"Weird."

Quentin was the last and, with that, a jet of dry ice filled the hall and the disco lights came rolling in with the music.

It seemed as though Dougie had decided to get drunk on his own. No sooner had he finished a beer, he was starting another. "You seen San?" Swimmingly, he looked around.

"Last time I saw San, she was off to see Quentin."

"God, San-Quentin – some kind of prison, ain't it?"

"Complete with Death Row," I said.

"That's what I'm on," said Dougie.

"You're only 30 for God's sake! Sounds like the car crash is getting to you?"

"The car crash got to me a long time ago. We only went through with this because it was all arranged, y'know?"

"Oh. Good job it wasn't a wedding, then."

"Yeah."

"Well – it's a great party. I mean, just look at it."

Oddbod was chasing the girl in the fur bikini, Emma Peel was dancing with Austin Powers as if they'd known each other all their lives, and Brains from Thunderbirds had just opened the top half of his square head to reveal a naked girl with a rifle rising from a birthday cake. I tried to forget the unfortunate circumstances of the party and join in the fun. I danced with the Gorgon and her snakes seem to rain down on my head.

The next time I saw Dougie he had subsided against a wall. By degrees, a bottle of Becks was slipping from his fingers – it landed upright on the floor. He blinked as Quentin blinked – slowly, over-glazed eyes that saw nothing in particular yet watched everything.

"She's left me," he said. "Gone off with that bloody muppet."

I could see that he was right, as someone had opened the only window that overlooked the cobbled street outside. Sandra was running up the road with Quentin and of the manic laughter that echoed from the walls, it was difficult to say whether it was his or hers, but the *tap tap tapping* of little feet sounded like someone up way beyond their bedtime.

CUP AND TABLE

Tim Pratt

Sigmund stepped over the New Doctor, dropping a subway token onto her devastated body. He stepped around the spreading shadow of his best friend, Carlsbad, who had died as he'd lived: inconclusively, and without fanfare. He stepped over the brutalised remains of Ray, up the steps, and kept his eyes focused on the shrine inside. This room in the temple at the top of the mountain at the top of the world was large and cold, and peer as he might back through the layers of time—visible to Sigmund as layers of gauze, translucent as sautéed onions, decade after decade peeling away under his gaze—he could not see a time when this room had not existed on this spot, bare but potent, as if only recently vacated by the God who'd created and abandoned the world.

Sigmund approached the shrine, and there it was. The cup. The prize and goal and purpose of a hundred generations of the Table. The other members of the Table were dead, the whole world was dead, except for Sigmund.

He did not reach for the cup. Instead, he walked to the arched window and looked out. Peering back in time he saw mountains and clouds and the passing of goats. But in the present he saw only fire, twisting and writhing, consuming rock as easily as trees, with a few mountain peaks rising as-yet-untouched from the flames. Sigmund had not loved the world much—he'd enjoyed the music of Bach, violent movies, and vast quantities of cocaine—and by and large he could have taken or left civilization. Still, knowing the world was consumed in fire made him profoundly sad.

Sigmund returned to the shrine and seized the cup—heavy, stone, more blunt object than drinking vessel—and prepared to sip.

But then, at the last moment, Sigmund didn't drink. He did something else instead.

But first:

Or, arguably, later:

Sigmund slumped in the back seat, Carlsbad lurking on the floorboards in his semi-liquid noctilescent form, Carlotta tapping her razored silver fingernails on the steering wheel, and Ray—the newest member of the Table—fiddling with the radio. He popped live scorpions from a plastic bag into his mouth. Tiny spines were rising out of Ray's skin, mostly on the nape of his neck and the back of his hands, their tips pearled with droplets of venom.

"It was a beautiful service," Sigmund said. "They sent the Old Doctor off with dignity."

Carlsbad's tarry body rippled. Ray turned around, frowning, face hard and plain as a sledgehammer, and said "What the fuck are you talking about, junkie? We haven't even gotten to the funeral home yet."

Sigmund sank down in his seat. This was, in a way, even more embarrassing than blacking out.

"Blood and honey," Carlotta said, voice all wither and bile. "How much of that shit did you snort this morning, that you can't even remember what day it is?"

Sigmund didn't speak. They all knew he could see into the past, but none of them knew the full extent of his recent gyrations through time. Lately he'd been jerking from future to past and back again without compass or guide. Only the Old Doctor had known about that, and now that he was dead, it was better kept a secret.

They reached the funeral home, and Sigmund had to go through the ceremony all over again. Grief—unlike sex, music, and cheating at cards—was not a skill that could be honed by practice.

The Old Doctor welcomed Sigmund, twenty years old and tormented by visions, into the library at the Table's headquarters. Shelves rose everywhere like battlements, the floors were old slate, and the lights were ancient crystal-dripping chandeliers, but the Old Doctor sat in a folding chair at a card table heaped with books.

"I expected, well, something more," Sigmund said, thumping the rickety table with his hairy knuckles. "A big slab of mahogany or something, a table with authority."

"We had a fine table once," the Old Doctor said, eternally middle-aged and absently professorial. "But it was chopped up for firewood during a siege in the 1600s." He tapped the side of his nose. "There's a lesson in that. No asset, human or material, is important compared to the continued existence of the organisation itself."

"But surely you're irreplaceable," Sigmund said, awkward attempt at job security through flattery. The room shivered and blurred at the edges of his vision, but it had not changed much in recent decades, a few books moving here and there, piles of dust shifting across the floor.

The Old Doctor shook his head. "I am the living history of the Table, but if I died, a new doctor would be sent from the archives to take over operations, and though his approach might differ from mine, his role would be the same—to protect the cup."

"The cup," Sigmund said, sensing the cusp of mysteries. "You mean the Holy Grail."

The Old Doctor ran his fingers along the spine of a dusty leatherbound book. "No. The Table predates the time of Christ. We guard a much older cup."

"The cup, is it here, in the vaults?"

"Well." The Old Doctor frowned at the book in his hands. "We don't actually know where the cup is anymore. The archives have... deteriorated over the centuries, and there are gaps in my knowledge. It would be accurate to say the agents of the Table now seek the cup, so that we may protect it properly again. That's why you're here, Sigmund. For your ability to see into the past. Though we'll have to train you to narrow your focus to the here-and-now, to peel back the gauze of time at will." He looked up from the book and met Sigmund's eyes. "As it stands, you're almost useless to me, but I've made useful tools out of things far more broken than you are."

Some vestigial part of Sigmund's ego bristled at being called broken, but not enough to stir him to his own defence. "But I can only look back thirty or forty years. How can that help you?"

"I have... a theory," the Old Doctor said. "When you were

found on the streets, you were raving about gruesome murders, yes?"

Sigmund nodded. "I don't know about raving, but yes."

"The murders you saw took place over a hundred years ago. On that occasion, you saw back many more years than usual. Do you know why?"

Sigmund shook his head. He thought he did know, but shame kept him from saying.

"I suspect your unusual acuity was the result of all that speed you snorted," the Old Doctor said. "The stimulants enabled you to see deeper into the past. I have, of course, vast quantities of very fine methamphetamines at my disposal, which you can use to aid me in my researches."

Sigmund said "Vast quantities?" His hands trembled, and he clasped them to make them stop.

"Enough to let you see centuries into the past," the Old Doctor said. "Though we'll work up to that, of course."

"When I agreed to join the Table, I was hoping to do field work."

The Old Doctor sniffed. "That business isn't what's important, Sigmund. Assassination, regime change, paltry corporate wars—that's just the hackwork our agents do to pay the bills. It's not worthy of your gifts."

"Still, it's what I want. I'll help with your research if you let me work in the field." Sigmund had spent a childhood in cramped apartments and hospital wards, beset by visions of the still-thrashing past. In those dark rooms he'd read comic books and dreamed of escaping the prison of circumstance—of being a superhero. But heroes like that weren't real. Anyone who put on a costume and went out on the streets to fight crime would be murdered long before morning. At some point in his teens Sigmund had graduated to spy thrillers and Cold War history, passing easily from fiction to non-fiction and back again, reading about double- and triple-agents with an interest that bordered on the fanatical. Becoming a spy—that idea had the ring of the plausible, in a way that becoming a superhero never could. Now, this close to that secret agent dream, he wouldn't let himself be shunted into a pure research position. This was his chance.

The Old Doctor sighed. "Very well."

"What's it like?" Carlotta said, the night after their first mission as a duo. She'd enthralled a Senator while Sigmund peered into the past to find out where the microfilm was hidden. Now, after, they were sitting at the counter in an all-night diner where even they didn't stand out from the crowd of weirdoes and freaks.

Sigmund sipped decaf coffee and looked around at the translucent figures of past customers, the crowd of nights gone by, every booth and stool occupied by ghosts. "It's like layers of gauze," he said. "Usually I just see the past distantly, shimmering, but if I concentrate I can sort of... shift my focus." He thumped his coffee cup and made the liquid inside ripple. "The Old Doctor taught me to keep my eyes on the here-and-now, unless I need to look back, and then I just sort of..." He gestured vaguely with his hands, trying to create a physical analogue for a psychic act, to mime the metaphysical. "I guess I sort of twitch the gauze aside, and pass through a curtain, and the present gets blurrier while the past comes into focus."

"That's a shitty description," Carlotta said, sawing away at the rare steak and eggs on her plate.

The steak, briefly, shifted in Sigmund's vision and became a living, moving part of a cow. Sigmund's eyes watered, and he looked away. He mostly ate vegetables for that very reason. "I've never seen the world any other way, so I don't know how to explain it better. I can't imagine what it's like for you, seeing just the present. It must seem very fragile."

"We had a guy once who could see into the future, just a little bit, a couple of minutes at most. Didn't stop him from getting killed, but he wet himself right before the axe hit him. He was a lot less boring than you are." Carlotta belched.

"Why haven't I met you before?" Sigmund shrank back against the cushions in the booth.

"I'm heavy ordnance," Carlsbad said, his voice low, a rumble felt in Sigmund's belly and bones as much as heard by his ears. "I've been with the Table since the beginning. They don't reveal secrets like me to research assistants." Carlsbad was tar-black, skin strangely reflective, face eyeless and mouthless, blank as a minimalist snowman's, human only in general outline. "But the Old Doctor says you've exceeded all expectations, so we'll be working together from time to time."

Sigmund looked into Carlsbad's past, as far as he could—which was quite far, given the cocktail of uppers singing in his blood—and Carlsbad never changed; black, placid, eternal. "What—" What are you, he'd nearly asked. "What do you do for the Table?"

"Whatever the Old Doctor tells me to," Carlsbad said.

Sigmund nodded. "Carlotta told me you're a fallen god of the underworld."

"That bitch lies," Carlsbad said, without disapproval. "I'm no god. I'm just, what's that line—'the evil that lurks in the hearts of men.' The Old Doctor says that as long as one evil person remains on Earth, I'll be alive."

"Well," Sigmund said. "I guess you'll be around for a while, then."

The first time Carlsbad saved his life, Sigmund lay panting in a snowbank, blood running from a ragged gash in his arm. "You could have let me die just then," Sigmund said. Then, after a moment's hesitation: "You could have benefited from my death."

Carlsbad shrugged, shockingly dark against the snow. "Yeah, I guess."

"I thought you were evil," Sigmund said, lightheaded from blood loss and exertion, more in the now than he'd ever felt before, the scent of pines and the bite of cold air immediate reminders of his miraculously ongoing life. "I mean, you're made of evil."

"You're made mostly of carbon atoms," Carlsbad said. "But you don't spend all your time thinking about forming long-chain molecules, do you? There's more to both of us than our raw materials."

"Thank you for saving me, Carlsbad."

"Any time, Sigmund." His tone was laid-back but pleased, the voice of someone who'd seen it all but could still sometimes be pleasantly surprised. "You're the first Table agent in four hundred years who's treated me like something other than a weapon or a monster. I know I scare you shitless, but you talk to me."

Exhaustion and exhilaration waxed and waned in Sigmund. "I like you because you don't change. When I look at most people I can see them as babies, teenagers, every step of their lives superimposed, and if I look back far enough they disappear—but not you. You're the same as far back as I can see." Sigmund's eyelids were heavy. He felt light. He thought he might float away.

"Hold on," Carlsbad said. "Help is on the way. Your death might not diminish me, but I'd still like to keep you around."

Sigmund blacked out, but not before hearing the whirr of approaching helicopters coming to take him away.

"I'm the New Doctor," the New Doctor said. Willowy, brunette, young, she stood behind a podium in the briefing room, looking at the assembled Table agents—Sigmund, Carlotta, Carlsbad, and the recently-promoted Ray. They were the alpha squad, the apex of the organisation, and the New Doctor had not impressed them yet. "We're going to have some changes around here. We need to get back to basics. We need to find the cup. These other jobs might fill our bank accounts, but they don't further our cause."

Ray popped a wasp into his mouth, chewed, swallowed, and said, "Fuck that mystic bullshit." His voice was accompanied by a deep, angry buzz, a sort of wasp-whisper in harmony with the normal workings of his voicebox. Ray got nasty and impatient when he ate wasps. "I joined up to make money and get a regular workout, not chase after some imaginary Grail." Sigmund knew Ray was lying—that he had a very specific interest in the cup—but Sigmund also understood why Ray was keeping that interest a secret. "You just stay in the library and read your books like the Old Doctor did, OK?"

The New Doctor shoved the podium over, and it fell toward Ray, who dove out of the way. While he was moving, the New Doctor came around and kicked him viciously in the ribs, her small boots wickedly pointed and probably steel-toed. Ray rolled away, panting and clutching his side.

Sigmund peered into the New Doctor's past. She looked young, but she'd looked young for decades.

"I'm not like the Old Doctor," she said. "He missed his old life in the archives, and was content with his books, piecing together the past. But I'm glad to be out of the archives, and under my leadership, we're going to make history, not study it."

"I'll kill you," Ray said. Stingers were growing out of his fingertips, and his voice was all buzz now.

"Spare me," the New Doctor said, and kicked him in the face.

By spying on their pasts and listening in on their private moments, Sigmund learned why the other agents wanted to find the cup, and see God:

Carlotta whispered to one of her lovers, the shade of a great courtesan conjured from an anteroom of Hell: "I want to castrate God, so he'll never create another world."

Ray told Carlotta, while they disposed of the body of a young archivist who'd discovered their secret past and present plans: "I want to eat God's heart and belch out words of creation."

Carlsbad, alone, staring at the night sky, (a lighted void, while his own darkness was utter), had imaginary conversations with God that always came down, fundamentally, to one question: "Why did you make me?"

The New Doctor, just before she poisoned the Old Doctor, (making it look like a natural death), answered his bewildered plea for mercy by saying, "No. As long as you're alive, we'll never find the cup, and I'll never see God, and I'll never know the answers to the ten great questions I've composed during my time in the archives."

Sigmund saw it all, every petty plan and purpose that drove his fellows, but he had no better purpose himself. The agents of the Table might succeed in finding the cup, not because they were worthy, but simply because they'd been trying for years upon years, and sometimes persistence led to success.

Sigmund knew their deepest reasons, and kept all their secrets, because past and present and cause and effect were scrambled for him. The Old Doctor's regime of meth, cocaine, and more exotic uppers had ravaged Sigmund's nasal cavities and set him adrift in time. At first, he'd only been able to see back in time, but sometimes taking the Old Doctor's experimental stimulants truly sent him back in time. Sometimes it was just his mind that travelled, sent back a few days to relive past events again in his own body, but other times, rarely, he physically travelled back, just a day or two at most, just for a little while, before being wrenched back to a present filled with headaches and nosebleeds.

On one of those rare occasions when he travelled physically back in time, Sigmund saw the Old Doctor's murder, and was snapped back to the future moments before the New Doctor could kill him, too.

Ray ate a Sherpa's brain two days out of base camp, and after that, he was able to guide them up the crags and paths toward the temple perfectly, though he was harder to converse with, his speech peppered with mountain idioms. He developed a taste for barley tea flavoured with rancid yak butter, and sometimes sang lonely songs that merged with the sound of the wind.

"We're going to Hell," the New Doctor said.

"Probably," Sigmund said, edging away.

She sighed. "No, really—we're going into the underworld. Or, well, sort of a visiting room for the underworld."

"I've heard rumours about that." Hell's anteroom was where Carlotta found her ghostly lovers. "One of the Table's last remaining mystic secrets. I'm surprised they didn't lose that, too, when they lost the key to the moon and the scryer's glass and all those other wonders in the first war with the Templars."

"Much has been lost." The New Doctor pushed a shelf, which swung easily away from the wall on secret hinges, revealing an iron grate. "But that means much can be regained." She pressed a red button. "Stop fidgeting, Sigmund. I'm not going to kill you. But I do want to know, how did you get into the Old Doctor's office and see me kill him, when I know you were on assignment with Carlsbad in Belize at the time? And how did you disappear afterward? Bodily bilocation? Ectoplasmic projection? What?"

"Time travel," Sigmund said. "I don't just see into the past. Sometimes I travel into the past physically."

"Huh. I didn't see anything about that in the Old Doctor's notes."

"Oh, no. He kept the most important notes in his head. So why aren't you going to kill me?"

Something hummed and clattered beneath the floor.

"Because I can use you. Why haven't you turned me in?"

Sigmund hesitated. He'd liked the Old Doctor, who was the closest thing he'd ever had to a father. He hated to disrespect the old man's memory, though he knew the Old Doctor had seen him as a research tool, a sort of ambulatory microfiche machine, and nothing more. "Because I'm ready for things to change. I thought I wanted to be an operative, but I'm tired of the endless pointless round-and-round, not to mention being shot and stabbed and thrown from moving trains. Under your leadership, I think the Table might actually achieve something."

"We will." The grinding and humming underground intensified, and she raised her voice. "We'll find the cup, and see God, and get answers. We'll find out why he created the world, only to immediately abandon his creation, letting chaos fill his wake. But first, to Hell. Here." She tossed something glittering toward him, a few old subway tokens. "To pay the attendant."

The grinding stopped, the grate sliding open to reveal a tarnished brass elevator car operated by a man in a cloak the colour of dust and spiderwebs. He held out his palm, and Sigmund and the New Doctor each dropped a token into his hand.

"Why are we going... down there?" Sigmund asked.

"To see the Old Doctor, and get some of that information he kept only in his head. I know where to find the cup—or where to find the map that leads to it, anyway—but I need to know what will happen once I have the cup in hand."

"Why take me?"

"Because only insane people, like Carlotta, risk going to Hell's anteroom alone. And if I took anyone else, they'd find out I was the one who killed the Old Doctor, and they might be less understanding about it than you are." She stepped into the elevator car, and Sigmund followed. He glanced into the attendant's past, almost reflexively, and the things he saw were so horrible that he threw himself back into the far corner of the tiny car; if the elevator hadn't already started moving, he would have pried open the doors and fled. The attendant turned his head to look at him, and Sigmund squeezed his eyes shut so that he didn't have to risk seeing the attendant frown, or worse, smile.

"Interesting," the New Doctor said.

After they returned from Hell, Sigmund and the New Doctor fucked furiously beneath the card table in the Old Doctor's library, because sex is an antidote to death, or at least, an adequate placebo.

"That's it, then," the New Doctor said. "We're going to the Himalayas."

"Fucking great," Ray said. "I always wanted to eat a Yeti."

"I think you're hairy enough already," Carlotta said.

Sigmund and the New Doctor sat beneath a ledge of rock, frigid wind howling across the face of the mountain. Carlsbad was out looking for Ray and Carlotta, who had stolen all the food and oxygen and gone looking for the temple of the cup alone. They wanted to kill God, not ask him questions, so their betrayal was troublesome but not surprising. Sigmund probably should have told someone about their planned betrayal, but he felt more and more like an actor outside time—a position which, he now realised, was likely to get him killed. He needed to take a more active role.

"Ray and Carlotta don't know the prophecy," Sigmund said. "Only the Old Doctor knew, and he only told us. They have no idea what they're going to cause, if they reach the Temple first."

"If they reach the Temple first, we'll die along with the rest of the world." The New Doctor was weak from oxygen deficiency. "If Carlsbad doesn't find them, we're doomed." She looked older, having left the safety of the library and the archives, and the past two years had been hard. They'd travelled to the edges and underside of the Earth, gathering fragments of the map to the temple of the cup, chasing down the obscure references the New Doctor had uncovered in the archives. First they'd gone deep into the African desert, into crumbling palaces carved from sentient rock; then they'd trekked through the Antarctic, looking for the secret entrance to the Earth's war-torn core, and finding it; they'd projected themselves, astrally and otherwise, into the mind of a sleeping demigod from the jungles of another world; and two months ago they'd descended to crush-depth in the Pacific Ocean to find the last fragment of the map in a coral temple guarded by spined, bioluminescent beings of infinite sadness. Ray had eaten one of those guardians, and ever since he'd been sweating purple ink and taking long, contemplative baths in salt water.

The New Doctor had ransacked the Table's coffers to pay for this last trip to the Himalayas, selling off long-hoarded art objects and dismissing even the poorly-paid hereditary janitorial staff to cover the expenses. And now they were on the edge of total failure, unless Sigmund did something.

Sigmund opened his pack and removed his last vial of the Old Doctor's most potent exotic upper. "Wish me bon voyage," he said, and snorted it all.

Time unspooled, and Sigmund found himself beneath the same ledge, but earlier, the ice unmarked by human passage, the weather more mild. Moving manically, driven by drugs and the need to stay warm, he piled up rocks above the trail and waited, pacing in an endless circle, until he heard Carlotta and Ray approaching, grunting under the weight of stolen supplies.

He pushed rocks down on them, and the witch and the phage were knocked down. Sigmund made his way to them, hoping they would be crushed—that the rocks would have done his work for him. Carlotta was mostly buried, but her long fingernails scraped furrows in the ice, and Sigmund gritted his teeth, cleared away enough rocks to expose her head, and finished her off with the ice axe. She did not speak, but Sigmund almost thought he saw respect in her expression before he obliterated it. Ray was only half-buried, but unmoving, his neck twisted unnaturally. Sigmund sank the point of the axe into Ray's thigh to make sure he was truly dead, and the phage did not react. Sigmund left the axe in Ray's leg. He turned his back on the dead and crouched, waiting for time to sweep him up again in its flow.

Carlsbad found Ray and Carlotta dead, and brought back the supplies. By then Sigmund was back from the past, and while the New Doctor ate and rested, he took Carlsbad aside to tell him the truth: "There's a good chance we might destroy the world."

"Hmm," Carlsbad said.

"There's a prophecy, in the deep archives of the Table, that God will only return when the world is destroyed by fire. But it's an article of faith—the basis of our faith—that when the contents of the cup are swallowed by an acolyte of the Table, God will return. So by approaching the cup—by intending to drink from it—we might collapse the probability wave in such a way that the end of the world begins, fire and all, in the moments before we even touch the cup."

"And you and the New Doctor are OK with that?"

"The New Doctor thinks she can convince God to spare the world from destruction, retroactively, if necessary."

"Huh," Carlsbad said.

"She can be very persuasive," Sigmund said.

"I'm sure," Carlsbad replied.

The fire began to fall just as they reached the temple, a structure so old it seemed part of the mountain itself. The sky went red, and great gobbets of flame cascaded down, the meteor shower to end all others. Snow flashed instantly to steam on all the surrounding mountains, though the temple peak was untouched, for now.

"That's it, then," Carlsbad said. "Only the evil in you two is keeping me alive."

"No turning back now," the New Doctor said, and started up the ancient steps to the temple.

Ray, bloodied and battered, left arm hanging broken, stepped from the shadows beside the temple. He held Sigmund's ice axe in his good hand, and he swung it at the New Doctor's head with phenomenal force, caving in her skull. She fell, and he fell upon her, bringing the axe down again and again, laying her body open. He looked up, face bruised and swollen, fur sprouting from his jaw, veins pulsing in his forehead, poison and ink and pus and hallucinogens oozing from his pores. "You can't kill me, junkie. I've eaten wolverines. I've eaten giants. I've eaten angels." As he said this last, he began to glow with a strange, blue-shifted light.

"Saving your life again," Carlsbad said, almost tenderly, and then he did what the Table always counted on him to do. He swelled, he stormed, he smashed, he tore Ray to pieces, and then tore up the pieces.

After that he began to melt. "Ah, shit, Sigmund," he said. "You just aren't evil enough." Before Sigmund could say thank you, or goodbye, all that remained of Carlsbad was a dark pool, like a slick of old axle grease on the snow.

There was nothing for Sigmund to do but go on.

"The cup holds the blood of God," the Old Doctor said. "Drink it, and God will return, and as you are made briefly divine by swallowing the substance of his body, he will treat you as an equal, and answer questions, and grant requests. For that moment, God will do whatever you ask." The Old Doctor placed his hand on Sigmund's own. "The Table exists to make sure the cup's power is not used for evil or trivial purposes. The question asked, the wish desired, has to be worth the cost, which is the world."

"What would you ask?" Sigmund said.

"I would ask why God created the world and walked away, leaving only a cupful of blood and a world of wonders behind.

But that is only curiosity, and not a worthy question."

"So anyway," Sigmund said, sniffing and wiping at his nose. "When can I start doing field work?" He wished he could see the future instead of the past. He thought this was going to be a lot of fun.

The cup in Sigmund's hands held blood, liquid at the centre, but dried and crusted on the cup's rim. Sigmund scraped the residue of dried blood up with his long pinky fingernail. He took a breath. Let it out. And snorted God's blood.

Time snapped.

Sigmund looked around the temple. It was white, bright, clean, and no longer on a mountaintop. The windows looked out on a placid sea. He was not alone.

God looked nothing like Sigmund had imagined, but at the same time, it was impossible to mistake him for anyone else. It was clear that God was on his way out, but he paused, and looked at Sigmund expectantly.

Sigmund had gone from the end of the world to the beginning. He was so high from snorting God's blood that he could see individual atoms in the air, vibrating. He knew he could be jerked back to the top of the ruined world at any moment.

Sigmund tried to think. He'd expected the New Doctor to ask the questions, to make the requests, so he didn't know what to say. God was clearly growing impatient, ready to leave his creation forever behind. If Sigmund spoke quickly, he could have anything he wanted. Anything at all.

"Hey," Sigmund said. "Don't go."

LIFT

Kate Moore

The lift was spacious. I wondered why he stood so close to me. He picked at his shirt.

"Are you here for the interview?"

"Yeah." I fiddled with my bag. "Is that what you're here for?"

He lowered his eyes. "It would appear so."

There was an extended silence, but somehow this was comfortable, comforting — I couldn't explain it.

"You know, this isn't really what I want."

I noticed his eyes were green. "What do you mean?"

He shrugged, so I answered for him. "Oh, I see. You're passionate about something, aren't you? So now you're going to do something you don't like, to do something you do like. And then you'll get lost in what you don't like."

He examined my face. "Is that how you feel? Do you feel trapped?"

"Well... yes. I'm a poet. It's what I do, what I am. But I can't make a living off poetry. Everyone knows that." I thought I heard a sniffle of music. It stopped as though a tissue had wiped it away.

"You're a poet? I'm talking to a poet in a lift. Recite one for me."

The carriage slowed right down, almost stopped. My stomach dipped. I hadn't been asked to do this before.

"Go on," he said. "Please? I'd really enjoy it."

The carriage picked up speed.

"Okay," I told him. "I'll do it."

His modest smile masked a generous one. He waited for me to speak.

The lift jolted. Artificial light flickered around us.

"It is scribbled along the body, impossible to even say a word. An alphabet has been stored beneath the ground. It is a practice alphabet, work of the hand. Yet not, not marks inside a box. For example, this is a mirror box. Spinoza designed such a box and called it the Eighth Sky."

He had loosened his tie, with what looked like the beginning of a smile.

"Michael Palmer wrote it," I added. It's called Eighth Sky. One of my favourites."

"It's quite beautiful, isn't it? Unusual."

"Yes."

"But what about your own? Can I hear one of yours?"

"I ... don't know if I can."

"Please. Just try. It's something I need to hear."

I liked the way he spoke to me. "There is one I could recite ... just a few lines, if you want."

"I do."

When he said that, I knew it was the right one. "Okay, well, it starts like this – He teaches story fragments, strange shards of tension. Pupils unaware of the home-tale, truth-tale. Weekday lungs drenched in heavy tide. Sand-grit throat. Gravel in, gravel out. All they hear is the same sentence. Tuesday is Wednesday, Thursday is Friday. But eyes are packed with pewter, as he rides the blackest horse of Monday's carousel."

I tugged at my earring, realised the poem maybe wasn't good enough, that maybe this was why I was there. The operating panel seemed to be broken. All floors were lucent.

He looked at me. I gripped the handrail, its chilled surface a relief. I waited a long time for him to speak.

"I want to tell you all the things I felt when you gave me those words, but there's too much to sift through. The person in your poem is you, and me, and the ones we don't understand."

His words came to me as a painful release of misadventure – an axe for the frozen sea within me. He understood.

"It's OK," he said. "I feel it too. You showed me in your poetry, and I showed you in my response."

The stark light grew into a small caramel sun – we stood there in its glow, close and connected, for some time.

I broke the silence. "The lift... has it moved at all in this time?"

We became aware of something other than ourselves – that we were bound by muted silver walls.

"I don't know." His fingers traced the numbers on the panel, floor six ablaze with vivid blue.

"I think we've passed the floor we need." I pressed the *open* button continually, but the door remained tightly shut.

"Are you afraid?" He took my hands.

"No."

The lift started to move. Seventh floor, eighth floor, ninth floor, tenth floor... it kept going, digit after digit, ascending effortlessly. Our hands laced together, I squeezed lightly. Floor six was a memory. There were twenty-one floors in the building, and we were still climbing. Still rising. Lifted.

LISTEN

Louise Coquio

Let me tell you how it really was. I'll try and remember how we felt, our fear. Sometimes it's like it didn't happen at all and I have to ask Ed "Was it real? Were we there?"

And he'll say, "Yup, but I don't think we're supposed to remember. I think it wipes itself clean out of your head if you let it, and that might well be the very right thing for it to do."

That's Ed, though. All practical. Grounded, I guess you'd call him. He tethers us. In a good way.

So it's been a while since it all happened, and here we are, going back again. I know it will be different now, but I'm not sure how. Of course, that house has changed way more than the rest of us over the years. I swear it's like it had surgery or something. It went in for a big, expensive makeover and came out all glossy and airbrushed, like some Hollywood star who's had a lot of work, but it's good work, you know, so good that people admire it instead of being all mean and cynical like they are usually with beautiful things. So the house is like a chameleon; it's changed itself on the outside so well that, even on the inside, you have to really look hard to see how it used to be.

9 Rue Corbeau; the name gives it a kind of glamour that our houses here in England can only dream of. A name can be misleading though. For all its glossy façade, 9 Rue Corbeau is a fraud, a charlatan at heart. Its front yard might now be full of scented lemon trees and red begonias in weathered antique pots, but we would do well to remember, your honour, that it is still the same yard in which old man Faveroux used to slit the throats of the pigs he had hand-reared, before curing the meat to make his famous *saussicon*. Its path is still the one the villagers lined up on, every Tuesday and Thursday, to buy their air-dried hams and thick, lumpy slabs of *pâté de campagne*. It's nearly twenty years since

the *charcuterie* shut its doors for the last time. The house stood empty then, forgotten until, inevitably, it joined all the other beautiful houses in this area and was bought up for peanuts by foreigners searching for the idyll we've all read about and feel we deserve somehow for ourselves.

"Jesus Gab that's not how it was!" Ed will say when I've just finished some anecdote or other about our time there.

"Yes it was. What have I said that didn't happen?" I'll ask him, all wide-eyed and innocent. I'll smile when I say this, and our friends will think we're joking around, but we're not, not really. We're challenging each other to battle. We love all that stuff. I've always thought that a bit of competition is healthy. Keeps things exciting. Ed would say that you should probably bring along a pinch of salt with this story, but I think you should listen, and then decide for yourselves.

So my family bought the house, ruin as it was back then, not because they wanted to live the dream, but because they were about to be living some kind of nightmare. They knew something bad was coming for them, and they wanted somewhere big and private to meet it, face to face. There is a vast garden, south-facing, at the front of the house, and that first summer my aunt spent two whole months moving rubble out of it with a small metal wheelbarrow, just so that they could clear enough space to plant a lawn. It was a barren wilderness, like those photos you see in the National Geographic of Afghanistan, where the odd stalk of grass fights for survival amongst rocks and dust. All that grew in the garden then were old fruit trees and a thicket of woody, parched stalks of asparagus that had survived, alone and inedible, since Madame Faveroux shuffled off this mortal coil the year before the *charcuterie* closed its doors for the last time.

The first time I saw the house, Ed and I had gone down on the TGV for a week. Of course we wanted a holiday, but we were full of curiosity. Ed, because he needed to see the place for himself to picture it properly, and me because I wondered how everyone had continued to exist so easily without me near them. As far as I could tell, I had lost them all in one fell swoop: my father, mother, grand-mother and aunt had de-camped four months previously. I expect that, had I stopped for a minute to really examine my own thoughts, I would have discovered that I was still grieving for them.

In France, it was my father who met us at the station. I remember that he was covered in a whitish film of plaster dust, because they were in the middle of knocking down walls in the front part of the house and reclaiming a kitchen from the ruins of the shop.

"Hope you don't mind a bit of mess," he'd said "but I think you'll like it."

And he was right, I did.

Even in its present state you could see that the house had once been grand and beautiful and could be again. It was big; three stories high and pleasingly symmetrical, with a red-brown roof of curled terracotta tiles above the small, square windows of the *grainier*. It had peeling shutters the colour of wine at the tall windows of the first two floors and a giant front door of carved wood. They'd only signed the papers with the *notaire* three weeks before and already you could tell that all of them had this kind of fervour; a shine in their eyes when they looked at it. That house had them the minute they started work on it and their passion has never waned.

"So, what do you think?" my aunt, Paulette, asked as she pulled off her workman's gloves and revealed the perfect manicure beneath. "She's a looker, this one, no?"

"Yes, she certainly will be," Ed said. "You look like you've been working hard, though."

"Her father is a hard task master, he works us dawn to dusk." Paulette winked conspiratorially at me. "But you remember what he is like, eh? Never mind, he knows we love him. You go in and see your mother. She is in the salon; this heat is no good for her."

I nodded, left Ed with Paulette, and went in through the open side door of the house. The inside was so dark after the glaring sunshine of the day that I was blinded for a minute. I could hear the sound of hammering somewhere above me, and the dust from the plaster was so heavy on the air that you could taste it, thick like chalk, on your tongue. I found myself in a makeshift kitchen. I recognised various things from home; though it was strange to see them here, out of their natural habitat. The old chest freezer, where my mother had stored the vast amounts of vegetables she had grown every year, was covered in a plastic-coated tablecloth and appeared to be the only work surface in the enormous room. Against the back wall was a range cooker with two blue bottles of gas standing neatly at its side. The village, a tiny hamlet, was too remote for gas to be supplied by pipelines. My father had told me that the place wasn't big enough to have its own *boulangerie* but that, every morning, a van laden with breads parked for fifteen minutes in the centre of the village, on the square in front of the stone church. Through the darkness of the kitchen I could hear the television, competing loudly with the relentless hammering. I walked towards the sound. I smiled. I swallowed the lump in my throat and I went into the salon to hug my mother.

After that first trip, each visit felt as if time had hurtled forward without us, too fast, throwing us off balance. Even Ed was disorientated by the changes. We couldn't keep up and sometimes I know that, secretly at least, I was afraid of what we might find there. The house gradually became habitable but still makeshift. More and more relics from my childhood found their way out of storage, until the place was filled, museum-like, with the artefacts of a past that teetered on the brink of extinction. Whenever we arrived I found I could spend the first hour or two walking round the house like a tourist, silently running my hands over memories and seeing them again. I felt as if some kind of wheel was turning and that I had to strain to see this view, to record it as a camera would, before it disappeared forever over the horizon.

There were changes, of course, that were not to do with the house but its occupants. Sometimes, things would be almost normal and parties were thrown, so we could meet the people who had become important in my parents' life. There were elaborate dinners, when my mother was well enough, at which she would hold court with a repertoire of filthy jokes, fuelled by her incredible capacity for whiskey.

Once, after such a night, she had leaned against me as I struggled to get her up the curving, polished stairs to bed, and whispered, "You know, I love this house so much that the only way they'll get me out is in a box, feet first."

"You're not going anywhere," I'd said quickly, uncomfortable with the truth of it all.

Other times, we would find that she would stare blankly at us when we spoke to her. One day she had simply forgotten how to hold her cigarette. We took it in turns, then, to hold it for her. I think we all figured that we had no right to take away that simple pleasure from her.

"Don't ever start smoking," she would say when it was my turn to do the honours. "It's a dirty, disgusting habit. Your father has never liked me smoking."

And I would smile and reassure her, with my fingers crossed against the lie because, by then, I had been smoking for fifteen years already.

The day before we were due to sail home from a holiday in the early autumn, my grandmother had taken my mother for a walk up the lane to the village, and I was helping Maria, a carer from the village, who sat with my mother in the afternoons. Maria washed the dishes after lunch while I dried, and as she worked, she held a cigarette clasped between her lips, her eyes squinting against the smoke.

"So these men at the window. She say they press their faces right up against the glass. They frighten your mother, no?" she said without stopping what she was doing.

"What men?" I asked, struggling to dry a huge iron pan that I could barely lift.

"She tell me she see men watching her through her window. She see them in the garden too."

"But how could anyone watch her through her window? She's on the second floor," I said.

"This is what she say. No one believe her but me. I seen."

I stopped drying and looked at Maria. She was small and fair-haired, in her early sixties. She smiled but she held my gaze.

"What have you seen, Maria?" I asked.

"I've seen marks on the glass after their faces press. I clean it away before your father see. He would be upset, I think."

"You said she was afraid."

"Yes, she wants to come downstairs to sleep."

My father and Paulette had driven into town after lunch to pick up shopping. We heard the sound of their car turning into the gravel-filled barn at the side of the house.

"I'll watch her. She'll be OK with me," said Maria. "No need for you to worry."

We didn't get a chance to speak again because Paulette came bustling into the kitchen laden with supplies. But that night I found myself staring nervously into the garden when I went up to close the shutters, and I couldn't help thinking about what Maria had said. From then on I began to see the house differently, as if all it had taken was that one suggestion for me to see beyond its smooth veneer. I found I was uneasy there and that I didn't like to be alone upstairs.

Things deteriorated, of course they did, though we all did our best to ignore the small changes that occurred; the way she could no longer lift a glass to her mouth, the way she forgot how to pick up cutlery or do up the buttons on her blouse. We all, without discussing it, simply began to take on these small tasks ourselves. Mostly, my mother was placid and accepting of our help. She would stand quietly, like a small child, while we buttoned her coat or combed her hair. She did get angry, violently so on occasion, but only ever with my father. Hostility was a common symptom, one we had been told to expect, and was reserved for those closest.

Each time we went back, we were aware that soon there would be greater changes that none of us could turn a blind eye to. At some point soon we would have to act. We would have to decide the future; it was just a question of when. We thought we were ready. Before the final visit there was a phone call.

"She's much worse. You must come," my father had told me, and a cold wave of fear washed over me.

"When?" I'd asked.

He had sounded calm. His voice was softer than usual, alien. "Now. We need you now. Tickets are waiting at the port."

And so we'd gone.

The next morning, we stood on the deck of the ferry in the cold half-light of the morning and watched as Portsmouth gradually slipped away into the past, but we didn't speak. Seagulls followed us out for a while, loudly hopeful, but even they sensed that the fate that followed us that day was not charitable and they quickly made their escape, trying instead for their breakfast, the pickings to be had along the empty, grey coast of the Isle of Wight. Ed probably wished he could join them and avoid all that lay ahead but, if this was the case, he didn't say so. Instead, he leaned against the railings on the front deck, his face pale and his hair blowing into his eyes, as he stared into a future that must have seemed bleak, even to him.

The journey took us the whole day. It was already close to midnight when we arrived and there were bright stars massed against the inky black of the sky. There was only one street lamp on the lane and this was turned off every night at eleven, leaving the house in almost total darkness so that its appearance, this time, remained a mystery. The lights were on in the kitchen, although the shutters had hidden them on our approach, and here Paulette, my father and my grandmother sat around the table halfway through a joyless game of whist. My mother was already asleep, had been for hours. She hadn't been sleeping well. Nights had become difficult for her; filled with disturbing dreams that she could no longer articulate to us, though they left her sweating and wakeful. We sat around the table drinking strong, bitter coffee and local cognac from small, tulip-shaped glasses.

Paulette kept her arm protectively around my grand-mother as she spoke; "Your father, he needs your help now. It is good you are here so quick." She smiled at me. "There are many big things to decide now."

My father stood up to empty Paulette's ashtray into the bin with practiced irritation. "These are things to decide tomorrow, not now. We must talk carefully, we have options now and we need to make the right choices for everyone," he said.

I must have had questions, but I didn't ask them. I wasn't ready for the answers.

I need a break now; my head has started to ache. I can't believe I'm telling you this. Ed thinks I'm mad to keep going over everything, when I can't change any of it, but I need to speak it to make sense of it. Do you know what I mean? Have you ever felt like that? I think talking's healthy. Things out in the open and all that. I read once that all the most terrible fears begin as something we repress. Freud I think it was, mad old bugger. Still, he may have been on to something, don't you think? So, where was I? Oh yes, decisions. Actually they were easy when it came down to it. There was only one path open to us really. We brought her home.

The last night we spent all together in that house started early, because we had to be up at four in the morning to make the 10.30 ferry from St Malo. We packed up our stuff and some of hers, the things we felt she loved most, although there ended up being far more than my father had wanted us to take, because we all had different memories of which things she'd told us were special over the years. I remember I tucked the tiny red pouch that held my own baby teeth into the leather vanity case that held her vast collection of perfume, and that this, more than anything along the way, made me want to cry. We sat down to eat some dinner, *mouclade* that Paulette had prepared, but no one really had their heart in it.

"Big day tomorrow," said Paulette to my mother.

"Is it?" she replied, although we had all told her over and over that we were taking her home.

"I'll stay here and look after the house," Paulette whispered, "so you won't have anything to worry about. I'll take care of everything."

My mother was tired and we put her to bed early that night. She slept, now, on a small single bed that had been set up in the corner of the living room. She was unsteady on her feet, and the polished wood stairs were too fraught with danger. Sometimes, at night, she still wandered around the house. Gates had been installed at the foot of the stairs to prevent her falling. She had not been sorry to move from her bedroom. Ed and I slept in there this time, out of necessity, because there was no other space for us, but it made us feel like impostors. Uncomfortable.

So, that last night, the night it happened, had a strange feeling from the beginning. Of course it did, you wouldn't expect anything else from me, would you? But I promised I would tell you the truth, didn't I? And I didn't cross my fingers when I said that. There really was a knot of fear in my stomach that I did my best to ignore; I didn't know whether this was because of the house and the men, or because we were taking her out of it for the last time. Of course, I felt different about sleeping in the bedroom, now I knew. I felt there was truth in her claims because I trusted her, even then, and I was angry that everyone else seemed so quick to dismiss her. Sometimes, of course, she was still there, just as we had been told she would be, and her presence at unexpected moments disorientated us all. It was as if the film of confusion would peel slowly away from her eyes, and there she'd be. Just how she used to be. I'd never had a single reason to doubt her my whole life. I don't ever remember her not telling the truth, not even when the truth was newly raw and painful, glistening like a wound. I wasn't sure I could discount her now. I expected to see those faces pressed against the window. I believe, as she did, that anything can happen, even things we cannot always explain. So if they were there, then I might come close to the window to see them better, these men. It was obvious to me that if I were to lean outside and look, then there they'd be, legs dangling, floating in the cool air with the scent of May blossom clinging to their clothes like death.

Ed and I went to bed early, and together, because, by that time, I was too afraid to go up there alone. He was annoyed, I could tell. He liked to watch the sport headlines on the English satellite channels when everyone else had gone to bed, so he probably felt he was missing out. My mother's room, for all our unease, was beautiful. It had an antique walnut sleigh bed and a polished oak floor. In the corner stood a vast cheval mirror that I remembered from her dressing-room when I was growing up. It had a tray at the bottom where my father would keep his watch, his cufflinks, his change. It was strange to see it empty, but this was no longer his room. He had moved to a small guest-room off the bathroom when she first became ill. I suppose they both needed some relief from the relentlessness of it all. Once it started, there seemed to be no respite. Her condition just marched on and on, causing destruction and devastation to anything in its path: to her, to him, to me, and to the life that we had once had, all together.

We lay in bed listening to the sounds of the others coming up the stairs, their voices soft as they said goodnight, so as not to wake her. We heard water running in the bathrooms, lights clicking on, then off. Then silence.

"I can't look at the mirror," I said, my back prickling with unease. I rolled over and propped myself up on an elbow to look at Ed instead. "I keep thinking that I'll see something that shouldn't be there." I waited for the reassurance, the amusement, but none came.

"I know," he said, "me too."

"You're supposed to be the voice of reason here."

"Gab, it feels weird tonight, even to me. Like we're all on the edge of something here. No one is talking about it really, are they? She loves this house and she must know she won't see it again."

I turned over to stop any more talk. It was uncomfortable. Ed took the hint and turned over himself, but I noticed he left his bedside light on and I was glad he did.

We had been quiet for ten minutes, maybe fifteen, when it started; it's difficult to tell. Time moves strangely at night; a few minutes feel like an hour in the darkness. It began with banging. It was sudden, jolting us into consciousness; shockingly loud and as fast as footfalls. As if someone was stamping along the wooden boards of the *grainier* floor above us.

Bang. Bang,

Sounding like it was over the right hand side of the house and coming closer.

Bang. Bang.

We clung to each other, Ed looking at me wide-eyed, me nodding to let him know that no, it wasn't just him. As the noise drew closer, we could hear the sound of something dragging right after the foot sound.

Bang. Bang. Drag.

We listened, transfixed, as it came right overhead. It was deafeningly loud. The others must be awake now. You couldn't sleep through this. I expected to hear them knocking on the door.

Bang. Bang.

The glass light fitting in the ceiling shook.

"Gab, what if it's your Mum up there?"

I looked at Ed, horrified, both at the possibility that it could be her, and that we would have to go up and see.

Bang. Bang.

At last it began to get fainter, to move away to the other side of the house. Still the sound of dragging followed it. Over my grandmother's room it went.

Bang. Bang. Drag.

Over the bathroom, over the guest room where my father slept.

And then silence.

As the noise stopped, the fear that had held us still and spellbound released its grip, and we shot out of bed.

"She could be hurt," Ed said, opening the door and snapping on the landing light. Unbelievably, no one else was up yet. The landing was in darkness, save for the dim, orange glow of a nightlight on the table. I followed Ed to the door that led to the *grainier* stairs and found myself flinching as he reached for the handle. The door was locked. We exchanged glances but there was no time to smile our relief.

Downstairs, my mother had begun to scream.

We ran along the landing. My father and then my grandmother emerged, blinking with confusion as if they had been woken, unbelievably, by the screaming, not by the banging that had preceded it. In the living room, the screaming had stopped before we opened the door, and we found her out of bed, standing in the dead centre of the room, but not seeing us. She stared towards the fireplace on the outer wall of the house. We were still for a minute, unsure of whether she was awake or asleep. Then I stepped forward and she turned towards me.

She smiled. "Look," she said. "Look who's come."

I followed her gaze towards the dying embers of the fire but I could see nothing, no one.

"Who is it?" I asked her and she looked at me as if I was stupid, but didn't answer.

We got her back onto her bed and she lay down without a fight. My father fetched a sleeping bag and sat heavily on the sofa. We went back upstairs in silence, but we left the landing light burning.

In the morning we swept out the last warm cinders from the fire and ate the breakfast Paulette prepared for us. My mother was cheerful as we loaded our luggage into the car, but she waved to Paulette long after we had turned the corner at the end of the lane. We didn't speak much on the drive to the port. There was nothing we could say.

Ed thinks it happened because my mother was angry to be taken from a place she loved so much. But when I look back, when I try to remember, I can't help thinking he is wrong. I don't think the fact she loved the house was the problem. I think what we heard that night was the anger and sorrow of a house that loved her back.

A LIFE IN PLASTIC

Andrew Hook

Oki usually took his green tea quietly. At one of his favourite establishments they brewed it at the table. He would watch as the waitress put approximately three grams of loose green tea into a ceramic cup with a filter. He preferred the taste of *sencha*, and the waitress would stand quietly as the water she had boiled cooled for several minutes before pouring it over the loose leaves and covering it. Again, they would wait for a few minutes, depending on the newness of the tea, then she would remove the cover and the filter and place the cup in front of him.

He always admired the colour before inhaling the aroma, then taking a sip. The tea rolled over his tongue as he savoured the subtle scent of the sweet grass. He would nod at the waitress and she would return to her station, whilst he returned his gaze to the department store opposite.

There was a young girl he sometimes saw window-dressing the mannequins who reminded him of his daughter. Today she wasn't there, or maybe it was too late. She usually performed her tasks early in the morning, often Thursdays. Oki decided not to wait too long. The store next door to the tearoom had been refurbished as a record shop, and it was their opening day. They were blasting music by Ayumi Hamasaki and if he watched carefully he could see the vibrations flutter the tea in the cup, individual ripples which touched the shore of his tongue.

He stood and beckoned the waitress over, dropping coins into her open palm. Then he opened the door of the establishment, glanced once in the direction of the record shop and swiftly crossed the road until he stood in front of the department store.

It was her work. That much was clear. There was a cleanness to her touch, which was almost a trademark, yet it was often matched by a quirkiness that was decidedly kooky. In the traditional salaryman's suit facing Oki a yellow handkerchief had been folded into the breast pocket in such a way that the corners resembled petals. He placed one hand against the window, aware that he was soiling the sheen with his fingerprints. Then, sighing once, he placed his hand into his trouser pocket and turned back to the street. Hailing a taxi, Oki departed for work.

In his thirty-third year he'd had one child, a girl, Keiko, with a partner he hadn't intended to be serious with. The girl's parents had pressed for them to get married, but she had also known that their relationship wasn't fated to work and had resisted. Oki should have known then that her stubbornness was a sign of great strength, and in retrospect he should have pursued the relationship and made it honourable. As it was, he hadn't seen his daughter until her first birthday. From a distance. She took a step and fell into the arms of her mother.

Oki realised then that the woman was indeed a mother and therefore she no longer and never would be his girl again. Even if they were reunited.

He sent a letter to his daughter's grandmother asking to be allowed into the child's life. With a gentle persistence the woman convinced her daughter that the child should be aware of her father. The first few meetings were tentative, then regular. When Keiko was six it was agreed that Oki might take her on a long weekend to Ōkunoshima.

The subsequent day the record shop had tempered its enthusiasm and Oki was able to enjoy his green tea in relative peace.

As he took his first sip the girl stepped into the window display and he associated the sweet aroma of the tea with her presence. He watched as she unbuttoned the yellow handkerchief mannequin, slipping the jacket off its shoulders. Involuntarily, Oki shivered. He imagined his own jacket slipping from his body. As the girl folded it in two and placed it on top of a cardboard box she looked directly across the street. Oki held his gaze, but was sure she hadn't seen him. And even if she had, she wouldn't have understood that he was looking.

Some people were interested in speculating what might happen should a mannequin come alive, but for Oki the reverse was true. He wondered what it would be like to be the mannequin. He couldn't imagine his emotions any more distanced than they already were, yet would like to try.

The girl crouched and unzipped the mannequin's trousers, then slid them down smooth white legs. Oki had seen a television programme, which had shown how mannequins were produced. Many of them had detachable limbs and torsos. A large proportion of mannequins had the same legs and lower body, whether they were male or female. Only the face, fingers and breasts, or absence of breasts, were necessary to distinguish their gender.

Two months after he had first seen the girl who resembled Keiko in the department store window he purchased a mannequin for himself. Yet it had taken another month for him to unpack it from the box.

Oki hadn't been sure what he expected, but had imagined some disappointment. The mannequin's structure was inflexible. There was some movement to be had from swivelling and positioning the limbs, but it was clear once the structure was complete that this wasn't what he was looking for. The mannequin might be immutable regarding its emotions, but even something emotionless needed a heart.

The task wasn't to recreate what he had seen in the privacy of his home, but to find himself thumping against the safety glass of the department store window as the girl he decided to call Keiko dressed him.

The day was crystal-bright. With Keiko's small hand in his they caught the Sanyō Shinkansen train to Mihara Station, then caught the Kure Line local train to Tadanoumi Station. A smiling cartoon rabbit greeted them from a sign for the island and they walked the short distance to the terminal before catching the twelve-minute ferry to Ōkunoshima.

Oki had taken Keiko to the island because he didn't know where else to go. He wasn't used to being around children, few of his friends had married and those who had children tended to keep themselves to themselves. The island, with its over-zealous population of rabbits and numerous walking trails, seemed a good destination to bond with Keiko. So far their occasional meetings had established an uneasy camaraderie and Oki felt they needed something specific to themselves and devoid of maternal influence which they could reflect on in later life and identify as theirs and theirs alone.

Other than the rabbits and the walking trails the island held a dark history. From 1927 until 1945 it had been home to a chemical weapons facility that produced over six kilotons of mustard gas and tear gas.

When Oki remembers it now—holding Keiko's hand as the ferry surged towards the island—he can no longer picture her face. She looks up at him blankly, the skin as featureless as a tan stocking spread over a mannequin. Her long black hair streaks away from the direction of the island as though in fear. It pains Oki that he cannot remember how she once was, that he has supplanted her face onto the face of Keiko the window-dresser and then aged it. Yet that is the only way he has been able to deal with the tragedy that unfolded.

Keiko squeaked at the sight of the rabbits. She chased them along the forecourt to the entrance of the hotel, their multiple bodies splitting into twos and threes, from Oki's perspective, skittering into the undergrowth. Rabbits had been used in the chemical munitions plant to test the effectiveness of the weapons during World War II. However, those rabbits had been killed when the buildings were demolished. According to official reports, the rabbits which now overran the island had no connection to those involved with the weapon tests.

Oki called out to Keiko and she returned her hand meekly into his. They checked into the hotel and Oki ran a bath as Keiko explored their room, emptying her backpack and putting the contents into a cabinet alongside her single bed.

Oki stood in the bathroom doorway, steam billowing behind him as though he were a monster stepping out of the mist. In that moment the privacy of the hotel room astounded him. Outside the four walls there might be no one in the world, but inside the cramped space he and his daughter quietly existed.

He had never felt more alone in his life.

Keiko had arranged two mannequins facing each other. One had an outstretched hand whilst the other, a gloved female, held her fingers close to the side of her face.

Oki stood with his back to the tea room, with the street separating him and the department store. Cars were grid-locked. He imagined hoisting himself onto the roof of the nearest

Daihatsu and stepping across the four lanes like a squirrel hopping across a stream on turtle backs. He watched with decreasing detachment as Keiko gently positioned the mannequins, her right hand held out ready to steady them if they tilted, her left hand smoothing down the clothes so they gave the appearance of a fit.

If his daughter were standing beside him he was sure she wouldn't see the connection between her and this older woman. True, he had extrapolated the years onto her, but she had already been created in Keiko's image and he considered he had simply found her rather than appropriated her. There was nothing sexual in his gaze, in his admiration of her slender form and the delicacy in which she performed her job, which she obviously loved.

If there was any emotion, it was that he was proud of her.

Oki crossed the street, placing his hands on the bonnets of the cars he passed, feeling the heat from their engines. He stood directly in front of Keiko standing within the window display. She didn't notice him, simply continued with her task like an actress forgetting an audience, or—more simply—a worker focussed on the work in hand. If she were to acknowledge the window then she would fail in her task. For Keiko to succeed she had to imagine the window to be a blank black wall. This would explain why she failed to acknowledge him.

That evening Oki dug out the Swiss Army Knife he had retained from his camping days and began to peel back the hard plastic from the arm of his mannequin. It came away like shaved wood. On an unobtrusive part of his right shoulder, where the limb would be concealed by his office shirt, he glued the fragment of plastic to his skin.

Keiko soon found the speed of the rabbits detrimental to her enjoyment. The morning after her arrival she sat on the front steps of the hotel with her arms folded across her chest.

Oki remembered that she asked for her mother.

Ōkunoshima had little—in retrospect—to pleasure a child. Even for an adult the six-hole golf course couldn't hold attention for more than a morning, and the Poison Gas Museum had limited appeal. One of the two rooms was devoted to donated artefacts from family members of the workers who had lived there. A display explained the inadequate conditions; how the gas would leak due to poor safety equipment. The second room had illustrations of how poison gas affects the human body through the lungs, eyes, skin and heart. Keiko looked at the images with scant understanding. In the afternoon they took one of the walking trails, passing the ruins of the gas manufacturing plant that were blackened and eyeless, their windows put out many years ago.

Oki spent some time examining the dilapidated building. Barriers were erected to prevent admission, but enough could be seen from the trail to imagine how life might have been. He considered the effects of war—not only on those who might be the recipients of a gas attack, but also on those who did the manufacturing. Sometimes his elder colleagues talked about war in terms which emphasised the immediacy of living a life constantly undermined by death, but Oki imagined it probably wasn't like that at all. In all likelihood, living in war would resemble being numbed. A desensitisation of emotion.

He began to wonder whether he would have liked to live in wartime, while Keiko ran after rabbits without any idea of what she might do should she catch one.

When Oki's colleagues mentioned how stiff he was looking at work, he held back a shrug and mentioned a recurring back problem.

In truth, the shards of plastic adhering to his skin restricted his movements. He had to be careful that none of them dislodged and fell through his shirtsleeves to the floor. That had happened on one occasion and he had quickly kicked the offending shard under his desk. That wasn't so easy now fifty percent of his legs were also covered in plastic, and even if the glue he had used recently was of greater strength there were no certainties to be had.

Even drinking his favourite green tea held difficulties. The regular waitress appeared to have noticed, as on two occasions concern had crossed her face and she almost broke the customer/staff relationship by asking if he was OK. Oki had been touched, and for a moment regarded her as more than a waitress. In effect, they had been companions for some months and he wondered if that might extend to years. Whether he could court her. Whether she might become his wife. Whether they would have children. But then the memories of Keiko rushed back and he erased the future by closing his eyes.

All that remained were the tiny pricks of the edges of the plastic on his skin.

Oki wondered what he might have been should he have married Keiko's mother. He wondered about the life he didn't have.

At night, dissecting the mannequin, he began to consider that it had more of an identity than he did. It was no longer a factory-identical model. Oki had ordered a male, but the genitalia were smooth. Now the gouges in its structure had come to resemble the scars invited by emotional distress; the invisibility of the soul made manifest on the visible body. Whereas Oki was transplanting those scars onto his form, both absolving and absorbing them. It was similar to a deletion of history.

For twenty minutes Oki had lost Keiko at Ōkunoshima. Transfixed by the shells of the buildings, he had turned his back on Keiko far longer than he should have. He didn't blame himself. He was not used to being around children. He should have realised that they had no fear, no conception of time, nor of their elders' concerns for them. Yet when he turned around and saw that she was missing, those abstract concepts of fear and time were riveted into the core of his being. As his fear increased so time slowed, as though he were forced to savour its intensity as a punishment for being remiss.

After those long minutes, when Keiko was returned to him by no more than a bend in the trail, squatting beside a rabbit hole and poking inside it with a stick, Oki bent down and clutched her in his arms and vowed never to allow those circumstances to happen again.

The following morning they returned to the mainland. The wind was once again in the same direction, and Keiko's hair blew around her face from behind, revealing and hiding it, revealing and hiding it, until they reached the land and took a taxi to her mother's house where Oki formerly handed over his responsibility once and for all.

It might only have been two years ago but it was easier for Oki's conscience to imagine Keiko all grown up and independent.

He needed to order another mannequin for parts. He had put on weight since first seeing Keiko in the window. Some of the plastic required buckling to make it fit. Unlike in phenotypic plasticity biology, where an organism has the ability to change its phenotype in responses to changes in the environment, Oki acknowledged his procedure was less natural. But that didn't mean it was any less effective.

On the morning before the substitution he stood directly before Keiko in the window. All of his body hidden by his clothes was covered by ill-fitting, often overlapping shards of plastic from his mannequin. None of this was evident from the outside. He simply resembled an almost forty-year-old undergoing a midlife crisis as he watched Keiko self-consciously dress the male mannequin in the display. He saw the curiosity in her eyes as she darted glances towards him, noticed her attempt to spy his reflection in the glass rather than view him directly, to try to understand—obliquely—where his attention fell. She wore a skirt that stopped just above her knees and Oki smiled at how beautiful Keiko had become. A human tear ran down from his right eye at the intervening years which had been lost. Yet it was a solitary tear, and he knew in his heart that if he had taken a greater place in Keiko's life, those tears would have been more damaging and more frequent.

He was about to leave when Keiko turned and stood still. Her limbs coalesced into a typical mannequin pose with almost fluid precision. For an instant she was perfect, and then her eyes dropped and her posture sagged. She forced a smile, then shrugged and exited the back of the display via the little door she needed to stoop through to use. After a moment a security guard poked his head through the same door, and after another moment Oki found himself sitting inside a taxi. He didn't look back to check if the guard had left the building, if he was standing outside the store.

That night Oki applied the last of the plastic to his face. He lay on his futon, eyes closed. He knew it would never happen, but he imagined breaking into the department store and replacing himself with the main male mannequin in the display. He watched as though from a distance, perhaps with the smell of green tea in his nostrils, as Keiko entered the display window and dressed him.

It was difficult to breathe.

Oki slipped into a fantasy whereby his subterfuge was evident and he was hauled from the display and thrown into a furnace. The heat melted the plastic until all that remained was his mouth as a blistered O.

Yet he had no illusions that this was an improbable ending, and that, in truth, when Keiko touched him, there would be nothing at all.

A Woman Talks to her Flesh as it Meets the Ground

Lisa Mansell

the curve of her back
                crabs a void of something blind
        volcanic and kin
as scrawl before the splay of shoulders anthem a myth
                        of lash upon the
ground
            alpine and vast as staves (music)

    to the head
              fed yellow and *sul-point* by neon
tubes
    buttressed on woollen linoleum
                 brutal and tight as latex
to the skin-hard heel of her left foot
             digging   digging
      giddy in the howl that gallows the
ground

METAWIFE

Kerry Fender

I woke up in the middle of the night with an itch on the back of my left hand. I scratched and scratched at it. I scratched so hard that Tom nudged me with his foot and grunted 'stop it' in a sleep-furred voice, but the itch got worse. It was as though my raking nails were paring away the flesh, exposing more and more of the irritation to the air, until it oozed hot over the whole appendage. I was now wide-awake, and all I could think of was slathering on some kind of cold, white cream to extinguish the sensation. I wriggled out of the bed and stumbled into the little shower-room that was only three steps away from the bed on my side, closed the door carefully and flicked on the light. What was eating at my hand? I expected to see broken skin at the site of the inflammation, or at least some redness. But I saw nothing.

Nothing.

The twin gold bands that constricted my ring finger were there, my favourite punctuated all round by little square-cut diamonds. I was still holding the white cotton handkerchief that I habitually clutched in sleep. It was compressed into folds where my fingers gripped it, the middle blurred slightly, like a heat-haze, perhaps from the vibration of the itching. But I saw no hand; no greyish-pink flesh mapped by blue venous pathways, sculpted by bone; no rosy short-pared nails with deep white half-moons. The bony protrusion of the wrist was absent, so too the white scar where a distressed dinner plate had finally snapped in the hot water and sliced me, turning the soap bubbles bloody pink. There was nothing but the rings, the handkerchief and the itch. My arm began and ended with the blue sleeves of my pyjamas.

I held up the other hand for comparison, and saw only the scalloped lace cuff with light shining through where it should have shown flesh. I dug my toes into the thick bath mat. I could feel its distinctive texture, and when I looked down I could see the fat, green velvety loops of the chenille. But I could not see my feet.

I was too tired for this nonsense. *Dreaming,* I said to myself. *You are dreaming.* It didn't feel like a dream. This was definitely my bathroom, in my current house, with no incongruous details to betray a fuddled, sleeping mind. All physical sensations were sharp and there had been no random, inexplicable leaps in time, place and logic. It felt like four a.m. If I went back to bed now I could get in a good couple of hours' sleep before the alarm went off, and in the morning everything would be fine. Well, normal.

I slid back into bed and huddled against Tom; he was solid and real, radiating heat in the darkness, his hairy shins rough against my calves. I thought he would push me away, he likes his own space in the bed, but instead he pulled me into his lap and pressed lazily against me. If he had been awake enough for speech he might have said "brace yourself", but he was on early morning autopilot. He pulled my hips into position as though he were heaving a sack around the garden and tugged at my pyjama bottoms just enough to allow him to penetrate. Faint, pleasant ripples spread out from the site of intrusion, but died before they reached my navel. I wondered, if I looked at my belly now, would I be able to see him inside me? Before I could reach over to flick on the light, he shuddered, and groaned quietly as he was relieved.

Pale light was bleeding in around the edges of the curtains. The alarm began to shriek, setting my heart racing; it can't be good for you. I kept my eyes closed as I stumbled into the bathroom again. I was acutely aware of Tom's wet trail on my thigh, and of my full bladder. I did not need to see to find the toilet and place myself on it, or to reach out with my hand and pull the cord that switched on the shower, or to remove my pyjamas. The cubicle door closed behind me with a hollow sound. At first my skin shrank away from the cool water, leaving my nipples and all the little hairs on my arms standing exposed. But as it warmed up I relaxed and enjoyed its soft trickle on every part of me. Without opening my eyes I raised my hand to wash my breast and felt the swell of it under my palm. With my other hand I found my knees, my neck, my ears. Everything was exactly where it should be. But when I opened my eyes there was nothing but running water and my wedding rings, flashing whenever I moved my 'hand'. I closed my eyes again, groped for the shower-head, turned it up to its harshest setting and let it scour the soap off my back, feeling present in the sensation. Above the sighing of the spray I heard an indistinct but imperative shout. I turned the water off, flung a towel around myself and padded damply into the bedroom.

"Liz ... Liz ... where are you?" Tom bellowed from the bottom of the stairs.

"I'm here".

"Oh, there you are," he said, not bothering to come up the stairs to find out where 'here' was. "Will you have a look for my ski jacket up the loft, later? The boys are going to Aviemore next month, I thought I might join them."

I went out onto the landing and called down to him: "Can you see me?" But by now he was sitting on the bottom step with his back to me, tying his shoes.

"Oh, don't start," he said. "I haven't got the time or the energy for an argument this morning."

Sophie emerged from her room, growling "Mum, I can't find my homework".

"Watch out," said Tom, "your mother's in one."

"Oh, God, what's up with her now?" wailed Sophie pounding down the stairs. Why do teenagers take the phrase 'throw your weight about' so literally in everything they do? I retreated into the bedroom as Jack wrenched his door open and crashed it shut with the force of a minor earthquake. Then he too dropped down the stairs like rolling thunder. There was a chorus of "goodbyes" in three different pitches, then the front door banged with a rattle of the letterbox and I was alone.

Did I need to get dressed if no one could see me? Well, if I was going into the attic, yes; for protection. It was a dusty, cobwebby space with lots of heavy objects and splinters. Tom knew how much I hated going up there. I went back up to the bedroom and dug out of the wardrobe the long pole for the loft hatch and some old clothes. They were streaked with bleach, and stiff in places with dried emulsion. I got dressed with my eyes closed; it was too disorientating to keep them open and not be able to see myself. With them closed everything felt normal, I knew exactly where my body was in relation to everything else.

Even with the long pole it was not easy to open the hatch, but after some impressive stretching, groaning and dancing about on tip-toe I managed it, and pulled the ladder down with a metallic clang. Usually I looked carefully to see exactly where I was placing each hand and foot as I climbed, but today I could not bear to. I put my trust instead in the feel of the hard grooved treads under my feet, and the cold handrail.

There were many boxes and knot-topped black plastic bags up there, and I tried them all without success. By now I felt gritty, my eyes were itchy and breathing was tight and difficult. I was about to admit defeat and lower myself down onto the ladder when I spotted, under an old sleeping bag, the corner of a white plastic crate.

I tugged at it, almost tipping myself off the rafter I was balancing on. The last thing I wanted to do was put my foot through the ceiling, but luckily as it shifted I was able to steady myself. I cracked the lid off. There was no jacket: it was full of old photographs.

I pulled a sheaf of them out. I recognised the girl in all the pictures, but I cannot say she was familiar. Her skin was smooth and flushed. She had a head of reddish-brown curls that, cut by a hairdresser and not her mother, would have turned heads. Her eyes and her smile were wide and bright. Her figure was not as skinny as she would have liked, though it was nice. Her bottom could have been used as a WMD – a weapon of masculine distraction. Yet she was never comfortable in her own skin. It made me sad to realise how little idea she had had of her own virtues. I could hardly believe she was a previous incarnation of me. I am ugly and frumpy and clumsy. My hair is dull and faded. And my smile. My eyes are so heavy that I spend most of my time looking down at the ground. I am not comfortable in my own skin, either. I would gladly strip it off and put on hers, any day.

Underneath the pictures in the crate was something that looked like crinkly, yellowed tissue paper. Intrigued, I fished it out. It was not tissue, it was a substance more like the strips of hard skin my mother used to pare off her feet with a corn blade, only drier and more brittle. It was much bigger, too. I stood up and held it against myself. It was almost as big as me, and vaguely person-shaped, with distinct 'arms' and 'legs'. With its limbs dangling down it looked like I had visible hands and feet again. I tried to put my left hand into the skin 'glove' that hung at the end of one arm. But the friable, yellowish substance crumbled. I was hardly conscious of what I was doing as I picked up the fragments and put them in my mouth.

How hungry I was. I had not eaten yet that day. I tore a great big strip off the 'skin', stuffed it in my face and chewed with relish. The texture was so satisfying. Like some bizarre pregnancy craving, once I'd tasted it I had to keep eating. Soon it was all gone. A leaden tiredness swept over me, as though the act of consumption had used up more energy than it had given. I dragged myself out of the loft hatch, and closed it up. My bed welcomed me with instant sleep.

When I woke again there appeared to be a dense translucent veil between me and the room, as though I was viewing it through contact lenses made of parchment paper. What the bloody hell was wrong with me? I closed my eyes and rubbed at them breathlessly, but it made no difference. If anything it was worse. Was I going blind? Was the whole world disappearing? I rubbed again, pressing my knuckles into my eyeballs until patterns flashed on the black. I felt something tear over my right eye, like breaking the skin of a blister, but no fluid leaked out. When I opened my eyes I found there was a narrow slit of clear vision. I rubbed at the other eye until I felt the same tearing sensation. Now I had two little embrasures I could see through. I made my way over to the wardrobe's mirrored doors.

Protruding from my clothes where my hands, feet and face should have been was some kind of thick, white cuticle, as though they had been coated in a layer of glue or latex that had dried into a ghostly facsimile of me. What disease was this? Would I die of it? I didn't feel like I was dying. What did that feel like, anyway? Did this carapace cover all of me? I tried to undress, but found that my fingers weren't nimble enough to cope with fastenings. I rubbed my hands together vigorously hoping the stuff would tear like it had around my eyes. It came away in cloudy yellowish scraps, which littered the floor like confetti. Underneath was visible, pink skin. Healthy skin. I peeled away the mask of stuff on my face. A few flakes of it clung stubbornly around my hairline. I flung off my clothes, now that my fingers were free, and rubbed and scraped at my body, until strips hung down like peeling wallpaper. It stuck in places, and had to be snatched off quickly like a plaster, releasing a stinging pain that made me curse.

Once I was satisfied that it had all been removed I surveyed myself in the mirror again. My skin had a new, rosy glow. My eyes were bright and saw everything in high definition. My hair, though it would never be auburn again, was no longer grey. It was silver. I was mature, not old. My breasts were round, my belly slight, smooth curve, and my bum...

I heard a car door slam right outside. Crossing my arms over my chest I ran to the window. On the drive, Tom was locking his car. I threw my dressing gown over the mess on the floor and ran, naked and radiant, down the stairs.

THE HIDE

Liz Williams

The birds were white as they flew over the marsh, across the reed-beds and the frosted meres, but as they drew level with the hide their shade changed, from white to black. I saw their crimson eyes, sparks in the cloudy dark, as they disappeared into the storm. Richard and I crouched in the hide and waited.

"Jude, can you see her? Can you see?" Richard whispered.

But all I could see was darkness.

People lived here once. A very long time ago, when this land was called the Summer Country – named not for cowslip meadows or hazy warmth, but because it only appeared in summer, when the waters had retreated towards the Severn Estuary and the marshes were dry enough to be negotiated on foot. At all other times of the year the gleaming wet of the marshes, the dense beds of dull golden reeds, the groves of alder and unpollarded willow, were the haunt only of ducks and herons, and the small people who lived along the causeways and in the lake villages.

Richard and my sister Clare and I had followed the Sweet Track the summer before when the heat hung heavily over the water meadows, with the damselflies zooming through the kingcups that grew along the margins of the dug-out peat beds. The Track, discovered years before by an academic named Sweet, is an old road, one of the oldest in the country. I was researching it, and Sweet's own research, at the Moors Centre, lying right in the middle of Sedgemoor.

Hard to imagine winter, in those dreaming meadows, but I knew that come September the fog would start drifting in from the Bristol Channel, smelling of salt mud and sea, hiding first the whale-humps of islands, then the arch of Brent Knoll, then the flat lands all the way to the Tor with its tower. After that would come flood and then frost, and the long, dim, damp winter.

I'd been there for six months, but it was Clare's first visit to the area – she was living in Manchester then, working as a fundraiser for some big arts project – and her New Age soul was enchanted by it all, by the faux-Arthuriana of Glastonbury and the rather more real claims of Cadbury, by the startling caverns of the Mendips and the flat lands between, where the lake villages had once stood. She and Richard had apparently met through some university bird-watching society – though I'd never known Clare to be interested in twitching before. She was more enthusiastic about it in summer, perhaps, out in the wilds with a couple of bottles of beer and a blanket, and that's how we discovered the hide.

I hadn't realised it was there, although I'd been to the bird reserve a couple of times before. I must have walked right past it, but it was Clare who spotted it, as we walked along the track with the remains of a picnic in a rucksack.

"Richie! Jude! There's a causeway, in the reeds. Can we go and look?"

Moments later, she was gone. I remember feeling an odd moment of panic, as though she'd performed some unnatural conjuring trick. Then her voice came from among the russet tassels nodding several inches above our heads. "Look at this! This is so cool!"

The causeway was built of slats placed on piles, close together and easy to walk on, with the addition of a handrail, which the Lake Village structures would not have had. Quite contemporary and not all that old, judging from the scrubbed pallor of the wood. I'd have told her all this, but I'd grown too used to the rather glazed expression that came over Clare's face whenever I talked about my work. We'd both had our noses in books as kids, but they hadn't been the same ones. She liked the myths. She was less interested in fact.

At first, I couldn't see where the causeway led. A dog-leg in the middle took it out of eye-line, deep into the reeds. Clare and Richard vanished around the bend. I stood for a moment, just before the turn. The reeds swallowed sound. Distant traffic and the lowing of cattle were cut off, and the sudden rattle of a coot in the rushes made me jump. When I turned the corner, I saw that the little causeway ended in a long low structure, also raised on pilings, but with a tarpaulin roof and a laminated National Trust information sheet tacked to the wall by the door. There was nothing ancient about this place; it was not even a reconstruction like the round houses at the Bronze Age information centre some miles away. It was a bird-watching hide.

As I came close to the door, I found something: a small black wing, very soft and dense. I didn't recognise the bird: this wasn't the right kind of terrain for blackbirds. Perhaps something – kestrel, maybe – had dropped it. It was clearly a recent kill; there was still a bloody fragment of meat on the bone, an electric red against the dull background of the planks. I picked it up and put it on the flat surface of the railing, not quite knowing why, as if it was a child's glove for which the owner might shortly return.

Inside, the hide was dark and still, stifling in the afternoon heat and filled with the limey odour of bird droppings. When my eyes adjusted, I saw that the floor was white with them. I looked up, but there was nothing in the rafters. Swifts, perhaps, but I couldn't see any round hummocks of nests and they'd be in residence at this time of the year.

"Richard?" Clare's voice cut through the gloom. "Come and see!"

I went around the corner of the central notice board. Clare and Richard were standing shoulder to shoulder and I stifled an old and familiar sensation. I allowed myself to wonder what would have happened if Richard had met me first – but I knew from experience that it wouldn't have made any difference.

When she saw me, Clare raised the hatch that looked out over the other side of the marsh, and fastened it with a wooden peg.

"Look."

There was a heron among the reeds, a common enough bird in this area but still alien, predatory, as startling as a pterodactyl in its blue and grey plumage. It was stalking through the shallow water at the edge of one of the reed beds and as we stared, breathless, the long beak stabbed downwards and came up with a fish. Silver caught the light. The heron flipped it up and swallowed, then was gone into the reeds in search of new prey.

We kept looking for a moment, hoping it would come back. Then Clare said, "What are those?"

There were three of them, gliding over the crest of the reed-beds. They had long necks, long beaks, but at first I thought they must be gulls because their wings caught a shaft of sunlight, gleaming white as they turned. Then they veered again and I saw that their wings were shadow-black, a strange trick of the light. Cormorants, perhaps. They were common along the coast and you frequently found them inland, sharing prey with the herons. They were flying west, towards the estuary.

We watched them go and then, as if some decision had been made, we filed out of the hide like obedient schoolchildren, into the hot day, and back along the track. Clare said she wanted to go back into Glastonbury and see some of the shops. She wanted to buy a crystal, or something. I just wanted a cup of tea. We headed back to where Richard had left the battered 2CV.

The car park had been empty when we'd arrived, but now there were a few more vehicles in it. One of them was a van, painted in rough red and green stripes, a homemade hippy job. As we came into the car park, a young man came around the side: typical of travellers in this part of the world, dreadlocks, mud-coloured clothes, a joint held between two fingers. There was a dog at his heels, a black and tan thing with heavy jowls that looked as if it might growl. But the young man was affable enough.

"Nice afternoon," he said. "Been out to the bird sanctuary?"

"Yes, just for a stroll. We saw a few things."

"You want to wait for evening. All the starlings come then – like a cloud. Thousands of 'em. This place is known for it."

"Starlings?" Clare asked. "Maybe we'll come back. We found the hide."

"Did you, now?" the young man said. He took a drag on the joint; sultry smoke coiled into the warm air. I thought there was a fractional sharpening of his interest, but perhaps it was only the dope. "See anything?"

"A heron," I said. He nodded, interest waning, until I added, "And some cormorants."

"You saw those?" He was staring at Clare, not me, half-amused, half-something else, an expression I could not identify. But that he was looking at her at all irritated me. "Black or white?"

"Black," I said, not understanding. "You don't get white ones, I thought."

"Sometimes you do." The young man spoke with assurance and I didn't know all that much about seabirds. I wasn't prepared to argue the toss. "How many?"

"Three. There were three of them."

"Okay. Well. Let's hope you don't see them again." I was about to ask him what he meant but he turned away, clicking his fingers at the dog, which was wandering. Richard opened the car and we drove into Glastonbury, where Richard and I spent the rest of the afternoon in one of the little cafes around the market cross. If I thought about the bird sanctuary at all, then or in the days that followed, it was simply as a fading memory of a half-pleasant, half-painful afternoon. I did not think about the cormorants at all.

I did not manage to return to the hide, but was busy with research in the Centre and elsewhere. Richard and Clare went back up north and I tried not to think about when I'd see Richard again. I knew I'd never be able to tell her how I'd started to feel about him and I didn't want to. There was something behind the New Age stuff in her, something competitive and deep, something sisterly, and not in a right-on feminist way. Anyway, it was too embarrassing to talk about and God knows it wasn't as if it hadn't happened before. Perhaps she knew what was going through my head, all the same. But I told myself that she seemed happy with Richard and I should be happy for them, and could not be. There should be a natural end to it, now they had gone back up north.

But when I next saw them, and summer itself was over, I found that things weren't as I'd thought.

I'd been to a conference at Lancaster, stopping off at Clare's on the way back. But when I got to her place, she wasn't there. Instead, I found Richard.

She'd been moody ever since they came back, Richard told me, over a beer in a nearby bar. It was October now. At first he'd put it down to anxiety over the coming months, the time when the success or failure of Clare's fundraising bid was going to be decided. She was snappy and short-tempered, which was new to Richard if not to me, and he'd deemed it wiser to leave her alone to get on with her work. At first, he thought this approach was a success: she was heading off to the office every morning, but three weeks or so later he had run into a colleague of Clare's, who asked how she was, given that she was on sick leave.

"I didn't want to ask her about it," Richard told me. He took a sip of his drink. "But it freaked me out. I thought – I thought she'd found someone else, but, you know, sick leave, it's not just sneaking off for an hour or two."

"Is there someone else?" I felt a cold growing elation at what he was about to say and I hated myself.

"No. I don't know. She said there wasn't, but I – I didn't believe her. I told her I did, then when she went out the next morning, I followed her. She went straight to the canal and sat on the bank. For the rest of the day, as far as I could see. I went to a pub for lunch, even, and when I came back, she was still there."

"Maybe she reckoned you'd follow her, and she thought she might as well lead you on."

"Maybe." He looked dubious. "I suppose I wouldn't have blamed her."

"Funny place to sit, the Ship Canal. It's not exactly Hawaii."

Richard looked suddenly defeated. I nearly reached out to him but stopped myself in time. "It's a shithole, Jude. They keep saying they cleaned it up for that sports bid, but it's still a murky, dirty drain. What appeal could it possibly have?"

Unless you were thinking of chucking yourself into it, I thought, but did not say, and I hated myself a little more. There was something gruesome about the idea of my sister sitting by the side of that grim channel of water, staring into grey scummy nothing, contemplating what?

"Did you follow her again?" I asked.

"A couple of times. She went back to the canal once, and then the next time she just wandered around. This was a few days ago."

"Do you think she's having some kind of breakdown?"

"I don't know. She's been worried about her work, thinks they screwed up on the funding bid, didn't have enough of the required elements. I tried talking about it last night and she said she thought she needed a break. I was wondering if she could come down to you for a few days. I know it's not exactly the weather for it, but it's not the weather for perching on the side of the bloody Ship Canal, either."

All I could see in his face was concern. I had the sense of a trap, closing. I bit back what I had so nearly told him and felt something brush my clenched hands under the table, something soft, like feathers.

"Of course she can come," I said.

Having her in the house was odd and awkward, even more so

because Clare exhibited none of the signs of anxiety or depression that I'd been expecting. That made me think that the main problem lay with Richard and that, of course, gave me hope. But I didn't want to overstep bounds that I didn't even know for sure were there. I told myself that I was being stupid. And there was relief, too, because at the end of the day she was my sister, in spite of all the covert rivalry, and I didn't like to think of her being suicidal and not saying anything.

We went out to dinner at the local pub on the night she arrived, and when we got back to the house I bolted up to bed before we really had a chance to talk, assuming that we were going to. She'd never been in the habit of opening up, after all, in spite of all the New Age stuff.

I went to sleep quickly, but in the middle of the night, something woke me up. I sat up in bed, clutching at the covers. There was no one in the room, but it smelled dank, like marsh water. Worrying about damp proofing and winter, I went back to sleep.

In the morning, Clare was gone. I sat at the kitchen table, wondering and worrying, in case she'd gone off like some marsh spirit, wandering the Levels in the morning mist. Twenty minutes after I'd drunk my second cup of tea, she was back, looking rosy-cheeked and cheerful, and announced that she'd been for a walk down the lane and had met a nice horse in a field. The canal-haunting woman whom Richard had described seemed to have flown like the mist itself, upwards into the sunlit air.

I had to go to the Centre that morning, so Clare said she'd come with me. I spent the next couple of hours going through records, while Clare – I learned at lunch – had passed the morning in looking through the information section, about the Lake Villagers.

"I'm surprised how much is known about them," she said, over soup and bread in the centre's café.

"Well, peat preserves things. If the structure's there, then you can build up guesstimates from that. I'll have to show you some of the computer reconstructions: I've got some on CD back at home."

"It's fascinating," Clare said. "Like a world built on water."

I stiffened, anticipating canal revelations, but all she said was, "It must have been bloody cold in the winter."

It wasn't exactly warm that afternoon. We went into Glastonbury for a cup of tea and there was a distinct sense of the year beginning to wind down, a faded quality to the light, a bite on the wind's breath.

"I keep thinking of that afternoon we spent down here," Clare said in the café. She was looking down at the table, playing with her teaspoon. "Do you remember? Everything golden and grey, and the birds in the reeds."

"That was the day we saw the cormorants."

"I've dreamed of them, you know." She spoke with a sudden rush, as if confessing something forbidden. "They keep changing. Sometimes they're black and sometimes they're white."

"Things stick in your mind," I said. "Do you remember, when we were kids, we went to Tenby that time – there was a fortress on a rock, just beyond the bay? I still dream about that sometimes."

She nodded, but she looked slightly disappointed, as though she had been expecting me to say something else and I'd let her down. We did not discuss when she might be going back.

Next day, I went to the Centre, but Clare did not come with me: she said she wanted to sleep in. Still nervy about signs of depression, I didn't attempt to dissuade her. When I got back to the house about mid-afternoon and found a note saying that she'd gone out for a walk, I wasn't worried.

But she didn't come back.

It was dark by six and I was starting to get seriously freaked out. I tried her mobile and got her answering service, left messages. I got the car out and drove into Glastonbury, wondering whether she'd gone into town. But I did not see her along the road, and she wasn't in any of the pubs. I drove back, hoping to find her at home, but the house was as dark and silent as I'd left it.

I didn't want to ring Richard, but if it turned out that something had happened to Clare, I wouldn't have been able to face myself. His landline rang and rang; I tried his own mobile and that, too, was switched off. I left more messages, tried to decide whether it was too early to call the police and then decided that I'd rather look like an idiot than risk Clare's life. It was cold outside, with the stars hanging heavy and burning over the low black land.

The police took me seriously, though with a certain weariness, but said there was little they could do. If Clare continued to be missing, then they'd initiate a search, but until then, all they could do was keep an eye out and wait. The implication was that I should do the same.

When the doorbell rang, all my foolishness came crashing in on me. She had got lost and forgotten her key, that was all. I threw the front door open.

"Clare, I'm so–" But it wasn't Clare. It was Richard.

He didn't seem to know anything about my phone messages. He said that he was there because he'd had a dream. He was dishevelled, a bit stare-eyed, and he smelled dank, the sort of smell you might acquire on too close an acquaintance with the greasy waters of the Ship Canal. Both this, and the account of his dream, were completely out of character: the only thing that made me listen to him at all, rather than insisting on rest and a bath, was the fact that he knew Clare was missing.

My mind, wandering in areas that I did not understand, started to invoke further paranoia. This was all some weird game, either involving me or, worse still, directed at me. They had set it up between them, it was all planned. But then Richard started to tell me about the dream itself.

"She was walking in a dark place. She was lost, and there was a storm, but no rain. I knew that it was cold, and then I saw that she was out on the mere. You know, where we went for a walk? Where we saw the hide? And the hide was in the dream, too – I knew that if she could get to it, she'd be OK, we could pull her back. But then I saw the birds."

"The birds?" But I already knew which ones he meant.

"The cormorants, or whatever they were. Long necks, sharp beaks. They were white when I first saw them and as they flew towards her, they changed to black. Then it started to snow and the snow was black, too, like little beads of jet, and it covered her, she stood still like a statue and when I touched her, I realised she had turned to peat and she crumbled into the water."

There was a long silence after he recounted his dream, but it was just a nightmare, nothing more. Wasn't it? Richard was staring ahead into the heart of the fire as if trying to conjure its warmth back into his bones. He said, "She's out there, Jude, and we have to find her. We have to bring her back."

His eyes were burning and he looked thinner since I had last seen him, as if he'd aged in the past few days. I did not know what to make of his dream, but it was easier to leap up and go out, knowing that I'd already contacted the police and could do no more if we stayed home, knowing that action was always easier than just sitting, with the unspoken accusation ringing in my head that it was under my care that Clare had become lost.

"Let's go, then," I said.

October had borrowed a winter's night; when we stepped outside it felt more like the middle of January, a raw moonless landscape with the mist breathing off the ditches. A bone-coldness, seeping in even through my Barbour jacket and fisherman's sweater. I thought of Clare, staring into a canal for hours at a time and I grew colder still.

We took the car out to the bird sanctuary, driving slowly with the window down so that Richard would spot her on the road, if she should come that way. But we passed no one on the road and once we had turned into the track that led to the bird sanctuary car park, the night closed in, a clammy dark with the stars swallowed by cloud and the reed beds swimming out of the mist.

Richard was out of the car even before I'd switched the engine off, walking quickly towards the hide. I had to run to catch up with him and when I did so, he did not turn to see whether I was with him or not. He was looking straight ahead, like someone possessed.

We reached the hide. As we did so, a breeze sprang up, but it didn't seem to make any difference to the mist. I thrust my hands further into my pockets and found something brittle and sticky in there. I pulled out the black bird's wing that I'd found on the way to the hide, the last time we'd come. I could have sworn I'd got rid of it months ago. There was no smell, but the bloody flesh had not clotted, it was still moist, and cold as ice. I was so revolted that I nearly dropped it, but then I heard Richard's voice, calling my name, and I stuffed the thing back into my pocket and ran along the walkway.

He was standing in the entrance to the hide, clutching both sides of the doorframe. His face was suffused with a kind of strange joy. He said, "Jude! It's OK. She's here."

"What? Is she all right?" I had visions of Clare collapsed, huddled against the wall in a disorientated daze, but when I pushed past him into the hide, limp with sudden relief, there was no one there.

"Richard, where is she?"

"She's there," he said. He gave me an odd look, as if I was behaving like an idiot. He pointed to the shuttered window of the hide. The shutters were raised, looking out onto the reed beds. It was pitch black in here, apart from the tiny light of my torch: I couldn't believe that he'd managed to see anything.

Then I looked through the shutter, and saw for myself.

There were more than three birds. This time, there was a flock, perhaps twenty or more, flying from east to west. I saw a smear of pale light in the east, like the grey minutes before dawn, and on the western horizon, just above the reeds, a thin red line in the sky with the stormclouds rising above it. The birds were straggling, and the ones in the east were white, but as they passed the hide, I saw the darkness melt over them, changing them to black.

Richard whispered, "Jude, can you see her? Can you see?"

The reedbeds were the same, but nothing else. There was a kind of house opposite the hide, a hut on stilts. It stood in a patch of reeds, as well, but I saw, as you see in dreams, that they were black, with crimson tips that looked like ragged bulbs of flesh. Clare stood on the balustrade that surrounded it. I leaned out, shouting.

"Clare! Clare, can you hear me?"

A shutter rattled, from across the water. A black oblong opened at Clare's shoulder, and something looked out of it. I saw myself looking at my own face, but it was changed: I looked older, lined, bitter. Across the water I saw myself raise something and wave it in mockery: something black and dripping, like the blood-drenched wing of a bird. Then the face changed and was no longer mine, was no longer anything human.

There was a splash. I looked down, and Richard was in the water, ploughing through the reeds towards the opposite hut.

"Richard! Don't go, come back!" I might as well have been whispering. As the last of the birds reached the hide and changed, I saw Clare bend over the rail and reach down a hand to pull Richard up. The bird changed to black. I saw its reflection, shining white in the water below, the light breaking the water up into a thousand dazzling splinters and the hide, the fleshy reeds, the gleam on both sides of the sky, everything was gone. I was alone, and it was night, and it was cold.

I would like to say that I woke up next day, and found that it had all been a dream. But Richard's rucksack was there to remind me, and Clare's belongings, and a message from the police to ask me to let them know if she appeared. She did not. There was a hunt, and they dragged the waters of the bird sanctuary. I went with them, although the place terrified me. They found nothing. They asked me a lot of questions, but I did not get the sense that I was under suspicion. The case made the papers, and after a while, the authorities and the media lost interest.

I had dreams, too. They were always the same: two dark birds, flying west. I thought a lot about the bird sanctuary, about the kind of place it might be. I thought of the people of the Summer Country, living in the liminal lands between sea and pasture, summer and winter, life and death. The area around Glastonbury was known to be the land of the dead, the Celtic lord of the dead dwelling beneath the Tor. I did not know if this was what I had seen, some kind of ancient conjured hell, filled with spirits that I, with my imperfect human sight, could only see as birds. But I gradually came to think that it was simpler than that: that just as we had gone to the hide to spy upon the life of birds, so something somewhere else had also set up a hide, to watch us, and when the time was right, to take.

A New Womann

Jack Fabian

I pull on my jacket and reach into the pocket for the door key.

I hold the key between my lips and zip up my coat, gurning like an old, toothless crone, so as not to bite the metal. I spit the key into the palm of my hand, open the front door and step into the darkness, locking the door behind me.

It's cold.

As I make my way towards the university, the street is empty. Dry leaves rattle along the tarmacked road. The scraping sounds echo in the silence. Victorian houses line the street on either side. Every so often a gap breaks up the brickwork and leads onto alleyways; rubbish bags clutter the passages.

The silence, as comforting as it is, feels stifling. It must be the first time, since moving in to my accommodation a few weeks ago, that I've walked down this street and not passed anybody. I prefer being alone. Actually, that's not true; I love being around people but I have a scar on my face – a hare lip. Since I was a kid I've been teased about it.

If I run my tongue along the inside of my mouth, I can feel a small indentation where the countless surgeries I had as a child have left suture marks. It isn't as pronounced as it was when I was younger, so I guess my face has kind of grown into it. Whenever I look in the mirror, though, it appears huge to me. I feel like that woman who's always in the papers; the one who had acid thrown in her face. It's a thought that fills me with guilt. Her scars are more noticeable and she has probably endured more pain than I ever will. Regardless, my scar bothers me, and I can't change that.

For the last month I have run to and from lessons and haven't really spoken to anybody in my classes, other than the obligatory 'hello' and 'goodbye'. Surrounded by groups of people has made me feel the loneliest I've ever felt. It doesn't help that I live in rented accommodation when everyone else has opted for halls. People make friends in halls, and already I can see their relationships forming, while I sit at the back of my English lectures, wishing I were one of them. I didn't go to any of my classes last week and nobody even noticed. Nobody asked me where I was and when I told my lecturer I was ill she asked who I was. That's why I'm on my way to university, to try and make some friends. To be part of the crowd, not just in it.

I reach into the inside pocket of my jacket and fish out a small black card. In the glare of the streetlamps I read the print, in raised white lettering:

Open Place

Sunday, 24th

10pm

The words seem cryptic.

The guy who gave it to me works in the student juice bar. He smiled when he placed it in my hand. Not a pity smile, either. We even made eye contact.

I haven't been to any of the campus parties yet, not even the fresher week events; this will be my first attempt to meet new people. And all because a cute guy didn't look as though he wanted to throw up when he looked at me. It's a wonder what we do for a pretty face.

Ahead of me, as I turn the corner, is the university; its tall roofs turret the skyline. Across the street is a line of off licenses and fish and chip shops. A post office sits in the middle, sticking out like a sore thumb – the only window in darkness.

I cross the road at the lights, just past 'Uni-Fish', and head towards a small archway, tucked between the campus library and a bistro type restaurant that opened at the start of term. The archway's shadow is elongated by a security light fixed to the library wall, its ornate swirls of metal silhouetted on the concrete.

The courtyard beyond is just an empty square that's usually, during the day, decked out with aluminium chairs and slatted wooden tables. Students sit here, cup in hand, cigarette in the other, and chat idly of how they hate their lectures, between discussions of who their friends left the club with last night. Now though, the tables and chairs are all stacked up neatly against the window inside. For a moment they seem to me to be like real people, longing to be outside, wooden faces begging for freedom.

Beside the bistro is Open Place. The name certainly fits, as it looks open, spacious. The ceiling is so high I have to crane my neck back to see it. A light is on inside it now. Long rectangular overheads hang from chains, casting yellow hues along the grey concrete.

A rush of warm air wafts over me as the doors hiss open. I step inside. After walking in the dark, the bright lights hurt my eyes. The doors close behind me, fling a cold hand of air at the back of my head.

I don't come here much because it's usually packed. The emptiness feels comforting, sets my nerves at rest. The beanbags, now in a tidy circle against the north wall, are seldom free and always strewn about the place. The bench seats upstairs, installed into the dugout walls, are usually just as crammed. Now though, the place feels inert, vast. Perfect.

The prospect of this huge space being filled with people suddenly pops into my head. I decide to head back home. Maybe I'm not ready for the student life just yet. The image of fifty students crammed together, maybe more, is so vivid in my head it's like they're already here.

I turn to leave but walk straight into the doors. Startled, it takes me a few seconds to realise they are stuck. The sensors must be broken.

What if nobody else turns up? I'll be stuck here all night. The bistro is not open again until Monday; nobody has any real reason to come here at all. The irony of my situation – of being fearful of no people rather than a crowd of them, now that I'm stuck – is not lost on me. I shouldn't have come. I should have stayed at home and watched TV.

I try to pry the doors open but they don't budge; my nails almost rip from their beds. It could be awhile before anybody comes and it's cold down here, so I head upstairs. If anybody *does* come, I can shout down to them to keep the doors open, so I can get out.

The upstairs is just as cavernous as downstairs. The bench seats are hideous; brown-burgundy woven covers. They are comfortable though. I spread myself out on one of them and try to relax.

As I rest my head back against the wall, I hear a faint patter of rain tapping against the roof. I'm thankful for the sound. Rain calms me and takes me back to the time I spent camping as a child. My mum and I would pack up the tent, load it into the back of the car and set off to nowhere in particular, until we came across a camping ground. During the day we'd explore the local area, and at night we would sit around a homemade campfire and cook hotdogs, while Mum would tell me stories from her youth. Whenever it rained, we'd huddle up in the tent with a cup of hot chocolate, made on the portable stove, and listen to the rain tap against the nylon roof.

I cross my arms on the table, rest my head in the crook of my elbows and listen to the gentle patter of raindrops.

When I wake it's difficult to tell how long I slept for. A minute? Ten? An hour? It's still raining outside. Moonlight shines a spotlight of glimmering dew on the window. I rise to my feet. My head aches and the tumult of rain on the roof sounds distorted. I'm unsure whether or not I'm still asleep, and this is a dream.

Created by the Art & Design students, along the west wall, is a line of art displays. I head over to them, to distract me from my thoughts – counting to ten never worked. The first thing I come to is a disfigured mannequin. A torso attached to a leg with no foot, to be exact. The torso has a small scar that runs along the middle, like a caesarean scar. A small plaque on the wall beside the piece reads:

Artwork by Anton Chong

This piece, entitled *Fashion Fears*, is a
comment on how we wear our fears and how
they define us like the clothes we choose.
Our clothes not only symbolise who we are
but also reflect our goals, attitude and
even our fears.
The scars on the mannequin represent
how our insecurities can hold us back.

A small brass brooch is perched on a tall stand beside the mannequin. The plaque for this one names the artist simply as 'Kishma' and claims that without fashion, we feel as naked as the small isolated brooch on the stand.

Hssshh.

The doors.

I look over the railings that fence the top deck. In the reflection of the glass doors, as they hiss shut, I see a figure step towards the toilets. A door squeals open, closes with a thud. Quietly, I make my way downstairs.

I sit on one of the sofas, placed in a square to the left of the doors, and wait for the person to return. While I wait, I take in the room some more. A television is bracketed to the wall. It's switched off and gives the room a motionless feel, as if it has been frozen in time. Emptiness often gives things that feeling – like the world is on pause.

Twenty minutes later, according to my phone, and still nobody has returned from the toilets.

I push the women's toilet door open, deciding that I should check if the girl – if it was a girl – is OK. The door gives the same shrieking creak as it did before. The room is dark. The lights in the on-campus toilets use motion sensors to save energy. I wait for a second, the door held open to let the light from outside shine in, as I wait for the lights to flicker on inside. The room remains in darkness.

"Hello?" No answer. I pull out my phone, switch on the camera's torchlight and let the door close behind me. Darkness envelops me. The mirrors lined along the wall reflect the light back; I point the glare to the ground.

"Hello?" Again there's no reply. I place my phone screen-side down on the side beside the sinks, the torchlight splaying a beam towards the ceiling.

I sigh, splash cold water onto my face and look into the mirror. The hare lip, as always, is the first thing I see. Hideous scar. If you look close enough you can see a small indent where the cut was made when I was a child, a fork of lightning connecting my mouth together like a patchwork doll. I try not to look closely at it anymore because it makes my stomach flip. It isn't always possible, though.

I dry my face with paper towels. Creeping to the end of the

room, phone held ahead of me like a torch, I bend down, peek beneath the stalls. They're all empty, no feet poking out.

I'm sure it was the girls' toilet door; it certainly had the same creak. It doesn't make any sense but I'm not staying in a dark toilet all night; I leave. Before I sit down, there are footsteps upstairs. I turn to the staircase and make my way up.

When I reach the top I see him. I know him. It's the guy who gave me the card. The reason I'm stuck here.

"Hi!" He says.

"Hey." I smile too. I sit beside him, not sure of how to hold myself.

"You came."

"Yeah." I'm not sure what to say. I'm nervous – he's more attractive than I remember. Or maybe I'm just happy to see the phantom toilet enterer.

"Have you seen my artwork?" He gets up and points to the mannequin. His jeans are baggy, grey hoodie roomy, Converse on his feet; I should have guessed he was an art student sooner.

"You're Anton? This is yours?"

"Yeah, do you like it? It's based on insecurities. See this scar here?" He points to the jagged cut down the centre of the abs, "It's one of my friends from class. She had a kid a few years ago." My eyes must have widened because he adds, with an adorable smile, "she's a little older than me. She was left with this scar. It's beautiful isn't it? I've always been fascinated with the patterns they make on a person. To me they're like veins in marble; sinuous, baroque." The smile that had started out as adorable changed as he traced the scar on the torso with his finger.

"Wow," is all I can say. I'd rather scars weren't the topic of conversation. "What's it made from? It looks so realistic."

"I use a mould to make sure all the veins and imperfections get caught and then use a thin lay of polymer clay to cover it."

"It sounds like a lot of work."

"Would you be a model?" He looks directly at the scar above my lip. Great! So this is why he invited me – to use me. Of course!

"Oh, I don't think so."

"Come on." He reaches out to touch my arm. I shrink from his grasp.

"Okay." He continues to stare at my lip but, with a faraway look in his eyes, I'm not sure he even sees anything.

I turn to leave. He grabs my shoulder.

"Hey, I'm sorry. Please, don't go. Let's sit and talk?" He gestures towards the bench seats beside the mannequin. I don't want to, but my only other option is to sit downstairs awkwardly and wait for somebody else to open the doors. I shrug my shoulders and nod.

He sits down and pats the empty space beside him. Reluctantly, I take the seat.

"So, what course are you studying?"

I tell him.

"I thought you'd say that. You look like the kind of girl to be interested in English."

He continues to ask me questions. I continue to give him one-word answers. We carry on like this for a few minutes. Then he puts an arm around my shoulder. I'm dying inside; as much as I'm offended by his attempt to invite me somewhere just to use me, he *is* still attractive. I try to hide my smile.

He may even like me, why else would he get this close to me? I think, as he begins to play with my hair. I try to give more than one-word answers, open myself up to him a little. Maybe a friend isn't the only thing I leave with tonight . . .

Within ten minutes we are discussing *Wuthering Heights*. His arm is still draped across my shoulder, his fingers twiddling with my hair. I really don't want to get up right now but if I don't, I'll wet myself.

"Is it OK if I just go to the bathroom?"

"Of course." He smiles at me, his gaze briefly hovering over my lip. I ignore it and make my way down the stairs. I hear his footsteps behind me. I turn to face him but before I can everything goes black.

My mouth feels numb, dry.

My vision comes back. Conversation and laughter bounce from the walls. A sharp pain nags at the back of my head. The sun streams in through a window, hurting my eyes. I try to shield them with my arms but I can't raise them.

When my eyes have adjusted to the light, I see I'm still in Open Place, only now it is the middle of the day. People sit all about me.

Why has no one tried to wake me?

I attempt to move but, like my arms, it's impossible to move my legs. I try to speak – ask for help – but it's just as useless as trying to walk.

Opposite where I'm standing, in one of the dugout areas, there's a picture. It hangs wonky, slightly to the left. Out of the bottom right corner I can faintly make out the mannequin from last night. From where I am it's difficult to make out any detail but there's a head attached to the torso now. It looks dark, like it's made of some kind of clay.

A guy and a girl walk towards me, hand in hand. The guy whispers into her ear. The girl laughs and pushes him gently into me. I wobble in place and the guy stills me. Something is wrong. Nobody seems to notice me and I just *wobbled*. The girl looks deep into my eyes. I look back at her and try desperately to say something.

"It's really creepy." She says.

Screw you, too! I scream. The words only make a sound in my head.

Little Miss Opinionated pipes up again, "They shouldn't have these where people eat." She takes one last disgusted look at me before sitting down, poking me. I don't feel anything but her finger landed somewhere on my forehead. Her boyfriend stills me again as he passes. They sit beside me on the bench seat. They are shorter than me by at least two feet. Little Miss Opinionated drapes her legs over the boy.

Out of the corner of my eye, to my right, is the small brass brooch that rested next to the mannequin. To my left, the couple are now getting far too intimate. Like in class, they do not notice me and I watch from afar, wishing I were one of them.

An End to Empire

Rosie Garland

I see her on the observation deck of the Empire State Building, where she is gazing through the bronze bars bolted round the perimeter. All for our own good: to deter the climbers, the jumpers and those who might itch to lob a bomb through the four-inch gap. I sidle up and make a snappy observation about King Kong and how he couldn't do his fateful climb these days. If she laughs, I'm in with a chance. *Go where your accent is an aphrodisiac*, the ad said. Two days in the Big Apple and not a sniff of interest from these hard-faced females. It's not my style to go hungry.

She shows no sign of having heard. I try again, give her the line about being the English guy lost in the city: artistic, lonely, sensitive and searching for his Muse. She raises a hand and crooks her fingers as though cradling an invisible apple. I think she's about to brush her knuckles against my face, but instead she cups her ear like she missed what I said and wants me to repeat it. The breeze up here is certainly stiff enough to toss the words aside. I take it as a good sign.

From this angle, all I can see is her left cheek; nose and chin sideways on. Her coat is buttoned to the throat, long sleeves covering her knuckles and the hem reaching halfway down the calf; the verging-on-the-unremarkable sort worn by women on the Upper East Side. She could stroll down Fifth Avenue and not turn a single head. A cloak of invisibility. To all but me.

I lean a little closer and she tucks a strand of hair behind her ear. Her skin is so bright it looks polished. Middling height, middling figure as far as I can tell. Maybe she is hiding voluptuous curves under the coat. It's a navy blue that on first glance could be taken as nun-like. No; an indigo cut from the night sky.

Not just any night sky.

As I watch, the cloth shivers and I am sucked back to that night I thought I'd forgotten. Three days after my seventh birthday. My father crashes into my bedroom, panting, gasping, the light from the landing shining in a halo around his head. My mother screaming for him to stop. Her fists hammering his chest. His promises never to do it, ever again. He grabs hold of the curtain, a drowning man grasping at straws. The rip of cheap polyester printed with stars and rockets. As I lie there I stare through the window, pour myself out of my body and into the cobalt bowl of the sky.

Just as I am doing now.

I stumble and just manage to catch myself from toppling into her. I mumble an apology: *the wind up here, it'll blow your hair off.* I am a clumsy Englishman once more. No threat. She folds her hands over her stomach as though she's carrying a flock of doves inside and is worried that they might escape.

I force myself to stop looking at that dangerous coat. I turn my attention to her hair. Not a strand stirs, despite the wind. It should strike me as odd, but I still have the luxury of naivety and I shrug it off as extra strong hairspray.

I glance at the other tourists. There's a tangle of girls to my right, hair blown in all directions. They are snapping photos of each other and shrieking in that way of holidaymakers on their first day. I could have any one of these giggling out-of-towners. The loudest and blondest throws me a look but I'm not interested. I want a challenge. I want to prove something to myself. Perhaps, if I'd admitted that to myself, I wouldn't be in my current situation. Perhaps. I have to believe that. I have to believe in something.

At this moment, I believe in this still, silent, self-contained woman. My right to have her, to have her smile at me, acknowledge me at least. I bring my mouth close to her cheek, so she'll feel my breath on that pretty ear of hers. I've done it dozens of times and they love the way it raises gooseflesh. I wait for the squirm, the giggle. It doesn't come.

Instead, I hear a sound coming from her ear. Like the voice of the sea, it whispers. The undertow beckons, sucks me into her head. The ocean tells me how it covered the earth a billion years ago and is jealous of what it has lost. How it hates us swarming across the land, dry-footed and uncaring. How we have forgotten where we came from, what birthed us and can swallow us again.

I raise my head. It's then that I see it; the East River lifting itself from its bed and overflowing its banks. The wave rolls in a luxuriant swell and takes First Avenue, Second Avenue, Third. I watch as it streams into Manhattan, gulping Murray Hill and Lexington, spreading south to Avenue A, north to Grand Central. The lights of Times Square wink out with a whimpering buzz. Saint Patrick's Cathedral and the Flatiron give up without a fight. Tiffany's drowns in a twinkle of diamonds. The tide engulfs the Lower East Side, Gramercy and Midtown, lapping along Fifth until it reaches the foot of the Empire State Building.

The idiots on the observation platform continue to act like nothing's wrong: squealing for pictures, shoving quarters into the telescopes, holding up their kids for a better view. I can't understand why they aren't screaming at the coming annihilation; why they don't hold their noses against the sudden stink of putrefaction, of a city going belly up, bloated with filthy gas.

I yell, *can't you see what's coming?* No-one notices or cares.

I turn to her for guidance. A word is all I need. She is smiling. Not at me, for that would be too obvious, but I know she's heard. She props her elbows on the wall, leans her chin on her knuckles and stares at the water as it makes its inexorable rise to the height of its ancient dominion. She is so calm I believe she could halt the destruction with a flick of her little finger. She does no such thing.

My mouth is close to her ear. I say, *why don't you help?*

It's then that I realise the reek of corruption is coming from her; radiating from her hair as though she's rinsed it in corpse-water. I stagger backwards and bury my nose in my shirtsleeve. I don't mean to offend. I should pretend I haven't noticed. Women are very touchy about how they smell.

She continues to smile. It's not enough to blot out this stench that blooms and blossoms around her. The sky sucks it up like blotting paper until it soaks into the twilight and blurs the moon. She glows brighter and brighter, wearing a sheaf of stars around her head. I reach to pick one from the night sky of her hair. I want to possess a piece of her light. I need to make sense of what is happening. She is laying on this show for me, in a bizarre flirtation. I should feel special. It's usually me who calls the shots with the ladies. I don't know what to do.

The tide climbs to the 86th floor, spills over the retaining wall and curls around my ankles. I lose all feeling in my toes and heels as frigid water slops over them. A few minutes more and I can't feel my shins. When my knees are swallowed in the icy surge I stumble, lurch forwards and throw my arms around her. The least she can do is break my fall.

My nose is running and the sobbing I can hear is coming from my throat. I'm past caring; it's too late for acting cool. The sightseers are up to their waists and shouting happily; pointing at the sky, the tip of the Chrysler Building, the One World Trade Centre, anywhere but at the rising water. I have no idea how long I'll be able to hold my breath. If it's worth trying. Whether it'll be faster and less painful if I dunk my head right now and breathe in deep.

You're behind all of this, aren't you? I say.

Her coat fans around her hips like the petals of a flower. Without glancing over her shoulder she gathers up her sopping clothing and swims between the bars. I don't know how she does it. The only way I can explain is that she closes herself up like a book and slides through. I climb on to the sill and try to catch hold of her ankle and pull her back. It is too late.

It's always too late.

Perhaps she says it, perhaps I do. I like to think she spoke to me, right at the end. I watch her disappear, tiptoeing west along the silver path laid down by the moon. The last thing I hear is one of the security guards yelling for me to get down. The waters close over my head. I lose the light.

THE SECRET GALLERY

Storm Constantine

Had I heard of the *Galleria Buiocuore*? Of course. Who hasn't? A hidden salon that houses a private collection of the most provocative of the *buiocuore* artists, who worked in the last century. People have always talked about it in my circle, but until I met Levayze, I'd never known anyone who'd claimed to have been there. I didn't believe it truly existed or, if it did, had to be fake, created by someone who ached to make it exist, because it *should* be real.

The Fellowship of the Darkened Heart had included both hedonists and ascetics among its members, who claimed they'd 'opened the door' into the *giardino crepusculo*, the 'dusk garden', and painted what they'd found there. They wandered, they said, the shadow of the world, the truth of nature, its darkness. They had a fondness for opiates, I was sure. The big pictures they had displayed at popular exhibitions had only been 'glamours' apparently – the true work of the Darkened Heart had never been shown in public. Some said these more mysterious works were dangerous to view; the secrets they revealed would haunt you.

I was living in Italy when I was introduced to Levayze. This was at a presentation of modern artists – a dull show, I thought, brassy and shallow. Critics called my own work 'antiquated', but in an indulgent, quasi-affectionate manner. I was harmless, I suppose, and invited to events like this because I was slightly famous, with a small but loyal clique of patrons. I was also a curiosity, a bauble to decorate their gatherings. Everyone had drifted out into the garden of the museum, into the breathing heat of that gilded summer evening. The chatter, the chink of talons against glass, melted into the sizzle of insects around me. All day, I'd been aware of this country's history, the prickle of the unseen against my skin. Something to do with the heat maybe, the weight of the past in the simmering air, ghosts of dryads among the trees in my garden. I suspected this heralded the germination of a new painting within me, its struggle for growth, but as yet it hid its face.

I'd dressed for the evening event to reflect my mood, in a pale gown like the robe of a Roman goddess. I still felt odd – full of excitement, a strange kind of yearning and expectation, yet simultaneously I was bored, wondering when it would be polite to leave. But then Signora Sanguerosa beckoned me to her with an enamelled claw. "Come here, Alex, you dove. There's someone you must meet."

She bought my work regularly. Of course I obeyed, my sandals sinking into the sweating lawn as I approached. The small crowd around her parted, and there *he* was: glorious and golden, the most devastating of poisons.

"This is Levayze," the lady said, "he *buys*."

Good reason enough, I supposed, to meet him. He smelled of opulence. Levayze was his family name, but he was addressed by no other. I knew his sort and was aware he saw that judgement in me. We bantered, crossed our swords lightly. He intrigued me, yes, because I like beautiful things, but I could always see through the dazzling camouflage of predators. The temptation he offered to win my approval was a visit to the *Galleria Buiocuore*. I laughed. "Really, Levayze?"

But he didn't laugh in return. He leaned towards me and said softly, "You may only find the gate at certain times of year. And even then you might not get in. But..." A killing smile. "I'm confident you'd be welcomed."

Only a fool would refuse. I doubted the experience he offered me would be genuine but, even so, entertaining. We arranged to meet at noon the next day.

I dressed scruffily in shorts and a loose shirt that was carelessly repaired in places, because I thought he'd expect the gliding twilight goddess of the previous evening. It amuses me to perplex people, so they're never sure what they've got. By daylight he was still glorious – a vain stallion of a man, his pale hair falling over his face. He treated me no differently than he had the night before. He had impeccable manners and a self-effacing manner. Quite the actor. He led me from the open piazza into the narrow ways of the city, into shadows – naturally. We didn't speak much, but the silence wasn't uncomfortable.

The entrance to the *galleria*, when we came to it, was unimposing, a cramped gate half hidden beneath draping ivy, in the high wall of a common, nameless lane. No plaque to announce what lay beyond. No bell to pull to advertise our arrival. The air there was close; the sounds of the baked city muted but for the frenzied rub of cicadas. Was there a warning in that chirring? It would be easy to think so.

"You see?" Levayze murmured. "We have found it. I knew we would."

Did he think me so gullible? "Let the adventure begin," I said lightly, smiling to show I shared the joke.

Beyond the gate was a courtyard, where tamed trees grew in pots decorated with gargoyles and mermaids. Tables of green wrought iron were set out, and chairs, but no one sat there. The paving was of pale marble; a barely visible emerald thread ran through the stone. The walls of the yard were blanketed in green, vines so clean it was as if every leaf had been polished, every stem dusted. No dead growth, no insects lurking there. Against the right hand wall was a rose garden; the blooms achingly white, the deep foliage behind them accentuating their purity.

Across the yard, the doorway to the *galleria* yawned open; beyond it darkness. I felt dizzy, and for a moment couldn't remember how we had got there; all memory of the walk had gone. Had I even agreed to come that day? When had I decided?

Focusing my mind, for I hate to feel vulnerable, I found the previous evening in my head, recalled the agreement, and then the walk earlier through the shimmering city, but even so I had become nervous, my breath shallow, one hand at my throat. I felt now my companion's claim was authentic, and I had perhaps been foolish not to believe him.

I didn't want Levayze to see how I was affected, but frankly it was impossible to hide. "The heat," I said, weakly, hoping that would be credible.

He took my right elbow, murmured sounds I couldn't

interpret, leading me into the shadows at the threshold.

The *galleria* was so dark within that at first I could see nothing, but I could smell wood polish, and an intensification of roses. I thought I heard a strain of music, but it vanished swiftly. There was no other sound, but for the squeak of our sandals on the glossy oak floor. There appeared to be no other visitors, no staff to be seen or sensed.

Gradually, my eyes adjusted to the dimness and I could make out the dark oblongs and ovals of the paintings hung around us – only four of them. The room had a shadowed domed ceiling and was roughly circular, yet even the largest of the paintings seemed to lie flat upon its curving wall.

I paused for a moment, reluctant to draw closer to the pictures, thinking there might be no going back. But Levayze was braver – after all, he had been here before, or claimed to have. He still held my elbow and now I put my other hand over his arm, like an invalid. His vague form seemed to swim towards the wall through the dimness, me drifting in his wake.

"This is the first salon," he whispered close to my ear. "The works are quieter perhaps, but a taste of what's to come… Look, Alex."

He led me to a picture, the first to our left, and now I could see that a narrow plank of sunlight fell down upon it from a slit in the domed ceiling, bringing certain details into high relief. A plaque to the left of the picture held the words *'Midsummer',* *Angelina Cuoroscuro*. The scene was painted from a viewpoint at the edge of a wood, where the foliage was thick and dark. The foreground was almost completely black, the vista beyond it startlingly bright. Standing before the picture, you peered through tangled branches and gazed out across a sunlit meadow, which sloped down towards a farm comprised of several low, pastel-coloured buildings and a high barn with a blue roof. White cows grazed in the meadow – you could almost smell their hot flanks. Beyond the buildings was a further meadow, leading to more forest, which loomed over the farm, its trees being incredibly tall. The pale stone farmhouse, glowing in the light, looked strangely *exposed* – menaced – but I was sure it didn't realise this. It was dreaming in sunlight, didn't feel the eyes upon it.

I couldn't help but murmur, "What happened?"

And Levayze squeezed my clutching hand and replied softly,

"That is for you to decide."

He led me on, not to the picture further to our left, but back across the doorway, to the first on the right.

This painting had no light upon it, but seemed to glow softly with its own faint radiance. The plaque beside it said: *'Rainy Day' Antoine Crevecoeur*. It depicted a window of four panes, puttied into an old frame of peeling paint and fibrous wood. The detail was incredible, almost photographic. Rain ran down the mottled glass. Thin blades of grass – brilliantly, acid green – grew at the corners of the sill, feeling its way through the mulchy wood; it must be spring time in the picture. You couldn't see into the room beyond the window; all was dark. But you could feel someone in there, looking back at you – desperately. I fancied I could hear the soft pat of rain, the hiss and shiver of it, and nearby the plink of drops falling from a blocked gutter into water, perhaps a barrel.

"What will happen?" I breathed.

Levayze laughed quietly in reply.

We moved on, further round the right-hand wall. I felt that by the time we reached the fourth picture something hideous would be revealed. Tension was building all around me in that dark chamber. My steps dragged but my blood pounded hungrily in my head. My apprehension had faded. I wanted to see.

The next picture was entitled *Path Across the Hills* and was another Cuoroscuro, perhaps even painted in the same countryside as *Midsummer*. The viewer stood upon a hill path that filled nearly all the foreground, tapering quickly as it snaked away into a late afternoon. There was one bush, a hawthorn, I think, to the right, a few feet up the path, but no other vegetation except for the sage green of the softly-bundling hills, here and there lightly smudged with pastel lilac heather. The horizon seemed farther away than it should be.

The scene was empty, plain even, but the more you peered at it, so a creeping fear spread across the pale of the sky. The landscape thrummed and hummed, not simply with heat, but the oppressive spirit of high summer, that which sends travellers mad, running like hares across the fields, through forests. It was as if an immense godlike being had been painted invisibly within the faint clouds, gazing down with a satyr smile.

"What is happening?" I asked, then added quickly before Levayze could answer, "No, don't say. I know. They have already escaped."

"Have they?" said Levayze.

I made to walk to the last painting in the room, but Levayze shook his head. "Not yet. The next salon."

The last painting of the first chamber hung in darkness, keeping its secrets.

The second salon was slightly brighter, but not much. It was again circular with no windows, but here the shafts of sun allowed through the upturned cup of the ceiling were less constrained. There was a smell of greenery, as if someone had recently removed plants from the room, and the leaves had been slightly crushed in the process. Again, only four paintings hung upon the wall.

The first picture, by an artist known only as Zuko, was *The Garden*. It featured a mirror in an ornate mahogany frame: carved wooden birds strained their heads backwards within a profusion of foliage. They looked as if they were being devoured by the vines. One stem, I noticed, entered the mouth of a bird, pierced its throat and emerged from its back, between the startled wings. In the mirror, you could see the reflection of French doors leading to an old-fashioned garden, where lavender grew in untrammelled abundance, and white daisies reached for the sun. There was a gravel pathway leading through a high dark hedge in the distance. Not much could be seen of the room where the mirror stood, but I knew that someone was standing where I stood. They looked into the glass, yet saw no reflection of themselves, only that sliver of summer beyond the shadowed room. Staring at the picture, I felt trapped.

"Are they a ghost?" I said aloud.

Levayze said nothing.

"These pictures are nearly all of summer time," I said.

Levayze murmured wordless assent, then said, "Have you never felt that fear?"

I had, but didn't say so.

"Some think that autumn is desperately sad, because it heralds the conclusion of life, and winter terrifying for the death it holds, the silence, but summer..." Levayze narrowed his eyes. "...that is when the secret is revealed for those hardy enough to withstand it. The secret of life, my friend, is horrifying."

I stared at him. "This is the theme of the gallery?"

"There is no theme," he said. "My words are whimsical."

We moved in the same pattern as before, to the painting to the right of the door. The gallery sought to surprise me. Here was a winter scene by Zinaida Safronov. It depicted a sprawling manor house in a snowscape, where the sky was the same colour as the land. Heavy snow bent the immense branches of stately trees that framed the building. Bulky tarpaulins of snow oppressed the ancient roof. You knew at once the house was empty, abandoned, desolate, yet a curl of smoke sneaked from one of the tall narrow chimneys. The banks of windows were the staring eyes of a lunatic. You wanted so badly to see a misshapen form in one of them, or a white face, or a hand pressed against the dull glass. None of that. Just the house with its deceitful smoking chimney. The painting was entitled *Tomorrow*.

The next picture featured a lawn, neatly-clipped and tamed. In the distance, a border of dark blue delphiniums could be glimpsed. But the subject of the painting, which I didn't or couldn't perceive until I was close, was a peacock. He emerged from the green to fill nearly the entire canvas. His tail was folded, but so huge it looked as if it would be almost impossible to drag around. A train of brilliant feathers. The peacock stood with his back to you, but had turned his head to look behind him. There was something bizarrely human in the gesture, and you knew then he wasn't really a bird, but something else, extraordinarily beautiful and yet in some way ungainly because he was earthed. Do you ever see a peacock fly, his tail like a kite on the wind? This picture was named *The Looking Glass* and the artist was Toby Smatterpond.

We walked then to *At Home*, a painting by Anna Winfrey. Evening was coming down over a white square house. Bare trees clawed at the coral sky around it. Lawns spread away like an ocean. The house was in darkness, but for one window, high up, right under the roof. Here, yellow light spilled out of tiny panes. You felt lonely at once, aching with it. But in this picture, there was a figure, the first I'd seen in the collection. Just a shadow, long and thin, upon the driveway to the house. You felt they weren't moving, and perhaps had no intention of going closer; they were watching.

I turned away. "These pictures are sad, Levayze. I'm

depressed now. Do we skip the last in this room and go to the next salon?"

"Not at all. We need to see if you may go in further."

"What?"

He smiled, guided me. The painting was huge, a forest scene, although there was little to see other than tangled roots and branches. You must lean in close to see the eyes. And then, you couldn't see them, realised what you'd taken for eyes were only green berries. There was something obscenely fecund about this picture, which unsettled me. You could almost hear things growing, crackling, sucking, rustling, slithering. And within all that fecundity something hid. And yet there were glimpses of it, the suggestion of bare brown skin that became a tree, a swatch of hair that became ivy. A softly echoing laugh that grew louder and became the call of a yaffle in the foliage. The artist, again Zuko, had named the painting *Threshold*.

"There is a story here," I said. "The paintings are chapters."

Levayze nodded. "In a way, although you may read the chapters in any order. I'm merely showing you the one I learned."

"How did you find it? Were you invited?"

"Of course. It's the only way to gain entrance. The *galleria* was built by the Fellowship's patron, Cosima Giocinta, an eccentric lady of wealth. I know her grandson."

This explanation seemed sadly prosaic. "Why the secrecy?"

Levayze smiled. "Oh, come now... isn't that what makes it interesting? Desirable?"

"I don't believe it's only here at certain times," I said. "You have a membership, of course."

Again he laughed and said, "no", taking my arm again. "Come, you can go further."

"But how can you tell?"

He didn't say.

"Oh stop it, Levayze, you're just being mysterious on purpose. Tell me."

"Leave your doubts at the gate, my friend."

He led me to the next doorway, which was curtained by thick drapery of deep crimson velvet. Swags of fabric, bound with golden rope, decorated its crown. I'd not noticed it before, yet now it seemed the most obvious feature of the salon. Before the entrance was a spindly table of gilded wood, upon which rested an old-fashioned oil lamp with a tall shade. It was lit, but the flame was low. Levayze lifted the lamp in one hand, drew aside the curtain a little with the other. "After you."

I gave him a hard glance but eeled through the gap into a darkened room. I felt space around me; the salon was no doubt circular like the rest, with a high, domed ceiling. Levayze's lamp cast a wan glow that didn't extend beyond us, creating a small vehicle of light for us to travel in. We walked to the left of the room as before, and eventually the light picked out the edge of a frame. As we drew closer, I saw that it was enormous, the painting within it yet hidden.

Levayze raised the lamp, illuminated a portion of the picture. I saw glimpses of jewels, spilling from gem-encrusted coffers, the fingers of a long, elegant hand, whose skin was almost golden, laid lightly upon the treasures. I drew closer, but could barely see beyond the small circle of light. Levayze took a few steps to the left and now more details bloomed. I saw a shapely leg – yet apparently male – its calf sandalled in coiling ivy. Levayze raised the lamp to reveal the figure's thigh. He was lying upon a couch of flowers, on his stomach, one leg beneath him, the other extended. A wisp of shimmering cloth, hardly more than air, covered his hips. Lush, fleshy blooms surrounded him, trailing over his body. I couldn't yet see his face but, in the shadows, the hand I had previously seen was still glowing.

"Who is it?" I murmured.

"Their model," Levayze whispered back. It was as if we were in a shrine, standing before the image of a god. "All of the pictures are of this... how would, you say it? *Espíritu?*"

"Were they all in love with him?"

"Enthralled," said Levayze.

I thought of the scenes of abandonment and bitter loneliness, the depictions of fear and menace in the most ordinary surroundings, the knowing peacock stumbling over his tail.

"Who painted this?"

"All of them."

"Show me the face."

Levayze lowered the lamp. "If I do that, you'll crave return, and you won't find the gate. Do you understand?"

"No, I don't. Don't be ridiculous."

Levayze took my elbow, began to propel me back towards the

entrance.

"The other paintings…" I said feebly.

"This is all we should see. You *will* understand why."

At these words, I felt suddenly and overwhelmingly exhausted, as if I might faint. I let Levayze guide me, craving now to be outside again, in the sunlight. We passed through the curtain, and Levayze replaced the lamp upon its table. As I faltered dazedly at his side through the previous chamber, I felt as if I'd looked for hours upon scenes of unutterable brutality and vileness. Were there pictures beneath the pictures, hidden by paint, but which I'd somehow penetrated? I couldn't speak because of nausea, couldn't ask.

In the first salon, he took me towards the painting we'd not yet seen. I struggled a little. I didn't want to see. Not now.

"Hush," he murmured at my protests, touching the fingers of one hand to my face. "You must, because this will end it – for now."

"How much more is there?" I asked.

He didn't answer the question, saying only, "I knew you should come."

The picture was of a filigree metal gate in a wall. Beyond it was darkness, but lamps upon the wall, to either side of the gate, spilled light upon the foreground. A figure was standing there, a woman… perhaps. The figure was veiled, dressed in black, but facing outwards, about to walk away. You could see that person was me.

When we went outside into the courtyard, evening had come. The air was warm and fragrant, a caress upon the skin. A veil had been lifted. We went out through the gate in the wall.

IN TOUCH

Paula Wakefield

They tell me it helps to write things down. I am being meticulous; taking my time with each letter, every word. Maybe all exorcisms are painful.

Some writing is meant for public consumption, discussion, but the words written to a lover are those scratched or hacked from our secret selves; words of midnight, salt sweat and tears, longing and lusting, regret and recrimination. These are the words that have travelled through centuries on the soft skin of young calves, scraped and stretched in fitting readiness for songs of desire and despair.

This is what I wrote yesterday:

The high street auction house is probably still very pleased with itself. Situated in that part of the city where yummy-mummies maraud coffee shops, shamelessly staking territory among the buzzy, equally bold young, it sells anything and everything to punters looking for pre-trend *objèts*, or stuff so post-trend it's fashionable again. Intuiting these developments is no mean feat. This is no land for the faint-hearted.

That scorched summer, the city's heat and smog seemed glamorous, as it always does, to newcomers, to outsiders. Beyond open doors, the large, low-ceilinged auction room was filled with seasoned city dwellers, so wholly invested in their stock of self-worth they were completely unaware of how cool they looked. My family would have thought the pre-owned furniture shoddy, but surrounded by these people it looked chic.

Metal fans, like the ones in old black and white movies, standing atop various pieces of big furniture, churned the thick air over and over. I wanted one of those fans. I wanted to be Gloria Grahame leaning against the kind of desk she would have graced. I couldn't afford the smallest table in that place.

It seemed to me the natives were dragging car fumes into the room with them. They might as well have been smoking cigarettes. I felt like Doris Day but without a secret love. *Que Sera Sera.* I had never been to an auction house before. Conscious of the sweat in my arm pits, I admitted the guide prices were higher than I could afford and turned to leave.

The searing pain on the back of my hand, just where the wrist begins, came from the contact with his forearm as I'd brushed past him, unaware he'd been standing, so close, behind me.

"Sorry, I'm so sorry." The red welt between his wrist and elbow, transformed itself, as I stared, into a tattooed shape, a small inflamed heart, visible beneath the dark hair furring his forearm. My arm looked as if it had been scorched with a branding iron. But then I didn't know that red is the hardest pain to bear.

"You're looking at the desk. Interested? I can get you a bid slip – or will you be at the auction?"

"Umm, no. No. I think it's... too big for my room and..." I tentatively rubbed the spot where his forearm had caught me, my glance flashing between the mark the contact appeared to have left on my skin and his tattoo. "Sorry, I was just leaving..."

"Vic, Vic Andrews." His palm felt as if some goddess had pressed hot metal into the flesh, leaving raised shapes where life-lines should have been. "Let's get a coffee, or a juice, there's a great deli round the corner. I haven't seen you here before. Hungry? They do food too."

This is the truth:

That night I dreamed of tortoise shells and oracles; sea-scripted shells crunching beneath my feet, and above me, a rolling, bruised sky-scape propelled by furious winds and rain. Dream time fast forwarded me across slippery barren wasteland, mud oozing through my toes, and in the dream distance, horizened, I saw stick figures scratching drier land with stones, scattering their first seed.

The tender underside of my toes stubbed something. I picked it up, letting the rain wash away the mud. It was a tiny clay tablet, impressed with a thumb print.

Dreams – nightmares – give us what we need. I threaded the small clay slab on the grainy gut-string of some animal that of course was lying ready to hand and that, in my dream consciousness, I knew was from some fresh kill. As I knotted the pendant behind my neck I understood the tablet contained a message that came before code.

The stick figures were getting nearer; a tribe, fleshing themselves out, moving towards me carrying reeds hacked from swamp. They wanted the clay tablet that my dream self also realised had bruised the thin stretch of skin across my throat. The string was rotting, fraying; I tore at it. A tentative cuneiform appeared in the clay under the slow sweep of my fingers. When I looked up, the stick people were nearer still and in their hands were crude lumps of metal. I was afraid but I didn't wake up.

It took time to become accustomed to the surprise I felt beneath my fingertips when I touched him. It was autumn. His skin fascinated me. It smelt of the must and dust of the dried-out drawers and storage cupboards in his properties, and his books.

I imagined the various textures of his skin were Braille, and that if I touched the vellum at his inner elbow enough times I would glean his meanings. I still had the mark on my arm from our first contact, but it was now bigger than his heart-shaped tattoo, which still felt hot when I touched it. After we'd made love I would trace the outline of it, trying to transcribe its ridges and valleys. The hair growing over it was coarse, like wire. While he snored I would peer at the heart, trying to decipher the letters raggedly scarred inside its crimson outline, guessing its secrets.

I knew this much: he had been married, he had fathered twins, girls. One day, long ago, when they were children, he'd taken them on a camping jaunt in the Lake District. His wife had stayed at home, working on some small painting commission she'd hoped would lead to greater things. The rocky outcrop he and the girls had clambered over wasn't high but one of them, Emily, had fallen, her head cracking open like an egg shunted from a nest. Grief; fury; blame; guilt. He'd had an affair. There was a divorce.

Sometimes I fingered the creases of his closed eyelids, imagining light behind them flashing and flickering like the beginnings of binary translated into cause and effect, like language as light on a screen.

On Sunday mornings, he would lie, propped under my arm, reading newspapers, munching croissant while I traced the lines across his forehead, deciphering censored battles that were never spoken of. In the pulse at his neck I thought I felt the throb of long-spilt blood, and in his deep nasal-labial lines I tracked a record of atrocities. I believed the creases around his eyes could teach me how witches fly, and that his toes were runes.

He was a collector and, as well as the auction house, there was a warehouse and a yard full of paraphernalia. The warehouse heaved with furniture piled high, paintings and posters leaning against other items for want of wall space. Moths fluttered out of dark corners and folds of fabric every time something was moved. Tiny skeletons littered stuffed boxes and bags, drawers, cabinets, wardrobes, and cupboards full of weird and ordinary things. Some of it he'd had for years, had been left outside, and was slowly rotting away, but he was unconcerned. He bought, he sold, and he traded. He gave some things away. But he always collected.

I was pleased – just because they were gifts from him – but perplexed by some of the things he gave me. I invested meanings in the bestowals: badly-painted plant pots, yellowing lace, the rusting manicure set, eyeless dolls, and stained Victorian underwear. He was always busy. He was a like a reliquary of anecdotes, information, instructions.

There was a garage for vans next to the warehouse and he employed people – women mostly – as drivers, though often he was away too, collecting things from France, Spain, and Italy. Sometimes he went to Canada, sending cargo back in crates. His drivers came and went with the work he gave them and when they were around, sometimes, on very rare occasions, he'd invite me to the bar-cum-restaurant they all frequented. We were young, students and migrants. He had cash, experience, energy, a wealth of stories from his travels; a local celebrity. The men who served us our over-priced cocktails were foreigners and they were in awe of him, on the make-or-take as much as those girls were.

"My father has things in Morocco, you might be interested. Okay if I show you pictures?"

"I have a business idea. May I speak with you?"

"I found a flat. You'll look? Yes? Check the papers, please."

"My brother needs this advice for his restaurant. Come and eat! I told him you know business."

The women chatted and laughed with me only because of my

proximity to him. I must have shone in his orbit, but I knew that if we split up they wouldn't even grace me with a glance. They were like a football subs bench; lean, well-trained, eager to prove themselves and waiting for an injury to happen; better still, a sending-off.

He collected books too, beautiful old – very old – volumes that he seemed as unconcerned about, in terms of value, as anything else in his serendipitous store. I pored over them while I waited for him to come back from a viewing, a collection, a delivery, a meeting, a family event. There were lots of those but I was never invited. "Other people's feelings are sensitive"; no matter how often I pointed out that my part in his story was nothing to do with their history.

Except when he was relating some anecdote, he didn't talk much. But he once told me I was the love of his life, and he invented a name for me: Honey, the colour of my hair; sweet, because that's how I tasted, he said.

"I've never called anyone that before."

The mark on the back of my hand was still there, the initial rawness of it deepened to the royal colour of plums. I thought it had become beautiful, with tendrils circling my wrist, crawling towards my inner elbow. He said I should get it looked at.

No matter how many specialists he paid for expensive consultations, none of them diagnosed the disease. It was spreading rapidly by the time our first Christmas arrived, inching across my chest and, as I peered at my back in the antique oval mirror in his bedroom, I realised I had a sapling, my very own Christmas tree, tiny purple branches budding from my spine. But Christmas wasn't 'ours'. It was theirs. I was reticent, pliant, patient. I thought I would be accepted, eventually. The Gloria Grahame desk was my Christmas present.

Before I went home, he shared the winter city with me, its quiet nooks and crannies, its blatant offerings. I held his hand and left no crumbs behind me as I wandered into spring, followed him into another parched summer, then another autumn, and another.

It became our custom to spend New Year (a belated Yule) at his get-away-from it-all place, a sturdy stone house in the Cornish countryside, set in generous grounds with woods and a stream. Unlike his barely-furnished, smart city flat, this place is packed with old furniture and curiosities.

On my first visit I saw, as the garden gave way to rough ground, an old clapped-out tractor, an ancient plough that probably should have been cared for in a museum. A wartime army surplus tent was collapsing with the weight of its own rain-sodden canvas and, inside, damp and mould smothered abandoned blankets and cushions. In the orchard, there was a large, sophisticated child's climbing frame, a tree house, and swings with wooden seats were roped to the fruit trees' branches. A forgotten teddy bear was half buried in wet leaves.

Inside, the house is filled with amusing antique novelties, there are photographs everywhere: his Edwardian ancestors, Marianne's – his ex-wife's – French forebears; and the extended family: his daughters, Eve and Emily before the accident, Eve with her own young brood, Eve and her cousins with their children, Vic and Marianne with their grandchildren, the family with their French relatives and Canadian friends who visit at Christmas. The pictures of Emily alone are flanked by candles. There is a playroom full of funny old toys and big shellac records for the wind-up gramophone in the corner. There were never any photographs of us.

This is what I'll talk about:

The longer we were together the more incidental I felt. If Marianne needed a piece of furniture moving, the boiler pilot light fixing, a door catch mending, a garden plant re-sited, she called Vic, and he went running. Once, he gave me the programme of a ballet he'd taken Marianne to see. It was one time he apologised, after I'd explained my anger. Another time, I was rushed to hospital with appendicitis. He didn't visit me because his relatives were staying with Marianne, and he had to see they were all OK.

When Eve wanted a bigger car for her gaggle of children, Vic gave her the money for it. She divorced soon after the birth of her fifth and last child, and decided that she wanted to live near her parents. Vic bought a house mid-way between his flat and Marianne's house, and Eve moved in. She rents out the house that she got in her divorce settlement. The older the grandchildren got, the more family holidays there were. Spring and early summer, Cornwall; summer France, and, or, Canada; autumn, Cornwall again. And in between there were all the birthday weekends, the special occasions, office parties, the anniversaries, especially Emily's. I was not invited. His penance was permanent, but I didn't understand that then.

The trees were bare again, pointing black fingers that didn't feel at all hackneyed to me. Vic had sponsored a Christmas entertainment about the history of a nearby school, the one his daughters had attended. There were meetings about scripts, songs, costumes, even the design of tickets and invitations. He'd arranged and paid for an after show party at the same restaurant bar he always went to. I offered to help, but he said it was all taken care of, by which he meant he'd already employed his subs bench to do everything. One day, I walked into his office and he was on the phone, saying: "It's OK, honey, leave it with me."

Whoever he was speaking to, that was my name. He'd promised he'd never call anyone else by that name. My lungs contracted as if I'd been poisoned. I thought I was going to vomit.

"So, do I get an invitation to this shindig, or just turn up with you?"

Silence.

My distress was souring to anger. "Will I see your family there? Will you introduce me?"

Silence. He shuffled papers around his desk.

Fury: "You might at least have the decency to answer me, *Honey!*"

He put the papers in a drawer; moved to a filing cabinet and pulled out some more. "It's complicated." His tone made it clear he found my questions tedious.

"What's complicated?" My voice sounded strangled.

He shut the office door, even though the rest of the building seemed silent; his employees holding their breath, taking diplomatic early lunches. Later he could say this was what he'd had to put up with.

The injustice of it surged through me. "How is it complicated?!"

"I mean other people's feelings are complicated!" He shouted back, exasperated.

"*Other people!* You mean your *ex*-wife? You mean your *adult* daughter?" He was heading for the door. "I don't understand, Vic!"

I was crying to his back. My anger got me to the door before

121

him. I stood in front of it barring his escape. "What about Christmas? Are you spending it with me or them again?"

I knew the answer. He'd dragged an enormous fir tree, like he did every year, to his wife's house – their former marital home – which was just round the corner from his flat, and still the seat of all their family gatherings. I knew when he'd been round there, even when he didn't tell me. His tattooed heart always looked redder, raw, like a palimpsest freshly scored in flesh.

He'd actually told me that "Uncle Tom Cobley and all" would be there this year, including, cousins, relatives from France, and friends from Canada. He thought it was funny, that I'd share his amusement about their large, eclectic gathering.

"Please let me leave." He was polite, knowing he'd won this battle as he'd won all the others, just by waiting for me to be desperate. Standing in front of the door had only justified this triumph. He didn't need to slam it, as I would have.

I opened the door and saw him walking along the hallway to the exit. "Am I invited?" I called after him. I didn't care who heard. I wanted them to hear. He was near the outer door. He said something to someone in a room off the hallway.

"What about my feelings, Vic!"

He'd gone.

My house mates rallied round. They'd encountered his generosity as a host and, at first, they'd been happy for me in my joy of him but they'd seen the writing on the wall and were already armed with the necessary comforts: tea, booze, soup, fruit, chocolate, hot water bottles, duvets, and films – all comedies.

Pritti was a hugger. "It's not fair. No-one could think it reasonable to be compartmentalised like that. He is a bad boyfriend."

Lucy was rational. "He'll never change – too old and set in his ways – he's got everything he needs and you – where, and when, he wants."

Agata was uncompromising. "He's fucking you every which-way. You're a fool, Alice! And he's a coward. A bully. Passive aggressive. And mean. Constipated!"

We stared at her, uncomprehending.

"Farting out little bits of time, attention, gifts!"

I think I laughed.

I went home for Christmas and I imagine it was nice, as always. Agata rang on Christmas day. "Don't be blue. He'll be eating his wife's food, and playing the *pater familias* before falling asleep in *her* armchair. He's exactly where he wants to be."

I imagined his tattoo glowing like a light on their Christmas tree. I quietly fretted about the fading Rosea on my chest. The tree on my back looked as if it had been felled. The vines and tendrils had disappeared from my arms. There was just a red blotch at the base of my spine. I sent him a card saying that I'd be in touch, but I didn't come back to the city then. That's when I got ill.

This is another secret:

I dreamed I was travelling, arriving first at Hadrian's Wall where the Vindolanda tablets sent me south and east to Delphi. The hillside looked beautiful still despite the grazing tourists. I think I dreamed that. I know I dreamed his body, and my fingers on it, teaching me how the Pythia had prophesised: the counting of sand grains, the hard shell tortoise and the soft-fleeced lamb's flesh, bronzed pot broiling; the gagging scent of fat in the humming heat, and hard-won coins given to gate-minding priests for news of weather, and wagers, and wars.

Asleep or awake I re-mapped the trade routes of his body. South and East: sweet tea, frankincense, coffee, sandalwood, lemons. In darkness I fevered over wrong turns I had taken. I picked and scored, and scratched out his north: blue ice, wild garlic, salted fish. Later I wanted cigarette butts to scorch out his permafrost in my own sub-cutis.

There are more nerve endings in our finger tips than anywhere else in our bodies. I threw away the rotting lace, the eyeless dolls, the broken pots, the rusty manicure set. I bought a surgical kit complete with scissors, swabs, anti-bacterial cleansing fluid. There's even a small scalpel and antiseptic cream.

My early, tentative narrative has healed to pale striae on my thighs and belly. The heart on my arm is new, raw and sticky, but the coda on my palm is now deeper than his. When I shake his hand I'll be in touch, just like I said I would, and he'll understand. I am a love story.

CARNIVORY

Lisa Mansell

a phantomized infanta shakes into her alum-tawed
skin

balletic in acid-bald
curls

of old blue and zinc-white easy
and her kingdomized miser rivals in the oval riverrun of
wrack

black and tempest-wrecked against her skirt-
folds

of rosin-mist and
toffee

easting

in the distance

wallons howl-wallow a dishevel of carnival
and a euphony of nosferati show-freak

man-strong and lady-beard

allegorical and liquorice
as wretches skirmish in their shell-skin sheen

a doxy of hamlets voodoo

then dovetail
supertonic as tortoiseshells

their   soles   nexus   to   a   midas-skinned   sax
and the theatre of teeth wraths

BRIAN

Glynis Charlton

There were this pigeon once, all mashed up, feathers stuck to track by its innards. Only wanted summat to eat, fluttered down for summat to eat. "Splat," I said. This bloke on platform, he looked at me like I were weird. I could see I'd got him. He didn't say owt, didn't need to. "Ever seen a dead body?" I said, and he smiled. Just a bit. Fancy, who smiles when someone asks them that?

I were having one of my dizzy spells, so there were two of him, then two pigeons, then two blokes coming toward me from station office. They just start, these spells, no warning. Plenty of folk get them, I said, it doesn't make me a nutter. I know everything that goes on. I've got a lot more nous than they give me credit for.

I had to lean on pillar, nearly fell over them tubs of flowers. That's another thing them blokes were always doing; watering flowers when they reckoned I'd not be there. If it weren't me they'd be saying that thing people like to say, "haven't you got a home to go to?" Nobody said it to me. They were too busy with all their little lists. Not everyone can write lists, you've got to earn the right. Money, anyone with half a brain can earn that, but rights, they're different. They think they've got permission, think they can look in at me, stare in, ask questions, write their lists.

Mam had lists, loads of them, on backs of cornflakes packets, envelopes, even cardboard from inside her pack of new tights. Do this, do that, got to do all these things. Tie shoe laces tight, straighten pictures, buy gravy granules.

It takes a special sort of person to write them lists and keep everything neat. He thought he could do that, Mr Kit Kat Man. Petrol, B&Q, postbox. He had me on there. Hadn't written me down, though. No, he thought he were too good for that, thought he'd just add me after postbox. Let's seal Brian away, let's see what he's got in his sandwiches, tell him about Katy, Carol, Candy or whatever her name is, her and her lovely shoes. He didn't know I'd already seen them. Heels all clean, with nice little rubber tips, price still underneath. Probably squeezing her feet into them after she'd put his Kit Kat in his lunchbox. Not a morning person, though. Used to think she was, but not since the shoes, not since the lovely shoes.

Lots of old Council Tax bills, that middle drawer in their living room, very messy, two years out of date, in there with rubber bands, a bottle opener, some other kind of gadget. Gliding drawers, though, I'll give them that. Nice glide, open, look, one fingertip, click. Opened the bottom one, knelt down, had a sniff. Old envelope smell, new wood, push, glide, click. There were an apple tree just out back, very nice. I could prune that for you I told him. I'm good with loppers.

I remember how it came on telly.

Mam were sitting in her chair, watching Six O'clock News and they did that bit at end. You know, bit where they say Coming Up, coming up in the news where you are. Good heavens, Mam goes, that's terrible. And she calls me in from kitchen to watch. I'm through there, making some more tea. She always had to have a fresh one at half past six, even though there were still some warm in pot. Take pot to kettle, Brian, she'd say, not other way round. Always teaching me them useless little things. But what were point?

And I'm standing in doorway, looking over top of her head, watching him. He's there, on telly, Kit Kat bloke. They're zooming in on him, some blurry picture taken on holiday, you can see all pores in his skin, all little lines round his eyes, probably even dandruff in his hair if they got any closer.

And they keep it there, camera, just fixed on his face, that smug smile, keeping his wife out of it. I only see her for a second; they're not interested in her. Not yet. Let her go back to her Tupperware boxes. He leaves a wife, they say. No children, they don't mention children. Thank goodness, says Mam, at least there are no poor kiddies left behind.

And they've been talking about him, telling half of Yorkshire what happened. Except they don't know, they've only got bits of story, them things they call gruesome and grim. Or a find, like it's summat you'd spot on a beach. And she's still watching is Mam, her knobbly fingers holding that mug and hanging on to every word them folk are saying.

There's a woman next, blond hair blowing across her face, standing outside some police station or other. It's drizzling, shining in special light they've put on her. They should give her an umbrella, says Mam. It's not right, poor lass, why don't they give them umbrellas?, and is that tea ready yet, Brian? You're taking your time in there.

And I watch that blue plastic tape flapping about in rain. Cordoned off, that's another thing they like to say. Police arrived on the scene, state of shock, quiet neighbourhood – them are all things they like to talk about.

Them words on blue tape are upside down. Look at them knots, though, they've tied them knots so neat and tight round fence post. I'll give them that.

And now blond woman turns to some bloke in a big overcoat. He's screwing his eyes up against rain, because it's fair pouring down now. White shirt, perfect tie, getting all wet, and she's pointing this big black microphone under his chin. Everything they can, he's going. All available resources, searching the area, urge anyone to come forward. And I'm in kitchen, watching, hearing kettle come to boil.

When I bring tray through, there's some old codger moaning about hospitals, and isn't it a disgrace, says Mam, I don't know what this world's coming to, I really don't and have I got her tablets, them red ones, don't go getting it wrong again. And I'm clicking top off childproof bottle, wondering how long before it reaches nationals.

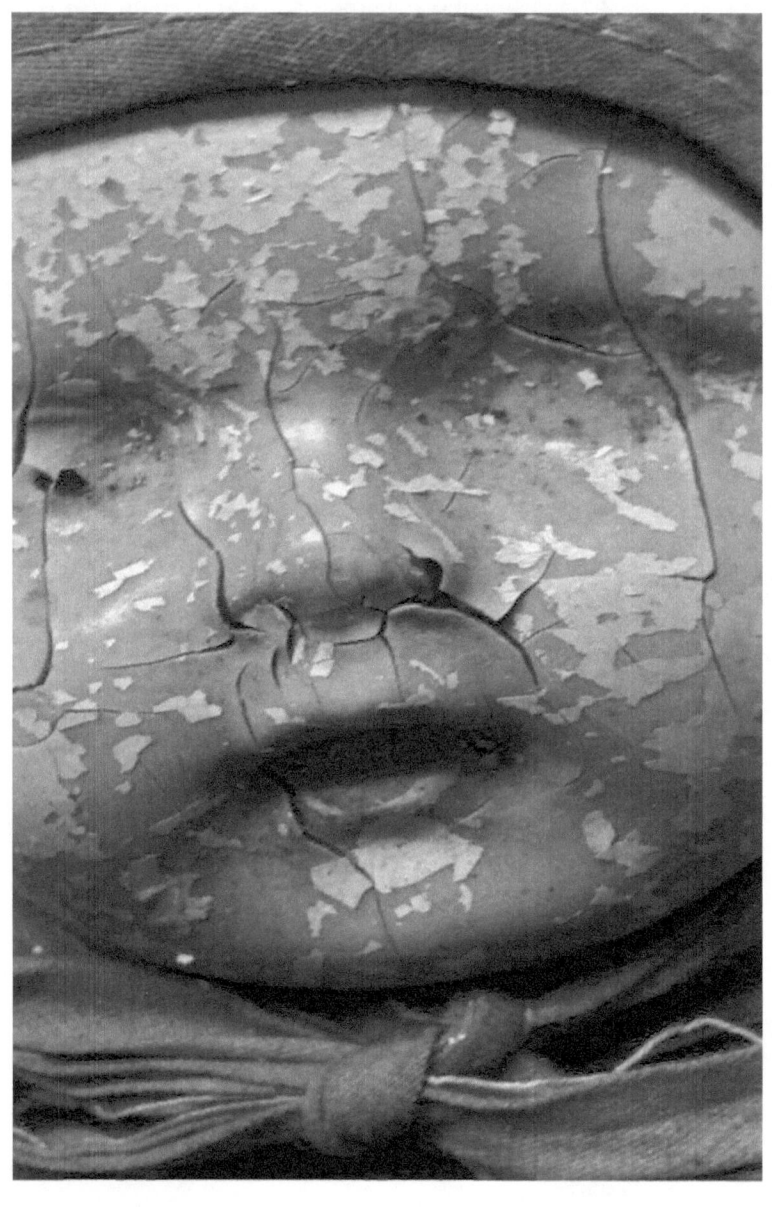

POST PARTUM

Siân Davies

Bethany rubbed the tip of her nose across the sleeping baby's fingers; little pink digits made of jelly-bones and impossible strength. She kissed the back of them, sniffed them, delighted in them when they wrapped around her manicured finger. The smile that stretched her cheeks and the softness in her gaze spoke of unconditional love. Awe. She put a loud kiss on the back of the baby's hand. "She's just . . . so perfect. Isn't she?"

Sam nodded with a plastic smile. "Yeah, of course."

Her sister devolved into kissy-sounds underscored by the gentle jingle of glass beads and dangling earrings.

Sam got to her feet, picked up their empty mugs – hand painted with black scrollwork, a wedding present – and excused herself to the kitchen. She put the radio on to drown out the incessant coos from the lounge. Rubbed her hands over her face. Her head hurt.

She wanted them gone.

It was her last chance to see her sister before she skipped off to America to direct a play she'd written. Californian wine, adventure, and a new man; that was Bethany. Everyone said she was making it big, knew she would. And Sam? She pushed her hair back. Unwashed, unstyled, uncut for too long. The kettle boiled noisily. The coffee – her favourite brand – smelled different. Burnt, and something else she couldn't place. Bethany babbled away in the background. Sam turned the radio up.

"Sammy! You'll – Oh, she's awake. Hey little one! Hi! You are *so* beautiful. Will you get her bottle? I think she's" – a wail interrupted her – "Oh, definitely hungry."

Sam closed her eyes. That shrill, needless cry. It made her insides twist in on themselves. She made the coffee up, deliberately slow. When she entered the lounge, Bethany was on her feet; she bounced the screaming baby gently against her front. Its red face contorted with each scream, its toothless mouth agape and slick with spit. Sam set the mugs down.

Bethany looked at them, then at Sam. No more love and awe. "Where's her bottle?" She narrowed her eyes. "Hello?"

"Oh. I'll get it."

Bethany hugged the baby closer. "I'll go."

The radio cut out after Bethany entered the kitchen. Cupboard doors slammed. The baby cried, and Bethany said, over and over, "I know, I know, I know."

Sam cradled her coffee in both hands. Felt the slight raise of scrollwork under her fingers. The heat from the mug seared her palms, and she didn't mind.

"I better go," Bethany said.

Cold panic dropped like a stone into Sam's stomach. "You sure you don't want to' – *take the baby with you?* – "stay a little longer?"

"I really need to go and finalise some things, and I'm sure you're itching for some alone time. Just you and the little one. Don't look like that; you'll be fine, Sammy."

The women stood in the middle of the lounge while the baby bouncer hummed a tune and the TV told them, in smooth, cultured tones that five more people were dead that day.

"I'll call you from California."

Sam waved a hand. "Don't worry about it."

"Just..." Bethany bit the inside of her lip. "Will you call Mum? If there're problems?"

Sam barked a laugh. "Yeah, sure."

"I mean it. She misses you."

"I bet."

Bethany opened her mouth, closed it. Then she was gone; a flurry of colourful scarves and expensive perfume. Off to America, far away. Jealousy washed over Sam in a green-tinted wave. She placed a hand flat against the ersatz-oak frame of the open door and took in the neighbourhood. The house – her husband's, not hers – was the jewel of a huge inheritance. It sat on the quietest, oldest street in Sevenoaks, decorated all around by perfect lawns and trimmed hedgerows and quaint elderly people. It was Stepford for the retired and dying.

She closed the door and put something on the TV, turned the

baby bouncer around to face it. She wasn't even sure the kid cared, but it felt like the right thing to do. Another mother might have stayed close, but she couldn't bring herself to sit beside the tiny, pink-faced stranger and pretend. It was asleep again. It must be exhausting, being newly alive. Having barely enough energy to eat and scream and dirty nappies. People said it looked like its dad but they were wrong. Aaron wasn't this baby's father, and Sam wasn't its mother. The baby was an imposter, the result of hospital incompetence.

She went back to the kitchen and closed the door so she wouldn't hear the kid unless it screamed. It was like this every day. She slid around the edges of her home, repelled from whatever space the kid took up. Not her kid. Someone else's kid. She wondered if there was another couple somewhere in Kent, fawning over their new baby, knowing something wasn't right.

Her feeling of wrongness – of having been robbed of a precious part of herself – became so intense that her hands balled into fists. The infant stranger did nothing for her but scream and vomit up its milk. Aaron insisted that breast feeding would fix it. Sam and the baby would settle, and they'd all be happy. He didn't understand why she couldn't do it, wouldn't even try. He'd been angry at her. He'd said terrible things.

Fatherhood fit Aaron like a tailored suit. Worry-induced hard work made him good at everything – on paper. A good boss. A good husband. A good dad. He picked all their baby necessities, always got the baby to take its bottle (and burp after), and he changed nappies like he'd been doing it for years. The kid always went to sleep for him. It always settled. Of course he'd never believe her story of some insidious hospital cockup when he had it so easy.

That's why she'd bought a paternity test.

Sam sat cross-legged in the middle of her bed, and pushed her orange-scented fingers over her tummy again. The ravages of pregnancy had left their initials in her skin like grotesque tiger stripes. The balm – Stretch Away – was pinker than she remembered. More greasy than oily. Didn't absorb into her skin like it had before. Her fingertips trailed along the top of the C-section's suture tape. She could take it off any time now, but she was convinced that if she did her guts would spill out into her lap.

Another bloody mess to clean up.

Aaron rapped his fingers on the door jamb and leant against it. Sam covered her stomach with her shirt. Her husband wore a smile that didn't meet his eyes. Dark blue shirt in black suit trousers, sleeves rolled up to his elbows. Completely creaseless. He didn't look like he'd just finished a stint at the office; he looked like he was about to go out.

"I noticed you threw the coffee away," he said. "Dare I ask why?"

"It smelled weird."

He laughed. "Post-pregnancy weird?"

"No." She screwed the top back onto her balm. "It smelled like it was burnt."

Aaron's smile tightened. "Did it taste fine?"

"No."

He pushed himself off the jamb and moved into the room. Hands in his pockets. Slow, easy steps. She'd never seen him more in control, or so unlike himself. He smirked when he caught her looking him over. Kicked an empty baby bottle out from under the bed and picked it up, dropped it on top of the long neglected vanity table.

"So Beth's gone for good?"

Sam scowled. "Not for good. For a little while."

"And you're OK with that?"

"Why wouldn't I be?"

He shrugged, perched on the edge of the table. The back of his head was reflected three ways and each way looked model-perfect. He laughed a little, blushed. Pulled his collar away from his neck.

"Stop staring at me like you've never seen me before."

"You just look different."

"Like your favourite coffee was different?"

"That wasn't my coffee."

"Like you threw out the clock my mother got for us? Stopped driving your car? Because they'd been what, replaced?"

"I didn't have a matte interior in the car, Aaron, it was lacquered. You wouldn't know, you never drove it, but someone changed it."

"Someone just swapped it?" He loosed a nasty laugh. "Like they just swapped your baby? You've been going crazy ever since you had Pip."

Hearing the name aloud made her tongue numb at the root and struck her dumb. They'd picked that name together: Philippa, Pip for short. It was a beautiful name for a beautiful, thoughtful little girl, one Sam had carried and loved and nurtured for nine months, and now she had nothing to show for it. A ruined body, a fragile marriage, and a baby that wasn't hers. She tried to speak.

"What was that?"

She tried again. Her throat was so tight it hurt to swallow.

"Sam?" Aaron's voice matched his stony expression. He was like that now. "What did you say?"

"I said, I bought a paternity test."

"Are you telling me I might not be Pip's father?"

"No! I mean, yes. Because neither of us are her parents." She flinched when he stood upright.

He stepped towards her and stabbed a finger in front of her face. "You need to stop this right fucking now."

"Will you do it?"

He grabbed her by the shoulders and shook her. "I'm telling you – *ordering you* – to cut this out. Right now, Sam. That baby is yours. Now, if what you're saying is that you *cheated* on me –"

"I didn't!"

"– and that's why you got a test, that's something else, Sam. That's something really fucking serious."

"I can't believe you'd ask me that."

His new, nasty laugh spread warm air across her face. "I can't believe half the shit you've pulled these last few months, Sam."

A cry from downstairs made them both turn towards the door. Aaron let her go, and slammed the door behind him when he left.

With the curtains drawn the lounge was almost cosy. No children played noisily in the street, and the only car Sam ever heard pulling up was Aaron's. No one argued loud enough to be heard through the walls, and no one revelled in midsummer drunkenness in any of the neighbouring gardens. Ten months earlier she would have felt lucky. Now she felt trapped.

She wasn't sure her elderly neighbours would open the door to her, or that anyone would believe her if they did. Proving that the baby wasn't hers was just a matter of DNA, but proving that Aaron wasn't Aaron would be something else. She watched the man with Aaron's face feed the baby and know just when to wind it. She couldn't remember a moment when he'd shown any new-father anxiety. He changed the channel from the news to the football.

"I thought you hated sports," she said.

Aaron shrugged. "Some guys at work got me into it."

"What team?"

"Arsenal."

"You're from Plymouth."

He gave her a crooked smile. "Why don't you put the kettle on?"

"We don't have any coffee."

He gaze slid back to the TV. He wiped milk off the baby's chin without looking. "Tea, then."

She watched him from the kitchen. He checked his phone, typed something, put it away. Repeated this two or three times. She lifted one of the filled mugs, and the handle came away. A clean break, gritty clay underneath. She felt gloss under her fingers. Pushed her thumb along the scrollwork. Flat. She dropped both mugs into the sink. When she turned, Aaron was in the door way, his phone in his hand.

"Mind if I head out for an hour?"

She blinked. "No, why?"

"Just something from work I've got to contain. You know how it is."

"Yeah," she forced a smile. "Yeah, I get it. Go ahead."

She waited until she couldn't hear the car anymore to look outside. No one around. She could leave. She grabbed her coat from the hook and strode back into the kitchen, started pulling drawers open to find the keys for her replacement car. She only needed to get as far as her mother's house, then she could ditch the imposter-car, the imposter-baby –

Keys in the backdoor made her stop. Aaron opened it, closed it, locked it again. They stared at each other.

"I was going to get coffee," she said.

"What?" He sounded out of breath. He'd put a black hoody on.

"I was going to get more coffee. You know. I can get you a few cans as well, for the football."

The landline chirped a shrill summons. She hurried to it, even as Aaron hissed for her to leave it.

"Hello?"

"Hey, Sam. I wanted to apologise. I feel bad about before. About the fight. Pip's been hard on us and I haven't looked after you. I'm going to come home."

Sam looked back into the kitchen.

Aaron leaned against the door jamb. "Put the phone down, Sammy."

She did.

Catafalque

Lisa Mansell

now it recurs
the shrug of shrink-wrap   corner-sogged and floral
oak leaves coda the tacit rain
(edge-torn by the crimp of sextons)

               it should be beech   like her
the shoulders are obliged to shrug
          not in indifference
but response to cold
        to recur indoors
        to illicit Lorca
there is nothing Canadian here
just voice   and rooms
in their limp flaps of breath
        knots suck and crucifix
amid the vuvuzelas and motorbikes that scythe the sog of
mourners

THE DUMMY

Nicholas Royle

The featureless road. The driving rain.

White lines, empty fields.

The endless rhythm of the stop-go shunt, a Newton's cradle of cars on the motorway heading north-west. The occasional church spire in the distance piercing the dark grey wadding of the clouds. The monotony is relieved by a fizzing spot of fluorescent yellow up ahead. You squint, peer through the windscreen, rub with your sleeve at a stubborn patch of fog on the glass. The view clears. The fluorescent spot grows, elongates, becomes a figure.

The motorway narrows from three lanes down to two. The traffic slows accordingly. The man in the high-visibility clothing moves his left arm up and down, telling you to slow down further. He's standing hard by the crash barrier on the central reservation. He's either suicidal or insane or both. There has to be a better way to warn drivers of impending hazards, you think. Sure, he's completely covered in hi-vis gear, from the hood of his jacket to the turn-ups of his trousers, but you can't imagine this man's UK counterpart happily standing that close to moving traffic in the fast lane of the M1. Maybe the Belgians pay danger money, or perhaps, as seems likely from the standard of the driving, all Belgians are clinically insane. Admittedly this may be the birthplace of surrealism, but still.

You twist your head for a closer look as you roll past. The planes of his face seem abnormally severe, his skin unnaturally smooth. Do motorway maintenance workers really shave every morning?

"Tell me where it comes from, this love of our country."

Asking the question was a striking young woman of slender build and average height, her irregularly cut mahogany-coloured hair framing a face shaped like a warning sign. Eyes that glittered;

a short, sharp nose, pointed like the bill of a goldfinch; lips painted a vivid red. When she leaned forward across the hotel breakfast table, peripheral vision gifted me a view down the front of her top.

"What's not to love about it?" I said, careful not to let my eyes drop. "Beer, chocolate, medieval architecture."

"In that order?"

She flashed her teeth; one was chipped at the corner. Either her lower lip was uneven or she twisted it unconsciously while she spoke. I remembered reading somewhere that beauty was all down to symmetry. I'd thought it was rubbish at the time and now here was proof.

"Definitely."

"No, but..." she started, signalling the switch to serious interview mode by picking up a sachet of sugar and turning it end on end on the tablecloth. "The Eddy De Groot novels are bestsellers. You're not telling me his creator is inspired by nothing more than a desire to sit drinking Duvel at pavement cafés in the Grote Markt."

"With a view of the Stadhuis."

"Exactly."

"No. In fact, just between you and me," I said, lowering my voice to a conspiratorial whisper, "I don't actually like Duvel."

She sat back, eyes wide.

"I know, I know," I said, hands in the air. "The man who didn't like Duvel. I don't like tripels either. I like blonde beers. I've always been partial to blondes." I gave her my winning grin.

"Only blondes?" she asked, sitting forward again.

"As you probably know if you've read the books, I like the brown beers best." My eyes flicked down momentarily. "Westmalle, Ename, Chimay – but only the red or the blue."

Around us, hotel staff were discreetly clearing tables.

"So, Eddy De Groot, your Flemish detective, is you?" she asked, bending the sugar sachet in half.

"It's easier than making stuff up."

"Your alter ego?"

"If you like. All I know is he's not Poirot and he's not Maigret, but he's not Van der Valk either. I saw a gap in the market for a Dutch-speaking Belgian detective. Written by an Englishman."

Now it was my turn to sit back in my chair. I took my eyes off her for a moment and looked around the breakfast room. She had described my Eddy De Groot novels as bestsellers. Which of course they weren't, not in the UK, but they did OK in Dutch translation. In addition, they probably sold as many English copies here in Belgium and in Holland as they did back home, there were that many English speakers in the Low Countries. In any case, the figures obviously added up, or I wouldn't get this treatment: five-star hotel, a reading slot at the Antwerp festival, a round of interviews with local and national media. The girl with the sexy mouth had come up from Brussels to do a piece for De Standaard. I wasn't kidding myself it was going to last for ever, but I might as well enjoy it while I could.

"It goes back to when I was a kid," I said, leaning forward and taking the sachet of sugar from her hand. "My dad used to bring me stamps off the ships. He was a customs officer and he used to rummage ships in the docks and bring me back stamps for my collection. The ones I liked best were the Belgian stamps. The picture of King Baudouin, the different colours. Pink, blue, green. Brown and grey. I liked the way the colours changed but the image remained the same. I wanted to own the whole set. I like having whole sets of things. Belgian stamps. Agatha Christie novels – Fontana paperbacks with the Tom Adams covers. No others." I toyed with the sugar sachet and shrugged my shoulders. "It's a man thing."

I watched her check the digital voice recorder.

"When's your deadline?" I asked. "Do you have to go away and write this up this morning?"

"I've got till tomorrow lunchtime," she said.

"So what do you say we do this over lunch?"

I held my breath and caught her looking at my wedding ring. I said nothing. She smiled.

Rain falls without end from a sky made of lead. Your eyes are gritty. Your head lolls momentarily over the wheel.

Microsleep.

You exit the motorway. Pull over, rub your face. Get out, walk up and down. Fresh air, pouring rain. Get back in the car. Sit there looking out at the rain. You get your phone out of your pocket and stare at it. You check that you haven't missed any calls or texts. You haven't. You remember the time you spent ten minutes going all over the house looking for the phone, while talking on what you thought was the cordless landline. You even told the person you were talking to that you were looking for your mobile, and all the while you were holding it in your hand and talking on it.

This wasn't so long ago.

You told your wife about it, hoping she would find it funny. She shook her head and said, "It's a bit early even for you, isn't it?" You had had a drink, as it happened, but nothing more than that. You wondered if she had a point and you decided that she may well have done, but that it was disappointing all the same that she didn't just laugh about it and then perhaps everything would have been all right.

It's a long time since everything has been all right.

You go to the messages on your phone and reread the last text she sent. There's no real need, there are no fresh insights to be gained. You're just tormenting yourself.

You put the phone back into your pocket and turn the key in the ignition.

More rain, more flat fields. Grey streets with occasional brick houses, shuttered, stark. More traffic cones, roadworks, another flash of fluorescent yellow. But the perspective's all wrong. It looks like he's lying down. You lean forward over the wheel, screwing up your eyes. He is lying down. Pull over, stop. Get out. Jacket over your head. Bend down. His hood over his face. Limbs at weird angles, as if he's been knocked down. Hit and run. You pull the hood back a little.

Jump.

The face isn't real. The rain doesn't roll off it in quite the right way. But the arms and legs look right; the torso is reassuringly bulky. You touch the leg. It's a real leg. You'd put money on it being a real leg. You haven't had a drink yet today. You squeeze harder. Maybe you're wrong. You look at the face again. Is it a mask? You remember the man on the tube, the blind man with the rubber eye mask. Two unblinking eyes painted on to a rubber mask held in place with elastic behind a pair of useless glasses. When you sat opposite, you stared at him so hard you ended up having to look away, because you became convinced he could see you doing it. Somehow.

When you took a photograph of him through a crowd on the

platform and showed it to your wife, she called you a sick fuck, but only after making sure the children were not in the room.

You took your camera with you when you went to say goodnight to the children, because you wanted to show that picture to them. You thought they'd get it. But they were both already asleep, their hands clenched into tiny fists, mouths slightly open. The infinitesimal rise and fall of the chest. You bent right down over their beds until you could feel their breath on your cheek. The faintly sour smell. You would never stop loving them, you told yourself, no matter what they did. Yes, you'd lose your temper with them and yell at them, and afterwards you would feel bad because the anger melted away leaving only the love behind.

You couldn't imagine life without them.

Sometimes you'd sit and watch them breathe, sitting with one and then the other. Until your wife would call you. I thought you'd gone to the pub, she would say when you went downstairs. No, you'd say, and you'd look into her eyes and see if it was still there, the glimmer in her eyes that had drawn you to her, what, twelve years ago? Thirteen? It had lost some of its candlepower, perhaps, but it was still there, and so you'd hold her and you'd hug each other tightly and you'd say you loved her and you hoped she'd be patient with you and she'd say nothing, but nor would she let go of you.

You try to loosen the collar on the shirt, just in case. The neck looks no more realistic than the face close up. You look up, look around. There's no one. The nearest buildings are some distance away. There's no traffic. You gather the dummy's legs and thread your arm under his back, taking care to support the head with your upper arm. He's lighter than a fully grown man. Heavier than either of your children. You carry him the few yards back to the car and manage to open the passenger door. Your heart is beating fast and the blood vessels in your head are throbbing. You position his legs in the footwell and once you've got the seatbelt around him he sits up OK. His head hangs forward just a little.

You check your mirrors. There's a car in the wing mirror, far enough away for its driver not to have seen anything. In any case, your car would have acted as a shield. The other car now drives past without slowing down. You wait for the ringing in your head, from the hiss of the tyres on the wet road surface, to die down and then you pull out and drive on.

I took her to the Entrepôt du Congo for lunch and between us we got through so many Rodenbachs neither of us thought it was a bad idea when I suggested we carry on the interview back at my hotel. Of course when we got back there, the lobby area was busy and returning to the breakfast room didn't feel like an attractive option, so although I know I could have asked the concierge for conference facilities, it just seemed easier to head upstairs to my room.

We did finish the interview, but let's just say it took a while to get started on the afternoon session. Hilde said it was the first interview she'd conducted in which both parties were completely naked.

"Both parties?" I said.

She smiled.

We could have perhaps left it at that and not gone on and ruined everything. But during the time we spent in my room there were moments of tenderness, interludes when we lay side by side catching our breath gazing into each other's eyes like lovers. Most of the time, admittedly, it felt like a one-night stand, but there were moments when it didn't. And there was a mutual reluctance to part once we were dressed and Hilde said the batteries on her digital recorder were exhausted but that it didn't matter because she'd already got far more material than she could use. Somehow we ended up at a bar not far from the hotel drinking shots. I switched my phone back on to see that my wife had been trying to get hold of me. Instead of calling her back I ordered another round of drinks and heard myself answering Hilde's question about the origins of my love of Belgium in greater depth.

"It wasn't just the stamps," I said. "Well, it was, but it wasn't just the stamps per se. It was what they symbolised. They were like the equivalent British stamps. Different colours, monarch's head. We had a queen, you had a king. I couldn't get my head around how strange it must be to have a king rather than a queen." I knocked back another shot and was about to order more, but checked myself and ordered two dark beers instead. "We should drink them slowly," I said. "Here was this country," I went on, "just across the Channel from us. A small country, a monarchy. In a way it was a mirror image of Britain. As I grew up, I imagined that it was like a parallel world to the one in which I lived."

Red light struck one side of her face, blue the other. I felt a compulsion to open up to her completely, to tell her everything about myself. In turn, I wanted to know everything there was to know about her. I took out my wallet and withdrew the battered picture of my kids that went everywhere with me.

"Jack and May," I said.

She grinned and tossed her hair back and asked me how old they were. I told her eight and six, but that the photograph was a year old. She handed it back and as I slipped it into my wallet I fell into a sort of fugue. I couldn't work out why. Eventually I wondered if it was because she'd been happy to see a picture of my children. If she was happy that I had kids, did that mean she would also be happy when I went home to them, which I both did and didn't want to do.

You went home, of course. But it was clear – not to them, but to your wife – that something was up. You can't dissemble, can't hide the truth. You said nothing, but within a week you were back in Belgium. Another book to research, you said, next in the series. You stayed with Hilde. She was single even if you weren't.

You scrapped a planned De Groot novel and started a new one. He'd fallen in love, with a journalist. His job was on the line, his life falling apart. De Groot's wife was suspicious; yours too. It wasn't as if she read your work-in-progress, not normally, but accessing your back-ups remotely on your iDisk was beyond neither her imagination nor her technical know-how. Getting the password right was the easy part, since you had never had any secrets. The drink and drug habits had never been kept from her. How could they be? Their effects were written all over your face and bank statements.

When you got home, your wife confronted you and you broke down and confessed. You sat at the kitchen table and looked out of the window while she threw crockery – wedding presents – at the wall. In the garden, perched on the handrail that runs around the outside of the deck area, was a small green bird, a greenfinch, seemingly completely oblivious to the mayhem taking place only a few feet away. You watched that bird, its tiny head shifting position in jerky increments, and were filled with a vague longing. If you could have put your feelings into words you would perhaps have said that you wanted to swap places with the bird. That you wanted your spirit or your soul to escape from your own body like smoke and drift under the kitchen door and then enter the greenfinch, which you would henceforth, in some strange incomprehensible way, become.

Do you even believe in a spirit or a soul? Or is there nothing but a mind? A consciousness? A sense of identity?

You see a sign for Westvleteren and leave the main road. Some say Westvleteren 12 is the best beer in the world and you would not disagree. None of the three Westvleteren beers can be bought anywhere other than direct from the Westvleteren Abbey brewery. You've heard they even require you to have an appointment, but if you turn up and say give me an appointment in five minutes' time, what are they going to do? Turn you away? Or sell you some of the best beer in the world?

You see his yellow jacket out of the corner of your eye and it startles you. You'd forgotten he was there, sitting right next to you, steam rising off him. His raised hood conceals his profile. Didn't you lower his hood? You must have raised it again, either deliberately or accidentally, while getting him into the car.

You keep driving, although the signs to Westvleteren have disappeared. There was a village, or a hamlet. A settlement. Three or four buildings, all shuttered, no gardens. Brick fronts hard by the road. But no crossroads, no turnings, unless you missed one while sneaking a look at your passenger. Here's something on the left. You slow down. A walled enclosure. Carefully cut grass. Regular lines of white headstones. Identical black lettering on each.

You accelerate slowly as if out of respect. There is no let-up in the rain. At the next turning you go left. The windscreen wipers sound like a heartbeat. A Coca-Cola sign shimmers out of the gloom on the right-hand side of the road. You pull over and stop. Some kind of café. Step out of the car and lock it, then look back in and hesitate, the rain drumming on your shoulders and the back of your neck, before unlocking it and turning to walk towards the café.

I took the Eurostar back to Brussels and jumped in a cab. We spent the afternoon in Hilde's flat on avenue Emile Max. When I finally looked out of the window I saw a flash of green as a bird the size of a jackdaw, but much more streamlined with pointed wings and a long tail, swooped down into the garden and then climbed back up from its dive just as quickly, like a BMXer on a ramp. I knew instantly what bird it was.

"Look," I said to Hilde, "a ringed-neck parakeet. They've become common in London, apparently, though I've never seen one. I had to come to Brussels to see my first one. It's an omen."

She asked me what had happened in London.

"She told me to fuck off," I said. And straight away, as a shadow seemed to pass across her face, I knew it was a strategic error. You don't tell your lover that your wife has kicked you out. It doesn't matter that you may have talked about the possibility. When it happens, you say nothing, unless what you want to end up with is precisely that, nothing.

We went out to a bar in Schaerbeek where a friend of Hilde's was celebrating a birthday. I drank steadily as I watched Hilde drinking and sitting with her arms around a succession of people, male and female, all of them younger than me, as she was herself of course, and I started to feel obscurely sad. Self-pity pricked at my eyes as I turned to look out of the window and thought about Jack and May.

And Sara. My wife.

I left the bar and walked in a random direction. Before long I realised I had entered the red light district by the Gare du Nord and I went into the next bar I came to. Pinewood panelling covered the walls. I ordered an Orval because it appeared to be the only beer they had. I detest Orval, so I drank it quickly and ordered another. And then another. It was dark when I left the bar. Red, blue and ultraviolet lights slid past me in a sickening blur. When I somehow found my way back to avenue Emile Max, I waited outside Hilde's building until someone came out. The door to her flat gave easily enough without causing too much damage, but really I was past caring. While I was blundering around inside looking for her car keys, I felt my phone vibrating in my pocket. A text message.

You don't like Jupiler any more than Orval, but when it's all they've got, you'll swallow it. Three small bottles. Take the edge off. A fat man sits at a till. You give him a handful of coins and go on through into a long narrow room filled with dusty display cases containing scraps of battle dress, a scabbard, a German helmet. Strange wooden boxes squat on tables. You put your eye to the eyepiece and twist the knob to change the photograph being viewed. Some optical trickery inside the box creates a 3D effect. Pictures of terrible wounds and corpses alternate with photographs of advancing columns of soldiers. The atrocity exhibition with slot machines. Somehow, their being in black and white makes it worse, but after a while, the pictures no longer shock. You become inured to the horror. At the far end of the room a doorway leads outside.

You follow a path into a field dotted with trees and lined, you now see, with passageways dug into the earth.

Trenches.

You remember the cemetery filled with war dead. Are these real trenches or some sick replica, a theme park, dug by the fat man? Or that the fat man had dug for him? From what you know of Belgium, it would not surprise you at all to learn that these are the real thing. In another country this would be a monument. Here it's a disgrace. You'd almost rather it were the fat man's plaything, that just one man was to blame instead of a federal state for failing to honour the sacrifice of others.

You half-clamber, half-slip down into one of the trenches and it's all you can do to remain on your feet in the mud. You feel a damp sensation on the left side of your chest. Something trickling. Sweat from all the exertion. You feel like a ghoul. Time to leave.

You collapse in the driver's seat. Turn to look at your passenger.

"Weird place," you say, and wait for a response. "Suit yourself. Let's go."

You realise you've not taken your coat off and Hilde's car will now be covered in mud.

"Too bad," you say. "She should have thought of that." And you laugh.

You know you shouldn't be driving, but you don't care. You can feel that wet sensation on the left side of your chest again. Still sweating? You look down, tugging at your coat. There's blood. Quite a lot of blood. Stop the car. Pull at your T-shirt, covered in blood.

There's a big hole in your chest. Fist-sized. As if something has been torn out of you.

You bend over to look more closely. Tentatively insert the tips of your fingers. Your hand slowly falls away and you look up through the windscreen at the ever-falling rain. The only sound you can hear, apart from the rattling of the rain, to which you have become so accustomed you don't notice it any more, is the ba-dum ba-dum ba-dum of the wipers.

The text said she had taken the kids and gone. I could come back, she said, but they wouldn't be there. I'd be coming back to an empty house.

It wasn't like she was kidnapping them and I'd never see them again. They'd be going to school as normal and I could hang around the school gate. But I wouldn't get to be with them properly. I could fight it, but I knew I didn't have a hope.

It was a long text.

I got in Hilde's car and drove out of Brussels, heading north-west towards the coast. Not that I had any kind of plan. It was already late and dark, and the combination of alcohol, tiredness and the constant rain meant I had to stop. I found a DIY superstore with a large car park on the outskirts of Gent. I parked by the wall facing the exit and slept on the back seat. In the morning I went in search of food, then sat in the car while waiting for the DIY store to open. I went in, got what I wanted and returned to the car with it coiled in a plastic bag, which I put in the boot. I then drove on with no fixed destination in mind.

There was a pain in my chest. From having slept badly, I presumed.

You drive until you reach the coast. Still it rains. The first cheap hotel you see, you leave the car and carry the dummy in over your shoulder. The woman gives you a twin room. You lay him on one of the beds and you take the other, kicking off your shoes. You turn and turn but sleep won't come. You get up and gently move him along a little so that you can get on the same bed. Facing away from him. You lie absolutely still, listening, but all you can hear is the rain hitting the window.

You turn to face him. There are raindrops on his yellow jacket. You pull the jacket to one side and rest your head on his chest. After a few moments you realise you can hear a noise like the windscreen wipers and you wonder if it's a kind of hypnagogic auditory hallucination or if it's the pulse in your temple.

You wake up in the original position you had occupied on the shared bed, facing away from him. A thin grey light from the window reveals large brown flowers on the wallpaper. You turn over and look at him. His face looks the same, smooth, unlined, eyes open. On his chest a line of stitching provides a point of detail on the otherwise featureless dark fabric that covers his frame and padding. Remembering the last thing that happened before you fell asleep, you press your ear to his chest. It's faint, but still there, but again, it could be the blood in your own head. Or it could be auto-suggestion.

You go into the bathroom and run the shower. When you come out, I'm sitting up on the edge of the bed staring at the floor.

"Shall we go?"

You drive along the coast towards Zeebrugge.

"What did you buy from the DIY store?"

My voice is flat, affectless.

"I think you know."

We take a ferry to England and are then faced with a long drive to London. By the time we reach the M25, it's late. In Upper Holloway you park Hilde's car outside the kids' school. It's a very short walk to your house. I follow you up the path. The house is in darkness. The kids' rooms are empty, their cupboards and drawers bare. You offer me your bedroom and say you're going to sleep in your son's room.

In the morning, you look in on me, your face blank, and you say goodbye before going downstairs. I hear the chink of a glass as a drink is poured, then another, and finally the sound of the front door. I get up and watch from the window as you cross the street. You open the boot of the car and look inside. The plastic bag from the DIY store is still sitting there. You close the boot, then open the driver's door and get in.

I feel a tiny stabbing pain on the left side of my chest as I think about what might be in that bag and what it could be used for.

It's not long before the street becomes busy with parents dropping off their kids, some on foot, others by car. I watch you watching the street and the school gate. A large black car stops in the middle of the road and two children get out. A boy and a girl. The black car moves off and you get out of Hilde's car and call them. They stop and look at each other, then run towards you and I see you holding them close to you. A short conversation takes place and you open the rear door of the car and they look at each other again before getting in. You start the engine and pull out of the parking space. As you move off down the street I have a last glimpse of the children sitting in the back seat, their heads nodding with the movement of the car. When you reach the end of the street, you turn left.

How far will you go before you stop and open the boot? The outskirts of London? Somewhere more remote?

It's usually somewhere remote.

THE PIANO SONG

Ian Whates

Kimberly Hobson was coming home; perhaps in the only way she ever *could* have come home.

Her mother's death had left her feeling oddly hollow. There was sadness, but only associated with the realisation that this marked an end in many senses – she was truly alone now. Her dad had gone first, claimed by lingering cancer which had made him feel he was being "evicted from his own body by a usurper". Those were his own words, spoken in a tone of frustrated injustice which she would never forget. And then Ed – killed in a head-on collision with a truck three years ago. Always cheerful, always there: Ed, her brother, who had been the one remaining link to the childhood she remembered. At least he'd gone quickly, or so the police assured her.

Now it was the turn of her mother, who had never really been a link to anything. Her death was difficult to accept – not for any deep-rooted emotional reason, but because Kim had somehow assumed that her mum would go on forever; this woman her father once referred to affectionately as "a force of nature", though Kim had always seen her more as feature of the landscape – a rocky outcropping, a mountain that blocked the view, refused to give ground and was impossible to get around.

Kim took a series of deep breaths and started to walk up the gravel drive. She'd parked on the road – a habit she couldn't break even now for some reason. Driving onto the property itself felt wrong, a trespass too far.

Why did this whole business make her want to reach for a cigarette that wasn't there? She had given up years ago, but right now would have killed for a smoke. A betraying hand had sneaked into her bag before she could stop it; she quickly converted the action into a general rummage, as if to kid herself that the thought of cigarettes had never even entered her mind. Questing fingers closed on something; a packet of mints.

Her feet stumbled to a halt as she drew the mints out, leaving her to simply stare at the house – this brooding presence that squatted there, waiting for her, a Pandora's Box of her past. Kim wished there was someone to come with her, someone she could lean on for support and look to share this ordeal with, but there wasn't. Paul had been excised from her life nearly ten years ago – no children and a swift divorce. Since then there'd been the occasional man, she'd 'dated' from time to time and had even slept with one or two, but none of these transient companions had touched her in a meaningful way and she'd always sidestepped anything that threatened to become a relationship, even Damon, who had been besotted and pursued her stubbornly for a while.

None of them had been allowed as close as Paul, and no one ever would be again.

In a way, she didn't even blame the girl. Mandy was a slut, always had been, even at school. She went through men like crisp packets, picking them up, emptying them and then chucking them away before moving onto the next one.

"Look out, girls, here comes Mandy; we'd better lock our husbands up," wasn't even something they whispered behind her back, it was something she laughed about with them.

No, she couldn't entirely blame Mandy, but Paul was another matter. If he were going to betray her with anyone, why did it have to be Mandy Gibson of all people? So blonde, so busty, and so fucking *obvious*.

In truth, she felt nearly as annoyed at her own missed opportunities as she did at Paul's actual betrayal. She remembered Martin from work; tall, buff Martin. The office party – now how was that for a cliché? – when it would have been so easy to succumb to the alcohol, his flattery, his attention, and her own desires. Yet she'd resisted, because she was married, because of *Paul*. One kiss; that was all they'd shared; that and the feeling of his impressive erection pressing against her midriff. The temptation was there, raging inside her, the desire to abandon caution and go with the flow, to reach down and caress that bulge, to cling to him and demand that he took her, that he satisfied her, but instead she'd broken the clinch, stepped away and told him that she couldn't; that she was married and this must never happen again. In defiance of her own racing heart and mounting lust, she stayed loyal.

Not that her abstinence had prevented her from feeling guilty as hell for months afterwards, causing her to work her socks off to be the best wife she could possibly be, desperate that Paul should never suspect her of that one stolen kiss. A *kiss*? And there was her precious husband banging Mandy Gibson's brains out with enough vigour to break the bloody bed!

The fact that she'd fought so hard to stay faithful while he'd rolled over and screwed the first slut who batted her false eyelashes was something she would never *ever* forgive him for.

She slipped a mint into her mouth and instantly wished she hadn't. Whatever a mint was, it was no substitute for a cigarette. The headache that had plagued her since first waking that morning threatened to get worse; a persistent throb of pain somewhere behind the eyes. She tried to ignore it and sucked hard on the mint.

The house was exactly as she remembered: flat-faced, pebble-dashed, imposing, and *big*. Someone had stripped the ivy away from around the door and never repainted, leaving a brown tattoo of the plant's former presence on the wall, looking as if all the colour and substance had somehow been leeched out of the paint and the brickwork where the creepers touched. That was about the only variance from the picture memory provided.

The door was just the same – solid wood and in need of a coat of varnish – while the cold metal of the key in her hand felt oddly awkward and out of place.

It was still hard to accept her mother's death as real, despite the funeral, the lawyers, the reading of the will and the abundance of black – they were things experienced by someone else, which she had merely observed.

There ought to have been more grief, but in truth Kim had been mourning her mother for nearly nine years. They'd only seen each other once in that time – at Ed's funeral – and spoken no more than twice otherwise, so her current sense of loss was minimal. Would it have been different if Mum had died first? Probably; she had always been a daddy's girl and would almost certainly have stayed close to her father had he been the surviving parent. Her mother on the other hand was a calculating bitch, a manipulator, wrapped up in her own version of how the world should be and determined to make life adapt to her vision rather than the other way around.

Particularly as regards her daughter's husband.

When Kim first suspected her mother of having a hand in Paul's infidelity, she went ballistic. The worst part was that the old shrew refused to either confirm or deny any involvement, insisting that her daughter shouldn't even think to make such an accusation.

The problem was that it would have been *so* like Mother to feign illness that weekend, knowing that Kim would come across and stay to look after her, while making sure that Mandy knew Paul was alone and suggesting she should pop in to check on how he was coping. That was Mandy's subsequent claim, and the more Kim mulled it over the more she tended to believe the slut.

Mum had disapproved of Paul from the start; not her choice of son-in-law at all.

Kim never did find out who her mother had lined up as replacement; by then, they weren't talking to each other.

The key slid into the ubiquitous Yale lock and Kim found herself hesitating. For some reason, she felt more trepidation about this moment than she had about any of it to date. Taking a deep breath, she turned the key and pushed. Brief resistance from the accumulated junk mail, which fanned out to form an irregular mat as she forced the door inward, then she was stepping inside.

Perhaps in retrospect she shouldn't have been surprised by what then happened. After all, she was receptive from the moment the door opened. As Kim stood there on the threshold of that old house and of her childhood, it was with a sense of expectation, as if she were simply waiting for the memories to wash over her, to swamp her, to carry her along on a wave of nostalgia all the way back to the girl she'd once been – her and Ed running along this hallway, laughing. Fun; that was another member of the family she's become estranged from in recent years. When exactly had she forgotten how to have fun?

Yet none of that happened, not immediately. At first the house felt lifeless, as if anything connected to her had seeped away long ago. She struggled to feel something, to connect with this place that had been her home for so many years, and failed. Then came the music. Not distinctly, not pervasively, but distant and half-heard, as if someone had left the radio on in another room. The piano. She strained to hear, recognising the song immediately. A dam broke inside her and all the memories came flooding back: that song... *her* song. No words, it didn't need lyrics; the rhythmic, melodic flow of notes spoke more poignantly than any verse man could ever articulate.

She sobbed, and was surprised to find tears welling up from the recesses of her eyes. *How could she have forgotten her song?*

Kim always assumed the haunting, rippling theme was something she had heard, perhaps on the radio; a snatch of tune that had connected to some element of her young mind and lodged there, but in all the years that intervened she had never managed to track it down, never succeeded in identifying that simple yet so effective melody. Never heard it *anywhere* except in her own head.

Mind you, that in itself amounted to hearing the song more frequently than any other piece of music. This tune, which she'd come to think of as simply *The Piano Song* for want of anything more definite, had provided the soundtrack to her childhood.

It was there when she played with her toys, when she read her books, when she was out somewhere with family or friends. As Barbie changed clothes for the third time in almost as many minutes, or sat wondering why Ken didn't take more notice of her, she'd be humming the tune in her head. When Kim's Pippa Dolls sat in their cardboard house on furniture made from matchboxes, yoghurt pots, sticky-back plastic and pipe cleaners – all based on designs taught her during recent episodes of *Blue Peter* – it was *her* tune that issued from the record player. As Mary Lennox nurtured *The Secret Garden*, she did so with *The Piano Song* playing in the background, and it was against this haunting melody that she first heard Colin Craven's weeping. When Lucy first tumbled out of the wardrobe and found herself in the magical realm of Narnia, there was only one tune that could possibly have accompanied her.

And as the adolescent Kim walked along a forest path, disdaining Ed's jibes and his yells for her to hurry up, *The Piano Song* added texture to the dappled sunlight, the sighing of the leaves in the gusting breeze, the distant bleating of sheep from somewhere beyond the trees, the sporadic birdsong, and the faint scent of wood smoke carried on the wind. The scene would have been beautiful without the music, but was complete only with it.

The adult Kim walked down a dark, carpeted hallway and imagined it was leaf mould and earth beneath her shoes; but she didn't have to dredge up memories of *The Piano Song*; it was there in her head, just as clear and beautiful as ever.

She wondered whether Mother had kept the piano. A grand – not a Steinway perhaps, but neither was it an electronic keyboard made of moulded plastic with pre-programmed rhythms and dozens of different voices. A *real* piano; a gracefully curved wonder in polished rosewood, with the words 'John Broadwood and Sons, London' inscribed in flowing script above the ivory keys. She didn't care that it was valuable, didn't care that it was rare. It was hers, and that was far more important.

The first door, on her left as she drew level with the stairs, led to the dining room. Kim's hand hovered over the handle for a moment, as she worried what memories might be pent-up inside waiting to pounce, but then she grasped and turned. The room smelt of stale polish and mustiness. How many times had it seen use in the past nine years? A dozen, perhaps? In truth she doubted if it was even that often. When left to her own devices her mum invariably ate meals in the lounge, in front of the TV, with a cushioned tray balanced precariously on her lap. On the rare occasions she entertained friends the kitchen table earned its keep. But the dining room? That was reserved only for 'special occasions'. The room's purpose had become eroded and diminished with the passage of time and changing lifestyles, until it was finally reduced to being what, a status symbol? A faded memory of the distant days when everyone had been expected to gather around it for the ritual of 'the family meal'?

Kim shivered and shut the door. She never had been especially keen on the dining room or the furniture trapped within.

But the song was still there.

The hall grew dimmer as she walked further into the house. Had it always been this dark in here? Memory suggested otherwise. And the song swelled around her, lightening her feet and easing the headache.

The piano had been bought for her. Not *entirely* for her (after all, what better status symbol could there be than having a grand piano in the house?), but primarily so. Ed had never been bothered about playing the piano. Kim wanted to learn, was *desperate* to learn; so that she could play her tune: *The Piano Song*.

She walked straight past the lounge, making her way to the far end of the hallway and the door that stood straight ahead of her. Had the song ever sounded so loud? Doubtful. It seemed that, after being neglected for so many years, the tune was determined that she should *never* forget it again. The door was almost upon her.

As a child, Kim had suffered from a low attention span – something which continued to plague her throughout her life, though it proved to be less of an issue as she grew older. Learning the piano took time; it required dedication and patience – qualities that Kim lacked in abundance. She gave up, exasperated by her inability to master the instrument overnight and annoyed with herself for not persisting. Kim knew that only her yearning to play that one song had kept her going for as long as she had, until long after it became obvious that she would never reach the standard necessary to actually master the stupid instrument. This realisation drove her to long sessions of sitting by herself at the piano, playing notes in ones and twos and threes, trying to find the proper sequence, to match the sounds her fumbling fingers created to the lilting beauty that tripped through her head. Once or twice she even thought she had something, but in the end these solo sessions too led only to frustration.

No one else in the house seemed bothered with playing the piano, but, as far as Kim knew, it was still here.

She heard the tune so clearly now; surely it wasn't just in her head. Kim rarely felt the need for anyone, but right then she wished there was someone beside her who could say, "Yes, I can hear it too." But there was only her.

It sounded for all the world as if somebody were actually *playing* it; her tune. Right here and right now – playing with an effortless surety that she could only envy, yet using her piano to do so. For the music was coming from just beyond this door, she was sure of it. Kim took a deep breath and reached for the handle. At the same instant she was struck by a fresh spasm of pain in her head. What the hell was going on? She'd never been one for headaches.

Then, the oddest thing; the door handle seemed to shift, to jump, almost as if trying to avoid her, to escape her touch. The illusion passed in an instant and her fingers fastened around the handle. For a moment she simply gripped the cold metal, squeezing it firmly, as if making sure it was real, that it was solid and not inclined to turn insubstantial and slip away from her grasp.

Still the music drew her on.

Kim turned the handle and pushed the door open.

Light flooded the hallway, causing her to squint. Suddenly she realised why the place had seemed so dark earlier – because of this door. Had she ever seen it closed before? Not that she could recall, except perhaps in the winter, at night, when it might be shut to keep the heat in. Otherwise, the door had always stood open, allowing light into this back-end of the house. Amazing what a difference such a simple thing could make.

The music never faltered.

She stepped into the room, dazzled by the light and the sound. There was her piano, looking exactly as she remembered... and there was a young girl, not yet a teen, sitting at the piano and playing. Playing *her* song.

But of course – what else would she be playing? After all, the young girl was *her*, as she'd been when she was, what, twelve? No, eleven – she remembered that dress, how much she'd hated the dark patterning of bright flowers set against a black background. Funny, it struck her as perfectly OK now – pretty in a prim and proper sort of way – but to her eleven-year old self it had been the ultimate humiliation to have to wear such a sombre, dreary thing, for all that her mother insisted it was 'smart and lovely'. This was the dress she was required to wear when her parents had 'guests' – smiling elderly faces to whom she and Ed were to be presented. Lord, how she loathed them – Mum and guests the same. Not Dad, of course, who seemed oblivious to how awful this all was for her. She was certain that he would have put a stop to such performances if only he'd realised. Yet never certain enough to actually test the theory by asking him to.

Kim watched in awe as the fingers of her girlhood self danced across the keyboard, playing her song as she had always dreamed of doing, as she had always yearned to do. She felt a great upwelling of joy as she realised that she *could* play this, that she had always been able to, that the music came from inside of her, was a part of her.

She blinked away tears, and knew this to be the happiest, proudest moment of her life.

The girl-that-was-her looked up, smiling, and invited Kim to join her with a shallow nod and a movement of the eyes. The woman sat on the stool beside this apparition from her past, and, after watching for a few careful moments, felt confident enough to join in. Her playing was effortless, unhesitating, the music seeming to flow from her, coursing throughout body and soul to direct her unpractised fingers. She closed her eyes, the tears running freely now, soft and warmly ticklish where they trailed down her cheeks. Somewhere along the way the girl had left or disappeared, leaving her to play the song, *her* song, alone. And it was beautiful.

Without warning the headache returned, but more, much more. She gasped, blinded by agony. Her fingers faltered, the song died...

As did she.

A month after her mother passed away, Kimberley Jeanette Hobson died of a brain aneurism. Discovered in the music room of her old family home, the broad smile on her features was put down to the effect of rigor mortis acting on the muscles of the face.

Her funeral was a quiet affair, with less than a dozen souls in attendance — her ex-husband unable to be there due to work commitments. Among those few who were present was an old school friend of the deceased: one Mandy Gibson.

Mandy had no real idea why she had come, except that she'd always regretted the loss of Kim's friendship and felt compelled to attend, perhaps to say goodbye, and perhaps to say 'sorry' with a sincerity she'd never quite managed while Kim was alive.

The sparseness of mourners saddened her; Kim deserved better.

At the funeral, as the coffin disappeared towards its fiery end, a rather lovely piece of music played over the sound system: a simple piano tune, rhythmic, haunting and melancholic, yet beautiful. It seemed entirely appropriate somehow, both for the occasion and for Kim. Mandy had never heard the tune before but instantly found herself humming it quietly as she walked out. She determined to ask someone what it was.

Of course, she never did, though the tune stayed with her.

She decided to think of it simply as *The Piano Song*.

WALLACE

Danielle Collard

Even in the beginning, when it was bare and the wooden floors were without the warm carpeting I later installed, I loved my first home. I had saved for years, though I still needed help from my parents to make the deposit, which made the whole event somewhat bitter-sweet, but I was fast becoming independent and was optimistic. I was twenty-six when I moved in, fresh from university and newly hired at a local hotel restaurant as an assistant manager.

The house was stylish and spacious, with a regal red hallway, from which dark, mahogany stairs curved up to the first floor. The open-plan living-room was decorated in pale colours and had rugs of soft cream. An archway led to the kitchen. Outside, the garden consisted of a tidy lawn, a paved path and flowerbeds; a wooden gate in the fence led straight into the woods so that they felt like an extension of my property.

After moving in, university was quickly forgotten and my only friend at work was my rather camp boss, Howard, who was twenty-five years older than me and whose only conversation beyond work was of his obsession with Kate Bush. Having begun work at management level, there was a distance between myself and the other employees. My loneliness was partly self-induced. I had broken up with my girlfriend at university. We'd been together for two years and had a strong relationship. But it was only after months of no other company that I regretted breaking it off, and I realised it was not so much that I missed her, but the companionship. I resolved this problem with the acquisition of a dog. I named him Barkley.

Several years later I was still working in the restaurant and earning several thousand more a year than before. The only other change in my circumstances was that I was seeing Christine, a sharp-minded blonde, who I happened to meet through my job.

One cold mid-February morning, after a night of heavy snow, I was walking Barkley in the woods behind the house. It was well after sunrise but even so, under the canopy of the snow-covered trees, it was perpetually twilight.

We had not gone far when Barkley—a well-trained bull-terrier—caught a scent and left the path. I called him, not too concerned, knowing we were far from the road. After a few minutes, he hadn't returned. Eventually I found him behind a row of bushes. He was fussing over what I thought initially was a strangely–shaped, grey rock. Drawing closer, I realised it was breathing.

When I saw the steam of its breath, I leapt backwards and collided with a tree. Then, carefully, I crept back to where it lay, and caught sight of its face. When I looked closely, I saw that it was remarkably human, and but for the skin and lack of any hair—and its primitive facial features—it could have been mistaken for a man. It lay naked on its side in an awkward position.

I stared for a long time—Barkley continuing to sniff the creature, who remained motionless. I wanted very much to run from the scene and forget ever seeing this thing. I faced the unknown, which gave strength to an instinctive urge in me, repugnant though it was, to stamp on the creature's skull.

But I didn't. My conscience was torn. Barkley and I were involved. We had been unfortunate enough to stumble upon this thing. Now, if I left, I felt I would kill it as surely as if I had trampled on it. I didn't know how long it had been here, but in this cold it would surely freeze in a few hours. Reassured by Barkley's lack of fear, I took off my jacket and wrapped the creature in it. Then, with some difficulty, I carried it back through the woods. Even in the cold, I noticed that it sweated far more than any human.

Back home, I laid it on the floor in front of the fire. Its sweat had soaked into my jacket while I'd carried it. It had an unpleasant odour, somewhere between petrol and pine needles.

Cringing, and deciding I would throw the jacket out afterwards, I fetched him—I decided it was a *he*—a blanket and waited while he warmed up by the fire. At least this would protect my furniture from his dreadful sweat.

When he stirred, the creature began to look about himself. He sat up, facing the fire, cross-legged. I worried that I had made an awful mistake. Barkley however, had hardly left the creature's side since we found him, and now nuzzled up to him closely. I decided to put my faith in his instincts once again, and in the possibility that this bizarre creature had within him some innate goodness that would keep us safe while he shared our home.

During the first few days of his stay, I learned a great deal about our guest while he continued to recover. First and most importantly, he appeared to be no danger to anyone around him. He had a powerful sense of empathy, and I believed he could feel the pain of others as much as his own. Secondly, he was incredibly intelligent, seeming to understand a good deal of his situation. He knew—without being told—not to go outside, or stand at the windows of the house, and that Barkley and I were his friends.

I learned a lot through his relationship with Barkley. On the second night, I had to work, and risked leaving the creature alone, curtains drawn and doors locked. He must have seen me securing the house, and when I returned, I discovered he'd not only unlocked the back door to let Barkley outside, but had also turned up the heating and poured himself a jug full of water. Later, I found him sitting comfortably at my dinner table, Barkley on his lap, sipping regularly from the jug in front of him.

That evening revealed more than just the creature's intelligence. It taught me one of the fundamental differences between his needs and a human's: I concluded that his over-active sweat glands meant he needed a constant source of fluid. He was cold at room temperature. Clearly, his sweat served a purpose beyond cooling his body. To my distaste, I decided this was probably to mark his territory.

On the morning of the third day, I replaced his blanket with a set of my old clothes, a tattered pair of jeans and a parka I no longer wore. I felt he needed a name too. I chose 'Wallace': his bald head reminded me of a television character of that name.

Already, my living-room was unrecognisable. Whenever I stepped inside, the tremendous power of his smell struck me. It

163

was always obvious what he'd been doing because everything he touched became moist: the taps, the door handles, the banister, the controls to the heating. After cleaning the room, I went upstairs to lie down and discovered him sitting on the bed.

"What the hell do you think you're doing coming in here?" In my rage, I hit him over the head. He fell to the floor with a moan, and I regretted what I'd done immediately. Hands on his head, he crouched in front of me. "I'm sorry," I said quickly. "Just, don't come into my room."

After he'd gone, I changed the sheets, and went to sleep.

That next morning, I tried to wash Wallace in the shower. He seemed to enjoy the water, but at first touch of soap he screamed and knocked it from my hand. I retrieved the soap, reprimanding him. "Wallace," I said. "You will be cleaned! Your smell is ghastly!" But when I returned, and made to repeat my action, he cowered away from me and I saw on his arm, where the soap had touched him, a raw, pink burn. I could only think of the smell, and the sweat, running like damp on my walls, and I persevered. I applied the soap again and Wallace screamed. It was a terrible, a rough, screeching sound—inhuman—like a wild animal in pain. Again, the skin came up pink and burned. I put the soap away, it was no use.

Wallace would not be cleaned, and my house would suffer for it. I don't deny I felt a good deal of resentment towards him either. Like a leech, he was sucking on my resources and my energy. I didn't know how much longer I could keep him here. That night at work, I wondered what I could do that might ease the situation, perhaps give him some independence, so that he might eventually leave?

I resolved to teach him English.

I stole a whiteboard from Howard's office and began working on the alphabet. Pointing at the letters, I made Wallace repeat the sounds, which he did without too much difficulty. But there was still a lot of work involved. I could only instruct him in the afternoon before my shifts at the restaurant, but Wallace made it easier by studying while I was away. I put stickers on objects around the house, and he learned the names of these objects and pronounced them for me when I returned. I brought children's books from the local library and he started learning to read. After I introduced him to television, with help from the subtitles, he would learn new words of his own accord.

After only a fortnight, Wallace began, on a rudimentary level, to communicate his thoughts and needs.

He had a peculiar voice, not gruff as I had expected, but instead somewhat poetic and lilting, with a certain intonation that inspired in me a kind of fear. To begin with, when he called my name, the hairs on my neck would lift and I would freeze in shock, but as it was with everything since finding him, I got used to it.

"Andy," he would say.

"What is it?"

"Hungry."

"Would you like something to eat?"

"Sandwich. Please."

"OK, Wallace."

"Thank you."

Though he spoke only single words at this time, his manners were always civilised. He would look at me with his grey, heavy eyes and I would see only a thoughtless expression. And yet he showed signs of tribal instincts, like the way he would systematically share his food with Barkley, who seemed to grow more attached to him every day. The speed at which his language developed was most remarkable. In that fortnight, his English became as good as my school-learnt French.

One night, I came home to find Wallace very disturbed, shaking as he had done when I found him in the woods. He was gesticulating at the television screen.

"Wallace, what is it now?"

"Andy. I. Don't. Like."

"Don't like what?"

"Television."

"What did you see?"

"Men. Killing. Shouting."

I turned to the screen to see what he'd been watching. It was an old movie, *Spartacus*; I almost laughed.

"For God's sake! Wallace, you don't need to be scared of that. It's just a film. It's pretend. It's not real."

"Pretend? You promise?"

"I promise, Wallace. Relax."

"Why. Do. They. Do. That?"

"It's supposed to be entertaining."

"Entahtanning?"

"Fun!"

He calmed down a little, and eventually seemed to forget about the whole thing.

On the Saturday of that week, I had the evening off and had been hoping to work on Wallace some more. My house reeked, and its former grandeur was reduced to squalor. But Christine had been similarly neglected the past few weeks, and had called me the day before, clearly believing I had lost interest in her.

"Why haven't you called me?"

"I've been busy ... at the restaurant."

"Bullshit."

"No, really ..."

"Andrew, be a decent guy. If you want to end it, just say so."

"Look, Christine. I like you, really, I mean it."

"I don't believe you, but fine, if you really mean it ..." She let the sentence hang.

"I do. Why don't we have dinner tomorrow, at the restaurant?"

"I'm sick of that place. Why won't you cook for me? You're always going on about how good you are at it."

"I'd much rather ..."

"No, Andy, you owe me this."

"Okay, okay ..." I sighed. "Come on over tomorrow. I'll cook you dinner."

"You mean it? You won't cancel?"

"Wait and see. We'll have a ball."

The moment she hung up the phone, I looked at Wallace and realised I had blundered into a disaster. There was no way I could cancel though; Christine had made that clear enough. I would just have to hope I could hide him—and his mess—for the evening.

After ruminating for a long while, I emptied out the cupboard under the stairs and put in his blanket, a bucket of water, as well as a fan heater to hold him for a few hours.

This following evening, while I cooked dinner, I tried to explain to Wallace what was about to happen, and emphasise the importance that he stay in the cupboard.

"If you balls this up for me," I told him, "I swear to God, I will throw you out on the street as though I'd never seen your face."

He looked at me fearfully, but at that moment I was beyond sympathy.

Before I put him in the cupboard, I gave him his own plate of carbonara. Even then he didn't forget to put some in Barkley's bowl, which was just outside the cupboard door. Minutes later, the bell rang.

"Christine!"

"Hi Andy, it's good to see you again, finally."

"You too, come in."

She'd hardly crossed the threshold when she flinched. "What's that smell?"

"What smell?"

"It smells like petrol in here."

"Oh, I'm sorry ... I'd hoped you wouldn't be able to tell. It must be worse than I thought."

"It's really strong!"

"Yeah, I was carrying a canister through the house earlier and I dropped it and ... I'm so sorry. You'll get used to it in a little while and it won't bother you."

There was a heavy silence.

Eventually she smiled, though I could tell it was insincere. "It's fine, don't worry. It happens ... I guess."

I led her through the hall, but after a few seconds she called out again.

"Oh, Andy!"

"What is it?" I cried.

She gestured at Barkley's bowl. "You gave Barkley some of our dinner."

"Oh, yeah, yeah I did."

"You're so sweet. I didn't think you were the sort."

We sat in the living-room. I poured us drinks and we talked. Barkley took only a second to greet Christine before seating himself next to the stairs. After a few minutes Christine couldn't help but notice.

"Is he all right?"

"Sure he is," I said.

"What's he doing?"

"That's just a spot he's taken up. You know how dogs are, they all have their spots."

Christine didn't seem entirely convinced. I wouldn't have been myself, it was a rather unnatural position to choose as a 'spot'. But she let it go.

The first half hour went as well as could be expected. She did comment on the warmth of the house, so I turned down the heat. Of course, given the circumstances, I found it impossible to absorb myself in any romantic atmosphere. From the moment she had stepped through the door I'd been on edge. It didn't help my nerves to see, at intervals, grey fingers sliding through the slats of the cupboard door, reaching for Barkley. Fortunately, Christine didn't notice them.

We finished the carbonara, and I was starting to feel Christine had forgiven me for the past few weeks. I let her do most of the talking, asking her to tell me more about herself, things she hadn't told me on our earlier dates. Stealing regular glances towards the stairs, I missed a great deal of what she said. She was telling me something about her troubles in high school when I saw the cupboard door open and a bald, grey forehead emerged.

Wallace seemed entranced. He stared at Christine, then left the cupboard and leaned around the wall to watch us eat.

Desperately, I waited for Christine to turn away from me, so that I could gesture to him, do anything to get him back in the cupboard. I was losing my cool, but even so I tried to maintain the conversation and sip my wine.

We finished the meal and Wallace was still there, in the periphery of my vision, when Christine got to her feet.

I jumped up too. "Where are you going?"

"To the bathroom, if that's all right?"

There was nothing else to say except, "Err ... okay. Fine, fine."

Christine frowned at me, then turned and walked towards the stairs.

I closed my eyes.

Christine screamed.

Wallace screamed too, that same rough, screeching sound I'd heard in the shower.

Christine ran back into the room and flattened herself against the wall.

"What in God's name is that?"

"Okay, calm down. Just calm down. There's no reason to be scared."

"No reason!" she cried maniacally. "No bloody reason! What is it?"

As she asked this, Wallace peered around the corner. He was visibly distressed. His usually heavy-lidded eyes were wide, and he was shaking as he often did when scared. He even seemed to have turned a paler shade of grey.

"Andy," he said quietly.

"Yes Wallace?"

"She is scared. I scared her."

"Yes Wallace, don't worry. Let me talk to her. Wait out there for me, OK?"

"OK."

Wallace disappeared again, and I implored Christine to take a seat next to me on the sofa. She sat, though she wouldn't turn her back to the hall.

"It can speak," she said.

"His name's Wallace."

"And what is *Wallace?*"

"I don't know."

"Where is *Wallace* from?"

"I don't know. I don't think he knows, doesn't remember."

"Why is *Wallace* in your house?"

"I found him, he was freezing to death. I didn't know what else to do."

"Do anything! Kick him out, call the police. Don't invite him into your fucking home!"

"What on earth do you think the police will do with him? I can't hand him over. He wouldn't be safe."

"Are you?" she asked.

"He's been here for weeks. He hasn't touched us."

Christine stared at the hall where Wallace waited.

"So he's living with you," she said. "You're just keeping him here."

"Yes."

It took a good while before Wallace and Christine could be reintroduced. When Wallace saw her again, he became incredibly shy, and was extremely apologetic. Christine—though perhaps still a little disgusted by him—seemed touched by his sensibility and began to make very polite, very tentative conversation.

"Barkley seems to like you," she observed.

"He. Is. A. Good. Dog."

"Do you like dogs?"

"I don't know."

"Barkley's the only one he knows," I said. "I think you're the first woman he's ever seen."

"You. Look. Nice," Wallace told her.

Christine blushed. "Thank you, Wallace. That's nice of you to say."

She then turned to me and intimated that she wanted to leave. I asked Wallace to stay with Barkley in the living-room while I showed Christine to the door. She agreed not to tell anyone else about him, and even considered coming back in a few days to help with him. In truth, I was relieved Wallace was no longer my secret.

Sundays at the restaurant were always busy. As part of the management, I usually worked throughout the day. That Sunday I got home near midnight. I was exhausted and planned to check on Wallace and Barkley, take a shower and go straight to bed. Instead, the moment I opened the door, I was accosted by Wallace.

"You're liar!"

"What?"

"You're liar! You said it was pretend."

"Said what was pretend?"

"Television!"

"It is!"

"You're liar!"

He grabbed my arm with his damp hand and dragged me into the living-room, pointing at the screen. On it was black and white footage of WWII tanks. Wallace had clearly discovered the history channels.

It seemed he cried in similar proportions to his sweating, far more profusely than any human. Again, he was pale and shaking. Altogether he was deeply unsettled.

"Wallace please, you're making yourself ill. Sit down."

I handed him his blanket and he sat down on the sofa. Quickly, I turned the TV off and fetched him some water.

"They said sixty million people died. How many is that?"

It took me a moment to answer. How, after all, could I help him comprehend how great a sum sixty million was?

"It's a lot. It was a terrible war, but it was a long time ago."

"It's bad. Andy, why did it happen?"

I shrugged. "There are bad people in the world. Sometimes we don't realise they're bad until it's too late. That war was caused by bad people with too much power."

"Why are they bad? Why don't they stop when people are hurt?"

He was calming down, but he seemed different to any time I'd seen him before. I thought carefully before answering.

"I think people only ever hurt one another because they ignore that hurt. They think about other things, about themselves, or power, or change; they justify it."

Wallace sat quietly, clearly thinking. I had nothing more to say, and I was too tired for any more drama. I left him on the sofa and went to bed.

Monday at lunch, I called Christine and told her what had happened. We had a long conversation about what we might do with him, but came to no conclusions. We both knew that he couldn't stay much longer in my home. My parents, a neighbour, a passer-by, someone would eventually find him and panic, just as Christine had. One of them would inevitably talk. God only knew what would happen to Wallace if that happened.

She asked me how I was. I was exhausted, and my work was suffering. Howard had spoken to me over the weekend, telling me that whatever was happening in my private life I had better sort it out quickly.

I was aware of all of these problems, but had no way of solving them. The truth was, I was ready to give up on Wallace; I wanted my old life back, and my home.

Christine came over that night to help. When I arrived, she and Barkley were with Wallace in the living-room and once again he looked dreadfully ill.

"What is it this time?" I said.

"He saw something on the news," Christine informed me.

"What was it?"

"Syria, I think."

"You said it happened long ago!" Wallace cried.

"It's a different war. Wallace, please stop this, it's nothing to do with us."

"Andy. You're lying!" His voice had lost its poetry. It had become a desperate groaning.

"I'm not lying, Wallace!"

His only reply was to give me a look that somehow—though I felt myself to be innocent—filled me with shame for my entire race. His grey face, pale, hairless, something between a baby's and an old man's, clearly showed his suffering, and there was nothing I could do.

"How can you live here, like this, when this is happening?"

"I don't know, Wallace," Christine answered for me. "We just do. What else can we do?"

"Make it stop."

"How, Wallace? If there was a way, we would do it, I swear."

Once again, he seemed to have run out of words. Christine and I couldn't console him, so we left him with Barkley in the living-room and spent an evening alone.

This routine continued throughout the week, and Wallace's condition grew steadily worse. It seemed the things he saw on TV were ruining his health. I tried more than once to unplug it, but he stopped me every time.

"I want to know," he said. "I don't want to be lied to."

He grew skinnier, and became so pale he was almost translucent. There was nothing I could do except watch in horror as he faded away before me, it seemed merely through conflicts and struggles on other continents or in other times. Barkley too could sense what was happening, but could do nothing more for Wallace than lie with him in my living-room that reeked of petrol.

On Sunday evening, I came home late from work, and Wallace was dead on the sofa. He'd been watching a documentary on the plague. He was wrapped in the blanket I had given him.

Monday morning, Christine and I buried him in the woods, still wrapped in the blanket, at the spot where Barkley found him.

Things were different afterwards. Barkley was distraught. No matter how much time I spent with him, he'd lost all of the energy he had before, as if he'd aged a decade.

The house took a long time to recover, though I scrubbed the living-room repeatedly. After a few months, I decided I could no longer stay there and—after an uncomfortable talk with Christine—moved to another town. On occasion, I would take Barkley back to the woods and he would return to the place where Wallace was buried. He would sit above the grave, and I would watch, and wonder how it was the creature felt pain so deep for those he never even knew.

THE VIGIL

J.E. Bryant

Mr Thomas' heavy-booted gait telegraphed his presence to all.
Here I come and here I am, each plodding step seemed to say. Not in
an overtly bombastic way, nor in the thuggish, cocksure tread of
what Mr Thomas would still term a 'bovver boy'. Rather, each
placed foot came with a sense of presence and purpose that
seemed fitting for a man of his size as he moved through the
capital on his way to work. It was a solid step, a dependable pace
driven by the sounds of Beethoven's *Emperor* that played out
through the floppy foam earpieces of his unfashionable
headphones.

His evening route, as for the past ten years, took him down
and through one of the idiosyncratic under-ways and across an
ancient stone bridge that still carried a pedestrian route over one
of the city's canal ways. He always paused momentarily at the
brow of this listed structure and marvelled at its survival,
surrounded as it was by a veritable forest of multi-tiered steel and
concrete. The stonework had obviously been treated, giving it a
varnished sheen beneath his heavy hands. Every evening he
promised himself that he'd look up the bridge's history – find out
why this one had been saved, or made in such a way, when further
up and down the waterway Victorian iron crossings dominated –
but something always came up to distract him. Maybe the fixture
listings for upcoming football matches, or some duty at his local
church managed to push the bridge out of mind on a daily basis.
When he was awake during daylight hours he had precious little
time to organise himself, such was the curse of working the
nightshift. As such, idle curiosity always dropped down his
personal rank of priority.

Mr Thomas strode on, John Tavener's *Protecting Veil* now
celebrating in his ears, doing its best to sustain a useful sense of
uplifting purpose to countermand the general despondency he had

once felt whenever walking to work.

Before he'd become a churchgoer, he'd found himself brooding on the negatives of the route, creating judgmental stories around the people and things he encountered. Drunkards and druggies staggering about in gutters filled with human waste. Malevolent youth in cowls, smelling of heady narcotics and spray paint. Each scene motivated a gradual pitch into bitterness, resentment, and a return to what Mr Thomas called 'coming over all peculiar'. His previous doctor had given a fancy label to what he had termed a 'condition', but Mr Thomas had long since forgotten its name.

In fact it was Father McLoughlin who had eventually helped him to navigate the increasing episodes of oddity, and Mr Thomas did his best to take his advice. *Just focus on the positives each and every day*, the priest had repeatedly suggested, *rather than feeling overwhelmed by troubling news and a world view dominated by the darker side of life.*

Mr Thomas was uncertain whether he actually believed in God, or heaven, but he owed the Father a debt of gratitude, and thus did his best to help out at the church wherever he could.

His commute had moved him from the sparsely-populated side streets to the traffic-heavy highway that led down to the hotel where he worked. Even though the city's rush hour had passed and it was early in the week, there were still a multitude of cars cruising in either direction. Their head and tail lights added to the overall brightness of the street lamps, creating a fractured reflection of Mr Thomas in the darkened shop windows. He glanced at himself, saw his shaved head, wrinkled eyes and compact features pulse in the fluctuating illumination, and turned his face away. Clean-shaven, despite his limited interaction with the public and yet, in his personal opinion, not much to look at. A typical 'don't mess with me' look for a typical night watchman.

The hotel itself had a tall, tinted glass facade that reached for ten floors – there were fourteen in total, counting basement parking levels and services. Not especially sizable in the world of hotels, but large enough to ensure a good forty minute tour of duty for Mr Thomas at a sluggish 4am in the morning pace. He ignored the company sign, the only noticeable outcropping on the building's sheer front, and walked around to the car park access ramp and staff entrance. One lumpy thumb instinctively followed the muscle memory of the pass code and the door's electronic lock clunked and allowed him access.

Back here, in the service corridors, it was all scuffed paint and concrete floors, the click of well-polished staff shoes announcing a person's presence well before you turned any of the multiple corridors. It was a warren of cluttered offices, service lifts and sliding doors. At least it was warm and dry and came with the added benefit of two free meals every shift.

Mr Thomas manoeuvred his bulk down the passageway towards the kitchens, scanning as he went for any boxes blocking fire exits, any day staff carelessness that he and the night porter would have to rectify and report upon.

The kitchen was typically deserted and spotlessly clean, the smell of the day's cooking masked by a chorus of cleaning products - citrus detergent vying for sensory dominance over bleach and the familiar aroma of dishwashers still diligently at work.

Dom, the head chef, was ensconced in a converted storage cupboard, his back to a sliding door that perpetually stood open, shoulders hunched as he clicked through a series of order sheets on a smudged computer monitor.

"Evenin', Dom." Mr Thomas's voice was deep, despite the nasal twang of his regional register.

The chef twisted his neck and glanced back over the shoulder of his white tunic. "Evenin', mate. Dinner's where it always is and fridges are stocked for Kev. But tell 'im a couple of things for me, will ya? One, the *petits fours* are not for his consumption – I've done a stock check – and two, he needs to *not* leave a stack of washing for the morning kitchen porter. Kev's got naff all to do the majority of the night, the least he can do is stick what he uses for room service in one of the washers."

"Right you are. And cheers, as ever, for dinner."

Dom twisted a bit further in his seat, a tired eye and ruddy jowl now visible to Mr Thomas. "Tha's alright mate. Least we can do. Don't know how you can stick it here all night."

"Don't know how you can stick the heat of the kitchen," said Mr Thomas.

"Yeah, well, each to their own." And with that the chef went back to clicking on a dull-looking web page, embellished only by a flurry of fruit and veg that clustered across the top of the screen.

Mr Thomas nodded to himself and walked further into the kitchen. Popping the heavy handle on a stainless steel refrigerator, he pulled a hermetically-sealed meal from one of the crowded shelves and wandered over to nearest microwave. Locating some napkin-wrapped cutlery, he extracted a gleaming fork and pierced the covering of the plate in several places. As he did so he peered through the plastic to see if he could identify today's meat. Fish maybe? Some kind of filo pastry ensemble that, knowing Dom's standards, would taste a hell of a lot better than anything he could personally cook.

The whirring of the microwave should have given Mr Thomas time to consider the next steps in his evening schedule, but so ingrained was his routine that his mind simply hovered in an indecisive state. Thoughts about how the food would taste once he sat down as his duty station were about as detailed as his higher functioning got until he'd properly woken up.

"Cheers, Dom. Always appreciated." Mr Thomas called in at the chef's door the hot plate balance on a requisitioned tray.

"Not a problem, chap," the chef replied, still not turning. "Have a good 'un".

The service lift clanked and rattled its way to the hotel's top floor, its interior spacious but showing the same levels of wear and tear as the rest of the service corridors. The automatic doors trundled open, and Mr Thomas walked down another uncarpeted passageway. He used his elbow to nudge open a door marked 'No Unauthorised Access', the words accompanied by the weird icon of a howling, black-handed man. Mr Thomas wobbled on into the short corridor that led past the camera monitoring suite and on to the rear fire escape. Finally, he negotiated the perpetually-open doorway into the room.

Daniel, the young day watchman, was slumped in the operations chair, his fingers a blur of activity across the surface of some mobile device or games console. He peeked at Mr Thomas as he navigated the doorway with the tray's precious cargo. "Evening." A few definitive raps on his handheld device and then Daniel sat up, giving Mr Thomas his full attention. He'd rinsed through naval training and had got himself his first job in security through a friend of his father's, but he knew how to respect his elders in his own way.

"Evening." Mr Thomas placed his tray on the desk opposite the bank of display screens and then turned to scan them all individually. "Anything to report on, Daniel?"

The younger man bristled at Mr Thomas' use of his full name, but stood up and passed across a clipboard containing a list of events from the afternoon. Mr Thomas noted that the younger man was actually a lot taller than he seemed when slumped in the chair.

"Nothing much, really. Usual loading bay, double parking negotiations with drivers, traffic wardens and the like. Monitoring deliveries, redirecting lost tourists... All patrols clear. That's about it, really. Mr Stocks' handover from the morning shift was equally as exciting."

"And now?" Mr Thomas nodded to indicate the screens in front of them.

"See for yourself. Quiet as the grave. Should be another easy gig for you tonight." Daniel immediately regretted what he'd just said. "I mean, aside from having to work the night shift an' all."

"Nah, don't you worry. Doesn't bother me too much. Always been more of an owl than a lark. Let's get this handover done and you can get off and I can get at me tea."

The transference between security managers was governed by an exchange of keys and bar codes. First Daniel had to sign into the handheld code reader, then pass the whirling laser over the bar code sitting just beneath Mr Thomas's name badge – perched, as it was, on his standard issue black V-neck sweater. Next the reader was passed ceremoniously to Mr Thomas who, in turn, signed in and read the younger man's bar code. Daniel then uncoupled a weighty bunch of keys from his belt and handed them over to Mr Thomas before bidding him a good evening. So adept had they become at the whole, elaborate process that Mr Thomas' meal was still piping hot by the time he sat and surveyed the bank of almost static images. He took his first mouthful and was delighted at the opening tastes. His eager fork returned to the plate and accidentally flicked a stray blob of white sauce onto the station's console. Swiftly retrieving this in a lifting swipe of one of his heavy fingers, he licked the digit clean and checked the office's doorway to ensure that Daniel hadn't lingered to watch him.

Overall the meal was delicious, and Mr Thomas paused after

its consumption to savour the flavours on his tongue and the weight of the food in his belly. He rose up quickly out of the swivel chair and stalked off on his first tour of the building, not so much to check on any security issues, but rather to ensure a visit to the drinks vending machine in reception. The can of fizzy drink was his single expenditure of any given evening, but he still looked forward to the purchase, its caffeine and his opening catch-up with Kevin the night porter.

Reception, however, had spawned a densely packed group of fidgety guests by the time he arrived. He thought back to the empty screens earlier, and puzzled at how he'd missed such a crowd. Perhaps they'd all arrived in the time it had taken him to journey from the top of the building. He rose slightly on his toes and watched Kevin bobbing about behind the long, high desk. The arrivals were obviously causing him some level of consternation, and the swarthy man's brows were knotted in concentration as he did his best to recall under-utilised skills within the hotel's check-in system. Mr Thomas wondered briefly if there was anything he could do to help, then discounted the notion. He swiftly grabbed his can of drink, scanned the reception bar code on the wall, and then retreated into the maintenance corridors. He glanced at the restless backs of the gathered guests, and felt a passing pang of regret at leaving Kevin in the lurch.

Taking a shortcut through a connecting service stairwell not accessible to the public, Mr Thomas emerged into the short passage that led to the gym and spa. Carpet gave way to polished flag stones, papered walls relinquished to frosted glass, as he lumbered his way towards another check point on his nocturnal rounds.

The heady scents of unguents and oils weren't entirely lost on him. He relished this part of the patrol, his senses waking up in this lingering atmosphere of the pampered. But it was more the orderly state the health and welfare team left their workplace in that gave him the greatest satisfaction. Management areas were a mess, cleaning cupboards were utter chaos, as was the parking office. Here though, in the spa and gym, gentle order reigned supreme.

He wound his way between low couches and polished marble tables, noticing the orderly, lined, pastel plastic tubs of aromatic creams. Stationed tastefully on glass shelves, their brand names were a seductive mix of science and self-improvement that baffled more than enticed him. Just what did a 'surface tissue exfoliate and dermatological revitaliser' actually do? he wondered, as he fumbled his way into the brightly-lit exercise room. Here too there was order, but in a more functional embodiment, captured perfectly in the rack of precisely-folded towels and the mechanical union of steel, rubber and leather. Mr Thomas placed one thick hand on his paunch and thought, as he always did, about getting back into shape. Sighing, he pointed the bar code gun at the tiny plaque on the wall and headed back to the lifts.

The monitoring station was just as he had left it, warm from all the clustered machines and practically silent, the muted hum of server fans providing the only ambient noise. He sat back in the swivel chair and began flicking through the numerous monitor feeds to see if there was anything occurring other than the slowly-dispersing crowd in reception.

One camera, set just behind a wide, glass automatic door, looked out into the courtyard at the centre of the building. The scene was unremarkable and flat in the low level evening lights, and Mr Thomas was still able to observe the base of the courtyard's impressive camera array. The pillar was designed to resemble an ornate Victorian lamp post but, at its apex, it contained one remotely-operated camera that could be swivelled around using a stubby, finger-sized joystick on the monitoring panel. He switched feeds and began to rotate the camera's vantage point taking in a vista of meticulously-clipped hedges and curtained windows. Imagining the lens swivelling in the hanging, blackened glass jogged something in Mr Thomas' memory.

There had been a feature on one of his favourite sports radio shows about vandalism and the rise of graffiti as an art form. He'd only been half listening in to this piece of filler content, which was only loosely sports-related due to an apparent rise in street football. The panellists had droned on, and it was only when one of the guests began talking about the work of a young 'guerrilla artist' that Mr Thomas' ears pricked up.

Over the next thirty minutes or so, what he could only describe as 'criminal activity' was presented as art. Graffiti was bad enough, in Mr Thomas's view, and yet the show seemed to be supporting the wanton destruction of corporate CCTV cameras globally. The host, to his credit, questioned whether such activity only heightened the need for more security cameras, to which the art critic responded that the artist didn't see it that way. His 'liberation' of monitored spaces was, he said, more to highlight the fact that society was sleepwalking into a world where everything was being observed, where the civic responsibility of providing light was being subverted into one where it was only captured. Mr Thomas hadn't really got the gist of that last part, but when the critic started to talk of the insincerity of cameras that disguised themselves as street lamps, he'd thought of the hotel's courtyard and promptly turned the radio off. Security wasn't about snooping or prying, it was about making sure an antisocial minority were less inclined to upset decent people.

It had been a while since Mr Thomas had to deal with a properly unpleasant incident. Thankfully, most troublemakers were drunk, or seeking sexual gratification, or both. Some couldn't pay, but there were a few who *wouldn't* pay, or had a chip on their shoulder or were showing off to their friends or partners. Then, in those rare moments, he'd have to gang up with Kevin and buy some time until the police arrived. It didn't faze him half as much as some little toe rag calling himself an artist destroying the very cameras that Mr Thomas believed kept people safe.

He paused in his observations and shook himself as he felt an immediate rush of blood to his head. Perhaps it was the unpleasant memory of this radio show that affected a change in Mr Thomas, or perhaps it was something completely arbitrary, but the unexpected shift from feeling clearheaded to decidedly odd came on as rapidly as it always did.

It started with his hands. A cold clamminess began to seep across his palms accompanied by a tingling itch across the knuckles. There was usually a moment's pause that followed, as Mr Thomas's perceptions skewed from natural and neutral to adrenaline-fuelled – the world suddenly popping into crisp-edged unreality. He'd experienced these episodes fairly frequently throughout his adult life, but he'd never got used to them, or was even remotely prepared for how the strangeness might uniquely manifest itself.

He reached a trembling hand towards his drink and saw something appear on one of the monitors. He blinked, trying to resolve the discrepancy between the sudden, stark relief of the monitor screen itself and the indistinct figure that had just moved through its field of vision somewhere on the seventh floor. The next camera on that level watched the fire escape and he was about to call it up quickly when his own face appeared on the screen.

Mr Thomas balked at the vision. He'd experienced mild visual peculiarities before, which he'd always shaken off, bullying himself to disregard their presence as simply part of his troubled mind, but never anything as tangible as this.

The Mr Thomas in the screen peered right down the throat of the lens into the monitoring suite and then moved off down the corridor, one hand holding the key ring tightly against his hip so it wouldn't rattle, the other held to his chest as if stress or exertion were getting the better of him.

As he witnessed this, the blood already gushing from his heart to his head made its absence felt in Mr Thomas's stomach and bowel. A dreaded, sinking fear descended through him, his pounding heart increasing its beat to a seemingly unsustainable repetition, as a dark shadow flitted across the door to the monitoring suite. Mr Thomas snapped his head around and tried to make peripheral sense of its transition. Was there someone there?

A lifetime of duty forced him to his feet, made him move faster than he had in years. He peered around the door frame into the corridor beyond. A single shadowy foot rose and followed an obscured but presumed body through the fire exit and onto the stairwell. *Must be Kevin*, a shaken Mr Thomas thought. He was the only one who'd have access to this part of the building, but why didn't he say something in passing, and where was he off to at such a pace?

Mr Thomas hit the crash bar on the safety door with way too much force, the sound of his entrance reverberating around the bare concrete shaft beyond. He peeked over the banister rail and spied what might have been a steadying hand clutching the rail a floor or so below.

"Hey! Who are you to be up here this time of night?"

The sound of his own voice brought some level of resolve to the pursuit and Mr Thomas took the stairs as quickly as his unhealthy feet would allow. Two sharp turns doubling back on himself, then a third and a fourth, alongside the sound of another fire exit opening just below him. He seemed to be catching up with the mysterious stranger.

Floor eight was as deserted as the cameras had suggested it would be, making it easy for Mr Thomas to make out the back of the receding figure as it took one of the corridor's four corners. Windowless and devoid of natural light, the route flanked the sides of the central courtyard and ran in a complete square around the building's perimeter. The already-labouring security guard considered heading in the opposite direction to the fleeing figure, in an attempt to meet whoever it was head on, but discounted the idea as he thought of the other emergency exit on the opposite side.

He set off in pursuit once again. Reaching the first turn, he noticed the dark lens of one of the security cameras nestled near the ceiling. He stared intently at the camera and shuddered as he recalled the uncanny moment at the monitoring desk just a few moments earlier. Was he still up there, even now, about to set off after the trespasser? He felt sickness well up inside as he imagined a cascade of other Mr Thomases all witnessing themselves on the screen and then tumbling out of the top of the building like lemmings off a cliff. He turned. *Just concentrate on catching up with whoever this is*, he told himself, *and the rest will figure it itself out*. It had done in the past, so why shouldn't it now? His previous episodes of disquiet and unsubstantiated panic had never reached such a full-blown level of manifestation, but he'd never had to deal with one in the midst of a work situation before. They usually crept in on non-work days, challenging him while he was doing his shopping, or on the way to or from the football ground.

He took the corner at a fast walk, almost a half jog and then, as he suspected, heard the click of the fire exit closing. Bumping through this, he increased his pace, took the following two switchbacks in quick succession and was rewarded with being able to watch the next fire door slowly swing to on its closing arc. He stuffed one of his steel toe-capped trainers into the diminishing gap and pushed the door back open. Then he was through and into an identical and similarly deserted corridor.

The figure turned, glanced back at Mr Thomas from under what appeared to be an ash grey hoodie, and then slowed to a casual walk before turning the next corner, almost as if it were taunting the security guard with its nonchalance.

Mr Thomas grasped the advantage, convinced that by catching up with his quarry he'd resolve the still-encroaching sense of wrongness about the whole situation. He'd be able to interrogate the person, whoever they were and, by doing so, he'd reassert his control over things. Order would be restored. As he moved, though, he was physically shoved from the centre of the corridor over towards the far right wall.

At first, more puzzled than frightened, he reasoned that perhaps the figure had raced around the quadrangle to tackle him from the rear. Looking quickly about, he assured himself that he was still alone. He reached out a hand to his left and encountered a resolute force as solid as a wall, but devoid of any tactile feedback to his fingertips. Exploring the phenomenon with a rising sense of unease, he discovered that it stretched from the floor to as high as he could reach, and continued to expand ahead of him. His eyes, however, relayed a perfectly normal-looking corridor, unchanged in its uniformity.

Mr Thomas was caught between this added layer of strangeness and the fact that he was being delayed by this obstruction. He thought again of the mocking gait of the figure and pressed on. If it was able to navigate this obstacle, then so could he.

Moving forward, Mr Thomas felt the swell of this invisible wall make the passage even narrower, pressing to a point where he was practically rubbing himself down the length of the doors to his right. He reached forward, his arms extended, as if he were feeling his way in pitch darkness, although the corridor remained fully lit. Taking another couple of tentative paces, he encountered a gradual recession of the mysterious barrier. It was as if something large and semicircular bulged out into the hallway. Unimpeded, once again, he continued the pursuit, albeit at a much slower pace with one arm perpetually held out in front of him.

Part of his mind, which was preparing to encounter another invisible obstruction, suddenly jumped to the capricious conclusion that such hidden obstacles could, in fact, manifest themselves in any shape. A spike say, or a knife edge, either serrated or straight. The remaining, rational part of his mind, however, was attempting to assert itself, to try and highlight just how out of control things had become. Its more measured approach was increasingly being swamped in a mire of adrenaline.

Another corner successfully navigated, only to reveal an empty passageway ahead. Mr Thomas cursed to himself and cracked open the fire door of the stairwell to see if he could hear any movement beyond. Nothing. He moved a few metres further, towards the mini foyer in front of the lifts and caught the sound of the hoists whirring in the distance above him. One of the lifts was in use.

He stabbed at the call button with one of his thick fingers and stepped back, straining his ears to define whether the stranger had headed up or down. His own lift scrambled the soundscape somewhat, but he was pretty sure he heard a muffled floor chime come from above. Above... Revelation cut through all his abstract fears with scalpel precision.

"Bollocks."

How could he have been so stupid? Why hadn't he followed procedure? He should have rung down to Kevin, called him up to cover the monitoring station while he headed off to apprehend whoever this interloper was. But no. Instead he'd freaked himself out with imaginings and had left his station, unlocked, open and exposed. The past twenty-four hours of security footage was all up there, sub-categorised in folders for ease of scanning, copying, or removal. Or theft! Mr Thomas pictured the mysterious figure expertly downloading whatever it wanted to take or erase. Frantically, he began pumping at the call button in the vain hope of speeding his ride.

It was the hotel's policy not to have piped music in the lifts, but its addition couldn't have made Mr Thomas's current conveyance less suited for swiftness. He pressed the button for floor twelve and then fidgeted throughout the agonising wait while the doors trundled shut. He half caught his own reflection in the back mirror of the vehicle's rear wall, and distracted himself absorbing, rather than reading, the wall listings of restaurant menus and gym services. His wide-eyed and sweating visage hovered just to his right, but he was in no fit state to see another replication of himself after the earlier monitor incident. Again, the drive of pursuit, of apprehension, kept him focused despite his florid misgivings.

Eventually the lift doors opened and he swept through, taking rapid strides, cursing himself again for being so stupid as the door with the "No Unauthorised Access" sign on it swung closed behind him; the black-handed sentinel, completely unnoticed this time.

He paused then, catching his breath in an anxious moment as he felt, more than heard, a presence down the corridor within the monitoring station. He listened intently as his mind raced over what he should say and how he should approach the interloper now that he, or she, was cornered. Nothing useful presented itself, so he sneaked towards the doorway he had so recently dashed through on this fruitless chase. A shaking hand strayed to his belt in the hope that he simply might not have noticed his baton-sized torch dangling there. It was empty. All his meagre defences were inside the room with the intruder.

He inched his head around the edge of the doorway, the interior of the station revealing itself in incremental vertical strips. The cluttered filing cabinet, the wall-mounted clock reading 03:13 – the overly rapid passage of the night only adding to his fear. A sparkling array of red, blue and green LED lights wrestled for his attention, and then he realised the figure was sitting in his chair.

Mr Thomas recoiled, but was unable to retreat, the horror of what he saw collapsing any sense of capturing the intruder or even comprehending its existence, let alone its purpose.

The entity was humanoid in shape, but made up entirely of smoke-like tentacles, or perhaps braids of drowned hair. It spilled out at its edges but, for the most part, held the vague form of a hooded figure. It turned on the chair's creaking spindle to face Mr Thomas fully. An involuntary whimper escaped from the big man's trembling lips. Maddeningly, though, he felt compelled to advance towards the apparition rather than flee. Two writhing arms were lifted as if in welcome and then the amorphous hands at their extremities did a most terrible thing. They fell and seemed to pat the seething lap that coated the top of the chair.

Was there a sound of hands tapping thighs? Mr Thomas's mind was beyond comprehension, but the implication was clear. Like his mother, father and all his dead relatives rolled into one. A basic gesture of body language made abhorrent by such a thing in such a place. And yet the beckoning had its desired effect. Mr Thomas' unwilling feet took him closer and closer to this epicentre of unreality in the midst of this night of oddity.

He stood in front of it, trying and failing to make sense of its squirming form and then, involuntarily, his body responded to the invitation to sit, and he did what he thought was unthinkable. He turned his back on the thing and lowered himself onto its proffered lap. A tingling sensation fluttered behind his knees, through the backs of his legs and buttocks and into the small of his back. He imagined a thousand little tendrils reaching, straining for him, all vibrating in anticipation at the approach of his trousers, his jumper, his flesh.

There was no resistance as his balance gave way and he tipped gently into the seat, no body to settle his sizable bulk against, just the customary huff of the seat's cushion expelling air. But there *was* something there. The thing had pressed itself into his back, neck and head and was now rapidly becoming part of him. Control over his body returned and he bolted up out of the seat, and turned... The chair was now completely empty.

He felt the figure's presence behind him and spun round to look back through the monitoring station's door, but it too was unoccupied. Sill he felt its presence, and then realised that it was almost as if it were clinging to his back, a warm, not unpleasant, sensation, like someone draping a heavy coat across his shoulders. He reached a shaking arm behind, patted his lumbar region and was reassured by the solid weight of his clothes and skin. The delusion had passed and he was, once again, alone.

More from nervous exhaustion than intention, he sat back heavily in the chair and immediately winced, imagining that the thing was still beneath him. He tested the seat, craned his neck around to his left and right to make sure that everything had returned to normal. Then he held his head in his hands - the aftermath of the chase and encounter draining him of any remaining energy, his rational mind trying and failing to marry up all the recent events.

He looked up, and felt a residual twinge of strangeness bring everything back into an edgy definition.

"What now?" He moaned, "What now?!"

Well, his inner voice came back, surprisingly calm and collected, *if you want to keep this job, I'd delete all footage from the past hour or so. We can't have management seeing a trusted night watchman flailing about like a mad man, now can we? Oh, and don't worry about what the day shift will say. Just put it down in the log book as a systems failure. Go on, have a look in there. You'll be surprised at just how often this sort of thing happens.*

Fearful and sick, Mr Thomas nodded to himself. It really was the only rational thing to do.

THE BEAST AND BEAUTY

Tanith Lee

We saw them married. We were all surprised, to various degrees; some of us were even shocked. She was so – we could hardly gloss over it amongst ourselves – so ugly, so graceless. And he was beautiful, such a handsome and couth young man, with his long, rich hair and slim, straight build. And this other – this *object*, standing there beside him.

To do her credit, if we can call it that, she seemed quite as amazed as we. But this only made her, we thought, less coordinated, more gauche and awkward. A parody. She was squat and short-legged, rather fat, and her wiry, frizzy hair hidden under a sort of exotic headdress, part hat perhaps, part bird's nest. She had small, pale, dull eyes, all of us noticed this, so unlike his own, that were dark, large and luminous.

We knew he had not married her for her money. She had none, and he was well-off. Had she then some terrible and inexorable hold over him? Some of us, I do believe, were constructing plots by which we could find out how she had suborned and captured him. But – and here the strangest thing of all – he seemed *happy*. And when they kissed – well, for a fact, he kissed her tenderly, sweetly. Even with – and we were worse horrified of course by this – with an element of actual physical desire.

We will never forget it, that day.

Not one of us.

They had a small house on the coast, which had belonged to him for two or three years. They went to the house at once. He had said, being by the sea, and the countryside there so appealing, they had no need of a honeymoon holiday.

There they lived then, the two of them. The town, quite a well-built and sophisticated place, was only a twenty minute drive from the house – or an hour's walk. Sometimes they did walk, along the cliffs, with the brilliant shifting shelves of water below, and off across the sunlit meadow-paths, between the tall hedges, the fields, the banks of wild flowers and the woods. A cycle of perfect summers. Had either of them ever before been so wonderfully happy? They told each other, he most often in fact, that they never had.

And between the walks and luxurious meals, and everyday or eccentric duties of their house and gardens, between – others had to suppose – their times of romance and sexual love-making – they continued with their usual work, he creating his rather excellent yet very crowd-pleasing art, and she writing her rather – it was generally agreed – *ordinary* little novels. His successes had begun early and had continued but hers, though at first she had been quite popular and sold well, had fallen off. In the end she hardly published at all, but still went on writing. She was, it seemed, nothing if not stubborn. Had that been the secret of her success with *him?*

By the second year they did not often see people, beyond the occasional, normally unplanned meetings in the town, or the city inland. They seemed wrapped up in each other. No one else had or could fathom why. That was, the rest of the world could see easily how *she* might be wrapped up in *him*. While with him, naturally, it stayed a mystery.

He had never painted her, for sure. But then, he very seldom, or now ever, painted people. His subjects were landscapes, skies, seas.

Another year passed.

Another year.

Nobody genuinely had grown at all used to their extraordinary liaison. Now and then it was still commented upon in amused disbelief, or even in a type of moral outrage. But less and less. An *unanswered* mystery can be irksome when it unalterably persists.

He had had, and he was the first to admit it, a limpidly-flowing and pleasant existence. Born into an emotionally and financially solvent family, blessed with great good looks, and strong yet accessible talent, he had prospered. His earliest memories, even, were nice ones. Happy: he grew *up* happily; popular, protected, yet independent, self-assured and enjoying his creative side, while revelling in friendships, not to mention love-affairs. Although, he would sometimes ruefully admit, the end of love-affairs, and exotic brief relationships, after say six months, a year, were often less delightful. He hated to hurt these women. But he had always had such luck with them. He need do very little more than be his handsome, charming, easy-going and gracious self, and girls cascaded from the boughs of earthly heaven into his life and bed. Saying goodbye was mournful, of course. It could sting. But quite frequently not only he, but a former lover, were soon established elsewhere, completely undamaged. He was never harsh, never cruel. He tried always to be kind. Kindness was – inherent in him, really. To distress another might distress him therefore. He liked the world sunny, even in rain. Intelligent, he *knew* he had a splendid time of it. And he honestly regretted the others, that he saw, heard of and read of, all about him, who did not. Things were unfair. Had he been able, he would have waved a magic wand, and put everything right. For this reason too, of course, he did not believe in a God. But then, it seemed he hardly needed one.

When he met her, the woman who would become his wife, he felt, immediately, compassion. She had just begun to work – actually her writing had for a while ceased to be lucrative enough to support her – in a small art shop in the back streets. He went in there occasionally for a particular primer not often available elsewhere. She served him politely and fairly efficiently, though she was slightly clumsy in her movements. Her body seemed uncoordinated and not properly to fit her psyche. He had noticed things like this before with plenty of people.

It must be said that the fact she was not herself attractive was *not* why he felt compassionate. Being himself so frankly beautiful, he did not, as some beautiful persons do not, bother very much with the looks either of others or himself beyond the obvious matters of grooming, hygiene and sanity. But he *could* see she was miserable. And though this, he had found, was often the case with people generally, he discovered her dejection rather pointedly disturbed him.

Covertly, he watched her as she dealt with his purchase and its payment.

Then, something happened.

A flock of quite ordinary birds lifted from the street outside and flew upward through the last of the afternoon sunlight. As a painter, he liked the image, and watched it. Then, turning back to her, saw that she had, too. And – for a split second, already ephemerally fading – he saw her face had flooded with its own soft light. A look of – *joy*. Pure joy. At seeing something beautiful, however everyday, or transitory, or unmeaningful. As if, he thought at the time, she had looked through a window into some other world, more lucent, more lovely, and immediately recognised.

It was not until he was almost at his apartment that it came to him that, for just one single second, she had looked at him, also, in the same way. And *in* that second, as in the longer moments with the birds, the misery had of course quite vanished from her face.

Perhaps this was irresistible. He was, as has been noted, normally inclined to kindness. To be kind filled him with pleasure. He had now and then given away his toys as a child.

He did not need to go back to the shop, but found himself passing about a month later.

Going in, there she was. She seemed if anything even more worn down and melancholy. But when he greeted her and she glanced up at him – why, there it was again. The wonderful sunrise.

That then, her charm for him. Her enchantment. Better than any mirror, to which inanimate species he never paid much attention beyond obvious necessity. Unlike a *human* mirror, too, which only returns the object of desire as a sort of faulty replica.

It was not he thought: *I can make her beautiful.* It was more somehow *I can make her happy.* Besides, it was not, and never could be with him, a *conscious* thought. He was unincluded in that tribe.

Adamantly, at first she would not lunch or dine with him. When he asked, she seemed almost frightened. Yet, the glow of light in her face persisted, fluttering on and off as the wings of the flying, sun-fringed birds had appeared to. After about a week of his constantly entering the shop, buying something, trying to persuade her, she agreed to drink a cup of coffee with him.

The café was discreet and serene, the coffee it served very good. They were there for half an hour.

It became a habit between them once, twice a week. After four weeks they ate sandwiches and drank, each, a glass of wine. They knew each other's names. They had started to discuss books, and plays. He took her to a play. He liked her reactions to such significant events.

She looked younger. Her cheeks had colour and she had had her hair cut more becomingly. Her eyes on him were always wide. Radiance existed in them. Her voice, though very low, was of an even timbre, not inarticulate or unmusical when she became animated.

They took a little holiday, four or five days in a quiet but opulent hotel. She had told him, flat and downcast as she did so, that her room must be separate. She was a restless sleeper, she snored, so she told him. He replied, untruthfully, that he too was, and did. On the third night he joined her for a drink in her room. Presently she insisted that all light be extinguished. *I hate to be looked at*, she whispered. *My body, I mean.*

He wondered what injury of birth or life had maimed her – some swollen or shrunken part, hidden when clothed – a rampant birthmark – a disease of the skin – but in the darkness she was simply a woman of short stature, clad in flesh that was, depending on a companion's view, heavy, or voluptuous. There were no deformities or lesions of scars of which he was made aware, nothing strange that, lacking full sight, the other senses stumbled on. Her skin was smooth and soft, her mouth tender, no part of her in any way offensive.

He knew as well, from her responses, what he would have seen in her face. Light transmuted to ecstasy.

He had painted the picture of a violin, once. She was like his violin. And her writing too, for him, was like her music; he had given it back to her.

She began to live with him for large amounts of each month. Unreluctantly she left her job, no longer needing it, since by then he was funding all her expenses, both with and apart from him. She did not seem even properly to notice this, and he preferred that reaction in her, for gratitude would have grated on him. All he wanted in exchange he saw in her eyes and face, heard and held, and glimpsed finally, when he made love to her: by then, she would permit a vague lamplight. He had, in all his benign existence until this point, never so relished, so basked in, so *needed* anyone other than himself.

To marriage also she made, now, no objections. Perhaps, during the wedding ceremony and the lavish feast that followed, she did not fully notice anyone but her lover. And he, for his part, was lost in her. Or found.

She, until she met, and then lived with her husband, had never been with anyone. Which is to say, she *had* been thrown in among a *huge* number of others, but with none who were ever concerned about or interested in her, let alone loving towards her.

Her parents had been uncomely and loutish, and both inclined to violence. Her couple of older siblings took after them. At an immature age she was rescued, or so it was termed, and cast instead into a sort of state orphanage, where all the cruelties and bullying continued in more elaborate form, not to mention the physical hideousness of natures, ambitions and surroundings, and the dearth of any food either for the heart or spirit; there was little enough for the stomach.

Somehow or other she had learned to read. Most probably this, and other more rudimentary knowledge, was beaten into her. But as she grew up, despite the menial factory work into which, at fifteen, she was processed, and the yet ever-expanding callousness of everyone about her, somehow she learned, of her own instinctive volition, to grasp at literature and to hold on. A fluke of circumstance put her, at the age of sixteen, into the position of entering a short story competition. She won it unrivalled, and was taken then under the wing of a quite prestigious publishing house.

Initially thrilled at her potential money-making ability, and her youth, they quickly lost momentum having once seen and met her. Gauche and awkward, clumsy and utterly unpretty, she had in herself no marketing power, as they were soon agreed. Only her writing had any worth which, in an age of instant visibility and supposed communication, would *never* be enough.

Some listless attempts *were* made physically to polish her up. But the smart garments and trendy hair-dos, the cosmetic specialists and speech-trainers soon gave up on her in impatient revulsion.

It was true, she had always seen about her, particularly on a screen, but even among her hair-dyeing and lip-glossing fellow citizens, persons who, lacking certain essential fleshly attributes, effected improvements. Some indeed underwent surgery, tooth-jobs, chin-jobs, face-jobs, body-jobs, gym therapy, hair transplants, wigs, waxes, revitalisations, skin-grafts. Though confused by all that, in her own muddled and entirely ineffectual way she had tried, or felt forced to try, to emulate the rest – who, she could see, did end up usually rather better for all the gruelling, costly, painful work put in on them.

But it was soon clear to her, as to her publishers it had already been, and quite swiftly, that *she* was beyond assistance. A lost cause. A lump best left in a cupboard of unforced privacy.

Lacking any solid publicity, and all promotion therefore, soon enough her talent too slid from the World Stage. At twenty she was a has-been. She retreated to a narrow one-room flat and various ill-paid employment and gradually, in exhaustion, smothered under that universal bucket, her light faltered down into coma.

It was he who woke her.

She had somehow, even bereft of so much, never been robbed completely of her fundamental passion for true beauty. Even for such as ill-made and crushed as she, stars and waves, leaves and lamps, sunrise, moonset, and the faces of non-human animals – all such abrupt and extraordinary miracles would drench her, for a few seconds, in the glow of paradise. Although a paradise from which she herself was forever banned.

She had seen, too, some naturally elegant and attractive people before, if normally from very far off. Confronted by him, so close, so apparent, she had been stunned.

Only her naivety later allowed her to give in to his persuasion. It was all a dream. She must start up from it soon enough, to find herself lying on a hot raw ground of reality and fact. Otherwise she could never have trusted the circumstance, let alone him.

Perhaps, *in* reality, she did *not* trust him. You are alone in darkness – a God or an angel appears. What map-reference is there, in such a case, to guide one? You can only give in.

But time ran by and over her, a clear river, all at once delicious and gentle. Amazement followed on amazement. The dream did not dissolve. It must, after all *be* real.

Of course, she had known one previous astonishment with her success in the competition. Maybe, even subconsciously, it had been *this* which soothed and lured her to accept a second gift. Choosing, as few would not, to forget how the first glory had been drained to dust.

In legends, even in contemporary stories such as she herself might have written, the gifts of gods are often suspect. Even if no evil plan of harm has been hatched against the recipient, *indigenous* to the glamour and wonder of the gift is its lethal flaw. The molten gold sears off the hand, the exquisite ring imparts a poisonous disease, the peerless wings are over-strong and hurl their wearer up against the sun. The kiss breaks the mirror.

We heard of it in disbelief. Where the marriage had shocked some of us in itself, the outcome, those five years later, sent us staggering.

Obviously, there was a lot of publicity, not least since he was so well-known and fashionable a painter. To the general public, of course, the blow was minimised by emotional distance. For us, however, particularly those of us who had never lost contact with him – even where keeping, when possible, out of *her* proximity – a kind of cloud of mourning settled. There was some anger as well. How not?

Inevitably, all the while, some of us had entirely foretold a reversal. That he *must*, at some junction, emerge from his unreasonable trance and realise his peculiar mistake. Or, more likely yet, that he must see another, no doubt a woman, somebody gorgeous and couth, and fall in love more logically with her.

Several of us had remained shattered that so far he had not seemed able to. While a few of us, certainly, once or twice over the years, may have tried to *cause* this to happen: *Oh, have you met so-and-so, she is such a fan of your work* – but no scheme bore fruit. He had gone on with *her*. Until *this*.

If only we could have undone the knots of that wicked fate which had inconceivably ensnared him–

But that, as we soon learn in this world, is as a rule out of our remit.

We must all make our own way. To Heaven, or to the Abyss.

And who could have predicted such a dreadful, vile – yet nearly laughable – thing? It was – *absurd*.

They had been at their house on the coast that day, as so often they were. It was a day like many they had already spent there.

It seems he painted in the morning, at a place in their gardens that overlooked the sea. It was glamorous summer weather, the temperature warm but mild, and a soft breeze blowing through the cedars and the scented lavender bushes.

They ate lunch on the patio above, a fresh salad with locally-caught fish, some wine and fruit. He had laid a rose by her plate.

About three o'clock they decided to stroll inland to the town, to buy a minor item necessary for the studio; this would then be delivered later in the week. After which they might take in a movie, dine early, and about ten be chauffeured home through the long blue dusk, the full moon out and stars glittering, all well with their world.

They never reached the town.

He was found on the beach, just above the tide-line, by that unlucky cliché – a person walking their dog. It was by then about 6a.m., and the sun up and streaming clear over the water. Any error was impossible.

He was covered in blood, which was not astounding. Most of his bones were broken too, also hardly inappropriate, under the circumstances.

His beauty was impaired, if not totally eradicated. He had stayed recognisable. Even the dog-walker knew him at once, if only from photographs and clips of TV footage. It seemed the dog-walker had very good prints of three of his paintings, and cried, and so the dog howled, and they cried and howled again when the police arrived.

Not long after that the beach grew very crowded.

She did not attend the funeral. It would hardly have been feasible that she could. She had vanished, disappeared rather as spent liquid slides down a drain into the sewer beneath. Had she *been* visible, accessible, it went without saying she must instead any way have been shut in jail, on trial, there found guilty, and either dispatched, or incarcerated for the remains of her time alive. She had killed him, her lover-husband, the painter. But why was this? *Had* he betrayed her with another lover? Or merely begun to be cruel, scorning her, insulting, bullying and abusing her, like all those others from her past? No, none of those. He had stayed faithful and adorable, ever cognisant of her, appreciative, eager to comprehend and interest, to make her smile or laugh, or sigh with pleasure. The perfect and most lovely of partners. Was it then *this* very thing – weird irony of an imperfect earth – this very faultlessness of his in his conduct, his charming attentions, his real care of her, his joy in bringing joy to *her* – had it somehow sickened or driven her away from him? Had he *smothered* her with his loving kindness? So that, only in order to breathe again, she had thrust out her sudden hand when they stood at the cliff's wild-flowery and unrailed brink, thrust out her graceless and stumpy hand and, catching him off-balance, spun him away and downwards, his fine face looking only surprised, and not even that very much. He struck his head mere moments following, and so made no complaint at all, striking all of himself next, and repeatedly, on the cliff, and ultimately the rocky beach two hundred and seventy feet below. He was already mostly dead, a task the beach had completed in six further seconds.

Or could it have been an accident?

No, it could not.

If she ever wrote about what had happened, what she had done at about half past three on that summer day, it never came to light. What happened subsequently to her, or where she had gone to – despite numerous sightings of her, all of which proved either false or too imprecise or dilatory to be of help – has never been learned. Maybe she too has died by now. Or else she is flourishing somewhere, in some theoretical country of the blind where, by a quirk of life's madness, it turns out she, after all, has some advantage. But this seems so very unlikely.

You may still ask, nevertheless, why did she kill him?

Turn back the pages of the memory she herself had – or has. Look carefully at its pictures, which only resemble, and attain, anything beautiful when they do not deal at all with contact by actual human things: the flying birds, purring cats, bounding dogs, the leaves, the lit lamps, the mountains, the sea, the sky, the sun, the moon and the stars. Even a paper written on, perhaps, a play seen, a book read. Yes, but turn quite fast past all those. Look now as she has at the faces of humanity. Not, as you might expect, while they leer and snarl at her – but as they make those corrective attempts upon themselves. As they put on the face-pack or undergo the nose-job, as they paint in and paint out what is missing and what should not be there. Such effort. Always that effort, which sometimes somewhat, and sometimes vastly improves them, makes them so much better, appealing, silky creatures, loveable and valid. Until the mask comes off, the wig, the special brassière or controlling device. Out with the tooth-implants, the plastic breasts, wipe away the make-up. And then – they are so much less. So much more...*her* people, though they will never agree. They survive by hiding in disguise. Although she, poor ruin, so badly-made – as they had always told her, and she learned *their* truth as she learned to read – beaten, beaten into her – she, she could never improve herself by such slender means. She had been thrown too far down that cliff of abysm. Nothing could *she* do. Her only consolation then perhaps, faint as a brush of pollen from some dying flower, to see that they at least must *work* at their survival.

But not so with everyone.

You will perhaps picture now how he was, her lover, her husband. Handsome, gracious, elegant – flawless. And to nurture this he need only – *be*. Asleep by night, waking in the morning, if a little unwell with a minor ailment, if sweating, hot and dishevelled from too long in the sun at a painting, irritated by some difficulty in his work, or grubby from some chore, or in the paroxysm of lust, which does not always beautify its subject – then, as at all times, by dark, by light, in shadow or in glare – he – *he* – *always* perfect. And to maintain perfection, all he need do was – *nothing*. Nothing at all.

On that walk, at the edge of the ocean, the afternoon sun, the clarity of the air – he turned his head to look away towards the water, speaking no doubt in his beautiful voice about the picture he had been making. His shining hair, his eyes, his expression, every feature of face and body, even that half step he took, so graceful, like that of a dancer or a duellist, in utter poise, if not quite in balance, that strong and eloquent movement of his hand – do you see? Do you *see?* As if across vast distances, the shrill scream of the revelation must at last have reached her. All this he has, and is. Even goodness and kindness belong to him. He needs do nothing. He *burns* the world.

Her hand too springs out. And he – is gone.

WICKEN FEN

Paul Finch

"It's not that me and Carly don't get on any more," Gerry said over his pint of Oakham's. "I mean, in *some* ways we don't get on not like we used to. Hell, I don't know. After you've been married twenty-five years you get bored with each other."

"Bored?" Trevor replied. "With Carly? Mate, she's what... forty-five?"

"Forty-six."

"She's forty-six, and whenever she walks down the road, there are still blokes eyeballing her with their tongues hanging out."

"Yeah ... because she's got blonde hair, a pretty face and big tits."

"Whoa!" Trevor glanced over his shoulder.

They were in a waterside pub called *The Kingfisher*. It was the hot and muggy end to a blazing July day, and the place was crammed; not just out in the beer garden and along the balcony overlooking the broad, but here in the taproom as well, rustic voices and gruff laughter echoing beneath the gnarled, smoky roof-beams. Not that they knew anyone here. Trevor and Gerry were Dagenham lads, currently sixty miles from home and 'getting away from it all'. It didn't matter if anyone overheard, but Trevor was discomforted these days when Gerry got into his cups and started discussing his own wife in that free, irreverent way.

"I know she's a looker, mate," Gerry said, elbows rested on the bar as he drained his tankard. "What're you having, same again?"

Trevor nodded, finishing his pint of Carlsberg.

"Yeah, I know she's a looker. That's why I married her in the first place. But once you've been handling the goods as long as I have, it all gets a bit samey."

Trevor supposed that might be true, but it was a shame to think of Carly, who was also a friend of his, and a very good friend of his wife, Josie's, in such crude terms.

"Tell the truth, mate," Gerry added, as he ordered two more drinks. "I'm not missing them at all."

Them, Trevor thought, interested. Them – as in Carly *and* Josie. He knew that his pal meant nothing personal by that. But it was increasingly Gerry's way that, whenever discussing whatever marital problems he imagined he was undergoing, and there seemed to be more and more of them, he tended to refer to 'their wives' rather than 'his wife', as if it was naturally the case that all men, Trevor included, should be going through the same kinds of midlife crises.

"I feel more and more that they hold us back," Gerry added. "You know … get in the way."

"Get in the way of what?" Trevor asked, not wishing to play devil's advocate but fascinated to know. He then apologised as a massive guy, his plaid shirt rolled back on meaty forearms, thick flaxen whiskers framing a beery red face, jostled against him at the bar. The whiskered guy made no apology of his own, nor acknowledged Trevor's.

Gerry noticed the incident but was too busy with his own thoughts to comment. He sank another mouthful of Oakham's. "We love them to bits … but after two decades married life is so *staid*. Is that the correct word?"

Trevor, who was a teacher, nodded.

Gerry, who was a mechanic and ran his own body-shop, pondered further. "I mean, we've been together so long everything's just routine."

"Isn't that what life eventually becomes?"

"Maybe for you. I don't consider I'm past *my* sell-by date yet."

"What else would you rather be doing?"

"Well… that lot, to start with." Gerry nodded past Trevor's shoulder to a nearby corner. Trevor looked around, and saw two girls beside the darts board.

They had their backs turned, but made a cute summer picture: one blonde, one brunette, both manes hanging wild and untamed, both figures slender but shapely. The blonde wore a t-shirt, a short denim skirt and Roman sandals, an ensemble that showed her sun-browned limbs to perfection; the brunette was in a sporty vest and denim cut-offs, 'Daisy Dukes' as Trevor had heard them referred to. She wore flip-flops and an ankle-chain with bells and stars; her legs were so smooth and tan you could have glazed them with honey.

"You want to …" Trevor said uncertainly, "you want to tap off with two …"

"With two lovely bits of stuff," Gerry replied. "What's not to like, eh?"

"You serious?"

Gerry sighed. "I suppose not. We can look though, can't we? At least they-who-must-be-obeyed aren't here to stop us doing that."

Trevor stole another glance. There was no denying it; the two lasses, who from this angle looked to be in their early twenties, had an aura. The sun slanting through the nearby window framed them in a golden glow, dazzled in their hair. If he'd come out now with some kind of pious statement to the effect that he and Josie, who had also been married twenty-five years, were still deeply in love and perfectly happy and never had any ups and downs, he'd be lying. They too had their problems, but didn't all married couples who'd been together so long? Certainly nothing had ever occurred that had set them so far apart that they'd gone looking for someone else. If Trevor was honest, he had occasionally – usually when he'd had too much to drink – wondered what it might be like to be approached by some, how had Gerry put it, 'lovely bit of stuff' – but at forty-eight and on a teacher's salary, he knew that was never going to happen .

"They haven't got blokes with them, either," Gerry said, furtively, like a man about to embark on a secret mission. "I've been watching them all evening, and they've been stood over there in that corner on their own."

"They'll just be on holiday, like us?"

"Or on the pull."

"We can dream, I guess."

Gerry's attention had now *fixed* on the two girls, his eyes adopting a predatory gleam. He was chunky lad – more chunky than was good for him, as Carly would often say – but the flat-cropped bristles on top of his head, the well-groomed moustache and trim goatee beard were still black rather than grey. His age-old Motorhead t-shirt revealed gym-toned arms covered with fashionable tattoos. In his macho 'wild beast' sort of way, he probably wouldn't be quite as unfanciable to younger females as

Trevor, who, though he wasn't grey either, had only a mouse-brown mop and was tall and lean, with wholesome 'Stan Laurel' features.

"I'll not be a minute," Gerry said, a change of tone suggesting the mission had commenced. He slid from his stool and lurched across the taproom, wiping the beer from his hands on the back of his over-large tennis shorts as he approached the door to the Gents.

Trevor hoped and prayed that he wasn't going in there to do something *really* stupid – like buy a packet of condoms. But he needn't have worried: no sooner had Gerry vanished from view than the two girls also made a move, drinking up and heading for the nearest exit, the brunette's flip-flops slapping against the soles of her naked feet.

Trevor watched them covertly. He still hadn't glimpsed their 'boat-races', as Gerry would refer to them, but he didn't doubt they'd both be beautiful and kittenish. They walked with a lithe, practised sway. He noticed that both had painted toenails; the blonde's crimson, the brunette's gold. They oozed sexiness and, if he was honest, availability. It was no surprise Gerry had been hooked. Trevor looked around, and was taken aback that the rest of the gathering – which was mostly men, a lot of them rugged outdoor types – weren't also drooling after the objects of desire. He edged to the window and stared down the grassy slope to the moorings, where various leisure craft bobbed and tilted on the sun-splashed waters. The two girls were heading towards an impressive-looking boat at the end of a short jetty: an old style twenty-footer, a river-cruiser type done in swish blue-and-white trim. He'd had them pegged for students, but was probably wrong given the quality of that vessel. That would have cost a pretty penny just to hire.

Gerry reappeared about three minutes after Trevor had idled back to his bar-stool. "Bloody hell, have you scared them off?"

Trevor sipped his beer. "Went of their own accord."

"And you didn't ..."

"What? Try to stop them? No, I bloody didn't. Look, Gez ..." Trevor assumed his common sense tone. "We've had a nice relaxed first day, we've had a few beers, we can have a few malts when we get back on the narrow-boat. It's going to be sunny tomorrow. We can do it all again. Why mess things up?"

Gerry still looked disappointed. He strode to the darts board window. Trevor joined him. There was no longer any sign of the girls. The river-cruiser was also absent. Gerry blew out a long, wistful breath. "Bloody stupid idea, I suppose. Ah well ... saves a shed-load of embarrassment. Let's have another round, if nothing else."

Happy to accommodate this lesser vice, Trevor returned to the bar and ordered two more pints.

"You're still wrong about Carly, though," Gerry said, perching back on his stool. "Blonde and pretty, I'll give you that. But big tits? Once, maybe. These days, she takes her bra off at night ..." He pulled an ugly face. "Spaniel's ears, mate."

The landscape was so flat that Trevor could see in every direction for miles – at least he would have been able to, had the heat-haze not imposed limitations of its own. The endless green of softly rippling reeds finally blended with a sky the colour of hammered steel. The sun reflected intensely from the brown waters undulating past.

The narrow-boat was travelling slowly but smoothly, the chugging of its engine little more than a gentle throb beneath Trevor's sneakered feet as he stood at the prow, shielding his eyes to peer along the broad; though he knew they weren't actually called 'broads', not here in Cambridgeshire – that was over in Norfolk. He thought this stretch was what the locals referred to as a 'lode', a kind of manmade channel connecting the natural waterways that networked this part of the county.

Trevor and Josie holidayed regularly in the Med, but even down there he hadn't known heat like this. He'd stripped off to a pair of shorts, but the sun was soon chafing his shoulders. Even the insects that swarmed these marshes in summer were stilled. If there were water-fowl around, and there should be every kind here – from bitterns and grebes to the rare black-tailed godwit – they were roosting among the sedge and bulrushes. There was no sound – none at all; it was almost eerie.

The ideal moment for him to sight what looked like a floating body.

In that disbelieving way familiar to folk throughout history who'd discovered corpses, he initially thought he was mistaken and then *hoped* that he was. Maybe it was just a sack of rubbish happening to resemble a torso and four limbs? Maybe it was a department store mannequin? But no – it was a body, male by the size of it, bobbing face-down. Trevor glimpsed what looked like a red t-shirt and a naked lower half. It was stationary in the water, but would pass them by a few feet to starboard.

"Gez!" he shouted over his shoulder. But Gerry was aft; he wouldn't be able to hear from so far back. Fortunately Trevor already had a pole to hand, with a hook on the end. He reached down, caught the corpse by its collar and lugged it towards him. It was heavy and awkward, perhaps snared on something underneath. He imagined thick bundles of weeds billowing up from the depths like ocean kelp, so platted and tangled together they were almost human in their outline: a central trunk swaying from side to side; even a head, a mass of green, spongy putrescence – possibly the upper portion of a log entrapped after decades, tresses of fronds coiling around it. And then the arms – more lengthy tangles of cable-thick weed, weaving back and forth as they reached up through the murk, not with ten fingers but hundreds: myriad mottled tendrils snaking towards the flickering sunlight.

When the body suddenly came loose, it turned over with such natural motion that Trevor thought the man might still be alive. But then he saw that where there'd once been a face there was now a jagged crimson cavity. The same was true of the chest. The guy had been hollowed out, gutted, reduced to a grisly shell by parasitic devils that had simply burrowed their way into him, voracious aquatic monstrosities, their needle teeth rending and slashing, their spiny claws digging, tearing …

Trevor shot up from his bunk so quickly that even though the ceiling was several feet above him, he almost clouted his head. He sat there in the darkness, panting, the thin sheets plastered to his sweat-slick skin.

It was pitch-black. Beyond the partition wall, Gerry snored noisily.

Shaking, Trevor clambered from the bunk and fumbled out of his cabin into the connecting passage. Though he wore only a pair of underpants, he made his way aft, unbolting the doors and climbing up onto the rear deck.

An awesome silence lay across the benighted fens. The occasional *slosh* disturbed it as wavelets slapped on the hull, but that was all. There was no moon, so nothing was visible – but he could sense it, that vast waterlogged wilderness stretching out on all sides. The air was warm and damp, rank with wetland odours.

Then he heard the cry.

It came from far away – a huge distance across the sodden wastes, but it sounded distinctly female. Trevor listened out. It hadn't seemed like someone in trouble; there'd been no pain or alarm there. It was as though the woman, whoever she was, had been calling someone's name. Was it his imagination that the name had sounded like 'Trevor'?

That was ridiculous. He must still be half-asleep.

They were no longer moored beside *The Kingfisher*. After they'd left the pub, they'd opted to press on a little way, but the dusk had soon dissipated to darkness and they'd had no option but to rope themselves to one of the many stone quays located along the tussocky embankments. He didn't think they were *officially* in the fens as yet – more likely they were still on one of the River Cam's many sidings, but it was much of a muchness in this part of the world; to an outsider like Trevor, the distinctions seemed trivial. That voice though – OK, he was tired, not to say a little shaken by the nightmare, but he was certain he hadn't dreamed it. Before he knew what he was doing, he'd gone back down into the narrow-boat's belly and re-emerged topside, this time with mobile in hand. It had just enough juice left in it for a single call.

"Hello?" came Josie's voice, heavy with sleep.

"Hi, it's me. Everything OK?"

"Erm … yeah. Why are you … Trevor, why are you calling at this hour?"

"Sorry, I just wanted to check you were … you know, that you'd had a good time."

"I've had an excellent time." She sounded puzzled, and not a little vexed. "It'd be perfect if I could get a good night's sleep to round it off."

"Yeah, sorry … I didn't realise what time it was. Erm, where are you?"

"Where do you think? Home."

He wasn't sure what he'd expected to hear in the background – rippling waterways, fen-fowl making night calls? None of that would have made any difference now. Just the sound of Josie's voice reassured him that she was exactly where she said she was.

But it felt awkward to suddenly ring off after he'd woken her up. "You and Carly were going out, weren't you?"

"To watch *The Woman In Black*. And now I'm back. Obviously I'm back ... Trevor, it's two in the morning. Are you drunk or something?"

Trevor had never noticed before how sensual Josie's voice sounded when she was sleepy. She didn't compare much to Carly when it came to full-on glamour, but she was still an attractive girl; in good physical shape thanks to a strict diet and exercise regime, and with her dark brown hair, hazel eyes, delicate cheekbones and that pert, dimpled chin, she'd always been handsome.

"No," he said. "Well, yeah. But not *that* drunk. Just wanted to hear your voice, that's all." It sounded lame even though it was completely true.

"Sweet of you. But perhaps we can save it 'til tomorrow?"

"I thought you were going out again tomorrow."

"We are ... *Shrek* in the afternoon and *Wicked* in the evening. But that still gives you a few windows of opportunity."

"Suppose so, yeah."

"Okay. Speak to you tomorrow. You sure everything's all right?"

"Everything's fine. Love you." Trevor probably hadn't voiced those words with quite so much feeling for a considerable time.

"You too," Josie replied, sounding less sure. And she hung up.

The darkness snuggled around the narrow-boat as it rode the lapping waters. They still weren't on the fens, Trevor reminded himself as he watched the lights wink out on his mobile. But the sense of isolation in this place was tangible. Sixty miles from home – that was all; yet he'd have given a lot to be back there now.

Trevor didn't call Josie the next day. There didn't seem to be much point once the sun had risen and chased away the night-time fantasies. In any case, his phone was dead. Gerry, who'd begun quaffing tins of beer as soon as they'd got underway again – around ten-thirty that morning – shrugged and said that he deliberately hadn't brought his own mobile. They were supposed to be on holiday; he didn't want bothering by "one of those monkeys back at the shop".

Of course they weren't really on holiday. Not in the true sense of the word. This was a weekend jaunt between Ely and Cambridge, taking in the fen country. It would be short and sweet, and the only reason they'd been allowed to do it was so that Josie and Carly could catch up on their West End shows. As a group, the two couples did almost everything together, but the men drew the line at theatre land, so this was an opportunity the women couldn't miss. Despite all this, Trevor still felt their wives would have enjoyed the narrow-boat, a cheerfully painted blue-and-pink affair called *The Sunny Dawn*. It was the last word in river-going comfort. Not only did it have a well-stocked galley kitchen, wherein he'd cooked an excellent bacon and eggs that morning (even if he did say so himself), its salon was roomy and well-furnished and its cabins small but luxurious. In the event of problems, it had lifejackets on board, and an 'emergency kit' which appeared to have thought of everything: a compass, first-aid items, water purification tablets, stay-light matches, candles, a solar blanket and even a flare-pistol with three flare shells.

But it was the sedate pace at which the vessel moved that was its most appealing feature, especially on a scorching day like today.

"These are beautiful," Gerry said, "filching another beer from the cooler at his feet. "Ice-cold, I'll tell you." They were out on the rear deck, Gerry leaning lazily on the tiller.

"You want to go easy on those," Trevor replied, poring over the map. "According to this, we've got a couple of locks to get through yet."

Gerry shrugged, at peace with the notion, basking amid the scenery. Once again an expanse of gently swaying reeds rolled to every horizon; only a lone stand of trees, the odd barn roof, the occasional boardwalk breaking its lush uniformity. Unlike Trevor, Gerry had vaguely green credentials. In his youth he'd been a biker – not some hard-ass Hell's Angel, but he'd ridden a hog, worn tasselled leathers and listened to metal. He'd also, or so he said, camped out a lot and smoked a ton of weed. That didn't perhaps qualify him as a paid-up tree-hugger, but it meant he was closer to nature than Trevor, whose teen years had been firmly suburban and middle-class. Alternatively, Gerry's tranquil mood might just mean that he was already drunk again. He too had stripped down to his shorts, and the hot sun was visibly reddening his big, hairy body, not to mention his face. It seemed highly unlikely he'd bothered to put any lotion on, but Trevor wasn't going to say anything – he was Gerry's mate, not his mother.

As it happened, they only had one lock-gate to negotiate, and this they managed with ease. Beyond that they were into the fens proper; in fact, according to Trevor's map, they were now on the legendary Wicken Fen, one of the largest and most picturesque in the whole of the UK – though the only initial difference this seemed to make was that suddenly there was less water traffic to be avoided. They hadn't seen a great deal the day before – surprising, given the time of year – but now it was astonishingly quiet; even the *whooping* and *whippering* of the fen-fowl, of which there'd been a preponderance at sunrise, seemed muted.

"This is as good as it gets," Gerry said, eyes closed.

"Telling me," Trevor replied. It was now mid-afternoon: on all sides lay a golden haze. The water rippled quietly past. The sun-burnished foliage was so still it resembled painted back-drops on a studio set. Occasional clusters of trees crowded onto the banks, paths winding away through them into green shadow. The sedate pace, the soothing motion of the craft, the heat soaking through them – and of course the beer – were combining to lull both men to sleep.

"Bloody hell!" Trevor suddenly said, eyes snapping open. "Hey, wake up, Dufus … you're the helmsman!"

Gerry snapped out of it as well. They were still mid-channel, chugging along in a safely straight line. Ducks skimmed by overhead, quacking.

They laughed, and cracked open more tins. "Where are we, anyway?" Gerry asked.

"Dunno." Trevor consulted the map again, but was enjoying the peace and ancientness of this place so much that it scarcely mattered. "How many turns have we made?"

Gerry shrugged. "Doesn't matter, does it? Probably come to another pub soon."

Trevor pursed his lips. "Not according to this. Look out for a windmill."

"A windmill?"

"Yeah. When we see that, we'll know where we are. There are as many hiking trails through Wicken Fen as there are waterways – we can't get lost for long."

Gerry pivoted round in his seat to scan the table-flat georama. "If it's anywhere in four or five miles we should be able to see it from here."

But no man-made structures came in sight. Even the occasional barns appeared to have vanished. Trevor put the map down and climbed onto the roof, to get a better view. They rounded another bend. Beyond it lay a kind of crossroads, channels leading off in various directions.

They each spotted the girls at the same time.

A small, grassy headland protruded from the left, and two shapely golden bodies were laid out on it. There was no doubt it was the same pair from *The Kingfisher*, even though they were face-down on blankets, their perfect peachy bottoms offered bare for the sun's kisses.

"Fuuuck me!" Gerry said slowly.

Even Trevor was briefly entranced; he stumbled down from the roof.

"Hey!" Gerry shouted. "Hey, girls!"

One of them, the blonde, glanced around from under her tumbling, tawny locks. She gave them a lazy wave as they cruised past.

"Get some clothes on, you saucy mares!" he laughed.

She made some comment to her friend, and a tinkle of laughter was heard.

"Fuck me," Gerry said again, as the channel curved and the heavenly forms passed from sight. "Stop this thing, I want to get off."

"If only we could," Trevor said, blowing fresh foam from a newly-opened tin, and he half-meant it. It had been a captivating sight, there was no point pretending otherwise.

"At least help me turn the bugger round!" Gerry leaned hard on the tiller. "Come on, Trev, this is the chance of a lifetime ..." The craft veered dangerously to the left.

"Gez ... what're you doing?"

"They're offering it, mate. You saw that as well as me. They want some company."

"Look, watch it, eh! You're going to run us aground!"

"Cut the engine or something."

"Gez, we can't just stop. This is a canal boat ... we need a proper mooring-point."

"Fucking bollocks!"

Trevor's good humour sagged as he saw how serious about

this Gerry was; the big galoot straightened the craft up again, but gazed backward along the lode, crestfallen as the prize fell further and further behind. "At least let's find some open space … we can pull a three-point turn."

"And like I say," Trevor replied tartly, "that'll run us aground."

Gerry rounded on him. "Anyone'd think you don't *want* to do this!"

"*I don't!* For Christ's sake, Gez, what about Carly and Josie?"

At first Gerry couldn't reply; he seemed to be struggling with some inner doubt. "A bit of harmless fun never hurt anyone," he finally said – he didn't look as if he believed that himself, but then he became excited and pointed left. "*There! Look!*"

A low section of brick embankment had emerged through the grass and sedge: maybe fifty yards in length, with occasional steel rings set into it.

"How convenient," Trevor said under his breath.

Gerry steered them shoreward eagerly. The quay was overhung by a canopy of willows. Behind those stood shadowy ranks of rowan and beech, gnats swarming in the sunlight shafting between them. They'd already followed the channel round in a near semi-circle, so, by Trevor's reckoning, the two girls were somewhere on the other side of the small wood – maybe fifty or so yards away, due southeast. Yet something about this place – and he couldn't quite pin it down – seemed wrong. The profusion of pondweed and marsh lilies, which he suddenly noticed half-choking this section of waterway, suggested that it wasn't used very often.

He scrutinised the map. "You know, Gez, there are no moorings at this point." Something scraped their underside as they approached the quay. He glanced again into the water. Thick reeds were trailing alongside the hull. "There aren't even any turns or side-channels, according to this map. That means we aren't on a public waterway and we shouldn't be here – probably because it isn't safe."

Gerry ignored him. He turned the key in the ignition, cutting the engine, and jumped ashore with the fore rope in hand. "Are you going to help, or what?"

Reluctantly, Trevor followed him onto the quay, taking charge of the central rope. "You realise this is, like … the worst plan ever. We came out here to relax, sail from pub to pub, have a few beers … not get into mischief."

"Listen to you," Gerry chuckled as he walked past. "*Mischief?*"

"What's wrong with just taking a boat ride?"

"It's a drag, that's what's wrong with it."

"It was *your* idea coming out here."

"That was before we got a better offer," Gerry said, tying them up at the rear as well.

"We haven't had an offer," Trevor protested. "Why would girls like that fancy us?"

"Dunno." Satisfied the craft was secure, Gerry climbed back on board, promptly reappearing with a fresh white t-shirt and a six-pack of beer from the cooler. "Let's ask 'em." He made to waltz off through the wood, but Trevor grabbed his wrist.

"Gez, wait a minute ... hey, just wait. Think about Carly."

"Do I have to?"

"Christ, mate ... this isn't funny!"

"Neither is getting old and what was that word, *staid.*" Gerry grabbed Trevor's wrist in return; his grip was tense and damp with sweat. "Look Trev, it's just a laugh, OK. And that's what we're out here for, isn't it? To have some fun, some R and R ... nothing heavy, no strings. What Carly and Josie don't know about will never hurt them."

He grinned feverishly as he said all this – as if it was exclusively about gratification, as if there was no moral issue at all. Trevor, who'd assumed all the lusty talk in *The Kingfisher* had been just that, talk, was genuinely amazed. Gerry might be the more bohemian of the two of them, he might be the one with the slightly more chequered past, but he was still a respectable married man these days, who ran his own business. Okay, he liked a few bevies, he told blue jokes and had a stash of sleazy porn on his hard-drive, but that didn't make him unusual. He'd never done anything as reckless and, frankly, ridiculous as this before. Of course, it wasn't as if there hadn't been signs that something like this might have been on the way.

"Mate ... you've got to get a rein on this," Trevor said slowly. "I mean seriously, you've got to grow up."

Gerry's impish grin faded. "And you've got to get yourself a new pair of slippers and a cardigan."

Trevor shook his head. "Okay ... fine, I'm boring, I'm unadventurous. But I'm also happily married and I don't want to jeopardise it all for two marsh floozies."

"Marsh floozies?" Gerry chuckled again. He was still trying to make light of what he was doing here, most likely because somewhere inside he was feeling a little guilty. "You make 'em sound like flowers."

"Yeah … well go and pluck them!" Trevor stepped backward. "But you're on your own."

Gerry shrugged. "Suits me." He turned and headed for the trees, stopping once to look back, his expression determinedly unconcerned. "I'd say don't wait up for me, but I suppose you've no choice."

"Hah! Don't count on that."

Gerry muttered something under his breath and continued into the wood, pulling on his t-shirt after first using it to waft at the gnats. Trevor wondered if he knew how ludicrous he looked in those tennis shorts, his big frame sagging down over the waistband. For all his tattoos and his gym work, Gerry was a still a middle-aged man with short, fat legs and an overly burly torso. He walked in the clumsy, plodding fashion of an ape pretending to be human. Those two nymphs would struggle not to laugh when he sat down and introduced himself.

"Hi, I'm Gerry Axewood from London. This is my mate, Trevor English … oh, he's not here. Well, never mind, he'll show his face when he stops being shy. So how do you like my beer-belly? …"

But in actual fact, none of this was very amusing. Trevor stood alone, perplexed at how quickly it had all happened. He gazed past the narrow-boat and across the water. Late afternoon sunlight flooded the dykes and reed-beds. The sky was still powder-blue, but the trees to his rear cast ever-longer shadows, reminding him that the day was waning. He didn't know how long he was expected to wait here, but they couldn't dally indefinitely. The boat-trip only covered thirty-eight miles and was scheduled to last three days and two nights. As such, there was plenty of leeway for them to proceed at their own pace, but they were still expected to book the boat in at the marina on the final day.

He wandered aimlessly along the bank, kicking through patches of bogbean and marsh marigolds, increasingly frustrated with himself that he hadn't been tougher – that he hadn't refused point-blank to stop here, that he hadn't insisted they keep moving. The more he thought about it, the more it struck him that it wasn't just a moral issue. They had to find their way through Wicken Fen before they could resume the trip. It covered at least two-thousand acres, and they didn't even know whereabouts on it they currently were. That said – he glanced at his watch. It wasn't yet six o'clock and wouldn't be getting dark for another two hours. He supposed there was no need to panic just yet.

He descended through a muddy hollow and rounded the exposed roots of an ancient, twisted willow, the multiple fingers of which trailed far out into the water, finally entering a narrow inlet – where he halted. At the opposite end of the inlet was the blue and white river-cruiser he'd seen at *The Kingfisher*. It wasn't moored or anchored – it appeared to be banked up amid a jungle of marsh-fern. Trevor peered at it, wondering what it was about the craft that now seemed odd. He advanced along the water-line, the ground squelching beneath his sneakers. The boat was tilted steeply to aft and starboard, as though it had run ashore. Had the two girls had some kind of accident? Only when he was very close did he realise that if they had, it could not have been in the recent past.

The boat was a derelict: rusted all over and crabbed with moss, its hull bashed and scraped, in some parts fissured clean through. Its upper woodwork had mildewed and rotted; all paint had flaked away. The glass panelling around the cockpit was grimy and broken. Marsh vegetation inundated the interior. And yet Trevor knew that this was the same boat he had seen at *The Kingfisher*. He didn't think it was; he *knew* it. Somehow or other this decayed relic, this gutted shell …

At once, the surrounding wetland seemed strangely still. All bird and insect life had hushed, as though anticipating an imminent dramatic event.

Trevor began to retreat, his eyes still riveted on the wreck. At twenty yards, he turned and walked swiftly back the way he had come, his sweat-damp hair prickling. He didn't know what this meant, if it meant anything at all. He tried to tell himself he was mistaken, but again he *knew* that wasn't the case. Some coincidences were just too great. When he reached *The Sunny Dawn*, his heart sank to find that Gerry was not already there, even though he hadn't really expected him to be. Several minutes passed as Trevor gazed into the wood. Bright sunlight still speared through it, now latticed with early-evening shadows. There was no movement in there.

Eventually, reluctantly, he strode forward. He imagined Gerry on the other side, settled down on the small headland with the two girls – they must have welcomed him by now, else even as proud a guy as Gerry would have returned with tail between legs. Trevor pictured the scene: Gerry, all fat and sunburned, grinning like the cat who'd got the cream as the two minxes, shamelessly naked, shared their wine and cheese with him.

"If only Carly could see me now?" he'd say, trying to play down his Cockney accent. "Carly? … she's my wife. Yes, merely my wife …" He'd laugh. "That's so correct, *merely* my wife."

Carly and Josie were merely their wives, Trevor thought, baffled by the imagined conversation. Mere wives, that was all.

Mere-wives.

Had he heard that curious phrase before? He didn't know, but it sent a shudder through him. The trunks ahead opened, and he saw thick ranks of sedge, though a path looked to have been beaten through these, beyond which the waterway sparkled. This had to be the headland. It was strange; he'd have thought to hear their conversation by now – their *real* conversation. But there was no sound of voices.

He emerged into sunlight, proceeding warily. The sedge was dense, at this time of year chest-high and emerald green, filled with the radiant purples and yellows of orchid, iris and marsh pea. Crickets and swallowtails darted back and forth through it. But Trevor saw none of this. When he stepped out onto the open headland, he was tense, nervous. He truthfully did not know what to expect, but even catching Gerry in the act of having sex with the two girls would have been a relief.

There was nobody there. Nobody at all.

He ambled forward, bewildered.

The headland, if such a word applied – it was really little more than a spur of dry ground in the waterway's elbow – was about twenty feet by thirty, the size of the average suburban lawn, and was strewn with old rushes, which had dried out and been flattened as if someone had indeed been lying on them. He glanced around – and spotted Gerry's six-pack of beer, or at least the six tins, all lying separate from each other, none of them opened.

A splash caught his attention. He glanced at the waterway:

large, concentric ripples spread across the otherwise motionless surface. A frog possibly? An otter? There'd be nothing unusual about that. But now Trevor noticed something else: a timber post, leaning sideways but jutting upward from the water at roughly mid-channel, splintered and jagged at its tip, with a rusty chain wound around it. The remnant of an old sign or tethering-pole, he surmised; a mile-marker or something. Either way, it clearly represented a dangerous obstruction, and yet they had sailed blithely past it. Now that he looked more carefully, he spied other potential hazards: an angled edge of rusted metal some three feet from shore. About the same distance from the opposing bank, the spiky branches of a lighting-struck bough protruding through the weed-choked surface.

How had they managed to navigate through all that unscathed? The luck of the drunken sailor? More to the point, this stretch of water was evidently not safe for recreational boating, so how had they blundered into it in the first place? Surely, in a well-managed nature reserve like this, all side-channels deemed unsafe would have been blocked off? In fact, Trevor knew that they were. He'd seen buoys floating at waterway entrances, chain-linked fences looping across them.

Such preventative fixtures could easily be removed, of course.

Another splash drew his interest to the far shore, where he fancied there was a brief flurry among the reeds, as if something had scuttled out of the water and gone quickly to ground. He stared hard, trying to penetrate the lush tangle with his eyes alone and having no success – but now feeling certain that another pair of eyes was staring back at him.

The obvious thing to do was call over there, to see if it was Gerry.

But Trevor did no such thing. Instead, he backed away. The sun was still some distance from setting, but it was now far behind him and the trees' lengthening shadows had reached the headland. The channel lay motionless again, pitch-dark.

He turned and headed back along the path. He'd wait on the narrow-boat. Lock himself in, if necessary – though why he felt the need for that, he couldn't really say. He was half way through the sedge when he heard a loud splashing somewhere behind. That started him running. A voice in his head asked if he shouldn't go back there, find out if it was Gerry; ask him what he was playing at. But another voice, a slightly crazier one, told him that he already knew where Gerry was – that he'd already seen him. Gerry had been wearing a white t-shirt that day, but it would be a different colour now.

Inside the wood, it was darker and cooler than earlier. Gnats and midges still flitted back and forth. He slapped at them as he stumbled along, sweat stinging his brow and eyes. He had a suspicion that someone was following him, but glanced back and saw no-one: just dark trunks and the odd beam of sunlight. He wondered with mild panic how long it would take him to untie the narrow-boat.

But why untie? Wasn't he going to be waiting for Gerry?

He didn't bother answering the question as *The Sunny Dawn* came into view.

His hands were greasy and shaking, and he fumbled as he tried to untie the aft rope.

"Shit!" he hissed, acutely aware of the silent woodland to his back. But this was bloody ridiculous. He didn't really know why he was doing it – the rope came loose and he lurched along the quay to the middle one – the last thing he wanted was to leave his best friend alone out here. But then it wouldn't be *so* outrageous. The fens weren't a total wilderness; they were dotted all over with visitor centres, ranger stations, bird-watcher hides. It wouldn't be difficult to get help and advice. People must get lost out here on their own all the time, especially in the dark. Surely there'd be protocols for such eventualities? And of course Gerry wasn't really out here on his own, was he – though that thought was no consolation.

The middle rope had been knotted tightly around its steel ring. Again, Trevor had difficulty working it loose. Again, he swore under his breath. Those two girls, whoever they were – how peculiar was it that neither he nor Gerry had so much as glimpsed their faces? It now seemed very intentional how, in the pub yesterday, the girls had been standing with their backs so firmly turned. He glanced up and over his shoulder.

Had a twig snapped in the wood? Had a leaf dropped?

All Trevor saw were the dim pillars of the trees and the even dimmer dells in between. Only faint remnants of reddish sunlight were visible back there.

He hurried along to the third rope, this one about six yards forward of the craft. His urgency to get away from here was becoming all-consuming. How had they finished up in this remote spot? Wicken Fen was not gigantic. Yet he pondered the blissful hours of idle, drunken boating. How far from civilisation had they somehow managed to travel? There was another sound behind him – and this one was real, not imaginary: a rustling of foliage. Trevor loosened the third rope, and pushed the boat away from the brick embankment, jumping across the narrow gap and alighting on its forward deck. Only then did he glance back, but if he saw anything, it was deep, deep in the wood, and it could only have been a heavy wad of undergrowth moving slightly in a breeze which for some reason he couldn't feel.

As he blundered through the salon and the galley, another thought came to mind. Suppose Gerry had got back here ahead of him? Suppose he was in bed right now with one of his conquests, or maybe both?

And they'd been in such a rush to get it on that he'd left his beers behind?

Trevor didn't think so. It was a near-comical image, like something from a 'Carry On' movie: middle-aged Gerry skipping through the woods, an eager dolly-bird on either arm. He didn't even bother to glance into the empty cabins as he made his way aft to the ignition-drive. The vessel was already drifting into mid-stream. He could feel it swaying. He also heard a scratching sound – as if something was bouncing along the underside of the hull. Tufts of pondweed, he thought; more loose branches. And then, as he climbed out onto the rear deck and turned the ignition key, he remembered the larger obstacles with which this stretch of waterway was cluttered. The scratching beneath his feet intensified; became a shrill squeal of twisting timber and tearing fibreglass, which seemed to run the entire length of the craft. *The Sunny Dawn* had lurched forward slightly when the engine churned to life, but still wasn't moving with any real velocity. Nevertheless, she now jerked to a halt, and Trevor was propelled violently down through the rear doors into the passage, catching his right temple on the steel lock en route.

The glancing impact was like a hammer-blow.

He wasn't exactly knocked unconscious, but for the next few moments was slumped on his hands and knees, dazed, trying to blink a hot stickiness from his right eye, and hallucinating that the floor was slowly tilting beneath him – though very soon it became apparent that this was no hallucination.

The floor angled upward so much that Trevor found himself sliding forward on the palms of his hands, and then tumbling, falling head-over-heels down the passage, past the cabins and into the galley, where he plunged face-first into the brackish water already swamping the cramped interior.

Spluttering and gagging, he re-surfaced and tottered to his feet. It was only thigh-deep, but it stank foully – not, as he'd expected, of mud and rotted verdure; but of petrol.

This revelation was shocking enough, but it was the craft tilting even further, listing sharply downward at the front, that had Trevor staggering again. The dark water continued to gurgle up around him, even as he struggled to balance. It was already at waist-depth, the light through the dusty portholes showing oily colours streaked in shifting patterns across its surface. Whatever object had torn through the hull had pierced the fuel-tanks. The stench was thickening, making it difficult to breathe. Trevor groped groggily around, wondering how he had made such an error, what this would cost – the enormity of his peril still not striking him.

"Gotta … gotta get out," he finally realised, the fumes dizzying his senses. Yes, getting out was all that mattered. If he could manage that, he was safe. He could make it to shore easily enough; he was a strong swimmer. But then he'd be out on the fens alone with darkness falling, wet and injured.

"The emergency kit!" he said aloud. It was here, in the galley – somewhere.

He plunged back beneath the acrid surface, opening one foot-locker after another, pulling out crockery and other useless junk – only to remember that the kit was actually in one of the higher storage units. Which meant it would still be dry. He gasped as he resurfaced, reaching up to the ceiling rack and immediately finding what he sought: a green zip-lock bag. He dragged it down, clutching it in both arms.

The water was still only waist-deep; whatever had holed the craft from beneath had now pinioned it in place – it wasn't sinking any further, so time was on his side. He still had to fight his way up the slanted galley, no easy task with its carpet tiles coated in pond-slime. But he made it. In front of him lay the cabin passage;

that section of the boat was dry but tilted so precariously that he had to scramble all the harder. Directly ahead, faded sunlight filtering down the rear stair filled him with hope.

Only as he reached it, did a shadow block out the orange glow. Trevor looked up, mouth agape. His blood-streaked face blanched with shock.

The female form coming down the stair was an hourglass silhouette on the setting sun. He glimpsed shimmering brown tresses, droplets of water gleaming on the most beautiful body he had ever seen – perfectly shaped and curved, bronzed by more suns than any human had a right to experience.

His rubber soles gave way beneath him as he retreated, and he slid back down the passage, grabbing out with his right hand but unable to stop himself floundering backward into the flooded galley, where the air was now almost unbreathable.

He coughed and retched, plunging again to his midriff, but the intruder followed him without difficulty, sliding silkily down into waters now swirling with iridescent colour and reflecting in rainbow hues on the walls and ceiling.

"I ... I don't want this," Trevor stammered. "I never wanted this."

"You came here of your own free will," she said, in a voice achingly familiar.

"Not for *this*."

"Nevertheless, you came. What is a woman to assume?"

"I'd die before I'd betray my wife."

"A brave threat ... but why go to such a length?"

There was only a yard between them, and he saw her face clearly for the first time. Such beauty would have brought a lump to his throat had it not already been filled with phlegm. And yet – those hazel eyes, those delicate cheekbones, that pert, dimpled chin ...

"You're not my Josie," he blurted.

"True ... was she ever this lovely?"

"Yes!" Trevor shouted, rage growing with his despair. "But even if she never was, that doesn't matter. I've seen what you do."

"Not all outcomes are the same." She reached a gentle, sun-browned hand towards him.

"I don't want you!" He retreated again. "Stay back."

"I can be all that Josie was and so much more."

"Never."

"Or I can be significantly less." Her eyes sank and darkened, her flesh drooped. The golden tan faded to a greenish tinge.

"And maybe even less than that!" Trevor shrieked, tossing the emergency kit aside and pointing the flare-pistol at her chest. "Your final warning!"

Snarling and slobbering, the fungoid horror advanced, its mottled tendrils flailing.

Trevor sobbed as he squeezed the trigger.

The flame took them.

CROCODILE AND ERLKING

Elizabeth Counihan

Two by two, bright coloured in their visibility jackets, a crocodile of eight-year-olds crossed the road beside the school and followed Mrs Styles across the road and down the track that lead to the park. Because the class contained an uneven number of kids Mrs Styles had put Kai Jones alone and last. He might be small for his age but he was a quiet, sensible boy - unlike Henry Jacobson.

Mrs Styles grabbed Henry's gloved hand as he raised it to throw something along the column.

"Oh Miss, that's my best conker. It's a niner!"

"Now you know they're not allowed any more, Henry - too dangerous! You can have it back after school." She put the wizened conker in her pocket.

They reached the park. Broomstick trees brushed at the cold January mist. The sun was a bright haze low in the sky. A few dead leaves left over from autumn stirred at their feet. Seagulls squawked and ruffled their feathers against the cold.

The front of the crocodile reached the football field, and let loose from their disciplined columns, the children ran and tumbled and wrestled like creatures just released from Noah's Ark.

Kai, still following, looked behind him uneasily then put his hood over his head.

"Hey, Kai, are you all right?" It was Miss Dene, the teaching assistant. He liked her. She was kind. Should he say something? He decided yes.

"There's a nasty man behind me."

Miss Dene hurried back the way they had come and peered into the bushes.

"What did you see, Kai?"

"Look, he's there Miss! He's wearing a crown!"

"Oh, I see what you mean, Kai. But it's just an old bush. The fog makes it look funny."

"But…"

"We're nearly there, Kai. Come on - race you to the field!"

She let him win and he knew it. Usually when the class came on their weekly visit to the park Kai preferred to wander around the edge of the field just looking at things or talking to his best friend Elliot. Today he dashed into the middle and played football with unusual enthusiasm.

On the way back Mrs Styles put him in the middle of the column with Elliot.

"Has the nasty man gone now?" she asked. Kai nodded. It was true; the crowned figure had disappeared.

As they walked across the school playground he heard Mrs Styles say to her assistant, "All this talk about paedophiles. It's very frightening for vulnerable children." Kai wondered what "vulnerable" meant. I can't be vulnerable, he reasoned, because I'm not frightened, not of that twiggy king. He was just fog anyway. Miss Dene said.

"Look Mormor, that's him!" He pulled the big picture book closer.

"Who is that, Kai?" His mother wiped her hands and came over to look.

"Now, Kai, you really shouldn't put your father's books on the kitchen table." She grabbed a cloth and wiped a spot of ketchup off the page.

"If you look at these pictures it is not a surprise you are having some bad dreams. This is a book for adults, not suitable for a small boy."

"But it's fairy tales."

"No, no Kai. These are scary Danish legends - not for little boys." She lapsed into her native tongue which he understood well.

"It's Da's book, to help him with his Danish. I'm not surprised you woke up screaming last night if you will look at pictures like that!"

"But I only just saw it," Kai answered her in Danish. "He's the nasty king I dreamed of last night."

"The one who wanted you to eat some chocolate? Now, now Kai, you must have seen this picture before. Maybe you forgot."

But Kai knew he had not forgotten. It was the person he had seen in the park and dreamed of last night.

The picture, old-fashioned in black and white, showed a man riding through a dark forest. One hand guided the horse, the other held a small child wrapped in his cloak. Their path, through trees bent by an unseen wind, was lit by a crooked moon. The child was looking back at a cloaked figure who beckoned him with twig-like fingers. Kai found his own face adopting the terrified expression of the little boy in the picture. The dark figure wore a crown. Was he holding chocolate out to the boy?

He asked, "Who is he?"

His mother scanned the Danish text. "It says here he is the *ellerkonge*. That means Elf King in English I think. Or Erlking maybe." She looked closely at her son's face.

"No, I am not going to read you the story. It's just a silly old legend and will only give you more nightmares."

"But…"

He stopped. Mormor never changed her mind. Instead he went upstairs to the computer and googled Elf King. After several misspellings and blind alleys he found a poem.

"Who rides so late through night so wild?
It is a father with his child.
He has the boy held in his arm.
He keeps him safe, he keeps him warm."

Kai read it through at an eight-year-old's pace right through to the terrible ending.

He read it again.

The strange use of English and some of the words defeated him but he understood the gist.

Even safe in your father's arms the Erlking would get you.

When Thursday came round again Kai said he felt ill and couldn't go to school. Da was concerned.

"Thought it was your best day, son. Running around in the park?"

"I've got a headache. I feel very ill." He shut his eyes. His mother put a hand to his forehead. She shook her head. "No fever."

"It's not like Kai to fake it. What's up son?" his father asked.

"You're worried about something, Kai," said his mother. "Tell us what's wrong or we can't fix it."

Kai took a deep breath and told them about the man in the park, the bad dream, the picture book. He thought they would laugh but they didn't. Dad assured him that the Erlking was just a bogeyman story. Mormor took action. She walked him to school herself and spoke to Mrs. Styles.

He thought everything would be all right.

But it wasn't.

The crocodile of eight-year-olds walked to the park.

Wispy white clouds fled across a blue sky. The park trees waved their heads in the breeze; snowdrops nodded at their feet. Pigeons strutted about on the pathways making chuckling noises in the hope of breadcrumbs.

Miss Dene held Kai's hand at the back of the column. As they passed the little stream on their way to the field she turned to him.

"Look, Kai, there's a crow on that willow tree. Do you think he's looking for a girlfriend?"

Kai shook his head. His heart thudded. A figure cloaked in bare willow branches smiled at him from high in the tree. The crow perched on his head like a black crown. The winter sun, caught behind the branches, shone through his eyes.

"Come with me," murmured a voice. *"We can play football all day long."*

"I hate football," said Kai.

"Oh, that's a pity Kai. You're good at it, you know," said Miss Dene. "But never mind, you can play with Elliot like you usually do."

He and Elliot wandered round the edge of the field. Elliot wanted to float dead leaves in the water but Kai wouldn't go near the stream and the willow.

"Elliot, do you think people who see things are mad?"

"You mean like, crazy?" Elliot said. Kai nodded.

Elliot dropped his voice. "I'll tell you a secret. I saw a Alien once!"

"Yeah? Well *I* can see a bad man in that tree." He tried to point the willow man out to his friend but the wind had blown him into rustling branches and the crow had flapped away. "He *was* there. Elliot, he wants to *get* me."

"Why?" said Elliot.

"I don't know. He's called the Erlking. I think it's what he does."

"Is he a invisible pedo?"

"I think so," Kai said.

"In the story the Erlking wins and the kid dies!"

Mormor frowned. "How do you know the story? I told you not to look at that book any more."

Da said, "It's great you've got such an imagination, Kai. But you mustn't let it run away with you. Freya, did you have a word with the teacher?"

She nodded. "He was with the assistant all the way to the park. There weren't any men hanging about; she told me."

"That's because she couldn't see him!" Kai was nearly crying. His parents exchanged glances. Mormor made him a special hot chocolate with marsh mallows and Da read to him until he fell asleep.

Again Thursday crept nearer. Kai surreptitiously re-read the story online. *Will he get me today?* he thought as Da took him to school. During the morning he kept feeling his heart to make sure it was still beating. He had to do it when Mrs. Styles wasn't looking. Da had had a long talk with her before school started and she was keeping an eye on him.

When the time came his teacher took him firmly by the hand.

"You can be column leader today Kai," she said. "If you see anything you don't like just tell me, OK?"

Kai grasped at a thin wisp of hope. *He offers the boy another present this time. He kills him the time after. I've got one more week.* He nodded dumbly.

The crocodile wound towards the park, guided carefully across the main road, where a trickle of water still ran in the gutters from last night's rain. The air was clean and fresh and a bright sun bounced along the treetops. When they reached the park newly opened daffodils brushed their ankles with rain drops.

"It's quite warm for February," said Mrs. Styles. "That pretty blossom is called blackthorn. It's not usually out so early." She sighed. The children were not paying attention to her efforts to teach them about the local ecology. She glanced around for something more attractive.

"Look at the squirrels, everyone. Do you know, if its cold enough they go to sleep in the winter? Who can remember what squirrels eat? Sophie?"

Sophie waved a bag of peanuts and chased after the squirrels, followed by Elliot.

"Go on, Kai, don't you want to feed the squirrels? You ought to run about a bit. Your hand is very cold. Didn't you bring your gloves?"

Kai could see the squirrels. They were running up and down a big grey tree. A tall man leaned against the tree, blending into it. He wore a grey cloak and a crown of dead leaves. The squirrels avoided him. As Kai watched the man reared upright and drifted away from the tree towards him.

"You can't get me this time!" Kai yelled. "Go away!" He snatched his hand free from the teacher's and shook his fist.

"Kai! What's got into you? I've never seen you like this!" Mrs. Styles tried to restrain him but he ran forward to confront his tormentor.

The man smiled and dead willow leaves fell from his mouth.

"Do you like games, dear child? I have the New 3DS."

Kai gasped. It was what he and Elliot wanted most in the world.

"You can play Mario and Pokemon forever with my other children."

The boy in the old picture wouldn't have known about modern games so the Erlking had promised that his daughters would sing and dance for him instead. It was the same thing all over again.

Kai screamed, "Leave me alone! I hate you! I won't come with you!"

Tears streamed down his face. He half-heard Mrs. Styles calling to Miss Dene to come and help her.

Background voices: "... some kind of seizure?"

"What's wrong with Kai, Miss?"

"Can you take over, Nicky? I must get him back to the

school."

"Miss, Miss, is he all right?"

Kai's eyes were fixed on the Erlking whose twiggy hand stretched to touch him. It was horribly real, greenish-brown with too many joints. There were hooked nails, translucent like cats' claws. He shrank back, still shouting his defiance. Just as the nail of one forefinger reached out to his chest it dissolved into drops of water as if melted by the sun. The rest of the figure shredded and fell away into leaves and twigs. Kai fainted.

Da, looking anxious, took him home and put him to bed. Mrs. Styles had said something about "counselling" and "psychologists" but Mormor took him to the doctor the next day who checked him over and said she would arrange some tests.

"Will they test my head?" Kai asked. "Have I got a brain tumour like Maria O'Dowd?"

The Doctor took him seriously. She said, "They will test your head and I don't think you have a brain tumour. I think you just have too much imagination."

Kai missed school for a week and that included Thursday. The Erlking did not appear at home but even so he felt miserable. Mormor and Da were very kind and concerned but he stopped telling them about the King. No one but himself could sense the malign presence of the "nasty man". He reasoned: *I know I haven't got too much imagination so either I've got a brain tumour or the King is real. Either way I'm dead.*

"Are you better?" Sophie asked. He was sitting next to her on his first day back at school. Elliot, sitting on his other side, said, "He wasn't there on Thursday." Before Kai could ask what he meant Miss Dene joined them. She hovered around their group all morning and Elliot wouldn't say anything more.

"How do you know he wasn't there on Thursday?" Kai demanded at break time.

"I think he was waiting for you to come back."

"Did you see him? Last time I mean?"

"The Invisible Pedo? Yeah, he looked really scary. I'm not surprised you passed out," Elliot answered matter-of-factly.

"I saw him too," said Sophie. "I threw pine cones at him.

Didn't you see?"

Kai explained that he hadn't been able to look at anything but the terrible King.

"Miss Dene thought I was throwing them at the squirrels but I never would - I think squirrels are cute," Sophie added.

Kai sat down suddenly. "Then I haven't got a brain tumour or imagination. The Erlking *is* real. I knew it." Then he remembered.

"He's going to kill me on Thursday."

"Kai," called the playground teacher, "get up from the ground, there's a good boy. You'll catch cold."

Kai googled "evil spirits" and "good luck charms" but didn't find anything useful. He wasn't too sure he had spelled "evil" correctly anyway. He certainly couldn't spell "paedophile". He was very quiet that evening and his parents exchanged anxious glances.

But that night he had a good dream. He was in the park again but the Erlking was not there. Instead there was an old gentleman with a white moustache. He and Kai sat on the bench that overlooked the football field.

"You must put my walking stick here," said the old man pointing under the bench. In the way of dreams, Kai simply nodded and said, "I won't forget."

When he woke up he felt sure the old man's face was familiar. Was it his Granddad? Hadn't he seen a picture of him in Mormor's album?

At breakfast he asked Da if Granddad had a moustache and Da said he did.

"Did I ever meet him?" Kai asked and Da said that Granddad had seen him when he was very little. "But he died when you were two. He was much older than Granma, you see."

"Has Granma got his walking stick?"

"No, she gave it to me...but how did you know about it?"

Kai shrugged and said he must have seen a picture. It didn't take much persuasion to get his father to find the old stick.

When Kai saw it after school that day he looked at it with respect. It was a great, black knobby thing, more like a weapon than a walking stick.

"It's a real shillelagh," Da explained, "made of blackthorn. Granddad got it when he visited Ireland."

Kai borrowed it and pretended it was a sword, though he

wasn't really pretending. He wished he could take it to school but he knew that weapons weren't allowed.

It was Wednesday.

Sophie said, "We ought to phone the police. They arrest pedos."

Elliot said, "He's a invisible pedo, stupid. Police are grown-ups. They won't be able to see him. But Kai, I know what you can do against a *demon*. I asked my Auntie Sandra. She's a white witch."

Kai didn't show any surprise. Brighton was a city where lots of people followed unusual religions.

Elliot continued. "She says blackthorn and holly are good. And she told me some, like, spells you can do."

"Blackthorn's that white stuff Mrs Styles was on about," Sophie said. "It's the flowers that are white. The tree's black, I suppose."

"And conkers. We asked Henry Jacobson. He said conkers are good against anything."

Kai remembered Henry's habit of throwing them at smaller kids, including Kai. Well, a big bully like Henry might be useful sometimes.

And now he understood his dream.

Miss Dene, who was playground teacher, watched the huddle of children from year five. The huddle expanded into a circle. She was going to intervene as she saw Henry push Kai's friend Elliot.

"No," squeaked a little girl; was it Sophie? "You have to go the other way, Henry."

She saw Henry grin and shuffle along behind Elliot. It must be some new game they'd thought of, probably one of Kai's ideas. The poor little kid had too much imagination. What had he said to her last term - that he had a pet dog called Ruffles who was an alien pirate from the planet Jupiter? And that weird behaviour in the park...

The kids were holding hands and moving round in orderly fashion. Now they were chanting. She couldn't hear the words but the rhythm reminded her of an old skipping rhyme that had been popular at her school when she was a kid and that she hadn't heard for years.

Well, Kai looked happy enough today and anything that kept the Jacobson boy out of mischief was a plus.

"Perhaps he should see a psychologist? Mrs Styles seems to think so," Kai's father said.

"No," said his mother, "he looks at too much scary stuff on TV and the internet that's all. He is not sick in the head."

"Shall we keep him at home tomorrow, Freya? He's really worried about going to the park."

His wife shook her head. "We can't let this fear get the better of him."

"Well, I'll take him in the morning and I'm going to take my Da's stick to the park like he asked."

"It might get stolen," Freya said, frowning.

Her husband shrugged and said, "If Kai thinks it'll help him it's worth the risk."

She smiled and took his hand.

The crocodile was more like a snake.

The children insisted on walking one by one in spite of all Miss Dene's cajoling. As they crossed the road there was a rumble of thunder. Dark clouds scudded across the sky.

"Hurry along, children," called Mrs Styles, "it looks like rain so let's make the most of it before we have to go back." She ran to and fro along the line trying to concertina them into pairs but they just raised their hoods against the wind. Several of the boys were fingering conkers. She felt uneasy. The children were too quiet - alien almost.

Once in the park they all raced off as usual - but, no, not quite as usual. No one was playing football. Instead they were tearing twigs and branches from the trees.

"No, children, stop that at once! It's vandalism." She and Nicky Dene ran after individuals but each child was acting independently.

Left to himself, Kai ran across the field to the park bench and drew out the blackthorn stick from where his father had hidden it. He thought his heart would explode.

He ran back to the middle of the football field, his eyes darting anxiously. A small black cloud paused above him, stationary while all the others blew past.

He knew what that cloud was.

The air grew cold. He heard a dog barking somewhere.

The cloud descended slowly and little flakes of snow fell onto Kai's face and into his eyes. His teeth chattered but he jumped back and held the thorny stick in front of him. The grass turned white where the cloud touched it.

Beautiful boy. I must have you. If you will not come with me then I must take you unwilling.

A dark tendril grew out from the grey shape before him and extended towards his heart.

"There he is!" a voice called.

"Quick, into the circle." That was Sophie.

"Dirty pedo!" Henry for sure

"*This* way. We got to go clockwise." That was Elliot.

The teachers watched in astonishment as the entire class circled Kai who stood with raised cudgel. His face was a deathly white and snow was falling all about him. A mist formed about his feet.

Mrs Styles darted forward.

"Wait!" said her assistant.

Each child held a branch of blackthorn or holly. They walked slowly around Kai. They were chanting.

"Pedo, pedo, sitting on a rainbow

Eating mouldy bread.

Along came a fly

Hit him in the eye

And the pedo dropped down dead!"

"What's that?" Mrs Styles peered into the mist rising at the centre of the circle. Was there a man's figure there?

"Dirty pedo go away.

Don't come back any day.

We don't want to come and play."

Henry and his friends hurled conkers into the centre. The creature raised dirty hands to fend off the blows.

All around the park seagulls and pigeons took to the air in fright, dogs barked from every direction. Somewhere a cat yowled.

"My God," said Mrs Styles, "there really is a man there! We'd better get the police."

Nicky Dene was already talking into her mobile phone. Mrs

Elizabeth Counihan

Styles ran forward and dragged Kai out of the way.

"It's all right, Kai. No one is going to hurt you!" she soothed.

But Kai looked at her, smiling, the light of triumph in his eyes.

Perhaps Their Parents Were at Fault

Martina Bellovičová

Upon the sunset of humanity, even the pulse of time was fading. The darkness was pregnant with silence, interrupted only by the unobtrusive whispering of waves. As far as the eye could see, there was only the endless stretch of murky waters. Like a fly resting on a flowing summer dress, a strange kind of raft occupied by a disparate two-man crew rocked upon the waves. A man and a little girl, who were not quite the last remainders of the human race, but might as well have been.

The young man, clad in a soaked black tail-coat, absentmindedly reached out with his right hand into nothing. "Can I have a glass of sherry, darling? I feel slight wistfulness and a lingering fear of manic-depressive symptoms of the absolute." His evenly shaped, diamond ring sparkled in the half light. A sickly looking individual with a lanky body, drawn features and limply hanging hair, he might have ranked anywhere between 21 and 30 on the scale of youth and sky-high on the scale of riches.

The girl pursed her lips in anger. "We haven't got any sherry. We don't even have any glasses. We haven't got anything! You seem to have missed it, but you've just saved yourself from drowning. You're sitting on a piece of a sunken ship and floating into open ocean!"

She was an unassuming, average, brown-haired child, dressed in a school uniform, but there was a hardness in her eyes found only in those who'd had to grow up fast. The young man wasn't paying any real attention to her, and she couldn't decide whether he was actually aware of her presence, or caught in his own utopian visions, populated by servants who never talked back to him and call-girls in skimpy dresses.

"Oh, no. I negate this option! Is there any other constant available?"

"What are you babbling about? I guess that in your mind, you are still lazing around on board, listening to classical music, playing chess and philosophising. Well, I have news for you: it's all gone!"

"Are you trying to tell me that in the present moment my existence is only a delusion of the eidolon?"

Alright then. She would give up on him. The girl went to sit as far from the man as possible, on the very edge of their piece of derelict – an imposing wedge of the "Astronomy Salon" designed in a flamboyant mix of the neo-neo-Victorian and deep-space style. Only a portion of the luxurious room was left, no more than five square metres of ebony floor, a chroniton clock (still working), a computerised card table, strewn with moist cards, a neo-neo-Victorian gold candleholder and a plush armchair, currently occupied by the insufferable young man. They couldn't expect a rescue party; everyone was too busy rescuing themselves. Thankfully, she could wait. At the moment, time was the only commodity of which she had an unlimited amount.

Suddenly a startling electronic "click" roused her from her thoughts. Of course; the chroniton clock served also as a data bank of all news reports that had ever been broadcast on the Global Network of the United Earth. Some of its controls must have been damaged during the disaster, and now it was going to grace them randomly by reciting something irrelevant. She didn't believe they could be as lucky as to receive an actual, live broadcast. The network had been down for days. And sure enough, the stoic neutral voice announced:

"*A 5-year-old boy was gravely injured when the hovercraft he was riding in crashed during a hail storm, in what is considered to be the biggest hovercraft chain accident in history. His left arm and right leg were fractured. Furthermore, he sustained other injuries, including three broken ribs, a bruised liver and a ruptured spleen. He also suffered the internal fracture of his skull from his spine. The unfortunate boy, Brandon Phelps, is currently in the care of the best surgeons of New New York.*"

"Fascinating," the young man commented in a tone that

implied he found great comfort in the misfortune of others.

The girl would bet that he'd liked to burn ants to ashes with a magnifying glass when he was a boy. She slipped out of her flats and dipped her ankles into the freezing ocean water. There were no lights on the horizon, no passing planes overhead. The endless, ink-blue surface was cloaked by a slightly cold fog, and the semi-darkness of late sunset framed the endless immeasurability of emptiness. Anywhere she looked – nothing, only the massive bluish-black body of their enemy: the ocean that had crushed their ship and was slowly swallowing the world, town by town, continent by continent. The insatiable waters had washed away all the blood that might have been shed in the accident; the only thing left behind was a lingering aftertaste, which reminded her of the stickiness of the cotton candy that had glued her small, hard fingers to her grandfather's calloused hand on their way home from the amusement park.

He worked as a crew member on a space ship, but she always thought he looked more like a sea wolf, a pirate, with his untamed beard and the sparkle of wit in his sea-blue eyes. His wife had a custom of chastising him for spending so much time with his granddaughter. She seemed to have an endless list of hurtful things to say always at the ready, such as "why do you keep reading to it, when it can just download everything" or "I don't understand this hobby of yours", and "I refuse to babysit it. Next time your daughter wants to go dancing, she can just let it sit in the closet. She doesn't have to bring it here". But the old space wolf always ignored her protests and kept rocking the girl on his knees, humming a restless, darkly-alluring melody of faraway places.

"I'm starting to feel somewhat cold," said the young man. "I would like to return to my cabin in order to taste the abstract principle of warmth."

The girl bit her lip so hard that it would have started bleeding, were she like him. The fop had a unique way of getting on her nerves, even when he wasn't offering any of his crazy insights. He was tall, lanky and kind of sleazy, with long, dangly earrings adorning both ears. Whenever she looked at him, an image of a creepy Christmas tree popped up in her mind.

"Well? How can I get to the delightfully bizarre staircase leading to the upper floor?"

"Go straight, sir. You can't miss it."

He thanked her and started walking across the derelict. After a few metres, he stopped in his tracks. Perhaps he had finally realised the nature of the situation they were in. "Oh."

The girl laughed, and even the delusional, decorative young man seemed to notice the mockery seeping through that little sound.

"This is tragic! Monstrous! Fiasco! Where is my phenomenal cabin with the artificial forest and holograms of Hawaiian dancers?" During this tirade, his voice would occasionally break and spiral a few octaves higher.

The girl thought that if there was anyone anywhere near, they'd had to have heard him. At least he wasn't *completely* good for nothing. She lay down on the boards with a deep sigh, observing the man's upside down image. It did nothing to improve his appearance. His skin had a pearly white sheen and seem to glimmer in the darkness; his bulging eyes shivered nervously in their sockets. Perhaps it was the stress caused by becoming aware of their situation, or else he had been injured during the disaster – she wasn't sure. But in any case, blood was starting to drip out of his nose, staining his satin shirt and the expensive tail coat. Drip. Drip. Drip. Splash.

She closed her eyes in exasperation. Would they ever be rescued? Would she be forced to spend the rest of eternity floating around with this human, slowly succumbing to madness due to his extensive, bizarre choice of words, until she started using newly coined phrases such as "participating nothingness" and "vertical vacuum" herself?

Click. *The police are investigating a reported theft of the newest model of SONY's high-intelligence personal android, which has been stolen directly from company's main office. Dr. Ooshi Kagawa, the principal developer of this unique line, is under the opinion that the unit, practically unrecognisable from a human, could have left the building of its own volition. This opens the old debate of whether self-aware androids can be considered an intelligent life form. Ing. Michael Pulaski, who was the last person to see the android, is of a different opinion. He believes that the unit seemed to "enjoy his life" in the company and that corporate rivalry was most likely behind the theft. Mr. Pulaski believes the perpetrator of the crime will use the android as a prototype and begin manufacturing his own line to sell on the black market.*

"Amazing," the man said, with an underlying tone of irony. "A petty thief, a whole line of intelligent androids, and I do not even have anyone to bring me a glass of sherry!"

She didn't consider his words worthy of an answer. Her ankles had been mostly immobilised by the cold water, so she pulled her feet back up and dried them on the damp Persian rug beneath the young man's chair. Meanwhile, the man had taken off his right shoe, pulled off his designer sock and was now using it to dag at his bleeding nose, producing unpleasant sounds somewhere between wheezing and bubbling. She detected tears in his eyes.

"I am very nervous!" he sobbed. "My sensitive nature bears tragedies of this kind with utmost difficulty!"

She disliked the sight of him crying with even more passion than she disliked him in general.

"Alone! In the middle of the ocean! The infinity of emptiness will senselessly apply itself on our credibility!" His nervously-flicking eyes kept shedding crocodile tears, soaking the reddened sock. "I am a writer! A renowned author! Not a cynical autocrat or an irrelevant landlord! An intellectual, not an instrumentalist! I am not manually skilled. I have a low stress resistance and the immediate proximity of the ocean renders me incompetent."

The girl rolled her eyes, wishing he would shut up. She was trying to do something practical, like light the candles protruding from the massive golden arms of the candleholder; the fop was shattering her concentration into shards. Or maybe it was the cold? She functioned best in temperatures between -10 and + 30 C. The sun had disappeared behind the horizon and the air had become significantly colder. Slowly, stealthily, fog spilled into the night and only the unfeeling, glistening eyes of hungry fish and other, unspoken beings dotted the now waveless surface.

Finally, she managed to produce a single, shivering flame, which lit the table and cast a foreboding shadow on the young man's armchair. He'd never offered her his place so she could sit down, even though he'd vacated his warm spot minutes ago; she settled down under the table instead, hugging her knees in the way children that no one wants to coddle often do. She was thinking of the dead bodies floating around. All the rich folks, who had been fooled into thinking they could save themselves on that ship: now the elegant ladies floated in mucous fascinators, electronic cigarettes in their stiff, pasty fingers. Dead white poodles in adorable sweaters and jingle bells on their necks. Deceased gentlemen with bloated faces, stuck in deep-salted suits like resting penguins. She was thinking of her parents too. The last time she had seen them, they were sailing away in a safety boat, not turning back, not waving at her, not saying good-bye.

"I write about love," the young man said suddenly.

The girl looked out from under the table to find out that he had thrown the soiled sock away, and had stopped crying; his nose was no longer dripping red. She didn't care about the content of his supposed books. In her mind, she was replaying the scene, in which her father's long, skeletal fingers had pushed her away. She felt they'd shivered in disapproval in the sea wind and then had retreated as if they'd touched something disgusting. She was too heavy. She would not have fitted into the boat. She was special; surely she could save herself? They had better go; hopefully they'd all see each other again. Have a nice rest of the day.

In the next moment, the ship broke into half and spat her out, high up in the air.

The scene stopped there, because she couldn't recall much from her flight. She might have short-circuited. Time and space had twisted their limbs into a single body.

She had flown through air and water, and then there'd been only darkness. The next thing she knew, she was stranded on a piece of the Astronomy Salon and someone wanted her to bring him a glass of sherry.

"It sounds banal," the young man was saying, "but I assure you, it is quite the opposite. Love is the fundamental prerequisite, which forms an individual's world image. Love preserves the philharmonic."

"If your writing is as intriguing as the way you talk, I doubt you're ever going to be famous."

"But of course I will." The man, whose face was only half-visible in the feeble candlelight, gave her a beatific smile worthy of an overzealous religious man. His satin shirt was beginning to smell of acidic sweat. "You know, Sugar, there is not enough love in the world. I can tell you all about that. You are trapped in your mourning and interference. Your deductions are plaguing you, if I am not mistaken."

"I'm plagued by your idiocy!"

He raised a curious brow. "Idiocy? I do not know that word. Is it, by any chance, something akin to blasphemy? By the way, we should have some sherry together." The man leaned over the table, so he could warm his fingers over the candle flame. He was obviously glad that the darkness of the night had swallowed the ocean, so he could pretend it wasn't there.

"I love candles. Such an antique, primitive source of light, yet so uniquely stimulating. I do, however, miss my servants. But meditating about love always fills my veins with an extra ergo. Looking at you in this warm candle light, illuminating your childlike brow so softly – ah, that was an amazing expression, I have to remember it – I have to ask... how old are you? Nine?"

"Eight, sir."

"Alright, alright, no need to be so economical. And where are your Argonauts?"

"Who do you mean?"

"Your parental units."

The girl pulled her knees to her chin and gave the man's shoes an unyielding glare. He leaned down, breaching the privacy of her bunker under the table, and looked into her face with his uncomfortably bulging, watery eyes. She could smell his breath. There was an unpleasant sweetness to it, as though he had spent his entire life sucking caramel candies and drinking dessert wine. If she could, she would have thrown up. The last time she had felt this sick was years ago, when she had accidentally eavesdropped on one of the nightly discussions that her parents liked to have when they thought she was in the dreamland.

("I still don't know if we have done the right thing. And she's cost us more than a new hovercar, or a trip to Mars!"

"You gave me two children, Ellen. Two. One of them was dead and the other retarded. You only have yourself to blame that we aren't going to spend our summer on Mars this year.")

"Away. They went away in the escape boat," she blurted out, so that he would leave her alone.

He did not. On the contrary, his pasty face drifted even closer. Boldly, he went down onto his knees and reached out to her – the two of them, alone, in cold darkness, on a piece of ebony floor, in the middle of the ocean, amidst the foul smell of fish, algae and decomposition. The long nails on his fingertips tentatively brushed her locks.

She shivered and pulled away.

"It is more than evident that you lack love. You are frustrated by the fatal absence of emotion! How relevant..."

On all fours, she quickly crawled to the chroniton clock and leaned back against its metal body. She kept her eyes fixed on the single candle flame, watching the wax drip down onto the card table. Was the candle visible enough to lead another ship to them? Rewind. The corpses returned to her mind view. All the people. They had believed themselves to be the chosen ones, intended to survive this catastrophe and, one day, when the ocean ebbed away, they would make landfall on a drying land and lay down the foundation stones of new civilisation. Now they were just floating corpses, thoroughly salted like herrings in a can. Noah's Ark gone wrong. She wondered where she would end up if she jumped into the water and joined them. How far would she be able to swim before the sea water immobilised her limbs? Would she find her parents?

Rewind. Her parents, sailing away in the safety boat, not waving good-bye. Not looking back.

The young man kept talking. He was saying an awful lot of words and none of them were important, nor made any sense. There was a badly-masked lewdness in his newest proclamations as he squatted under the table next to her, refusing to return to his armchair. She had once downloaded a quote from the galaxy net, one she was really fond of. It read: "The negation of evil is the emptiness, because each evil holds a glimmer of good and each good holds a glimmer of evil." She was trying hard now to find the proverbial bit of good in the thoroughly unlikeable young writer.

Perhaps his parents were at fault. Perhaps they had abandoned him at some point, too. Or maybe they had just never been at home and he'd had to spend the majority of his childhood with an old, stern governess in thick glasses, who used to read him a daily dose of philosophical essays instead of fairy tales. Maybe they had never bought him any toys and all he'd had to amuse himself with were old dictionaries from his father's library. But as the night grew darker, so did his boldness, and it was becoming impossible to keep looking for that glimmer. He was talking about himself a lot, too. He didn't ask her ask her questions about herself, or indeed *any* questions at all. That was why he never found out how strong her tiny hand could be, or that she had been eight years old for over a decade.

CLICK. *"An all-consuming tsunami is rising in the East. In Twilight Falls, dozens of houses have been flooded by saltwater in the last few hours. The city hall has reported that enormous water snails have covered the building in a thick layer of slime that resists all attempts at removal. The people are afraid are afraid are afraid are afraid are afraid are afraid are afraid are afraid are afraid are afraid are afraid are afraid..."*

She saw a tremor run through the writer's entire body, watched him cover his ears with his hands, try to tune the mechanical voice out, crawl from under the table, run up and down, right and left, round and round their derelict like a headless chicken. She heard his manic laughter; he tipped the clock over and stomped on it in a wild kind of dance that was clearly not sophisticated enough to match his clothing. After ridding the machine of its voice, he collapsed on the floor and knelt there with an expression of agony.

The girl tiptoed over to him and placed her ice-cold palm on his shoulder in a comforting manner. "Come on, let's take off our shoes and dip our feet in the ocean! Isn't that what writers do? They are... spontaneous and shocking and bold."

Subdued, but ever so hopeful, he covered her hand with his own larger one. "And then... Will you allow me...?"

She smiled and nodded. They sat down on the edge of the ebony floor and the girl let him hold her hand, which felt superglued to his by a clammy dampness. And then, without warning, she jumped to her feet, pushed against his back with all her strength and tipped the ornate young man into the deep, unforgiving ocean. His slowing breath would soon attract unseen water creatures from the depths. Though eyeless, they could *see*. Their impeccable senses would lead them right to him. But perhaps they would pass him by, finding him too gross a meal.

With the lone candle in her hand, she watched the surface in silent fascination until the bubbles signifying a battle of life and death disappeared. She stretched her limbs, walked across the the Astronomy Salon and settled down in the armchair. Finally. And as she tipped her head back to look at the sky, she noticed a falling star cutting a searing hot line through the darkness. *This is how butterflies are born*, she thought. Her last thoughts, before falling into a dreamless slumber, were of her grandfather.

Somewhere up there, his space ship was looking for new worlds. One day soon, the entire Earth would be drowned by the insatiable ocean. Her parents would be dead, her teacher and her classmates would follow suit. Water would take even the postman, the holograph movie stars, the brown-white cat that used to come to their garden until father chased it away with a phaser. It would swallow the president, and her mother's psychologists, and hundreds of thousands of other people that had never been of much use either. Her grandfather, though, would still be alive, and perhaps he would settle down on a different planet, somewhere in the Vega system perhaps, which was populated by a nicer species that valued each life it had created, even the artificial ones.

She saw the young man float near her derelict a week later. His bloated, pasty body was missing both arms and a leg and reeked of rotten apples. The girl closed her eyes and pulled up her feet that she had dipped into the ocean again – as if the corpse could have tainted it more than it already had been. She waited patiently for the unsightly thing to disappear behind her. All the while, her head was filled with thoughts of a rescue ship or a hover craft – that would certainly find her one day – of her parents not turning back, and of the fatal absence of emotion.

Pyramid and Thisbe

Rhys Hughes

Thisbe was an anti-vampire who looked and acted like a normal vampire, but her wings carried a positive charge. The undead are mostly negative in outlook and aura, so physical contact between Thisbe and a cousin would result in annihilation for both. Thus was she doubly cursed, forced to shun the company of other bloodsuckers as well as humans. A smoking crater does not make a fitting memorial for her kind of beauty. She was lonely and dreadful and lithe.

I watched over her, having caught her one hilarious night in a net. She rested in a cage that swung from a hook in the attic. She did not require much feeding. Contrary to popular belief, these creatures have modest habits. Blood is essential, yes; but they supplement their diet with conventional food. Thisbe had developed a taste for chocolates. I brought her the richest examples, in a coffin-shaped box, and the strawberry creams made her laugh.

The attic was not a real attic, but my house was not a real house. A shimmering pyramid, it rose out of the crimson desert. Tall dunes and ignorance protected it from prying eyes. There were no windows and only one door. Thisbe's room was at the apex of the structure. I chose the chamber at the base. Mine was larger, and stuffed with forbidden books, but hers was more pleasant. Two ventilation shafts connected our rooms. Along these conduits we communicated our dreams.

One evening, studying a papyrus of spells, I came across a curious footnote. The text was concerned with how to master the elements. There were spells to flood rivers, raise tempests and ignite volcanoes. Under a passage on electrical storms there was a description of Thisbe. "You are a *daednu*," I called up, placing my mouth to one of the shafts. "You do the usual vampiric things, but won't be put off by stakes or garlic. It is shoelaces and chillies you must avoid." The next time we met, she knelt and traced the delicate bones of my foot with her icy lips. "You prefer nipping heels to necks," I added.

Our mutual affection soon putrefied into lust. I was studying stars outside when she crept up and placed a hand between my legs. I lost no time tearing off her clothes, leaving untouched only her high boots and veil. The finer details, as meteors licked the sky, can be imagined. I shall content myself with offering a handful of key words: tongue, ache, blossom, sticky, decay.

The region was prone to earthquakes. As we thrust into each other, a tremor assisted our coitus. So violent was my climax, I was sure my soul had followed my seed into her sweet tomb. But I felt alive, pierced by a fang dipped not in poison but some stimulating drug. We laughed at the constellations and I pointed out Algol, most baleful of suns, as many light-years distant as the number of ways to torment an astrologer. We raided my store for wine and relished the antique stuff in the gloom of the internal passages, bloated on peculiar feelings like drunken worms in a rotten cheese.

This was perhaps the happiest period of my existence. For centuries I knew no company save that of the occasional nomad. I maintained my links with the outside world through these billowing folk, purchasing my modern lifestyle from them with silver measured from my sarcophagus. They came at irregular intervals, camels laden with tinned vegetables, fuel for my generator, newspapers and cutlery. We discussed the weather and politics. But Thisbe was a dearer friend, sharing my pleasures, alternately inspiring and terrifying me.

"Where are you from, Thisbe?" I asked, and she cried, "Old Vienna, wet and vain, where dark families eat sausage with their blood. The city has changed, the people no longer care. I was born in a cellar near the river. I heard the suicides knocking against my walls at night. Father was a respectable vampire, he worked in the graveyard. Always brought home some giblets for the children."

I was uncomfortable with her nostalgia, it cloyed like burnt honey. "How did you lose your innocence?" I demanded, and she said, "One night, as a treat, he took me to the big Ferris wheel. Up alone I went, higher than his gaze. At the top I was struck by lightning. When I came down, I had changed. My father would not touch me. My polarity had reversed, he said. So I was exiled. I grew up wandering the world. When I flew into your net you took me in."

I was cheered by her gratitude. She asked about my own life and I shrugged my shoulders. There was little to tell. I was a minor Pharaoh, I was embalmed alive. My priests were too impatient. I still do not know whether to be grateful or angry. Becoming immortal was sore. Since that ancient time, my nomads had kept me up to date with trends. Three weeks before Thisbe moved in, they delivered a washing machine. But my coffers were almost empty, the silver nearly exhausted.

The following month, standing in front of the huge brass mirror in my room, I prodded my stomach with worried fingers. There was a bulge. It had been hiding from my consciousness for some time, but now it was too large to ignore. I called for Thisbe and she placed her ear to my abdomen. Her eyes widened and she exposed her teeth. "Congratulations are in order. You're pregnant."

"Nonsense!" I was stunned.

"Why? Because you are a man? Yet that is not strictly true. You are so withered the distinction is meaningless. What did you expect when you ruptured my hymen and filled me with powdery seed? That I would brush off the experience as casually as dandruff? That I would suffer alone? But I'm a *daednu*, so these things work backwards. Our child grows inside you. There will be at least one."

"I have no placenta," I responded miserably. "My organs were taken out and placed in canopic jars. The child will have to be aborted. How will my waters break? I am completely desiccated."

Touching my stomach, Thisbe smiled languidly. "But vampires do not give birth to live young. They lay eggs, spherical and black as cracked leather. You will have to cut them out, sit on them in the cool dark. I will help you. When they hatch, they will follow you around. You'll be their mother. You will suckle them on shadows and teach them to ferment the blood of jackals."

I told her I did not want the responsibility at my age, I was far too weary. I had no wish to be woken in the middle of the day by little bats. Thisbe was amused by my reaction. As the days wore on, my attitude softened. I was as completely under her spell as I once thought she was under mine. We wandered the passages arm in arm and I showed her all the secret rooms, false doors and mechanical traps. I was lucky in having an imaginative architect.

When the time came, she helped me unwrap the bandages and we opened my lower stomach. Already eviscerated, there was plenty of room inside. Six black pearls glittered fearfully; she placed them on soft cushions arranged for the purpose. She stroked the objects tenderly. In this form she could caress her children, but when they hatched the laws of physics would disrupt the relationship like a cosmic social worker. Such is the thermonuclear family's lot.

My task was to incubate the eggs. Deprived of my constant attention Thisbe grew bored, trying to amuse herself by flying further afield. The desert animals were grateful for her absence. Anaemic hyenas crowded the dunes, sniggering with relief. Sometimes I did not see her from dusk to dawn. I adjusted myself on the cushions and sighed. Beneath me the eggs pulsated with horrible life.

"What would you do if we were discovered?" she asked me, after one jaunt. I shrugged my shoulders. I had been haunted by this prospect for centuries. A team of explorers might easily chance upon our abode. If nomads could find their way here, why not the pale men with their picks and shovels? I would make a fine exhibit in the British Museum. It was fortunate our desert had no fossil fuels to exploit, no military value. Yet it was a cruel question. She could fly away whenever danger loomed, unless I locked her cage.

When the eggs finally hatched, three boys and three girls, Thisbe and I drank a mordant toast of ancient red. We decided on suitable names for them: Edgar, Vernon, Poppy, Bram, Carmilla and Desmond. We kept them in a wooden chest in the attic and took it in turns striking them with a stick. We did not want to spoil them. Like all baby vampires they were quick to learn the rudiments of speech. Thisbe talked to them in German. I used Hungarian and Sanskrit.

They called me mummy. They called her *daednu.*

After the mock christening, I took Thisbe aside and questioned her about her escapades. "What's out there that is so fascinating?" I asked. She was reluctant to tell; this suggested she had discovered something of interest. Finally, she gave in. "For the past nine weeks, a group of explorers have been making their way towards the pyramid. They are led by a nomad who knows you are short on silver. He has sold your secret. They'll be here within a day or two."

I was shattered by this news. I decided to defend my home with all the strength of my shrivelled limbs. The treachery of the nomad saddened me. But I wished to be a presentable villain, an elegant adversary, so I wasted no time in brooding. I cleaned the pyramid from top to bottom, setting the traps as I worked my way down.

When I had finished, the dust of dynasties had been swept up and given to the winds. All that remained was to clean my grubby bandages, return to my sarcophagus and await the siege. I unwrapped the bindings and coiled them into the washing machine. Adding soap powder, I shut the door and started the device. I watched as the contents tumbled in a sea of foam. On spin cycle the screams began.

Somehow, one of the children had climbed into the machine. Peering closely into the whirling drum, I glimpsed a tiny face with milk fangs. It was Desmond, who was always falling asleep in strange places. As soon as the machine shuddered to a halt, I opened the door and retrieved him. I saw at once that he had changed.

I called for Thisbe at the top of my voice. She was by my side in an instant. "What's wrong?"

"It's Desmond. His wings have turned green. He has become a *daednu*! It must be something to do with rotation. You mentioned the Ferris wheel and the lightning. The combination of centrifugal force and electricity seems to reverse the polarity of vampires. I wonder if this holds true for all supernatural beings?"

Thisbe was delighted. At long last she was able to hold one of her offspring without detonating. If it was possible for Desmond, it should also be possible for his brothers and sisters. There was no reason why we could not become a normal family.

There were, however, problems of an ethical nature. We had hoped to release the children into the vampire community. We wanted the best for them. I had set the residue of my heart on seeing them enter the medical profession. If we now span them all into *daednus*, we would be condemning them to an unlife of exile.

This dilemma required much thought, but time was limited. Tomorrow the explorers would be knocking on our capstone. While Thisbe retired to her cage to mull the issues, I frantically searched through my spellbook for a way to delay them. In the musty papyrus, I found a seismic answer, an incantation of tectonic splendour.

The resulting earthquake, big enough to swallow expeditions whole, was much more powerful than I had bargained for. Possibly

I overdid the chants. The pyramid twisted on its axis, snapping at the base. Mortar of long ages was ground to nothing. The crack extended along all four walls of my chamber. My home was suddenly detached from the ground, separated at its widest point, a loose wonder.

Thisbe made a reconnaissance flight of the epicentre, one day's journey from our position. The explorers had vanished. In many ways it was an unsatisfying vengeance, but our purpose had been served. I told Thisbe, "We are safe again."

She shook her dark head, holding me to her grave-scented bosom. I nestled like a maggot in her cleavage. "Such an unnatural shock will intrigue geologists. We have destroyed one set of researchers only to encourage another. Before long someone will find us. The world is too small, there is no more room for our kind."

This time I was too tired to argue. With a broken home and a host of dependents, I had been eroded away to nothing. I felt as drained as if my veins were full again and Thisbe was drinking me dry. I wanted to escape to some silent and mindless void. As I pounded my crumbling brow with my fist, the idea came.

I nudged Thisbe and we raced up to her attic. On the way, I paused to collect Desmond and one other. It was vital to hold them apart. At the top of the building, beneath the cage, I suspended Desmond and his sister over the two ventilation shafts.

"The pyramid is no longer fixed to the ground. With enough thrust we can launch it out of the desert. The shafts converge at the base. If I drop Desmond down one and Poppy down the other, they will meet at the bottom. My room will act like a combustion chamber. The force might even be powerful enough to enable us to escape Earth's gravity. We'll be free of interference forever!"

Thisbe frowned. She wrestled with her conscience. Could she allow her children to be used as rocket fuel? I reminded her of our potential to make more. Provided we kept one breeding pair for emergencies, there was nothing to stop us reaching the stars. The washing machine would ensure enough *daednus* to keep us going indefinitely. Food and wine was no problem, we were well stocked. Besides, being supernatural, we did not need to eat. Nor would vacuum bother us. "Algol is pleasant at this time of aeon," I joked.

With a slight inclination of her head, Thisbe gave me permission to drop Desmond and Poppy down the shafts. There was a long minute in which nothing was audible save the hiss of falling offspring. I held my musty breath. Then the inconceivable happened. The details of the explosion cannot really be imagined. But again I shall be content with offering a key word: *blagharghtakm!*

My knowledge of physics was never very good. We were squashed flat, pyramid and occupants. Being immortal, it did not matter. At least we were rushing through the atmosphere, into space. The cosmos is one big coffin. So we began to feel at home.

We like it up here, cold and mute. We slide like shadows across the inner surface of our compressed vessel. My dreams about steering to the stars have also been squashed. We have gone into orbit around the moon. And yet, strangely enough, the washing machine survived the blast. I am tempted to enter it myself and change my own polarity. Too long have I been a mummy. Now I want to be an anti.

THE LONG LEATHER BOOT

Elizabeth Davidson

My name is Thomas Rutherford and I know who did it.

It has been pulling at me since I arrived: a flinch, a shiver. And now I have proof. It is there in the cold glue that grips my bones, and in the scarred landscape behind the house where the Forestry Commission has left its brutal mark; hillsides raked and vandalised by freshly planted trees; a pine graveyard beginning its creep.

I walk to the top of a nearby hill, and on to the next farm and then the next. The more I walk, the more I ache, as though the cold earth is reaching up to drag me down to my roots. The only signs of human life are cars on the long ribbon of road below and the distant buzz of quad bikes on the horizon — it is strange how the acoustics work up here. For a while, a small herd of heifers canter behind me, wide-eyed and snorting spittle. Soon, I think, they too will be replaced by trees.

A man is at the gate when I return, his jacket too clean for a local. He must be lost.

I shout a greeting, and he turns to me with a bewildered expression.

"Do you live here?"

I see his point. It's a remote location.

"Sort of." I explain that it was my grandfather's house, now mine but usually let out to holidaymakers. And him?

"I'm here because of the body." He smiles at the expression on my face. "Don't worry. It's not what you think."

It's the forestry machines, he explains. They've carved up more than their usual slice of earth this time, a remarkable relic from the past: the body of a man preserved in peat. And, despite the strength of the machines, the body emerged unharmed.

"Just up there." He points to the hill behind the house. "I thought you would have heard. It's the talk of the valley, although I suppose…" He looks round at the single-track road and laughs, but I don't join in. I cannot explain it, other than to say that there is cold glue in my veins.

"Would you like to come in? You can tell me more about it."

"Sure." His face lights up with enthusiasm. "It's in pristine condition," he tells me. "Peat is an excellent preservative. We've got it at the hospital."

He follows me into the kitchen. I turn my back to switch on the kettle.

"I can take you to see it, if you like," he says. "After all, it turned up on your doorstep."

The hills, of course, never change their shape but these days there are houses where previously there were fields. The tower overlooking the village is now inhabited, with Porsches and Range Rovers parked outside. I point at it. "That was a ruin when I lived here last."

"Progress, huh?"

I shrug. The road is still familiar, and as he drives, he tells me about the body. It dates from the late seventeenth century. That's the only downside: its relative youth reduces archaeological interest and potential funding although it is well preserved. The date of death, around the 1680s, suggests it could be one of the Covenanters.

"You know about them, right?"

"Of course."

"Ever heard of the 'Killing Time'?"

I haven't.

"Persecution of Presbyterians, all round the south of Scotland. The fifty years struggle. You know how many people died?"

I don't.

"Thousands." He shakes his head, smiling as if it's funny. "All around here. Bloodthirsty times. And look at this place now. I bet nothing ever happens."

Alternatively, he tells me, the body could be that of a thief dealt justice. A cattle rustler. There are many possibilities. It could have been gangrene. He looks at me as he says this last thing, and I immediately turn to stare out the window.

"You'll see what I mean when you see it." His voice is knowing.

I don't reply. It is difficult to breathe.

He sighs. "We've got problems with the church. The kirk minister. Do you know him?"

I shake my head. "I haven't been back here for thirty years."

He nods, not passing comment. "He wants the body given a Christian burial. That was part of the persecution, you see, if they found out a Covenanter had been buried in a kirkyard, they dug them up again. The minister's on a mission to right a historic wrong." Another sigh. "He's got up a petition. There were protesters at the hospital the other day. You'd think people would have better things to do."

We are pulling into a parking space. I am climbing out, unsteady, as a rare shaft of sunlight shines down, and watching him take a key from the tray in the car door. I am following him into Reception and down some stairs, through some plastic curtains and into a room, through it and through another, and then he unlocks the door and ushers me in.

It is cold, of course, but I wasn't expecting the dull light that fills the room. There are no windows. I hang there, in the semi-darkness, feeling the pain grow. There is a shape on the table.

"Hold on." He is milling about at the edges, fiddling with something.

The overhead light goes on, suddenly, and is dazzling. I need water, air, open space. My tongue is coated in a slick of repellent saliva. I blink.

Its head is wrapped in a scarf of wool, and its remaining leg encased in a boot and leather chaps that rise past the majority of its thigh. The fabric of its clothes is torn and frayed in parts, exposing the skin. Centuries in the peat bog have mummified the body, leaving it tanned and polished. Burnished. Even from the door, I can trace the lines of veins and finely detailed muscle in the arms and neck. It gleams beneath the laboratory lights. My fear turns to fascination. Edging closer, I see how well preserved it is: the eyelashes and brows still in place, and days-old stubble pushing through the cheeks. Its fingernails are intact.

"It's incredible," I whisper. I bend down so that my face is on

257

a level with its head. As I do so, I imagine that its jaws might grin their terrible truth. Nevertheless, I press on, examining its face, its high cheekbones and forehead. I turn to find the archaeologist observing me with interest.

"You know, he looks like you," he says. "I mean," he stifles a smirk, "like you if you had been buried in a peat bog for a few centuries. Of course, people were smaller in those days." He pauses. "You're from round here though, aren't you, your family I mean, probably go back a few centuries?"

I nod.

"Maybe you're related."

It is then that the twitching starts: mindless jerks and spasms. It is as though my body belongs to someone else, an unknown third party pulling levers to manipulate my muscle and bone.

An unknown...

A covenanter...

A thief...

"Are you all right?" The man is concerned but something stops him coming near me, even though it must be obvious I am about to fall. Instead, he stands at the opposite end of the room, with the body between him and me, and speaks. It strikes me that he has not stopped speaking since we first met. His voice never stops. It seeps into me, like water through the porous earth.

I am sitting in the hospital lobby and there is sunshine at my back. The woman at the reception desk has been joined by two others, all three faces ripe with pleasure at the thought of me, a grown man, fainting at the sight of a dead body. Beside me is the archaeology man. I realise, instantly, that banter has been exchanged at my expense, but I am too preoccupied with the thought of what comes next to care.

He holds out a paper cup of steaming tea. "I'll take you home," is all he says. As we stand up to leave, I see him turn towards the reception and wink.

We don't speak much on the journey back. I say nothing, and he gives up after a few attempts.

When we eventually pull up outside my house, he looks thoughtful. "Can you look at something for me?" He hands me some photographs and a photocopy of a diagram. One photo shows a shape cut into the body's chest. Another one is cut into the top of its remaining leg. The shape has been drawn out in scale on the photocopy: two triangles interlinked.

"Carved by a metal blade," the archaeology man says. "Probably the same one that chopped off his leg. It must mean something. I wondered if it was religious but nobody has seen it before. It's almost like he's been branded."

I realise that he is speaking more slowly than before, and that the reason is so he can watch my reaction.

"I don't suppose this symbol means anything to you? Does it have local significance, perhaps?"

I shake my head.

"Have you ever seen them before?"

"Thank you for the lift." I push the door open, stand in the stone yard, lift my hand in a wave and trudge indoors.

At night, I lie awake repeating the words, "I am innocent. I am innocent." If I can say it enough times then it will infect my dreams. Then I fall asleep and the dreams come anyway. They always start the same, with a terrifying slowness, first the heavy swell of movement and then I am face down, suspended above him.

I'd be lying if I said it began after my divorce, it began long before then, but perhaps that's when I began to fully understand. Once you notice the scars, you begin to see them everywhere. They take many shapes and forms. There are many thieves in this world but some are worse than others.

She said to me, please could I just forgive her. It would be easier for me – as well as them – if only I could do that. That is actually what she said.

My wife. My brother.

I am innocent.

But I am not.

I've seen things.

Since I arrived, I have taken to walking around at night, sometimes even into the forest. A person could get lost in the maze of forestry roads, walk round in circles, perish. It has happened before. No such fate for me, however. I always know my way home.

Indoors, I pace the kitchen and go up and down the stairs, checking the rooms. The itching is intense. I have pain and numbness: the top of my leg and my chest.

Sometimes, I think of her and wonder if she is happy. If he is happy. One man pushed under and the other afloat. Happy memories buried beneath pain.

The minister comes to my door the following day with a leaflet. "We are all God's children", it reads, and then in large writing, "Campaign for a Christian burial".

"I'd rather not have anything to do with it," I say.

He invites me to a whist drive and attempts to strike up conversation about the church roof. He comments on the state of the roads. There is a problem with potholes. He stays long after it has become embarrassing that I haven't invited him in. I've obviously broken local etiquette. After he leaves, I limp upstairs and take off my shirt. The rash has got worse.

In the back pantry, I wipe away spiders' webs and heave open a trunk. Inside, a cardboard box with my old jotters and notebooks: scribblings from my boyhood. I carry them through to the sitting room and set them on the floor, and begin to rummage, and there it is: the two triangles drawn over and over, the twins; him and I, twin arms stretching up to a joined future; measured and equal; the inseparable brothers, two lives duplicate; and strong.

Two lives stretching toward the same point, but which one will reach it first and render the other obsolete?

The minister does not come back. The archaeology man does not come back. I live in the house. I put the jotters away. I walk through marshy ground under cover of night, just like I did so many centuries before. It feels like I am floating.

When the itching grows worse and I can stand it no longer, I call Mr Robertson. It seems appropriate that he is head of the kirk session. More than that, he knew my family and I want to confess.

Looking back, it was an odd thing to be told as a child. And told in such a fairytale way...

"And do you know what he found?" My mother would smile. "A long boot, all the way up to the thigh! And do you know what was in the boot? You'll never guess." My mother's voice would break into a laugh. "Go on, can you guess?"

My grandfather was a shepherd, and later on he was a farmer, but all the time he and his family didn't have much money and, in order to get fuel for heating and cooking, they cut peat. Until recently, I didn't know what peat felt like but I knew it preserved things; anything organic.

Outside, I hear a vehicle draw up. Mr Robertson has arrived, his enormous 4X4 – they go in for big cars in these remote areas – dominating the yard.

This is a true confession and Mr Robertson is my witness. My grandfather was cutting peat when he made the discovery. I can picture it as if I saw it with my own eyes: the clouds of smoke rising from their pipes; the noise of the cutting machine; each man and woman in turn, looking in the boot and delivering their verdict, that, yes, the dark substance inside the leather sheath was human flesh.

Nobody knew whose leg it was, or who had cut it off. My grandfather gave it to the local schoolteacher, who promised to give it to a museum.

"Mr Robertson," I begin. "I asked you here because I want your advice. It concerns my grandfather. My grandfather lived in this very same house a long time ago."

Uhah, he wheezes. He is a long-time smoker, uhah! He is red in the face, like most of the farmers round here, accustomed to walking about in the drizzle and the cold all day. It must be good for them because they have long lives. We are distantly related, like most people in the area, and I wonder if we have mutual ancestors out there in the hills, buried deep. Perhaps we share the same sickle-shaped cheek bone. Perhaps, if placed side by side, our rib cages would look the same.

"I believe in paying my debts," I say.

I usher him through to the dining room, where I have set a fire. Uhah!

"I want to show you something," I say.

A hooded, alarmed look creeps over his face as I unbutton my shirt. He shrinks back in his chair and struggles to affect a look of sympathy.

"Look at this," I say. "Look!"

Mr Robertson's grim embarrassment gives way to a glow of curiosity. He steps forward and examines the two triangles on my chest, whipping out a pair of reading glasses from his jacket pocket.

"It just appeared," I say. "Mr Robertson, it matches *exactly* a symbol carved into the chest of the body. You know, the *body*."

He nods, and studies it some more. Then he shrugs, smiles and says a word that I don't want to hear. "Doppelganger."

I join in his laughter, swiftly pulling my shirt back down. Yes, the best response is to laugh it off. What else can you do?

"Okay," I say. I sit down. "I want to confess," I tell him.

He looks terrified. "To what?"

"I'm being punished."

There is a long silence. The only sound is the wind singing in the trees outside and the rhythmic tap of a branch on the window pane.

"Who do you think is punishing you?"

I can tell that, despite his position as head of the kirk session, he is willing me not to say the fall-guy of the insane – God. I know also that he is wary of asking me why I think I'm being punished. People round here don't like to know too much about their neighbours. Nor do they like to judge.

"I think that my brother is. But not my brother in his current form."

Silence. His hand squeezes the arm of the couch. "I'm not sure I follow you," he says.

I sigh. "I know I sound like I'm talking riddles but there's no other way of saying it. I know it now. I have proof."

I point to my leg.

"What about it?" he asks, quickly: I can tell he is worried after my unbuttoning of my shirt that I might now take my trousers off.

"I've lost a leg."

His eyelids crinkle. He looks down and then up again. "It's still there."

"It's not," I say. "It's an illusion."

He hesitates.

"It looks like it's there," I agree, "I can walk on it. I can move it."

He nods more vigorously than necessary.

"I have a reflex. Look." I cross my legs and tap my knee. It jerks. "But I can't feel anything. It's numb as ice. Everything works but there's no feeling."

A look of relief crosses his face.

"It's numb all the way up to here." I point to midway between my hip and my knee. "Here! Just like the—" I don't need to finish my sentence.

His face blanches.

"I shouldn't be able to keep my balance but I can."

I feel scared about what I am about to say, not just for me but for him.

"The thing is," I say, "the body and I, we have something in common. He was attacked. He lost his leg. That's why he, it,' I stumble over my words, "*this*, is happening. Now it's him who is attacking me, and there is nothing I can do to stop what is going to happen." I cannot bear to look at him, but I must confess. "I know," I lower my head, "what *is* happening."

"Well, I'm not sure what to think about all this," Mr Robertson says.

"You know who the body is, don't you? You can guess."

His face pales. He stands, and says he has to go.

I follow him, mute. What was I looking for? Absolution? Someone to stop me?

At the door, he turns to me. "Perhaps you're diabetic? That's a symptom, isn't it? Your leg, I mean."

I shake my head, and he hurries away.

I return to the sitting room, where I wait for the 4X4 to pass the window, which it duly does a few seconds later. They drive quickly round these parts, but he is moving with excessive speed.

I switch on the television and watch for a while. "Police are investigating," the smooth-toned newsreader says, "the disappearance of a three hundred year-old corpse."

I walk through to the back pantry and rip open the top of the plastic bags on the floor. I roll the body over, and its mouth seems to open a fraction. It looks like a smile, but perhaps it is my imagination.

My brother, I say, I am innocent because you got what you deserved. She was mine and you were a thief. I will take us to the forest, where everything will be hidden. You thought you could get away with it but you couldn't, and you will never get the revenge you crave.

Twice now, it has happened to me. My name is Thomas Rutherford, and I know why I did it.

CITY IN THE DUSK

Matt Colborn

Night was falling. I wouldn't have long to wait before I could rid myself of an irritant. The fierce vermilion of the sunset had faded over the towers of Simeon, leaving them phallic silhouettes against a deep ocean blue.

The room was like the others in the former palace; spacious, the walls of cracked white plaster tastefully draped with cloths of Malachite weave. A thick, patterned rug lay on the marble floor before the fireplace, and a huge bed, perfectly made, sat in the corner. On the dressing table was a broken Nikon camera. I'd tried to get replacement parts for it days before - but they don't go in for technological sophistication in Simeon.

One thing I had managed to purchase in the medina had been a large glass jar, which now sat on the bedside table, its lid lying beside it. It had been hard punching holes in the rusted top with my blunt penknife.

I sat on the window sill, enjoying the first cool breeze of the evening. I could hear the wind in the eucalyptus trees behind me, in the hotel garden, as well as the occasional cry from one of those bloody peacocks. I took out a cigarette and lit it thoughtfully, sucking the smoke into my lungs.

Alison, I thought. *Alison's responsible for this.*

She had left days before. There hadn't been an argument; that wasn't Alison's style. There had been a widening gulf between us ever since our arrival which had ended in a lazy but irrevocable straying. She was down there, somewhere, amongst the drowsy labyrinths of Simeon and I found myself not caring overmuch. She had always been capable.

We had come to the city a month previously. We had spent much of the voyage on deck, watching the sky turn to a deep blue and the sun arc as each day progressed. We had left all the junk and trash of our world behind. I remember the transfer party the crew had held, an evening crowded with elegant silks, penguin suits, balloons and spitting champagne. I held her hand tight as the rails began to glow and crackle with the St. Elmo's fire that announced the transfer. Moments later, calculated to the second by our hosts, the sun rose on the sea of another plane.

And Alison threw up over the guard rail.

"I've left something behind," she muttered, "I've lost something."

"You certainly have," I joked, patting her back gently and watching the vomit dispersing on the seething wake.

We set to work as soon as we arrived. She was carrying sketchbooks, pencils, chalk and paint. I sported my camera.

I marvelled at her fascination with figures and her skill at setting their movements down. I would watch her in the Medina occasionally, her eye flickering across the scene, one mark capturing a body, another a building, a heavy line a shadow, a shallow one a highlight. Her drawings pulsed with light, immortalizing the beggars, the hawkers, the wandering preachers.

But for me, the inhabitants seemed like shadows flickering on the city walls, hardly discernible in a bright sun. The real character came from brick, tile and stone. I would wander the back streets, looking for *that* crumbling rampart or *this* ruined courtyard with the extinct, litter choked fountain. This was where the city was truly alive. The blocky torsos of temples, the sprawling limbs of the slums, the cloacal mystery of the overgrown archways captivated me from the first day.

A week into the trip, the dream arrived. The daintiest of dragonflies crawled across the lens of my eye as it would crawl across the lens of my camera. Focus was perfect. Legs worked and wings glistened. The thing reached the edge of my visual field and was lost.

I hadn't liked the nights from the beginning. Alison and I would spend our evenings in the great square beyond the walls of our hotel, where benches were set out, and meat was cooked at the ends in huge cauldrons. Orange sellers would try to entice with freshly squeezed fruit grown in the irrigated fields outside the city walls; hawkers would thrust baubles at us as we passed; and donkeys and goats wandered through the crowds.

We both avoided the meat on sale and stuck to falafel. I always stayed close to her. I felt watched from the first night, claustrophobic, hemmed in by the sweaty bodies and the rich stenches.

Then there was the deep night, when Alison and I would lie side by side, too exhausted by the heat to have sex. She always slept soundly, which had become rare for me. I was plagued by dreams.

"Come and see what I've discovered," Alison said gently one morning, her hand on my shoulder. I had sat staring into my coffee all that morning. She hadn't interfered. She was used to my black moods. When they took hold, they isolated me, destroying any intimacy with others.

That morning she led me to the Temple of the Moon, where the frescoes were. The frescoes – which are not actually in the temple itself, but in its grounds – were, we discovered, amongst Simeon's great treasures.

They are hidden behind a riotous growth of bougainvillea. The walls on which the frescoes are painted are the remains of some immense tomb of one of the archaic kings of the ancient city-state, which once extended its influence far over the seas, perhaps as far as the awakened lands. The king is displayed in his chariot, bow drawn, the arrow pointing to the enemy. He is flanked by his best soldiers, all named in lists written in Simeon Script B in the blank spaces between the depictions. Behind the king is his retinue, an orderly multitude of servants and slaves, asses and camels.

Only a small portion of the enemy lines still exists; much has been lost over the thirty centuries since the wall was painted. The opponents seem to well up from a great darkness. The troops have tusks protruding from their mouths, bright red skin and many arms. Some carry daggers, whilst others hold severed heads. Their war animals are dragons. And above them, fly tiny, naked figures with huge, crystalline wings.

"The Script," announced Alison, scanning the guide book, "says it was a holy war against the demons of night and the souls of the dead."

I was awake in the dark and I could not move. A terrible weight perched on my chest. I was a bug under a stone, wriggling, powerless to shift.

Then I could move and my hand fled to my breast. I moaned. There was a hideous insect bite there, crowned with a pinprick of blood. I got up and staggered to the drawer where we kept the medical kit. I cleaned my chest of sweat with cotton wool, disinfecting the wound with iodine and dressing it with a big plaster. Then I smeared more insect repellent onto my body, which later on began to run as I continued to sweat in bed. Alison did not stir.

Some days after that, Alison failed to turn up at a rendezvous and I was forced to go and look for her. She had fled beyond the narrow streets of the medina that morning, to the poor quarter, which huddled in the wreckage of a different age.

No one knew how old those blocks were, or who had raised the buildings of which they had been a part. Many of them had been broken up for building materials in Simeon several centuries before. Each whole block, and there were about a hundred and fifty left, was fifteen feet high and twenty-five across. Some even had fragments of what might have been script carved on one side. Scholars had discovered that each block only had part of one glyph. Any attempt to discover what language they were written in had been futile. What was certain was that most of the blocks were now under the sea. My imagination strained to picture the titanic building they must have come from.

Alison, naturally, was more interested in the poor. I sometimes marvelled at her fascination with such squalor.

I searched for her amongst the maze of blocks, ducking under washing lines of barely cleaned rags, past chicken pens and over firewood. Toothless youngsters in tie-dyed, grubby T-shirts laughed at me and some tried to beg money. I tried to avoid anyone's eye and sped on, zig-zagging around the stones. At one point, I rounded a corner and almost collided with a large old man with no left foot, who regarded me stonily with his one good eye, the other being clouded with cataracts. He sat on what smelt like a crate of rotting fruit.

I ducked round another corner and finally found Alison. She looked up, distracted, her pencil tip resting on paper. She put the pad under her arm and let herself be led out of the maze. I waded before her, fending off more beggars. The next time she got lost, I didn't bother to go after her.

I had finished my cigarette and the sun had finally sunk. I flicked the butt into the scented dark.

I went over to the drawer and fished out some Pro-Plus, downing several tablets before getting onto the bed, sitting up against the headboard with an ash tray beside me. The curtains still billowed in the breeze and after a time, despite my resolution, and the Pro-Plus, I dozed.

The bright memories of the days before crept into my mind. I once again saw worn, crumbling blocks of stone, the towers and intricate streets of Simeon. Somewhere, a Muezzin was calling and in the air wheeled two storks like magical kites. I looked about me and the city had been stripped of the moving shadows of people. I dreamed Simeon as it would be in a thousand years. The endless deserts would invade, clogging the streets, a more permanent cover than the scurrying people.

The ash tray clattered to the floor, spilling its contents and jerking me awake. I didn't bother to clear up the mess. But the rush of adrenalin was enough to keep me awake for the next minutes.

There was a fluttering at the window. I lay still in the dark, wide awake and not daring to move. Something hummed stealthily, mosquito-like, in the dark above me. Then the noise stopped and a second later I felt a light touch on my chest.

I half opened my eyes and saw, in the dim light, a diminutive but perfect human figure perched upon my chest, six inches in height. She had grown.

She squatted over me. Dragonfly wings poked out of her shoulder blades at ungainly angles, twitching in anticipation. Miniscule lips brushed eagerly at my breast. I felt pain, sharper than before and there was a little blood.

I had guessed that, once attached to me, the little creature would take several seconds to free her teeth from my skin. But there must have been some kind of soporific venom in her spit, as consciousness began to slip quickly. Time was short, so I grabbed her. In return she bit my hand, hard. The pain and the adrenalin rush brought me to full wakefulness.

Blood flowed down my right hand. I fumbled with my left at the jar, stuffed her in and screwed the lid in place.

I set it down on the table. The tiny woman squatted, hair tangled, face bloody, her wings crumpled like discarded cellophane. She hugged herself and regarded me with tiny, bright eyes.

I awoke the next day with a start. Golden sunlight was pouring into the room. I looked over at the jar; the little creature was awake, tiny and mantis-like, apparently unharmed by the sun's rays. I suppose I had half believed that she would have vanished in a puff of mist with the dawn.

I peered closer. There was no trace of blood on her face. It was perfect, like one of the miniature faces on the figures they modelled in porcelain and sold in the medina. Her wings, which I had expected to find still crumpled, were smooth, and glittered in the sunlight. There was something very familiar about her.

Gingerly, I lifted the jar and placed it in the cupboard. It was so light that she might not have been in it at all. She was still staring at me when I closed the door.

I sat on my bed for a few moments, unsure what to do next. Then I stood and walked out. I would spend the day in Simeon. I needed the sun on my back and the thoughtless freedom of an eternal high summer.

I went to the ports, braving the odours of oil and fish and guano. The ocean lapped on greened concrete, plastic bottles and Coke cans bobbing in the froth of a departing ship. There was a jellyfish hanging in the green water, pulsing just below the surface. I could just see the wire thin, stinging tentacles below the waves. It was a peculiar, protean thing to watch. Maybe I should have made the effort, got my camera repaired, so that I could have photographed such a sight. Or maybe not.

Later, wandering back up the narrow streets to the hotel, I found myself thinking about Alison. She had caught me looking at her sketch book the evening after I'd fetched her from the poor quarter. She snatched it away, hurt at my presumption. Her mouth quivered, as if she was trying to express something. She didn't have to. Her eyes had become as utterly blank as the pages of that sketchbook.

"You're not inspired?" I'd volunteered, knowing that it ran deeper than that.

She hadn't replied, just stared out of the window.

Her blank sketchbook.

My broken, useless camera.

Neither of us could capture the place, not in any way that counted.

She was there at reception when I returned, haggling with the Parsee. The fans spun in the great arched hall in a futile attempt to wave the heat away.

She was thin, painfully so. Her faded green shirt was sodden with sweat under the armpits and across the back - the liquid scars of the small pack she had taken with her when she abandoned the hotel.

She smiled at me when I came in, as if we'd just been together that morning. There were black rings under her eyes and her skin was slightly yellow: a grinning skeleton welcoming me back.

"Oh, John, I'm so glad you're here. He wouldn't let me have the spare key." She gestured at the Parsee, who frowned and muttered at me.

"It's okay," I said to him.

"There's something in the room I need." She said, panting between the words. Perhaps she was malarial.

"Something important," she continued. "I just wanted to get it."

"All right" I said, starting to mount the wide, cracked marble stairs. She followed, hand on the banister, walking painfully slowly just behind me.

I prayed that I wouldn't have to talk to her, but she didn't attempt to start a conversation. The wall between us was left safely intact.

As soon as I unlocked the door, all fatigue evaporated from her. She barged past me before I could even cry out, throwing open the door of the cupboard and snatching the jar as if she'd known it was there all along.

She unscrewed it viciously and stuck her hand inside. The thing bit her as she held it: blood ran down her hand, but she

271

ignored this, possessed, opening her mouth wide and stuffing the homunculus into her mouth in one gulp. For a sickening moment, I saw a lump pass under her larynx, and then she belched, loudly, and flopped panting onto the bed. She lay there, gasping, for some moments.

Then she sat up and looked at me. There was something, someone, in her eyes that there hadn't been before.

She smiled, wearily, but jubilantly, and held out her hands to me.

"I'm back, Johnny, I'm back."

I had retreated to the door, shocked and uncomprehending.

"What's the matter?" She frowned.

"You went away," I replied, "You went away and left me."

She stood, weak, a shadow of what she had been, but whole. She hobbled over to the window. The wind was blowing from the east and the scents of cinnamon and ginger floated in from the market. Palm doves cooed on the sill.

"That wasn't me. Not all of me, anyway." She sighed.

I didn't reply.

"Come home with me this time, Johnny?"

"I'm sorry, Alison," I said, surprising myself with a sudden resolution. "I can't do it."

"But I can't stay here!" she said, "It didn't want to let all of me in, doesn't want me here, even now! Not the real me."

She sighed at my silence, turning to her bags, which I had packed away in the corner of the room some time before. Seeing that they were in order, she picked up the telephone and called room service.

"I'm sailing tomorrow, at dawn. I'm spending the night at a hostel on the quay front." She wrote the number down on a piece of her art paper with a pencil stub. "It's up to you," she finished, "Just remember, I'm not going to risk going to sleep tonight, or at all until I'm back home."

The Porter was at the door, the bags loaded onto a trolley.

"I'm not losing myself again," she finished, with determination.

"Not even for you." And she closed the door.

I didn't go back to the port until I heard the liner announce its departure early next day. I couldn't sleep for the last hours of the night, so I sat up in bed reading a battered copy of *the Iliad* and smoking cigarettes. The only movement in the room was the fan.

The deep throaty moan came with the morning, and after it stopped, I dressed and walked the mile and a half to the quay. The liner had already made its way out of the harbour, and I thought I saw her on deck, standing with all the other diminutive folk.

And as I watched, I became aware that I was not alone. Beside me was a woman wearing an elegant silk shirt and torn combat trousers. Her boots spoke of many hours tramping the streets and the shirt was smeared yellow from days of dust and sweat. Her hair, maybe carefully styled once, was knotted and tangled and bleached by the sun. Her skin was covered in a fine layer of grime. I decided to take a chance.

"They couldn't stay, could they?" I said.

She looked at me in surprise, then shook her head.

"No." She turned back to the sea. Not everyone could stay. But not everyone had to, or wished to, leave.

About me, two dozen other travellers, mostly grubby and city-worn, stared out to sea. The chosen.

I stayed at the hotel for a few more days, but funds were running low. The day came when they turfed me and my luggage out. I was happier wandering the streets, anyway.

No one is a native here. We all came from somewhere else, whether that other place is miles or leagues or centuries away.

I will never leave the streets of Simeon. The city calls to me too loudly. I do not know how long I will be alive, but I savour every day that I am permitted to wander its winding streets or sit in the blistering sun with the other beggars.

Each day that passes, the hubbub fades a little more, and I feel the stony, dusty reality jump into sharper focus. And maybe when I finally die, my soul will flit through the city's night on dragonfly wings, an eternal ghost amongst the heavy majesty of eternal stone.

Angels of Anarchy

Lisa Mansell

shells like grandmothers
    umber the bipartite phiz in the gender of conches
in sinciput taupes and taxidermy
    that tint a dribble of bead from a gag-lipped pout

    a stitch of peacock in the ruckus of clay
           orange before the glisten-soak of black
a brocade of mute and feather-choke
             and the mechanic gust-spill of twist
                dynastic and
backcomb

and the tile-quarry stain of fir-trees
             beneath the hallux of victorian warp
    lace-booted and tort
          chintz and custard-thick on the crisp suck
of a horse-rock that maps ancient in couchant sienna
       its teeth-meat pearl amid the pubic coral
           cloud-pink in puck-heavy folds

as yachts project from the drip of vultures
a sphinx-foetus harlequins   sequin and phosphorous

The Dark Land

Michael Marshall Smith

It started with the bed.

After three years at college I'd come back home, returning to the bedroom I'd grown up in. It was going to be a while before I could afford to move out for good, and so in the intervening month I'd redecorated the room: covering the very 1970s orange with a more soothing shade, and badgering my mother into getting some new curtains that didn't look like they had been designed on drugs by someone who liked the colour brown a great deal. I'd also moved most of the furniture around, trying to breathe new life into a space I'd known since I was ten. It hadn't worked. It still felt as if I should be doing French verbs or preparing conkers, musing on what girls might be like. I knew it was largely an excuse for not doing anything more constructive – like filling out the pile of job applications which sat on the desk – but that afternoon I decided to move the bed away from its traditional place by the wall and try it in another couple of positions. It was hard work. One of the legs was rather fragile and the bed had to be virtually lifted off the floor rather than dragged around – which is why I hadn't tried moving it before, I remembered. After half an hour I was hot and irritated and developing a stoop. I had also become convinced that the original position had been not only the optimal but in fact the only place the bed could go.

It was as I struggled to shove it back up against the wall that I began to feel a bit strange. Light-headed, nauseous. Out of breath, I assumed. When the bed was finally back in place I lay back on it for a moment, feeling rather ill – and I suppose I just fell asleep.

I woke up about half an hour later, half-remembering a dream in which I had been doing nothing more than lying on my bed and remembering that my parents had said that they were going to extend the wood panelling in the downstairs hallway. For a moment I was disorientated, confused by being in the same place in reality as I had been in the dream, and then I drifted off again.

Some time later I awoke once more. I found it very difficult to fight my way up out of sleep, but eventually managed to haul myself sluggishly upright, struggling with eyelids made of lead. After a while I lurched to my feet and across to the sink to get a glass of water. Drinking it made the inside of my mouth a little less dry, but no more appealing. I decided that a cup of tea would be a good idea, and headed out of the bedroom to go downstairs.

As I reached the top of the staircase I remembered the dream about the panelling, and wondered where a strange notion like that could have come from. I'd worked hard for my psychology paper at college, and was confident that Freud hadn't felt that wood panelling was even worth a mention. I trudged downstairs, still feeling odd, my thoughts dislocated and fragmented.

When I reached the halfway landing I ground to a halt, and stared around me, astonished. They had extended the panelling.

When you enter my parents' house you come into a two story hallway, with a staircase that climbs up three walls to the second floor. The panelling used to only go about eight feet up the wall of the front hall, but now it soared right up to the ceiling. And they'd done it in exactly the same wood as the original. There wasn't a join to be seen. How had they managed that? Come to that, when had they managed it? It hadn't been like this that morning, but both my parents were at work and would be for hours and... well, it was just impossible. I reached out and touched the wood, bewildered at how even the grain matched, and that the new wood looked just as aged as the original, which had been there fifty years.

Then: Wait a minute, I thought. That isn't right. There hadn't used to be any panelling in the hall. Just simple white walls. The stairs themselves had been panelled in wood, but the walls were just plain white plaster. How could I have forgotten that? What had made me think that the front hall had been panelled, and think it so unquestioningly? I remembered that I'd recently noticed, sensitised to these things by having repainted my room, that the white in the hall was a little grubby, especially round the light switches. So what was all this panelling doing here? Where had it come from? And why had I been so sure that at least some of it had always been there?

Something wasn't right. I walked into the kitchen, casting bewildered glances back into the hall. I absently-mindedly registered a soft clinking sound outside, and automatically headed to the back door – too puzzled about the panelling to realise that it was rather late in the day for a milk delivery.

Both the front and back doors of the house open onto the driveway, the back door from a little corridor full of muddy shoes and rusting tools, which connects the kitchen to the garage. I threaded my way through the gardening implements and wrenched the stiff door open. It was late afternoon by then, but the light outside seemed very intense, the colours rich as they are before a storm.

I looked down and saw the milk bottle holder, with four bottles of milk in it. They weren't normal milk bottles, however, but large American-style quart containers somehow jammed into slots meant to take pints. Someone had taken the silver tops off.

A movement at the periphery of my vision caught my attention, and I glanced up towards the top of the driveway. There, about thirty yards away, were two children. One was fat and sitting on a bike, the other slim and standing by his side. I was seized with sudden irritation, and started quickly up the drive towards them – convinced that the clinking sound I'd heard was them stealing the tops off the milk.

I had covered scarcely five yards when someone who'd been at my school appeared from behind me, and walked quickly past me up the drive, staring straight ahead. I couldn't remember his name, had barely known him. He'd been two or three years older than me, and I'd completely forgotten that he'd existed, but as I stared after him I remembered he'd been one of the more amiable seniors. I could recall being proud of having some small kind of communication with one of the big boys, how it had made me feel a bit older myself, more a man of the world. And I remembered the way he used to greet my yelling his nickname, with a half-smile and a coolly raised eyebrow. All this came back with the instantaneous impact of memory, but something was wrong. The man didn't seem to register that I was there. I felt disturbed, not by the genuinely strange fact that he was in the driveway – or that he was wearing school athletic gear – but merely because he didn't smile and tilt his head back the way he used to. It was so bizarre that I wondered briefly if I was dreaming, but if you can ask yourself the question you always know the answer. I wasn't.

My attention was distracted by a reflection in the glass of the window in the back hallway. A man seemed to be standing behind me. He wore glasses, had a chubby face and basin-cut blond hair, and was carrying a bicycle. I whirled round to face where he should have been, but he wasn't there.

Then I remembered the kids at the top of the driveway, and turned to shout at them again, needing something to take my bewilderment out on. Almost immediately a tall slim man in a dark suit came walking down the drive; briskly, as if slightly late. Maybe it was a trick of the light in the gathering dusk, but I couldn't seem to fix on his face. My eyes just seemed to slide off it, as if it were slippery, or made of ice.

"Stop shouting at them," he snapped. He strode past me, towards the back door. I stared at him open-mouthed. "They're not doing anything wrong," he said. "Leave them alone."

The kids took themselves off, one on the bike, the other walking alongside, and I turned to the suited man. For some reason I felt anxious to placate him, and yet at the same time I was outraged at his invasion of our property.

"I'm sorry," I said, "It's just, well, I'm a bit confused. I thought I saw someone I knew in the drive. Did you see him? Wavy brown hair, athletics kit?"

For some reason I thought that the man would say that he had, and that that would make me feel better. All I got was a curt "No" as he entered the back hallway.

Then another voice spoke. "Well then. Shall we go into your old house?"

I realised that someone else was already standing in the back hall. The man with the blond hair and glasses. And he really was carrying a bicycle. He wasn't talking to me, but to the man in the suit.

"What?" I said, and hurried after them, catching a glimpse of the suited man's face. "But it's you..." I stopped again, baffled, as I realised that the man in the suit was the same man who had been in athletics gear.

The two men marched straight into the kitchen. I followed them, impotently enraged. Was this his old house? Even so, wasn't it customary to ask the current occupants' permission if you wanted to visit? The suited man was peering round the kitchen, which looked very messy. He poked at some fried rice I'd left cooling in a pan on the stove. At least, I seemed to have left it there, though I wasn't sure when I would have done so. I don't just cook up rice in the afternoon for the pure hell of it. I still felt the urge to placate the man, however, and hoped he would eat some of the rice.

He merely grimaced with distaste and joined his colleague at the window, looking out onto the drive, hands on hips. "Dear God," he muttered. The other man grunted in agreement.

I noticed that I'd picked up the milk from outside the back door, and appeared to have spilt some of it on the floor. I tried to clean it up with a piece of kitchen roll which seemed very dirty and yellowed as if with age. I was trying to buy time. I felt very strongly that there must be some sense to the situation somewhere, some logic I was missing. Even if the man had lived here once he had no right to just march in here with his friend, but as I continued trying to swab up the milk before he noticed it – why? – I realised that there was something far more wrong than a mere breach of protocol at stake.

The suited man looked about thirty five, much older than he should have been if he was indeed the guy I'd been to school with. Yet that would still leave him far too young to ever have lived here. Between our family and the previous occupants I knew who'd lived in the house for the last forty years. So how could it be his old house? It didn't make sense. And was it actually him? The boy from my school? Apart from being too old, it looked like him, but was it actually him?

I did the best I could with the milk, and then straightened up, staggering slightly. My perception seemed to have become both heightened and jumbled, as if I was very drunk. Everything pulsed with an unusual intensity and exaggerated emotional charge, yet there also seemed to be gaps in what I was perceiving, as if I was receiving an edited version of what was going on. Things began to flick from one state to another – with the bits in between, the becoming, missing like a series of jump cuts. I felt hot and dizzy and the kitchen looked small and indescribably messy, the orange of the walls – the same colour my bedroom had once been painted – seeming to push in at me beneath a low and unsteady ceiling. I wondered confusedly if I was seeing the kitchen as they saw it, and then immediately wondered what I meant.

Meanwhile they stood at the window, occasionally turning to stare balefully at me, radiating distaste and impatience. They were evidently waiting for something. But what? Noticing that I still had the piece of kitchen roll in my hand, I stepped over all the rubbish on the floor – what the hell had been going on in this kitchen? – to put it in the overflowing bin. I squeezed my temples with my fingers, struggling to stand upright against the weight of the air, and squared up to the men.

"L-look", I stuttered, leaning on the fridge for support, "What exactly is going on?"

I immediately wished I'd kept quiet. The suited man slowly turned his head. It kept turning and turning, until it was looking directly at me – while his body remained stayed facing the other way. Like an owl, though, he wasn't blinking. I could feel my stomach trying to crawl away and fought the need to gag. I sensed he'd done it deliberately, done it because he knew it would make me want to throw up, and I thought he might well be right.

"Why don't you just shut up?" he said. Then he twisted his head slowly back round until he was looking out onto the drive once more.

I decided not to ask any more questions.

Meanwhile, the mess in the kitchen seemed to be getting worse. Every time I looked there were more dirty pans and bits of rubbish and old food on the floor. My head felt thicker and heavier, as if everything was slipping away from me. I slumped against the fridge and clung to it, almost pulling it away from the wall. I began to cry too, my tears cutting channels in the thick grime on the fridge door. I dimly remembered that my parents had bought a brand new one only a few weeks before, but they must have changed it again. This one looked like something out of the 1950s. Very retro. Or original. To be honest it was hard to tell, because it was swimming back and forth and there was a lot of white in my eyes. Both the men were both watching me now, as if mildly interested to see when I'd fall.

Suddenly there was a terrible jangling impact in my head. I flapped hysterically at my ears, as if to stop someone hammering pencils into them. Then the pain happened again, and I recognised first that it was a sound rather than a blow, and then that it was the doorbell.

Someone was at the front door.

The two men glanced at each other, and the blond one nodded wearily. The suited man turned to me.

"Do you know what that is?" he asked.

"It's the front door" I said quickly, still trying to please him.

"So you'd better answer it, hadn't you?"

"Yes."

"Answer the door."

"Should I answer it?" I queried, stupidly. I couldn't seem to remember what words meant anymore.

"Yes!" he shouted, and picked up a mug – my mug, the mug I'd came downstairs, I remembered, to put tea in – and hurled it straight at me. It smashed into the fridge door by my face. I struggled to pull myself upright, head aching and ears ringing, aware of a soft crump as a fragment of the mug broke under my foot. The doorbell jangled again, the harshness of the noise making me realise how muted all other sounds had become. I fell towards the kitchen door, sliding across the front of the fridge, my feet tangling in the boxes and cartons that now covered the filthy floor. I could feel the orange of the walls seeping in through my ears and mouth, and kept missing whole seconds of time – as if I was blacking out and coming to like a stroboscope.

As I lurched across to the kitchen door and grabbed the handle to hold myself up, I heard the blond man say "He may not go through. If he does, we wait."

It didn't mean anything to me. None of it did.

I made my way towards the front door, ploughing clumsily through drifts of rubbish in the hallway. The chime of the doorbell had pushed the air hard, and I could see it lapping towards me in waves. Ducking to avoid the sound, I slipped on the mat and almost fell into the living room. As I crouched there on my hands I knees, it was getting dark in there, really dark, and I could hear the plants talking. I couldn't catch the words, but they were definitely conversing, beneath the night sounds and a soft rustling which sounded a hundred yards away. The living room must have grown.

I picked myself up and turned to the front door. The bell clanged again, and this time the sound caught me full in the face, stinging bitterly. It should have been about four paces across the hall from the living room door to the front door, but I thought it was only going to take one and then it took twenty, past all the panelling and over the huge folds in the mat. It was not an easy journey.

Then I had my hand on the doorknob and then the door was open and I stepped out of the house.

"Oh hello, Michael," said a voice. "I thought someone must be in, because all the lights were on."

"Wuh?" I said, blinking in the fading sunlight.

The woman in front of me smiled. "I hope I didn't disturb you?"

"No, that's fine." Suddenly I recognised her. It was Mrs. Steinberg, the woman who brings us our cat food in bulk. "Fine. Sorry." I glanced covertly behind me into the hallway, which was solid and unpanelled and four paces wide and led to the living room – which was light and airy and the size it had always been.

"I've brought your delivery," the woman said, and then frowned. "Look, are you alright?"

"I'm fine," I replied, turning to grin broadly at her. My mind felt like a runaway lift, soaring back upwards to reality. "I just nodded off for a moment, in the kitchen. I still feel a bit... you know."

Mrs. Steinberg smiled. "Of course. Give me a hand?"

I followed her to the top of the drive and heaved a box of cat food out of her van, watching the house. There was nothing to see. I thanked her and then carried the box back down the drive as she drove off. I walked back into the house and shut the front door behind me.

I felt absolutely fine.

I walked into the kitchen. As I'd expected, the men had disappeared. I looked slowly around a kitchen which looked exactly as it had since before I was too young to remember. Everything was normal. Of course.

I must have fallen asleep making tea, and then struggled over to the front door to open it while still half asleep. I could remember asking myself if I was having a dream, and deciding I wasn't – but that just showed how wrong you could be. It had been unusually vivid, and it was odd how I'd been suddenly awake and alright again as soon as I stepped out of the front door. But it had been a dream. Here I was in the kitchen again, and everything was normal. Clean and tidy, spick and span, with all the rubbish in the bin and the pans in the right places and the milk in the fridge and a smashed mug on the floor.

That was less good. It was my mug, and it lay smashed at the bottom of the fridge. How had that happened?

Maybe I'd fallen asleep holding it. Not terribly likely, but possible. Or perhaps I'd knocked it over on waking, and incorporated the sound into my dream. This was slightly more credible, but where exactly was I supposed to have fallen asleep? Just leaning against the counter – or actually stretched out on it, using the kettle as a pillow?

Then I noticed the fridge door. There was a little dent in it, with a couple of flecks of paint missing. At about head height. That wasn't good either.

I cleared up the mug and switched the kettle on. While it was boiling I wandered into the hall and the living room. Everything was fine, tidy, normal. Super. I went back into the kitchen. The same. Great. Apart from a little dent in the fridge door at about head height.

I made my cup of tea in a different, non-broken mug, and drank it looking out of the kitchen window at the drive. I felt unsettled and nervous, and unsure of what to do with either of those emotions. Even if it had been a dream, it was a very odd one, particularly the way it had fought so hard against melting away. Maybe I was much more tired than I realised. Or ill. Food poisoning could make your head go very strange, as I'd learned after a couple of college friends' attempts at cooking anything more complex than toast. But I felt fine. Physically, at least.

I carried the box of cat food into the pantry, unpacked it, and stacked the cans in the corner. Then I switched the kettle on again. Suddenly my heart seemed to stop.

Before I had time to realise why, the cause repeated itself. A soft chinking noise outside the back door. I moved quickly to the window and looked out. There was no-one in the drive. I craned my neck, trying to see around to the back door, but could only see the large pile of firewood that lay to one side of it.

Then I heard the noise again. I walked slowly into the back hallway and listened, slowly clenching my fists. I could hear nothing except the sound of blood pumping in my ears. I grabbed the knob and swung the door open.

Stillness outside. A rectangle of late afternoon light, a patch of driveway, and a dark hedge waving quietly. I stepped out into the drive, and stood and listened again.

After a moment I heard a very faint crunching noise. It sounded like pebbles softly rubbing against each other. Then I heard it again. I looked more closely at the drive, peering at the actual stones, and noticed that a small patch about ten yards in front of me appeared to be moving slightly. Wriggling, almost.

They stopped, and then the sound came again – and another patch stirred briefly, about a yard closer than the first. As if registering the weight of invisible feet.

I was so engrossed that I didn't notice the whistling straight away. When I did, I looked up. The blond man was back. He was standing at the top of the driveway, carrying a bicycle with the wheels slowly spinning in the dusk. He whistled the top line of a perfect harmony, the lower line just the sound of the wind. As I stared at him, backing slowly towards the house, the crunching noise got louder and louder.

Then the suited man was standing with his nose almost touching mine. "Hello again," he said.

The blond man started down the driveway. "Greetings indeed," he laughed. "Come on, in we go."

Abruptly I realised that the very last thing I should do was let them back into the house.

I leapt back through the door into the hallway. The suited man, caught by surprise, started forward but I was quick and whipped the door shut in his face and locked it. That felt good, but then he started banging on the door very hard, grotesquely hard, and I saw that the kitchen was getting messy again, and the fridge was old, and I could barely see out of the window because it was so grimy. A slight flicker in my mind made me think that maybe I'd missed the smallest fraction of a second, and I realised that it really hadn't been a dream. I was back in the bad place. As I backed into the kitchen I tripped and fell, sprawling amongst cartons and bacon rind and dirt and what appeared to be puke on the floor. The banging on the back door got louder, and louder, and louder. He was going to break it, I knew. He was going to break the door down. I'd let them back and they had to come in through the back door. I'd come in through the wrong door...

Suddenly understanding what I must do, I scrambled to my feet and kicked my way through the rubbish. The fridge door swung open in my way. The inside was dark and dirty and there was something rotted inside, but I slammed it out of the way, biting hard on my lip to keep my head clear.

I had to get to the front door. I had to open it, step out, and then step back in again. The front door was the right door. And I had to do it soon, before the back door broke and let them in. I could already hear a splintering quality to the sound of the blows. And the back door was about two inches thick.

The hallway was worse than I expected. I skidded to a halt, at first unable to even see the front door. I thought that I must be looking in the wrong direction, but I wasn't, because I finally spotted it over to the left, where it was supposed to be. But the angles were all wrong, and to see it I had to look behind me and to the right, although when I saw it I could see that in reality it was still over to the left. And it looked so close – could it really be less than a yard away? – but when I held my hand out to it I groped into nothing, the fingers still in front of the door when it should have been past it.

I stared wildly around, disorientated and unsure even of which way to go. Suddenly the banging behind me got markedly louder, probably as the blond man joined in, and this helped marginally to restore my sense of direction. I found the front door again, concentrated hard on its apparent position, and started to walk towards it. I immediately fell over, because the floor was much lower than I expected. It actually seemed be tilted in some way, although it looked flat and level, because although one of my legs reached it easily enough the other dangled in space. I pulled myself up onto my knees and found I was looking at a sort of sloped wall between the wall and the ceiling, a wall which bent back from the wall and yet out from the ceiling. The door was still over on the left, although to see it I now had to look straight ahead and up.

Then I noticed another sound beneath the eternal banging, and whirled to face the direction it was coming from. I found that I was looking through the living room door, and that it gave into sheer darkness, a darkness which was seeping out into the hallway like smoke, clinging to the angles in the air like the inside of a dark prism. I heard the noise again. It was a deep rumbling growl, far, far away in there, almost obscured by the night noises and the sound of vegetation moving in the wind. The sound didn't seem to be getting any closer, but I knew that was because the living room now extended out far beyond the house, into hundreds and hundreds of miles of dense jungle. As I listened carefully I could hear the gurgling of some dark river far off to the right, the sound of water mixing with the warm rustling of the breeze in the darkness. It sounded very peaceful and for a moment I was still, transfixed.

Then the sound of another splintering crack wrenched me away, and I turned my back on the living room and flailed towards where the front door must be. The hall table loomed above me and I thought I could walk upright beneath it – but tripped over it and fell again, headlong onto the cool floorboards. The mat had moved, no, was moving, sliding slowly up the stairs like in a draft, and as I rolled over and looked at the ceiling I saw the floor coming towards me, the walls shortening in little jerks.

As I lay there panting, a clear cool waft of air stroked my cheek. At first I thought that it must have come from the living room, although it had been warm in there, but then I remembered that I was lying on the floor. The breeze had to be a draft coming under the front door. I must nearly be there. I looked all around me but all I could see was panelling and floor and what was behind me. I closed my eyes and tried to grope for it, but it was even worse inside my head so I opened them again. Then I caught a glimpse of the door, far away, obscured from view round a corner but just visible once you knew where to look. On impulse I reached my hand out in not quite the opposite direction and felt it fall upon warm grainy wood.

The door. I'd found it.

I pulled myself along the floor towards it, and tried to stand up. I got no more than a few inches before I fell back down again. I tried once more, with the same result, feeling as if I was trying to do something entirely against nature. Again, and this time I reached a semi-crouching position, muscles straining. I started to slump almost immediately – but as I did so I threw myself forwards. I found myself curled up, my feet a couple of feet from the floor, lying on the door. Electing to not even try to come to terms with this, I groped by my side and found the doorknob. I tried to twist it but the sweat on my hand made it spin uselessly on the shiny metal. I wiped it on my shirt and tried again, and this time I got some purchase and heard the catch withdraw as the knob turned. Exultantly I tugged at it, as with a tremendous crash the back door finally gave way.

The door wouldn't budge. Panicking, I tried again. Nothing. By peering down the crack I could see that no lock or bolt was impeding it, so why wouldn't it bloody move?

There were footsteps in the back hall.

Suddenly I realised that I was lying on the door, and trying to pull it towards me against my own weight.

The footsteps reached the kitchen.

I rolled over off the door onto the wall beside it and reached for the handle, but I'd slid too far. As the footsteps came closer I scrambled back across the slippery wall, grabbed and twisted the doorknob with all my strength. It opened just as they entered the hall and I rolled out through it, fell and landed awkwardly and painfully on something hard and bristly and for a few moments had no clear idea of where or who I was, and just lay there fighting for breath.

After some time I sat up slowly. I was sitting outside the house on the doormat, my back to the front door. At the top of the drive a young couple were staring at me curiously. I stood up and smiled, trying to suggest that I often sat on the doormat and that they ought to try it, as it was actually a lot of fun – hoping that they hadn't seen me fall there from about two-thirds of the way up the door. They smiled back and carried on walking, mollified or maybe even hurrying off home to try it for themselves.

I turned hesitantly back towards the door and looked in.

It had worked. It was all okay again. The mat was on the floor, right angles looked like 90°, and the ceiling was back where it was supposed to be. I stepped back a pace and looked down the driveway at the back door. It had been utterly smashed, and now looked like little more than an extension of the firewood pile.

I stepped back into the house through the front door, the right door, and shut it behind me. I walked carefully and quietly into the living room, and then the kitchen. Everything was fine, everything was normal. It was just a nice normal house. If you came in through the right door.

The wrong door was in about a thousand pieces. I thought about that for some time, with another cup of tea and what felt like my first cigarette in months. I saw with frank disbelief that less than half an hour had elapsed since I'd first come downstairs. The back door. The wrong door. It was coming in through there that took me to wherever it was that the house became. Coming in through the front door brought me back to where I normally lived. So presumably I was safe, so long as I didn't leave the house and come back in through the back door. They couldn't get me. Presumably.

But I didn't like having that door in pieces. Being safe was only half of the issue. I wasn't going to feel secure until that portal was well and truly closed.

I walked into the back hall and looked nervously out through the wreckage onto the drive. Everything was fine. There was nothing I needed protecting from. But I still didn't like it. Did it have to be me who came through the door? What if a falling leaf or maybe even just a soft breeze came inside? Would that be enough?

Could I take the risk?

As I stood there indecisively, I noticed once more the pile of firewood propped up against the outside wall of the back hall. I probably still wouldn't have put two and two together had not a very large proportion of the pile been thick old floorboards – a donation from a neighbour. I looked at the tool shelf on the inside wall and saw a hammer and a big box of good long nails. Then I looked at the wood again.

I could nail the damn thing shut.

I flicked my cigarette butt out onto the drive and rolled up my sleeves. The hammer was big and heavy, which was just as well because when I nailed the planks across the door frame I'd be hammering into solid brickwork. I was going to have to board right the way up, but that was alright as there were loads of planks, and if I reinforced it enough it should be well-nigh impregnable.

Feeling much better, I set to work. I may even have hummed. Kneeling just inside the door, I reached out and began pulling the floorboards in, taking care to select the thickest and least weathered. I judged that I'd need about fifteen to make the doorway really secure, although that was largely guesswork as I'd never tried to turn the back hall into a fortress before. Pulling them in was heavy work. I had to stretch out to reach them, and I began to get hot and tired, and anxious to begin the nailing. Outside it was getting darker as the evening began, and the air was very cool and still.

As the pile in the back hall increased in size it became more difficult, and I had to lean further and further out to reach the next plank. This made me nervous. I was still inside, and my feet were still on the ground in the back hall. I wasn't 'coming back in'. I was just leaning out and then, well, sort of coming back in, but not really, because my feet never left the back hall. But it made me nervous, and I began to work quicker and quicker, perspiration running down my face as, clinging to the doorframe with my left hand, I stretched out to bring the last few boards in. Eleven, twelve. Just a couple more. Now the last one I could possibly reach: that would have to be enough. Hooking my left foot behind the frame and gripping it hard with my left hand, I stretched out towards the plank, waving fingers little more than an inch from the end. Just a little further... I let my hooking foot slide slightly, allowed my fingers to slip round half an inch, and tried to extend my back as far as it would go. My fingers just scraping the end, I tried a last yearning lunge.

And then suddenly a stray thought struck me. Here I was, pulled out as if on some invisible rack. Why hadn't I just gone out of the front door, picked up piles of wood, and brought them back into the house through the front door? It would have been easier, it would have been quicker, and it wouldn't have involved all this monkeying around at the wrong door. Not that it mattered now, because as it happened even if I didn't get this last plank I'd probably have plenty, but I wouldn't have been so hot and tired. It was also worrying that in my haste I'd been putting myself in needless danger. I'd better slow down, calm down, take a rest.

It was an unimportant, contemplative thought, but one that distracted me for a fraction of a second too long. As I finally got the tips of my fingers round the plank I realised with horror that the hand on the doorframe was slipping. Desperately I tried to scrabble back, but my hands were too sweaty and the doorframe itself was slippery now. I felt the tendons in my hand stretch as I tried to defy my centre of gravity and think my weight backwards, and then suddenly my forehead walloped onto the ground and I was lying flat on my face.

I was up in a second, and I swear to God that both feet never left the hall floor at once. I leapt back into the hallway, grabbing that last bloody piece of wood without even noticing it.

I crouched in the doorframe, panting hysterically. Everything looked normal outside. The driveway was quiet, the pebbles were still and there was none of the faint deadening of sound that I associated with the other place. I was furious with myself for having taken the risk, for not having thought to bring them in through the front door – and especially for falling, which had been painful quite apart from anything else. But I hadn't fallen out, not really. I hadn't come back in, as such. The drive was fine, the kitchen was fine. Everything was okay.

Soothed by the sounds of early evening traffic in the distance, my heart gradually slowed to about only twice its normal rate. I forced myself to take a break, and had a quiet cigarette, perched on the pile of planks. During the fall my right foot had caught the tool shelf, and there were nails all over the place, both inside and outside the door. But there were plenty left and the ones outside could stay there. I wasn't going to make the same damn fool mistake twice.

Gathering up the hammer and a fistful of nails, I laid a plank across the door and started work. Getting the nails through the wood and into the masonry was even harder than I'd expected, but within a couple of minutes it was in place, and felt reassuringly solid. I heaved another plank into position and set about securing it. This was actually going to work.

After half an hour I was into the swing of it and the wood now reached almost halfway up the doorframe. My arms were aching and head ringing from the hammering, which was very loud in the confined space of the back hall. I had a break leaning on the completed section, staring blankly out onto the drive. I was jolted back from reverie by the realisation that a piece of dust or something must have landed in my eye, distorting my vision. I blinked to remove it, but it didn't disappear. It didn't hurt, just made a small patch of the drive up near the road look a bit ruffled. I rubbed and shut both eyes individually, and discovered with mounting unease that the distortion was present in both.

I stood upright. Something was definitely going on at the top of the drive. The patch still looked crumpled, as if seen through a heat haze, and whichever way I turned my head the patch stayed in the same place. It was flickering very slightly now too, like a bad quality film print, although the flecks weren't white, they were dark. I rubbed my eyes hard again, but once I'd stopped seeing stars I saw that the effect was still there. I peered at it, trying to discern something that I could interpret. The flecks seemed to organise into broken and shifting vertical lines as I watched, as if something was hidden behind a curtain of rain, rain so coloured as to make up a picture of that patch of the drive. This impression gradually strengthened until it was like looking at one of those plastic strip doors, where you walk through the hanging strips. It was as if there was one of those at the top of the drive, a patch of driveway pictured on it in living three dimensions. With something moving just the other side.

Then suddenly the balance shifted, like one of those drawings made up of black and white dots where if you stare at it long enough you can see a Dalmatian. I dropped to my knees behind the partially completed barrier.

They were back.

Standing at the top of the drive, their images both underlying and superimposed on it as if woven together, were the two men. They were standing in a frozen and unnatural position, like a freeze-frame. Their faces looked pallid and washed out, the colours uneven and the image flickering and dancing in front of my eyes. And still they stood, not there, and yet in some sense there.

As I stared, transfixed, I noticed that the suited man's foot appeared to be moving. It was hard to focus on, and happening incomprehensibly slowly, but it was moving, gradually leaving the ground. Over the course of a minute it was raised and then lowered back onto the ground a couple of feet in front of its original position, leaving the man's body leaning slightly forward.

I realised what I was seeing. In extraordinary and flickering slow motion, somehow projected onto the drive like an old home movie, the suited man was beginning to walk down towards the house. The image wasn't flickering so much anymore, the colours were getting stronger, and I could no longer see the driveway through them. Somehow they were coming back through. I thought I'd got away with it, but I hadn't. I'd fallen out. Not very far by anyone's standards, but far enough. Far enough to have come back in through the wrong door. And now they were tearing their way back into the world, or hauling me back towards theirs. And very slowly they were getting closer.

Fighting to stay calm, I grabbed a plank, put it into position above the others and nailed it into place. Then another, and another, not pausing for breath or thought. Through the narrowing gap I could see them getting closer. They didn't look two-dimensional any longer, and they were moving more quickly too. As I leaned towards the kitchen for a plank I saw that there was a single dusty carton on the floor. It had started.

I smacked another plank into place and hammered it down. The men were real again, and they were also much nearer to the house, though still moving at a weirdly graceful tenth of normal speed. Hammering wildly, ignoring increasingly frequent whacks on the fingers, I cast occasional wild glances aside into the kitchen. The fridge was beginning to look strange, the stark 1990s geometry softening, regressing, and the rubbish was gathering. I never saw any of it arrive, but each time I looked there was another piece of cardboard, a few more scraps, one more layer of grime. It had only just started, and was still happening very slowly, maybe because I'd barely fallen out. But it was happening. The house was going over.

I kept on hammering. I knew that at some point I must run to the front door, go out and come back in again, come in through the right door. But that could wait, would have to wait. It was coming on very slowly this time, and I still felt completely clear-headed. What I had to do first was seal off the back door, and soon. The two men, always at the vanguard of the change, were well and truly here, and getting closer all the time. I had to make sure that the back door was secure against anything those two could do to it, for long enough for me to get to the front door and jump out. I had no idea what the front hall would be like by the time I got there, and if I left the back door unfinished and got lost trying to get to the front door, I'd be in real trouble.

I slammed planks into place as fast as I could. Outside they got steadily closer and closer, and inside another carton appeared in the kitchen. As I jammed the last horizontal board into place the suited man and the blond man were only a couple of yards away, now moving at full pace. I'd barely nailed it in before the first blow crashed into it, bending it and making me leap back with shock. I hurriedly picked up more wood and slapped planks over the barrier in vertical slats and crosses, nailing them in hard, reinforcing and making sure that the barrier was securely fastened to the wall on all sides, furiously hammering and building.

After a while I couldn't feel the ache in my back or see the blood on my hands: all I could hear was the beating of the hammer, and all I could see was the heads of the nails as I piled more and more wood onto the barrier. I had wood to spare – I hadn't even needed that last bloody plank – and by the time I finished it was four pieces thick in some places, with the reinforcing strips spread several feet either side of the frame. I used the last three pieces as bracing struts, forcing them horizontally across the hallway, one end of each lodged in niches in the barrier, the other jammed tight against the opposite wall.

Finally it was finished, and I stood back and looked at it. It looked pretty damn solid. "Let's see you get through that," I shouted, half sitting and half collapsing to the ground. After a moment I noticed how quiet it was. At some point they must have stopped banging against the door. I'd been making far too much noise to notice, and my head was still ringing. I put my ear against the barrier and listened. Silence.

I lit a cigarette and let tiredness and a blessed feeling of safeness wash over me. The sound of the match striking was slightly muted, but that could've been the ringing in my ears as much as anything, and the kitchen looked pretty grubby but no more than that. I felt fine. I wondered what the two outside were up to, and whether there was any chance that they might have given up and be waiting for the change to take its course – not realising that I understood about the right door and the wrong door. For a few minutes I actually savoured the sensation of being balanced between two worlds, secure in the knowledge that in a moment I would just walk out that front door and the house would come back and none of it would matter at all.

Eventually I stood up, wincing in pain. I was really going to ache tomorrow. I stepped into the kitchen, narrowly avoiding a large black spider that scuttled out of one of the cartons. The floor was getting very messy now, scraps of dried-up meat covered with the corpses of dead maggots, and small piles of stuff

I really didn't want to look too closely at. I threaded my way over to the door, past the now bizarrely misshapen fridge, and into the front hall.

The hallway was still clear of debris, and as far as I could see, utterly normal. As I crossed towards the front door, anxious now to get the whole thing over with – and wondering how I was going to explain the state of the back door to my parents – I noticed a faint tapping sound in the far distance. After a moment it stopped, and then restarted from a slightly different direction. Odd, but scarcely a primary concern. Right now my priority was getting out of that front door before the hall got any stranger. Feeling like an actor about to bound on stage, I reached out to the doorknob, twisted it and pulled it towards me.

At first I couldn't take it in. I couldn't work out why instead of the driveway all I could see was brown. Brown flatness.

Then as I adjusted my focal length, pulling it in for something much closer than the drive I'd been expecting, I understood. The view looked rather familiar. I'd seen something like it very recently.

It was a barrier. An impregnable wooden barrier nailed across the door into the walls from the outside. Now I knew what they'd been doing as I finished nailing them out.

They'd been nailing me in.

I tried everything I could think of. My fists, my shoulder, a chair. The planks were there to stay. I couldn't get out. I couldn't come back in through the right door, and for the moment they couldn't get in through the wrong door. A sort of stalemate. But a very poor sort for me, because they were much the stronger and getting more so all the time, and because the house was still going over and now I couldn't stop it.

I strode into the kitchen, rubbing my bruised shoulder and thinking furiously. There had to be something I could do, and I had to do it fast. The change was speeding up. Although the hall still looked normal the kitchen was now filthy, and the fifties fridge was fully back. In a retro kind of way it was quite attractive. But it was wrong.

In the background I could still hear the faint tapping noise. Maybe they were trying to get in through the roof.

I had to get out, had to find a way. I tried lateral thinking. You leave a house by a door. How else? No other way. You always leave by a door. But was there any other way you could leave, if you were in, say, a desperate emergency? The doors... The windows. What about the windows? If there was a right door and a wrong door, maybe there were right and wrong windows too, and perhaps the right ones looked out onto the real world. Maybe, just maybe, you could smash one and then climb out and then back in again. Perhaps that would work.

I had no idea whether it would or not. I wasn't kidding myself that I understood anything, and God alone knew where I might land if I chose the wrong window. Perhaps I'd go out the wrong one and then be chased round the house by the two maniacs outside, as I tried to find a right window to break back in through. That would be a barrel of laughs. That would be Fun City. But what choice did I have? I ran into the living room, heading for the big picture window.

I don't know how I could have missed making the connection. Possibly because the taps were so quiet. I stood in the living room, my mouth open. This time they were one jump ahead. They'd boarded up the fucking windows.

I ran back into the hall, through into the dining room, then upstairs to the bedrooms. Every single window was boarded up. I knew where they'd got the nails from, because I'd spilt more then enough when I fell, but how.... Then I realised how they'd nailed them in without a hammer, why the tapping had been so quiet. With sudden unpleasant clarity I could imagine the suited man clubbing the nails in with his fists, smashing them in with his forehead and grinning while he did it.

Oh Jesus.

I walked downstairs again, slowly now. Every single window was boarded up, even the ones that were too small to climb through. As I stood once more in the kitchen, amidst the growing piles of shit, the pounding on the back door started. There was no way I could get out of the house, and I couldn't stop what was happening. This time it was going over all the way, and taking me with it. And meanwhile they were going to smash their way in to come along for the ride. To get me. I listened, watching the rubbish, as the pounding got louder and louder.

It's still getting louder, and I can tell from the sound that some of the planks are beginning to give way. The house stopped balancing long ago, and the change is coming on more quickly. The kitchen looks like a bomb site and there are an awful lot of spiders in there now. Eventually I left them to it and came through the hall into here, only making one or two wrong turnings. Into the living room.

And that's where I am now, just sitting and waiting. There is nothing I can do about the change, nothing. I can't get out. I can't stop them getting in.

But there is one thing I can do. I'm going to stay here, in the living room. I can see small shadows now, gathering in corners and darting out from under the chairs, and it's quite dark down by the end wall. The wall itself seems less important now, less substantial, no longer a barrier. I think I can hear the sound of running water somewhere far away, and smell the faintest hint of the of dark and lush vegetation.

I won't let them get me. I'll wait, in the gathering darkness, listening to the coming of the night sounds and feeling a soft breeze on my face as I sense the room opening out as the walls shade away, as I sit here quietly in the dark warm air. And then I'll get up and start walking, walking out into the dark land, into the jungle and amidst the trees that stand all around behind the darkness, smelling the greenness that surrounds me and hearing the gentle river off somewhere to the right. And I'll feel happy walking away into the night, and maybe far away I'll meet whatever makes the growling sounds I begin to hear in the distance, and we'll sit together by running water and be at peace in the darkness.

AROUND THE APPLE TREE

Jessica Gilling

A gentle tap at the window stirs Margaret from her thoughts. Mr Hotfoot Jackson waits patiently on the sill for the leftovers that sit in a bowl on the table. With great effort she heaves her body out of the chair and hobbles to the window. The raven caws thankfully as she places the cold mutton stew in front of him. She has not touched it this evening; her appetite has left her.

For many years, the raven has been her only companion; a pet to some, to others a familiar. Yet despite the locals' suspicions, the single ritual performed in this house is the one she is performing now; giving her only friend the food she cannot eat.

Margaret sits back in her chair, pulled up close to the hearth, in the single room of her broken-down cottage. Her dirty, moth-eaten shawl, along with the jar of gin she's drinking only does so much to fight the cold, but the embers in the grate emit just enough warmth to stop her shaking. This winter has been a long one. The pain that courses through her bones, and the hacking cough that has wracked her body for the entire season, tell Margaret only one thing; she will die, and soon. Perished and forsaken, she sits alone night after night, as she has not just for the whole of this winter, but for years before it. Her parents, the only people who had loved and cared for her, died when she was very young; she can't remember exactly when, but could recall she had started to sprout teats. Her hips had grown wider too, and she had begun to get her monthly visitor. It was also then that Parson Spencer first noticed her.

A familiar feeling rises in her stomach; a mixture of bile and anger. White-hot prickles of indignation puncture her chest, and she swallows this feeling with the last of her gin. She wipes snot from her nose with the cuff of her gown; the faint odour of mildew lingers in the fabric.

Pappy died first, and then Mother within a few weeks, leaving Margaret alone. Her only other relatives refused to take her in. She was abandoned, with only a herd of cattle for company. The cottage wasn't fit for habitation either; its thatched roof neither use nor ornament when the weather got rough. It was built in the centre of the Hamil, about two miles from the Leek to Burslem road. In the valley below, and through the woodland along her boundary, lies the town of Burslem, and the parish of Nortone high up on the moors to the east.

Yes, it was after the death of Margaret's parents that Parson Spencer began to do his duties as a man of God. He would come to the cottage once or twice a week to make sure that she was 'alright'. Oh yes, doing his duties! But not as a man of God; as a man serving his manhood and nothing else. He used his position to prey on the weak-minded, people whose shame would eat them alive if anyone were to know; the poor necessitous widows who had too many mouths to feed and would do anything for the crust of a half-penny loaf.

Margaret winces at the thought of his rough hands over her, the stink of stale beer on his breath, the stench of his sweat invading her nostrils. He had only attempted to violate her once. His wet lips had roamed her face, sucking at her like a hungry new-born babe, trying blindly to attach itself to its mother's nipple. Once was enough for him to see that she was not a girl to be taken advantage of. She bit his nose, hard, and spat his blood back in his face. No, Margaret Leigh was not a fool. She, like her mother before her, had been born with a fire in her belly.

As Margaret grew older, people started to avoid her altogether. Parson Spencer had made sure of that. Rumours were circulated about the hamlet; stories of her being born deformed, with jagged teeth, craving crusts of bread and suckling on the animals her family kept, from just a few hours old. It was easily done; the people of Burslem rarely saw Margaret any more, and when they did, only a handful knew who she was. She had stood outside St John's church on a Sunday once or twice and listened, bemused by the fact that people would not question the word of a drunk. After a while she understood, both of them shared something; it was something that was invisible to others, a darkness that people not inflicted with it were blind to. She, and the Parson had sought to find light at the bottom of a bottle, and no matter how many they searched, the light was never found.

Margaret lived a solitary life, eking a living by selling milk on market days to the people of Burslem. She would shuffle over the cobbles with her milk pails straddling her shoulders, longing for someone to talk to. Anybody would do, an acquaintance to wave a cheery hello to, a friend that she could invite to the cottage, but there was no one. She provided a service and nothing more to them. One day she opened the door of her cottage to find a raven perched on the lower branches of her hawthorn bush. She ignored him at first, but as time went on she realised that he wasn't going to leave, and she started to feed him. Eventually he became a great source of comfort for Margaret; a friend. He joined her on market days and would settle on her shoulder, while she called out to customers

Once, she had been a very beautiful girl, with dark brown hair that cascaded down her back in waves and curls. Her eyes were a deep blue colour, and her soft skin sun-kissed from working hard around her farm. She tended to the animals and did the work of ten men as well, to prove to herself and others that she needed no man; she needed no-one. But from early on, the laughing and the taunting began to take its toll. Margaret was only human, after all. She liked to act hard-faced to the people of Burslem, allowing them to believe she had a bitter and spiteful temper, and a ferocious and vindictive nature. They would never see her for what she truly was: a lone girl, outcast because she did not wish to give her body to a man. No, they didn't see that at all. They saw a girl who lived alone for most of her life, with nothing aside from her animals for company. They saw a woman who never attended church. They saw exactly what they wanted to see.

The passing years have taken their toll. Living her life, shrinking away from their serpentine tongues, has forced her to retreat within herself. She has ducked away from the society that ridiculed her, unknowing of the truth. She has spent most of her adult life walking over the cobbles of Swan Square, with nothing but a raven for a companion.

It has been years since she last went to market to sell milk; Margaret had sold most of her herd to a farmer from Brown

Edge, a village beyond the valley, and her land to her cousin in Chester. It fetched a modest sum, but unfortunately her living costs exceeded the money she had left. The last time she was able to visit Burslem, the older people looked down upon her, and children sniggered behind their hands.

"*Weight and measure, sold I never; milk and water sold I ever,*" she heard them whisper, mocking her.

"Really, milk and fucking water?" She spits into the embers, causing them to hiss, and grimaces bitterly. She doesn't like to look of herself anymore; the skin of her face looks like cow hide after it has been flayed and tanned by inept and unskilled hands. Deep crevices line her forehead and crow's-feet frame her eyes. The left side of her body sags slightly as if under an unseen weight. She's aware this is more noticeable in her face, because she can't control all her facial muscles. Her lips droop and strings of saliva often hang from them. She must be a gruesome sight. Margaret coughs and hacks once more and convulses with the pain of the savage disease running amok throughout her body.

She sits up as much as her curved spine will allow, and wipes her bloodied lips on the sleeve of her dress. She closes her eyes and sighs deeply. There is not even enough wood to keep the fire in until morning. Margaret grasps the last half-log on the hearth with her gnarled, work-worn hands and throws it onto the fire. She has never known any different, so why does her misery cause her so much anguish now? Then, the realisation strikes her like a scorching iron poker: she has brought this on herself. If only she had tried, if only she had stuck up for herself, if only she knew what their problem was with her. Why had they taken it upon themselves to destroy her life? She can understand, and possibly forgive, the people of the town, for they knew no better. But the Parson? His obsession with her had ensured that he was consumed completely by madness before he died, and for this she can think of no real reason.

For the first time in a long time, she cries. Tears stream down her ashen face, sobs and coughs wrack her body. Margaret cries for the family and friends she does not have, the husband she never knew, and the babes she never carried. The Hamil Witch is dying, with nothing and no-one to her name, but a raven, a lump of ash wood in her grate and that pitiful excuse for a hawthorn bush outside that refuses to bud every year.

Yes, she has brought it all on herself, and there is nothing that can be done now. Perhaps, if she could have just made them see that she wasn't a witch. She had never made a pact with the Devil, and, as sure as the sky is blue, had never intended any malice towards a person in her entire life. But, as she sits by the fire, watching the flames flicker as they consume the last freshly chopped log, she comes to understand that nothing can be done. It is all too late.

With this thought Margaret settles back into her rocking chair. The heat of the embers barely reaches her now. She rocks back and forth slowly. The wind whistles through the thatched roof and the cracks in the brick-work. The hawthorn bush scrapes at the window; the sound taunts her.

Oblivion is coming and she welcomes it with open arms. No more sorrow, no more pain. No more gin! She smiles, the traces of the former beauty that she had held in her youth, gone forever. Margaret would mourn the lack of gin, wherever she was going. No more of those bastard kids in the town teasing her with that stupid rhyme…

"Molly Leigh, Molly Leigh, chase me around the apple tree
Molly Leigh, Molly Leigh, you can't catch me."

If she could, she would curse this whole Godforsaken town, starting with the daft bastards that drink in The Turk's Head. If she *were* a witch, that ignorant bastard Spencer would be the first to go. She chuckles at the thought, but she knows in her heart that she would never be able to harm another that way, even if there was a chance that she could. With the brief lapse in emotions aside, Margaret can't wait to shed her mortal coil and leave the Hamil. Forever.

She closes her eyes once more and continues to rock in her chair. The motion is almost hypnotic and comforts her. Her breathing becomes more laboured, the rancid air escapes her lungs in long, drawn out wheezes. She smiles one last time as oblivion starts to consume her.

Mr Hotfoot Jackson starts to tap at the window again, this time with more urgency. Margaret shifts in her chair, and wonders what the commotion is all about. Her cottage door swings open; and there, standing in the doorway, is a man. The light of the moon casts his silhouette over the cold stone floor.

"Good evening Molly, my old friend." His voice is merely a whisper, and sounds if it is being carried by the wind, through the open door.

"I was wondering if it would be you who would take me, Spencer," Margaret says and laughs bitterly.

"I wanted to accompany you, on your last journey," he replies.

"I knew there was something wrong with you. The bastards in the valley down there would not know insanity, even if it does preach to them every Sunday." She turns to face the man standing in the doorway, and laughs.

"Quite, but they seem to have you figured out, do they not? Sitting here on your own, day after day, year after year. Is it any wonder you've gone a bit mad?"

"It's you that's taken leave of your senses, or should I say *had*?" she sneers at him.

"Me? I died surrounded by people who loved me, comfortable. You, however, are a lonely old witch, reduced to living in her own filth, talking to things that aren't there? I assume that is for the bird?" he mocks, and points at the bowl full of food on the sill.

"Mr Hotfoot Jackson is there." Her eyes narrow, and she points at the top of the open door. "Or are you blind as well as dead?"

"I don't think he is, Margaret, and I don't think he ever was,"

"Bah! He's there, and as real as you or I. It's you that's clearly mad," Margaret says, almost spitting through her gritted teeth.

"If you don't mind, Molly…" Spencer strides up to Margaret's chair.

"I shall go with you, but my destiny is not to be shared with you," she says, and looks at the old Parson. I've made my peace with the Lord, and he is waiting for me. Death has not been kind to you, I see."

Once a broad man, the Parson is now reduced to merely skin and bone.

"Come." He holds out his hand, and slowly helps Margaret to her feet.

"The problem with putting your trust in a liar." Margaret lets him take her by the elbow and lead her out into the brisk night air.

"I am quite sure I don't understand?"

"Were you quite certain that I would spend eternity with you? Quid pro quo, Parson Spencer, you never get something for free."

"Name your price." He turns to look at the old woman.

"Why me? What made you hate me so much?" She frowns, and searches his face for an answer.

"You and your land were the only things I wanted," he replies, "the only things I could never have. You were the only one to deny me. You know all too well that obsession will devour you in time." He points to the empty cup on the table.

"You drove me to that." She lets out a brief sigh. "I have nothing left, and look at what it has come to. Land and possessions aren't everything. You made my life a misery because of greed, and I can never forgive you for that."

"I had hoped that you would, Margaret," he replies.

"How could I? Have the other women that you took advantage of?"

"No," he says, "but have you never had a need for something? A need so strong it made you shake at the thought of it, that feels like a pressure in your chest constricting your heart. The need never dissipates. Eventually it dominates your every waking moment. The pressure mounts until it seizes every bone right down to the marrow. It rots you from the inside, and you are left with nothing but this feeling."

"Justifying your reasons doesn't give you the right to forgiveness, Spencer."

Then she pulls away from him and closes her eyes for the last time. They listen as a little way off in the distance they can hear the bells of St. John's church chime out midnight.

"You've come to take me in death, proving that the thought of owning me and mine haunts you still. You didn't want forgiveness, and you'll not be getting it this evening." She smiles. "Enjoy your eternity walking this earth." She turns and starts her journey down the garden path. "Goodbye, Parson. I shan't be thinking of you, while I am up there, sat on my cloud. Mr Hotfoot Jackson is going to stay on for a while. He'll keep an eye on you, while you atone for your sins." Margaret laughs and winks at the Parson, before she vanishes into the night air. She leaves nothing behind, but the moonlight filtering through the trees, and her empty vessel in the rocking chair.

Mr Hotfoot-Jackson perches on the roof of the cottage now, and caws mournfully. Then he takes off on a short journey through the night air from Jackfields to the centre of Burslem. There he sits on the sign of The Turk's Head public house. He watches, and waits.

PUBLISHING HISTORY OF THE STORIES

Martina Bellovičová – *Perhaps Their Parents Were at Fault* © 2016 – Original to this Collection

J. E. Bryant – *The Vigil* © 2016 – Original to this Collection

Glynis Charlton – *Brian* © 2016 – Original to this Collection

Matt Colborn – City in the Dusk © 2001 first published in *Interzone, issue 165, March 2001*

Danielle Collard – *Wallace* © 2016 – Original to this Collection

Storm Constantine – *The Secret Gallery* © 2016 – Original to this Collection

Louise Coquio – *Listen* © 2016 – Original to this Collection

Elizabeth Counihan – *Crocodile and Erlking* © 2016 – Original to this Collection

Krishan Coupland – *The House of My Grandfather* © 2014, first published in *Liars' League*, 2014

Elizabeth Davidson – *The Long Leather Boot* © 2016 – Original to this collection

Siân Davies – *Post Partum* © 2016 – Original to this Collection

Jack Fabian – *The New Womann* © 2016 – Original to this Collection

Kerri Fender – *Meta Wife* © 2016 – Original to this Collection

Paul Finch – *Wicken Fen*, © 2012, first published in *Terror Tales of East Anglia*, Gray Friar Press, 2012

Rosie Garland – *An End to Empire* © 2016 – Original to this Collection

Jessica Gilling – *Around the Apple Tree* © 2016 – Original to this Collection

Andrew Hook – *A Life in Plastic* © 2015 – first published in *Strange Tales V*, Tartarus Press, 2015

Paul Houghton – *The Strange Case of Quentin Wilde* © 2016 – Original to this Collection

Rhys Hughes – *Pyramid and Thisbe* © 2002, first published in *Stories from a Lost Anthology*, Tartarus Press, 2002

Tanith Lee – *The Beast and Beauty* © 2016 – Original to this Collection

Lisa Mansell – all poems © 2016 – Original to this Collection

Kate Moore – Lift © 2016 – Original to this Collection

Tim Pratt – *Cup and Table* © 2012, first published in Lightspeedmagazine.com, issue 25, June 2012

Nicholas Royle – The Dummy © 2008 – first published in *The New Uncanny* (Comma Press) edited by Sarah Eyre and Ra Page, 2008

Michael Marshall Smith – The Dark Land © 1991 – first published in *Darklands*, Egerton Press, 1991

Paula Wakefield – In Touch © 2016 – Original to this Collection

Ian Whates – The Piano Song © 2011 – first published in *Scenes from the Second Storey*, Morrigan Books, 2011, and in *Growing Pains*, PS Publishing, 2013

Liz Williams – The Hide © 2007 – first published in *Strange Horizons*, reprinted in *The Year's Best Fantasy and Horror, ed. Gavin Grant, Kelly Link, Ellen Datlow* and in *The Light Warden*, NewCon Press, 2015

About the
Contributors

Storm Constantine: is the creator of the Wraeththu Mythos, the first trilogy of which was published in the 1980s, which was boundary-breaking science fantasy. She has since written a further 21 novels, across genres, (including *Hermetech* and *Burying the Shadow*), and is currently working on a book of 3 linked novellas. Storm has 88 published short stories, 10 full-length non-fiction titles, including *Sekhem Heka* and *Whatnots and Curios,* (both through Immanion Press) and 10 short story collections, including *Splinters of Truth* (NewCon Press 2016). She is the founder of Immanion Press, created initially to publish her out-of-print back catalogue, but which evolved into the thriving venture it is today. Her interests include magic and spirituality, movies, music and MMOs. She is a long-time fan of weird fiction and old ghost stories, of which she has a large collection. She lives in the Midlands of the UK, with her husband and four demanding cats. She can be found on Facebook at https://www.facebook.com/storm.constantine and has a new web site, still in progress, at http://www.stormconstantine.co.uk. She tweets so rarely it's not really worth mentioning, but has a blog she makes every effort to update now and again at https://dreamsofdarkangels.wordpress.com/

Paul Houghton studied fine art, and then creative writing at UEA, under Malcolm Bradbury and Angela Carter. His first novel won a Society of Authors Betty Trask Award and he has since published stories in magazines and anthologies such as *Panurge, The Fiction Magazine, Cutting Teeth, Mouth, Gutter Magazine, You Are Here* (edited by Bill Broady) and *Magical* (edited by Kelly Ann Jacobson). He has worked as a freelance journalist, a screenwriter and a Writer-in-Residence working in various settings: libraries, prisons, hospitals and literary festivals, as well as being the recipient of several writing fellowships in the USA: at Yaddo, The MacDowell Colony, and The Virginia Center for the Creative Arts. His short art films have been shown in the ICA, and he co-wrote, directed and produced *Faith*, a short weird film for Scottish TV. He is currently writing a Gothic novel under PhD supervision and working as a Senior Lecturer in Creative Writing at Staffordshire University.

Martina Bellovičová was born in Brno, Czech Republic, where she received an English and German MA Degree at the Masaryk University. Her interest in literature and creative writing made her pursue a second degree at the Academy of Literature in Prague. She is currently working as a freelance translator, language teacher and copywriter. Her first published short story, *A Piece of Meat* appeared in the fantasy collection *Rytiny; The Day Music Died* (Kočas 2014) followed, and *Waiting Room*, a winning comic of KomiksFEST! 2010. Weird fantasy and steampunk are her favourite genres and she participates in various cons and festivals in an attempt to bring them closer to general public. Prior to focusing on writing, she devoted years of her life to theatre and music, and is currently involved in the cyberpunk band Neuromancy. She considers herself a lifestyle Goth and spins CDs at alternative parties under the pseudonym DJ Zlyhad. In the last few years, she has devoted most of her free time to organising subculture events. She can be found on Facebook at https://www.facebook.com/zlyhad/

J. E. Bryant has worked as a journalist and PR manager for the past eighteen years. In that time he has written for publications as diverse as the *Royal Pharmaceutical Journal* and the *Fortean Times*, but has concentrated mainly on video game magazines and web sites. His published works to date include short stories in *Asthetica* Magazine, *Looking Landwards* (NewCon Press) and *Dark Tales from the Secret War* (Modiphius). He also runs Drozbot.com, an ongoing blog focusing on science, speculative media and robotics.

His love of sci-fi and fantastical fiction stretches back to watching *The Clangers* as a child, and the discovery of a collection of Michael Moorcock stories left behind when one of his brothers departed the family fold. He lives with his wife Jo and two children - Will, 17 and Eliza, 13 - in the small village of Stapleford outside Cambridge. When not reading, or writing, or writing about writing, he does his best to cycle. He can be found on Twitter at @Drozbotdotcom and has a blog at www.drozbot.com

Glynis Charlton had a late start with her writing. Twenty years after leaving school, she put pen to paper again, and has never stopped since. She began with an Arts Council project, found workshops taking over her life and, before she knew it, had ditched the day job. Thinking 'better late than never', Glynis then enrolled for her degree and emerged – six years of Monday nights later – with a First in Creative Writing.

Now she writes all sorts. She's come fairly close with the Bridport Prize a couple of times – a short story and a poem both shortlisted - and has run workshops in countless places, including the West Yorkshire Playhouse, the Bronte Parsonage Museum, and Ilkley Literature

Festival. Glynis has also contributed to resource books on therapeutic writing and has had a film short screened as part of Leeds Film Festival. Prose remains her first love, especially creating characters like Brian and seeing what they get up to. Recently, Glynis has begun taking her writing further afield, and now runs writing retreats on a little Italian island. She can be found on Facebook at www.facebook.com/glynischarltonwriter and her web site is www.glynischarlton.com

Matt Colborn is a freelance writer and academic with a doctorate in cognitive science. He has written for The Guardian as well as SFX and Interzone magazines. He writes non-fiction on consciousness, science and the future and across the spectrum of speculative fiction. He published a collection of short fiction, *City in the Dusk and Other Stories*, in 2013 and is currently completing a novel. Matt's website is http://mattcolbornwriter.blogspot.co.uk. He can be found on Twitter at Mattcolborn2 and https://www.facebook.com/matt.colborn1

Danielle Collard is a 23-year-old writer studying English and Creative Writing at Staffordshire University. Born in Solihull and raised in Norfolk, she aspires to be a published novelist and is developing a writing philosophy in which prose is fuelled by economic and conversational style, but framed and complimented with richer language in scenes of epiphany and reflection. She cites Hemingway, Colette, and Orwell as key influences for their distinctive styles and the effective portrayal of their respective themes enabled by those styles. In her spare time she enjoys music (she plays the piano, guitar and saxophone), exercise (running and squash, among many other sports) and is a lover of indie films (her favourites are the Before films).

Louise Coquio is a sometime writer, free-lance editor and world-class procrastinator. She is currently a post-graduate student at Staffordshire University, where she studies Creative Writing and specialises in Gothic fiction. Having previously worked in assorted jobs including; chef, local government minion and professional pillow plumper, she returned to education full-time in her late thirties, after which she qualified as a teacher and taught Creative Writing at Stafford college. Now working in student support while she completes her studies, she has at last achieved her long-cherished dream of being paid to attend lectures. When not working on a Gothic novel with a mind of its own, and two ghost-filled children's books, she can be found attending to the every whim of her cats, watching deeply uncool teen movies and cooking obsessively. She can be found on Twitter at @Louisecoquio

Elizabeth Counihan was a NHS family doctor for many years before retiring early to concentrate on writing. She's had stories published in *Asimov's*, *Interzone* and many anthologies, and her novella *Forests of Eden* came out in 2012 with PS. At the moment she's concentrating on a rather complicated science fantasy novel which is taking much longer than it should.

The story in this collection was inspired by watching the children from the primary school across the road from where she lives troupe off to the local park and wondering what would happen if the evil Erlking from Schubert's scary song tried to take one of them. She can be found on Facebook at https://www.facebook.com/elizabeth.counihan.7, and on Twitter at @shezcounihan and you can visit her web site at elizabethcounihan.wordpress.com

Krishan Coupland is a graduate from the University of East Anglia MA Creative Writing programme. His writing has appeared in *Ambit*, *Aesthetica*, *Litro* and *Fractured West*. He won the Manchester Fiction Prize in 2011, and the Bare Fiction Prize in 2016. In his spare time he runs and edits *Neon Literary Magazine*. He is unduly pre-occupied with theme parks. His website is www.krishancoupland.co.uk and his blog can be found at http://www.krishancoupland.co.uk/ and he is on Twitter at @KrishanCoupland

Elizabeth Davidson gained her MA in Novel Writing at City University. An extract of her first novel was published in the anthology, City Novel 2010, and the book was later shortlisted for both the 2011 Unbound Press Best Novel Award and the Impress Prize for New Writers 2011. She is currently working on a new novel. She is interested in psychological suspense of all depths, from Patricia Highsmith to Patrick McGrath. By day, she works as a freelance writer and journalist. She lives in South London with her partner and frequently escapes to the rainy Scottish valley where she grew up.

Siân Davies is a fiction writer from Shropshire, England, studying Creative Writing at Staffordshire University. Her writing has motifs of domestic trauma and endeavours to make the commonplace surreal, primarily with a female 'voice' or narrator. She won the first *Poempigeon* competition with *Bonapigeon* in 2013, and won the Dragon Poems For Smiles competition with *Body of Flesh* in the same year. More recently, her short story *164 from Stoke* appeared in Scout Media's *A Journey of Words* anthology (2016). Her blog is https://crashage.wordpress.com/ and she is on Twitter as @crashage

Jack Fabian is an undergraduate student at Staffordshire University in the UK, studying Creative Writing. His interests include dystopian fiction and pugs. His writing focuses on gritty, urban dystopia, and in his spare time he listens to The Smiths and hopelessly pursues a healthy lifestyle. He is on Twitter as @jackfabdirtbag

Kerry Fender is a freelance writer, blogger and Down's Syndrome advocate from North Staffordshire. In 2013, thirty years after leaving formal education with a 'mediocre clutch of O levels', she walked back into the classroom to study for a BA in Creative Writing at Staffordshire University, which she completed this year. She lives in Newcastle-under-Lyme with her husband and children. She says that when she's not prostituting her literacy for money, she blogs about life as the mother of a child with Down's Syndrome, and sometimes draws rude cartoons. Her motto is: "It's never too late to be who you want to be." Her blog is pinkisthenewgrey.wordpress.com. She can be found on Twitter at @kerryannfender and on Facebook at https://m.facebook.com/Pink-is-the-new-Grey-413364315522288/

Paul Finch is a former cop and journalist. He cut his literary teeth penning episodes of the British TV crime drama, *The Bill*, and has written extensively in the field of children's animation. His crime debut novel, *Stalkers*, introducing DS Mark 'Heck' Heckenburg, was followed by four more books in the series. A new crime novel, *Strangers*, is published in September 2016.

Paul has had nearly 300 stories published. His first collection, *After Shocks*, won the British Fantasy Award in 2002, while he won the award again in 2007 for his novella, *Kid*. Later in 2007, he won the International Horror Guild Award for *The Old North Road*. He has written three *Dr Who* audio dramas for Big Finish, and his *Dr Who* novel, *Hunter's Moon* was published by BBC Books in 2011. Two of his movies, *Spirit Trap* and *The Devil's Rock*, were released in 2005 and 2011 respectively, while his new script, *War Wolf*, will be shot in the autumn of 2016.

Paul Finch lives in Lancashire, UK, with his wife Cathy and his children, Eleanor and Harry.

Rosie Garland was recently named 'literary hero' by *The Skinny*, and is a novelist, poet and singer with post-punk band The March Violets. She also performs twisted cabaret as Rosie Lugosi the Vampire Queen. With a passion for language nurtured by libraries, she started out in spoken word, garnering praise from *Apples and Snakes* as 'one of the country's finest performance poets'. Her award-winning short stories, poems and essays have been widely anthologised. She has five solo collections of poetry and forthcoming in 2016 is the sixth, *As In Judy* (Flapjack Press).

Rosie has received the DaDa Award for Performance Artist of the Year, the Diva Award for Solo Performer, and a Poetry Award from the People's Café, New York.

Her firm belief in the power of persistence stems from personal experience. Following twelve years at a reputable literary agency (who failed to place her novels), in 2011 she entered the inaugural Mslexia Novel Competition and won. This debut novel was published as *The Palace of Curiosities* (HarperCollins 2013) and was nominated for both The Desmond Elliott and the Polari First Book Prize. Her second novel, *Vixen*, was a Green Carnation Prize nominee. Her next novel, *The Night Brother* is due out in Spring 2017. Her web site is www.rosiegarland.com. She can be found on Twitter at @rosieauthor and on Facebook at https://www.facebook.com/rosielugosi

Jessica Gilling, based in North Staffordshire, is a graduate of Staffordshire University, with a Bachelor's degree in creative writing. She is the proud mother of a wonderful little girl, and is also an advocate for mental health. Jessica writes anything that pops into her head, and her taste in literature is broad. She likes to read anything from James Herbert to Tennessee Williams (everything in between is fair game too, but she will always hold a special place in her heart for *Snuggle Piggy and the Magic Blanket*). When she is not working (writing or actual grown up work), she likes to relax with rum-flavoured tea, but normally can be found rambling to herself on Twitter about her daughter and tweeting pictures of the squirrels that live in her garden. She likes herbal teas, ornamental cats, (and her own eighteen year old feline friend called Custard), is allergic to cats, can fit a whole wagon wheel in her mouth, and likes to clean, a lot.

Andrew Hook has over 130 short stories in print, alongside several books. His most recent titles include the neo-noir crime novels: *The Immortalists* and *Church Of Wire* (Telos Publishing). 2016 will see the publication of his fifth short story collection *Human Maps* (Eibonvale), a SF/F/H hybrid novella *The Greens* (Snowbooks), and a collaborative collection of stories co-written with Allen Ashley (*Slow Motion Wars*, Eibonvale Press). When not writing Andrew can be found writing. Andrew's web site is www.andrew-hook.com. He can be found on Twitter at @AndrewHookUK and his blog is at http://andrew-hook.blogspot.co.uk/

Rhys Hughes was born in 1966. His first book, *Worming the Harpy*, was published in 1995, and since that time he has published more than thirty other books. His fiction is generally fantastical and his main influences are Italo Calvino, Boris Vian, Flann O'Brien and Donald Barthelme. His most recent book is the collection *Brutal Pantomimes* and he is now at work on a weird Western called *The Honeymoon Gorillas*. His work has been translated into ten languages. Rhys's blog is http://rhyshughes.blogspot.co.uk/ and he can be found on Facebook at https://www.facebook.com/rhysaurus and Twitter @rhysaurus.

Tanith Lee (1947-2015) was one of the most influential writers of genre fiction, who inspired a generation of authors of weird fiction and fantasy with her unique voice and writing style. She wrote over 100 novels and hundreds of short stories. Her first novel, *The Birthgrave* (1975), changed the face of British fantasy, bringing an innovative approach and vitality to the genre. Among her most well-known works are *The Silver Metal Lover* and its sequel *Metallic Love*, and the *Flat Earth* sequence, which included *Death's Master* and *Night's Master*. Ms Lee wrote in and across many genres, including Horror, SF and Fantasy, Historical, Detective, Contemporary-Psychological, Children and Young Adult. Her preoccupation, though, was always people. Several of Tanith Lee's weird fiction novels are available through Immanion Press, as well as some of her short story collections. Tanith's complete bibliography can be found at http://www.daughterofthenight.com/

Lisa Mansell is a poet and critic based in Stoke, born in Glamorgan. She is interested in avant-garde music and poetics and is currently writing a monograph on the work of John Cage. Her writing experiments with language and form, departures from the traditional and expected, embrace the strange. More of her work can be read in *Tears in the Fence*, *Blackbox Manifold*, *Equinox*, *French Literary Review*, and *Interdisciplinary Science Reviews*. Lisa is the course leader for Creative Writing at Staffordshire University. She can be found on Twitter @limansell and on Facebook at https://www.facebook.com/limansell

Kate Moore is a writer hailing from Australia ("the one with kangaroos jumping through the streets") and a poet to her core. Experimenting with words brings her untold joy. She loves to play with books, magazines and other materials to create text art combinations. She writes open-field/experimental poetry, as well as prose with often difficult themes. She can sing, and act, but says she doesn't do a thing about it, adding: "Maybe one day, I'll set myself free." Kate's blog is at http://glassmushroom.blogspot.co.uk/. She can be found on Twitter at @WordsRoamFree and https://www.facebook.com/katiej.moore.921

Tim Pratt is the author of over 20 novels, most recently *The Deep Woods* and *Heirs of Grace*, and many short stories. His work has appeared in *The Best American Short Stories*, *The Year's Best Fantasy*, *The Mammoth Book of Best*

New Horror, and other nice places. He's a Hugo Award winner, and has been a finalist for World Fantasy, Sturgeon, Stoker, Mythopoeic, and Nebula Awards, among others. He lives in Berkeley CA and works as a senior editor at *Locus*, a trade magazine devoted to science fiction and fantasy publishing. He publishes a new short story every month for his Patreon supporters at https://www.patreon.com/timpratt

Nicholas Royle is the author of seven novels, including *Counterparts*, *Antwerp*, *Regicide* and *First Novel*, and a short story collection, *Mortality*. He has won three British Fantasy Awards. He has edited twenty anthologies and is series editor of *Best British Short Stories* (Salt). A senior lecturer in creative writing at the Manchester Writing School at Manchester Metropolitan University, and head judge of the annual Manchester Fiction Prize, he also runs Nightjar Press, publishing signed limited-edition chapbooks, and is an editor at Salt Publishing. His latest publication is *In Camera* (Negative Press London), a collaboration with artist David Gledhill. @nicholasroyle @nightjarpress

Michael Marshall Smith is a novelist and screenwriter. Under this name he has published over eighty short stories, and four novels — *Only Forward*, *Spares*, *One of Us* and *The Servants* — winning the Philip K. Dick, International Horror Guild, and August Derleth awards, along with the Prix Bob Morane in France. He has won the British Fantasy Award for Best Short Fiction four times, more than any other author.

Writing as Michael Marshall he has published seven internationally-bestselling thrillers including *The Straw Men* series, *The Intruders* — recently a BBC series starring John Simm and Mira Sorvino — and *Killer Move*. His most recent novel is *We Are Here*.

He lives in Santa Cruz, California, with his wife, son, and two cats. He can be found on Twitter at @ememess and his web site is www.michaelmarshallsmith.com

Paula Wakefield trained and worked as a journalist after graduating from university. Following that, she worked in industry, and in the health and social care sector, in adult mental health and an alcohol recovery project. She is also a qualified teacher. Her short stories have appeared in numerous women's mags over the last few decades. Her genre stories include *The If Game* and *The Fur Boot*, which appeared in the Midnight Rose anthologies, edited by Neil Gaiman, Rose Kaveney and others. Her tale *The Gift of Love* appeared in Interzone magazine. Her most recent work, *Red in Tooth and Claw*, was published in the anthology *Noir* from NewCon Press in 2015. She says that all her work explores love, sex and power – the tales we tell and re-tell to express our desires, regrets and revenge, our loves and losses. She is also interested in how stories live on through generations and cultures. Paula is currently communing with the dead for her first novel – part of her PhD project.

Ian Whates is a writer and editor of science fiction, fantasy, and occasionally horror. He is the author of six novels (three space opera and three urban fantasy with steampunk overtones), the co-author of two more (military SF), has seen sixty-odd of his short stories published in a variety of venues, and is responsible for editing around thirty anthologies. His work has been shortlisted for the Philip K Dick Award and twice for a BSFA Award. His latest novel, the Firefly-esque space opera romp *Pelquin's Comet*, was an Amazon UK #1 best seller, and his most recent short fiction appeared in *Galaxy's Edge* magazine (March 2016) John Joseph Adams' *Nightmare* (April 2016) and the science journal *Nature* (May 2016). His third collection, *Dark Travellings*, came out in June 2016 from Fox Spirit. In 2006 Ian founded multiple award-winning independent publisher NewCon Press by accident.

Liz Williams is a science fiction and fantasy writer living in Glastonbury, England, where she is co-director of a witchcraft supply business. She has been published by Bantam Spectra (US) and Tor Macmillan (UK), also Night Shade Press and appears regularly in *Asimov's* and other magazines. She is the secretary of the Milford SF Writers' Workshop, and also teaches creative writing. Her novels include *The Ghost Sister*, *Empire of Bones*, *The Banner of Souls* and *Winterstrike*. Her Chen series is currently being published by Open Road. Her first short story collection *The Banquet of the Lords of Night* was published by Night Shade Press, and her second, *A Glass of Shadow*, by New Con Press. *The Witchcraft Shop Diaries* (1 and 2) are published by New Con Press.

Her novel *Banner of Souls* has been nominated for the Philip K Dick Memorial Award, along with 3 previous novels, and the Arthur C Clarke Award. Liz writes a regular CIF column for the Guardian.

IMMANION PRESS
Purveyors of Speculative Fiction

Para Animalia Edited by Storm Constantine & Wendy Darling

Based on the world created by Storm Constantine for her Wraeththu novels, the stories in this collection explore how various Wraeththu tribes interact with animals, have spiritual or working relationships with them, or have encountered zoological mysteries out in the world. From the wolves of frozen forests, and a har's obsession with spiders, to the snakes of parched deserts and the hunting dogs of what was once the African plains, hara confront a strengthening natural world that is now free of humanity.

'Para Animalia' features stories from nine writers, some of whom are well known within Wraeththu fandom and/or have written Wraeththu Mythos novels published by Immanion Press. Also included are two new stories each by Storm Constantine and Wendy Darling.
ISBN: 978-1-907737-70-1 £11.99, $18.99

Night's Nieces: the Legacy of Tanith Lee

In the footsteps of the High Priestess of Fantasy… Tanith Lee was a huge influence on fantasy literature, and a generation of writers were captivated by her iconic prose and surreal visions. Here is a collection of stories by female writers, for whom Tanith Lee was a friend and mentor, and an inspiration. Each 'niece' has written a short story inspired by Tanith's work, as well as an accompanying article. The book, edited by Storm Constantine, also includes previously unpublished photographs from Tanith's life, as well as artwork by the authors.
Contributors include Storm Constantine, Cecilia Dart-Thornton, Vera Nazarian, Sarah Singleton, Kari Sperring, Sam Stone, Freda Warrington and Liz Williams. With an introduction by John Kaiine.
ISBN: 978-1-907737-71-8 £11.99 $18.99

Immanion Press
http://www.immanion-press.com
info@immanion-press.com

NEWCON PRESS

http://newconpress.co.uk/

The very best in fantasy, science fiction, and horror

The Sign in the Moonlight by David Tallerman

Steeped in the rich imagery of Victoriana, this collection recalls the very best of classic horror and adventure. Reminiscent of Machan, Conan Doyle, Lovecraft, M.R. James and H.G. Wells, these stories transport us to an age when the world still harbours dark mysteries that defy human knowledge and understanding. From the wind-swept peaks of the Himalayas to the desperate horror of the trenches, from the stuffy warmth of gentlemen's clubs to the haunted corridors of country hotels, the author challenges us to venture with him into realms where only the brave dare tread…

ISBN: 978-1-910935-15-6 £28.99 casebound limited edition, numbered hardback.

Splinters of Truth by Storm Constantine

Storm Constantine is one of our finest writers of genre fiction. This new collection, Splinters of Truth, features fifteen stories, four of them original to this volume, that transport the reader to richly imagined realms one moment and shine a light on our own world's darkest corners the next. A writer of rare passion, Storm delivers here some of her most accomplished work to date.

"Storm Constantine is a literary fantasist of outstanding power and originality. Her work is rich, idiosyncratic and completely engaging. Her themes have much in common with Philip K Dick – the nature of identify, the nature of reality, the creative power of the human imagination – while her sensibility reminds me of Angela Carter at her most inventive."

– Michael Moorcock
ISBN: 978-1-910935-08-8 paperback £12.99

www.ingramcontent.com/pod-product-compliance
Lightning Source LLC
Chambersburg PA
CBHW020429030726
47495CB00006B/1726